Charlie Owen enjoyed a thirty-year career in the police service, serving with two forces in the Home Counties and London, reaching the rank of Inspector. His first novel, *Horse's Arse*, was widely acclaimed. He is married with six children.

Praise for Charlie Owen:

'It's like *Life on Mars* without the time travelling' *Zoo* magazine

'Will have you gripped from page one. The characters, the plotlines and the dialogue are so vivid' *Daily Record*

'Charlie Owen has a talent for humorously exposing the dark world of British street crime' *Leicester Mercury*

'If you love dinosaur DCI Gene Hunt in TV hit *Life on Mars*, you'll find this violent, yet hilarious thriller a delight' *Peterborough Evening Telegraph*

Also by Charlie Owen and available from Headline

Horse's Arse

FOXTROT OSCAR

CHARLIE OWEN

headline

First published in 2007
by HEADLINE PUBLISHING GROUP

First published in paperback in 2008
by HEADLINE PUBLISHING GROUP

1

Cataloguing in Publication Data is available from the British Library

ISBN 978 0 7553 3687 6

Typeset in AGaramond by Avon DataSet Ltd,
Bidford on Avon, Warwickshire

Printed and bound in Great Britain by Mackays Of Chatham, Chatham, Kent

Headline's policy is to use papers that are natural, renewable and recyclable
products and made from wood grown in sustainable forests. The logging
and manufacturing processes are expected to conform to the
environmental regulations of the country of origin.

HEADLINE PUBLISHING GROUP
An Hachette Livre UK Company
338 Euston Road
London NW1 3BH

www.headline.co.uk
www.hachettelivre.co.uk

This book is dedicated to my children: Lucy, Elizabeth, Hannah, Oliver, Poppy and Maisie, who have seen the best and worst of me and have always forgiven me. Their lives were inexorably shaped by my years as a police officer, not always for the best, and the least I can do by way of apology is to say, This book is for you – you little buggers. I'm sorry and I love you. Dad xxxxxx

Acknowledgements

I'd like to say a huge thank you to the amazing team at Headline who have guided me through the trauma of writing a second book to a deadline. My editor, Martin Fletcher, was his usual quiet and thoughtful tower of strength who, whilst always encouraging me, never failed to rein me in when appropriate.

Kerr MacRae has been a constant supporter throughout the writing of this book, whilst Jo Matthews, James Horobin, Jo Liddiard and Emily Furniss have been unstinting in their efforts to bring both this and *Horse's Arse* into the public eye.

My very old friend (old in that I have known him a long time!) and agent, Richard Tucker, has proved invaluable to me with his wealth of knowledge of the publishing industry. I had accumulated the usual pile of rejection letters from agents and publishers before Richard introduced me to Headline and ensured that first *Horse's Arse*, and now *Foxtrot*

Oscar were published. This is an opportune moment to apologise publicly to him and his long-suffering wife Judy for vomiting on their bedroom carpet during cricket week at Welwyn Garden City Cricket Club. We have remained good friends despite that, and his involvement in the writing of these two books is a source of gratification to me.

Finally, I could not have written this book without the continued encouragement and support of my wife Karen. She told me to write that or else there'd be trouble.

Chapter One

The two petrol bombs arced away from the fifteenth-floor balcony of the Grant Flowers flats, their fiery tails flowing behind them in the night sky, briefly illuminating a group of masked youths on the balcony, before falling towards the three liveried police vans parked below. By the early summer of 1976, Handstead New Town, which lay fifteen miles north of Manchester, was a simmering cauldron of discontent. It had long been used by Manchester City Council as a social dustbin for its more troublesome tenants, and as a penal colony by the local police, who staffed it with their own malcontents. Such was the loathing they felt for the town that they had bastardised its phonetic code – Hotel Alpha – and now referred to it by the more appropriate name of Horse's Arse.

Of all Handstead's dismal estates, the worst without question was the Park Royal. Built on the former rolling acres of a long-disappeared Tudor royal residence, the majority of its rodent-like residents spent their waking hours engaged in every kind of criminal enterprise. They regularly went head to head with the local police, who quite unwittingly had embraced the ancient doctrine of the Stoics and resolved to make a difference in a place they hated. The biggest problems in the town as a whole were posed by a gang based on the estate, the self-styled Park Royal Mafia. They were a group of young, lawless hoodlums who regularly ran amok and had become quite dangerous. Even more so when, in January, one of their number had murdered PC Dave Baines. Since his murder, and the subsequent roll-up of the Mafia's hierarchy, Handstead had seen virtually nonstop outbreaks of disorder, but particularly on the Park Royal.

The knot of police officers standing around the vans moved away swiftly, watching dispassionately as the bombs crashed with loud explosions on to the roof of one of the vehicles, blazing petrol enveloping it and lighting up the surrounding area. Loud raucous cheers went up from dozens of unseen people gathered on the darkened balconies of the flats, and were quickly echoed by the police officers as they noticed that one of the throwers on the fifteenth floor was himself ablaze. Making a petrol bomb was extremely simple, but throwing one required a little care. The two milk bottles had been half filled with petrol, and rags sodden with fuel had been stuffed into the necks before being lit. It was important that the bottle was thrown with the wick upright, but one of the bombers had tipped his upside down, and petrol had gushed over his arm and upper body and ignited as he threw it. As he thrashed about on the balcony, desperately trying to extinguish himself, his mate left him to it.

Down below, a police officer stepped forward and used an extinguisher to kill the flames engulfing the police van. It was a well-practised routine. All three vans bore the scars of past petrol bombings and stonings. The patrol group to whom the vans belonged, the county's elite rapid response unit, had spent the last eight days on the Park Royal estate dealing with sporadic outbreaks of violence as the local hooligans flexed their muscles in a show of defiance ahead of the impending trials of the hard-core Park Royal Mafia. The estate was simmering in the early summer heat and the local police were hard pushed to keep it under control. Hence the presence of the patrol group, with a simple brief to deal with the problem in any way they saw fit.

'Delta Hotel, this is Ranger One,' reported the group's senior sergeant. 'We've just taken two petrol bombs from the Grant Flowers flats. We're redeploying in the vicinity.' As he spoke, the three vans were being moved to the far side of the road, adjacent to some waste ground.

The operator in the main control room looked anxiously over to her young, recently promoted inspector, who was hovering nervously at her shoulder, listening to the transmission over the speaker. Whilst the patrol group were under attack at the Grant Flowers flats, other local units were also being subjected to random ambushes around the estate. Hands trembling, the inspector leafed quickly through the well-thumbed operation order detailing police operations on the estate, then glanced at the large situation board at the front of the room that showed the locations of units deployed in Handstead. The situation had recently become so serious that resources from around the county were being deployed into Horse's Arse to deal with it. The county's fire-breathing shit-kicker, Chief Constable Daniels, was determined that the town would not go up in smoke without a fight. The control room inspector, however, was a spineless jellyfish with no confidence in himself, and little street experience, and deciding that discretion was the better part of valour, he resolved to withdraw the patrol group.

'Get the patrol group out of there,' he commanded in a shaky voice. 'Deploy back to Hotel Alpha and we'll reconsider.'

The operator looked quizzically at him for clarification. She was well aware that the bottom line of the operation order was that the town should not be surrendered without a fight.

'Get them out of there,' the inspector repeated in what he hoped was a firmer tone.

Shrugging in mute but obvious disagreement, the operator turned back to her microphone.

'Ranger One, Ranger One from Oscar One, get your

vehicles away from the flats and redeploy to Hotel Alpha. Oscar One will contact you there.'

As the patrol group officers digested this decision and the sergeant responded with a terse 'Understood', a mile away the night-duty Hotel Alpha inspector was listening aghast to the transmission. He was made of sterner stuff. Grabbing his vehicle's handset, he quickly intervened.

'Delta Hotel, this is Bravo Two, cancel your last, I repeat, cancel your last. We withdraw from the estate now, we'll never get back. This is my call – Ranger One, you keep your officers up there and deploy as you see fit. All Hotel Alpha units will hold their ground on the estate. We're not going anywhere. This is our ground, Delta Hotel; we're going to keep it. Bravo Two out.'

'Nice one, guv'nor,' smiled his sergeant as the inspector slammed the handset back on to its rack. 'Want to go and meet up with the patrol group boys?'

'Yeah, come on, Roy, get us up there. Fucking Control, what the fuck was all that about? Withdraw? Christ, we'd never get back. Wankers,' the inspector spat contemptuously.

In the control room, the operator acknowledged Bravo Two's very concise instructions and turned back to her inspector, who had turned crimson with embarrassment. He was aware that all the staff in the room were glaring at him, his weak decision exposed by an operational officer with balls.

'It's his funeral,' he finally spluttered, before throwing the operation order on to the operator's desk and slinking away to his supervisor's pod on the dais in the middle of the room. The operation order had been drafted personally by Chief Constable Daniels and deliberately included a caveat that the duty inspectors at Handstead would have primacy if there was ever a dispute about tactics on the ground. He had little faith in any of his control room inspectors, preferring to trust the judgement of the officers in the hot seat.

The patrol group nodded their agreement with what had transpired and, keeping a weary eye on the looming, forbidding flats behind them, gathered around their sergeant as he quickly came up with a new strategy. All of them were in fire-resistant overalls and NATO riot helmets, and they were all shattered by eight straight days in Horse's Arse. They were working twelve-hour night shifts, permanently deployed in and around the Park Royal estate, and would remain there until the trouble died down. There was no immediate prospect of that. The only consolation was that they were earning a small fortune in overtime, though the opportunity to spend it seemed a long way off. In reality their working days were a lot longer than twelve hours. Without fail, each unit was taking prisoners every night, and their practice was that a unit would not book off duty until every member had finished. Not good for the bean-counters at Headquarters, but vital to the camaraderie that bound the three units together.

The patrol group was a rapid deployment unit, comprising three units each of ten constables and a sergeant, overseen by an inspector at Headquarters. The inspector was strictly a figurehead, rarely going out with the vans; the real power lay with the three sergeants. The constables were volunteers from divisions around the county, all of whom had first proved themselves as decent thief-takers and handy in a punch-up. They were an elite unit who revelled in their elitism – a three-year attachment to the patrol group was regarded as a real feather in the cap for all of them. They were there to deal with public disorder wherever it sprang up and had acquired a reputation around the county for preferring to punch first and ask questions later. Unit Three, which covered the Handstead division, accounted for the majority of complaints of assault made against the patrol group as a whole, and they particularly welcomed the decision to remain on the Park Royal estate. They were more aware than most that a withdrawal would seriously undermine their credibility with the local scumbags. At the moment, their arrival in their dark blue liveried Ford Transit vans with grilled windows and lights, heavy rubber skirts and the menacing hooded cobra emblem on the door panels was enough to send the hoodlums hurrying for cover or risk a good hammering. The patrol group was keen to keep it that way.

The night-duty inspector's intervention had also struck a chord with a serial of officers from an outlying nick, deployed in the town for the first time. They had been patrolling the outskirts of the Park Royal, as instructed, but had moved on to the estate when the first call about the petrol bombs had come over the air. They pulled their van up on the waste ground opposite the flats and watched as the patrol group extinguished the flames on their own vehicle and then gathered around their sergeant for redeployment. The ambitious Sergeant Miller, in charge of the serial, was no fan of the patrol group, viewing them as hugely over-rated, with egos to match. He had also previously failed to secure a position on the group as either a PC or a sergeant, and his failure still rankled with him.

'Look at that lot,' he sneered to his PCs in the back seats, 'standing around discussing what to do next. Thought it'd be pretty obvious. Got to get into those flats and secure them.' His constables laughed their agreement, and cast nervous glances at the flats, where they could see shadowy figures moving around the balconies and walkways. They had grown used to listening to the sergeant bad-mouth the group. Militarily he was probably right, but without the option of using lethal force to secure the flats, it was a non-starter. Setting foot in the maze of walkways and stairwells, seemingly built for ambushes, would be a disaster, but it was exactly what Miller decided to do.

'Come on, guys, whilst they're screwing about, we'll get into the flats and sort them out,' he announced, seeing an opportunity to make a name for himself and show the patrol group what they had missed out on.

His crew showed little enthusiasm for what he was proposing, looking at him as though he'd taken leave of his senses.

'You sure, Sarge?' ventured one of the more experienced officers. 'The flats are fucking huge and there's only six of us. What good are we going to be?'

'Don't you worry yourself about it. Soon as they see coppers, they'll be off on their toes. Come on, you lot, with me now!' he shouted, brooking no argument.

Reluctantly his crew left the van and set off at a jog behind their sergeant. They were all in normal street uniforms and helmets, albeit with flimsy plastic visors fastened to the front rim of the helmet by an elastic strap, and were totally unprepared for what awaited them. Keeping close to a line of saplings and away from the streetlights, Miller led them across the waste ground and halted them behind a grass mound, with just the road in front separating them from the main entrance to the Grant Flowers flats. Keen eyes on the darkened balconies were watching their progress with interest. Miller and his officers were not in the best of shape and were all panting from the exertion of the short jog. The pause at the grass mound was a welcome break for his troops, who were praying that he'd have a change of heart as he got closer to the flats and realised their true size. No such luck.

'You lot ready then?' he panted. 'On my shout, we're across the road and into the main entrance. Don't use the lift, keep to the stairs. We'll secure the first-floor landings and then call the heroes in.' He laughed, indicating the still-briefing patrol group.

'Sarge, this is fucking bollocks,' hissed the PC who had posed the question in the van.

'Just wind your fucking neck in,' snapped Miller. 'Come on, with me,' he finished loudly, and crested the grass mound, followed by his reluctant cannon fodder. As the group crossed the road at the run, the patrol group sergeant caught sight of them out of the corner of his eye.

'Oh sweet Jesus, no!' he shouted, before stepping away from his officers and bellowing, 'STOP!'

Miller glanced in the direction of the shout, knowing full well who was calling and why, but he didn't slacken his pace until he crashed through the front doors to the tower block, holding them open for the rest of the group. The main foyer was dimly lit, covered in graffiti – most of it concerning the local police – and stank of urine. Rubbish littered the floor, and their feet crunched on numerous discarded and bloody syringes. Hearts pumping, wide eyed and fearful, the officers looked desperately to Miller, hoping against hope that he'd see sense and cancel this ludicrous escapade.

'Don't use the lifts,' he repeated, dashing their hopes. 'Up the stairs with me and we'll take the first floor. Stay close,' and he launched himself up the filthy concrete stairs two at a time.

They had reached the second landing, still well short of the first level of flats, when as one they stopped and looked down at the floor. It was soaking wet, liquid running in a steady flood down the steps, and the stench of urine had been replaced by another overwhelming smell. Their boots and lower legs were soaked. Horrified, they looked at each other and then up into the dark stairwell for the source of the torrent.

'Fucking hell, it's petrol!' screamed a young PC. As he did so, they all heard a loud pop and saw a brilliant flash of light. A split second later, the staircase above them burst into flames. Momentarily stunned, the officers watched the fire speed towards them, as overhead, unseen in the echoing darkness, voices screamed abuse. Then they turned, and flew in a panicked dash back down the stairs, pursued by the fiery river, bawling at each other to go faster. Loudest of all was the ambitious Sergeant Miller, right at the back, desperately trying to fight his way through his own officers. None of them was about to make way for him in their frantic dash to escape, leaping two or three steps at a time to get away.

Miller was the first to go up as the fire caught him at the top of the last landing, racing across his feet and up his trousers, quickly enveloping him. He continued to run, the flames flowing behind him as his shoes and uniform trousers began to burn fiercely. The group crashed down into the main foyer, glancing back in horror at the screaming fiery figure that was Sergeant Miller, and then the whole foyer erupted in flames, mocking laughter from the darkness above adding to the impression of hell.

As the officers fell out of the main doors and on to the scrub grass in front of the flats, the patrol group sergeant and his boys, waiting in the shadows alongside the flats, stepped forward with fire extinguishers, swiftly killing the flames in a huge cloud of choking white powder.

'You fucking twat!' bellowed the sergeant, hauling the shaken, scorched Miller to his feet. 'What the fuck were you thinking of? You could have got them all killed. Quickly, away from the building, all of you.' The patrol group were hoisting their smoking colleagues to their feet and dragging them back to the road as petrol bombs began to land where they had been lying. Soon the grass in front of the foyer doors was ablaze, flames twenty feet high licking the front of the building, black smoke billowing up towards the balconies, where an unseen crowd was raucously celebrating its victory.

The two groups of police officers staggered back to the relative safety of the vans, where Ranger One pulled Miller close to him by his still warm lapels.

'What the fuck were you doing?' he snarled. 'Those flats are a death trap. Why do you think no one else has tried getting in there?'

Miller remained silent, eyes down, but before Ranger One could continue with his questions, he felt a tap on his shoulder and turned to see one of Miller's PCs.

'Mind if I deal with this, Sarge?' the constable enquired pleasantly.

Suspecting what was about to happen, but not disapproving, Ranger One let go of Miller's lapels and stepped away from him. The PC took a step forward and glared at his sergeant.

'You useless bastard,' he began quietly. 'You took us into a death trap. It's a fucking miracle we got out of there unharmed.' And then he head-butted Miller square between the eyes, flattening him.

Miller lay unconscious for some time before being doused with water from the patrol group vans, bundled into the back of his own vehicle and taken back to Handstead nick, where his actions had already become public knowledge.

Back on the Park Royal estate, the patrol group and other serials held their ground until the sun came up and the rats scurried back to their holes. The following evening promised more of the same.

Chapter Two

As had been expected, the trial at Manchester Crown Court was a dirty affair. Witnesses were intimidated, and evidence was challenged, particularly that concerning Alan Baker's involvement in the shooting of PC Dave 'Bovril' Baines. Baker had been the number two in the Park Royal Mafia, serving as Bobby Driscoll's enforcer, and had been responsible for buying the gun used to kill Bovril. Since Driscoll's recent and still unexplained death whilst out on bail, Baker had continued to run the Mafia from his cell in Strangeways. However, DCs Benson and Clarke were hugely experienced detectives who had seen it all before. Benson had been a detective for fourteen years, eight of them at Handstead, where he fitted in just right, and his career was littered with legendary stories, the latest and best involving a recent trial at the local crown court. His defendant in that case had been a German national who had made a living cashing stolen cheques around Europe before he was unfortunate enough to cash one in a hotel in Handstead where Benson was on close personal terms with one of the receptionists. She had telephoned Benson when she became aware that the suspicious German was packing his bags to leave, and he had been unceremoniously lifted from his taxi by his hair by a jubilant Benson, who recovered dozens of stolen chequebooks from his suitcases.

After the euphoria of the arrest, Benson found himself with months of inquiries to complete. He was required to locate and take statements from every victim, and that involved an extended trip to mainland Europe. Because of the scale of the inquiry, he had travelled with another DC from Handstead, Jeff Cronin, and for two weeks they had roamed around Europe by train, taking statements and getting drunk. As was the norm when planning trips like this, they had liaised with local law enforcement by falsely identifying themselves as detectives from Scotland Yard. The rationale behind that was that experience had shown that foreign coppers were always hugely impressed by such a claim and would roll out the red carpet, and in the event that things went wrong, the Met would get the blame. The last statement on the trip was due to be taken from a woman in the small Swiss village of Burgdorf, a six-hour train journey from Hanover in West Germany. Benson had telephoned the Chief of Police in Burgdorf and given him the usual story, and the local policeman, ecstatic that

Scotland Yard were coming on to his patch, had hurried off to make suitable arrangements. These included having the unfortunate woman dragged to the police station to save the great detectives the trouble of finding her house. In his mind's eye he visualised two enormously tall, serious men, probably wearing three-piece tweed suits and with a bit of luck deerstalkers, emerging from the train carrying Gladstone bags and magnifying glasses and with names like Nipper or Farquar. He briefly considered asking them to cast their all-seeing eyes over a couple of inquiries he had on the go but eventually dismissed that idea – the great men would be far too busy.

To alleviate the tedium of the train journey, Benson and Cronin had located the restaurant car and taken up residence, emptying the bar of all its beer and two bottles of Schnapps before retiring to their first-class accommodation and falling into a deep drunken stupor. When at last the train pulled sedately into the station at Burgdorf, the local police chief was waiting with his entire department of uniformed officers (three), the mayor and the town brass band to greet the fabled Scotland Yard detectives. Two of the officers were holding a large sign that read, 'Welcome Detectives from the Yard'. Cronin had rolled off the cushioned bench seat and was asleep on the floor, blissfully unaware of the reception. Benson, however, had fallen asleep with his face against the window, drooled like a bloodhound and become stuck to the glass. From the platform he resembled the Elephant Man. As the train came to a stop opposite the welcoming party, he fully opened the bloodshot eye stuck to the glass and tried to prise his mouth free. Despite his thumping hangover, he quickly realised that the reception committee was there for them.

'Fucking hell, Jeff, wake up,' he hissed urgently, starting to kick the prostrate Cronin. 'There's a bloody reception committee.'

The assembled spectators stood patiently while other passengers disembarked, until Benson and Cronin appeared sheepishly at the open doors and peered out through swollen, red eyes. Their faces were creased and distorted, their hair dishevelled and their clothes soiled and crumpled. The brass band launched into 'God Save the Queen' and the mayor stepped forward to shake hands, having first confirmed with his Chief of Police that the two shambling drunks in front of him were indeed their famous guests. Deeply unsure, but reluctant to get it wrong and spoil the town's biggest day for years, the Chief of Police had answered in the affirmative, and saluted as Benson stepped unsteadily on to the platform. Behind him the bilious Cronin, his face the colour of parchment, caught a whiff of food cooking in the station restaurant and vomited profusely into the stairwell of the carriage. That set off Benson, who promptly leant against the side of the train and spewed on the tracks.

After several minutes of frenzied honking and gagging, Benson and Cronin stood swaying gently in front of the local dignitaries, looking for all the world as though they should be on a park bench or curled up in a cardboard box under some railway arches. The brass band had now moved on to a Beatles medley and were halfway through 'Yellow Submarine' when Cronin again lost control and sought refuge down the side of the train. Having deposited his entire stomach contents, he apologised in that special slurred way drunks have, hanging his head, waving his hands about aimlessly and using short nonsensical sentences that made perfect sense to him.

The disbelieving Chief of Police, having hesitantly confirmed with Benson and Cronin that they were indeed their expected guests, now led them to a car to take them to the police station where their reluctant witness waited. The short journey took considerably longer than normal, interrupted as it was by two stops, one for Benson to clear his stomach out, the other for both men to empty their straining bladders. The mayor and his wife, travelling in a car behind them, pulled into the layby for the toilet stop, where they sat in horrified silence as the two shambling drunks pissed like horses just a couple of feet from the lady mayoress's window.

The rambling statement that Benson eventually took from their bemused witness was never introduced into evidence as it made so little sense, disappearing instead into a large box of 'unused material'. That box was still in a property store at Handstead on the morning of the first committal hearing at the magistrates' court two months later. The prisoner had been brought through the underground tunnel to the court cells direct from the Handstead nick cells by a seriously pissed-off PC Sean 'Psycho' Pearce. He had been called in off the street to help the early-turn gaoler and had been detailed to take the remand prisoners to court. He now sat disinterestedly alongside the dock where the nervous German prisoner, Joachim Gunter, sat on the edge of his seat watching proceedings unfold. 'For you, my friend, the war is over,' Psycho had whispered to him as he took his seat. Psycho was the real monster in the pack, whose career to date was a litany of outrageous abuses. He was a beast in every sense. Pig ugly and built like a brick shithouse, he feared nothing and no one, and certainly not getting the sack. He had escaped dismissal from the Force once after he had attacked a toilet fairy and Complaints and Discipline had screwed up the inquiry. Initially suspended, he had been reinstated and sent to Horse's Arse, where he fitted in perfectly and was virtually fireproof.

The clerk of the court eventually directed the court to rise, and in strode the presiding magistrates, led by none other than the formidable Colonel Mortimer. The unfortunate German hadn't a chance, but was blissfully unaware of the fact. The three magistrates took their seats and the clerk turned to inform them of their first piece of business: the case of Joachim Gunter, charged with twelve counts of obtaining property by deception around the United Kingdom and various thefts of chequebooks and guarantee cards. The police, he informed them, were seeking to remand Gunter in custody until his proposed trial at the local crown court.

'On what grounds are we to remand the prisoner, Mr Drake?' asked Mortimer pleasantly, glancing over the top of his half-moon spectacles.

'Your worships, the police consider the prisoner is likely to abscond prior to trial as he has no local ties, is of no fixed abode and is a foreign national.'

'A foreign national? From where?'

'He's German, your worships.'

'GERMAN?' shouted Mortimer, who despised the sausage-eating bastards even more than he did the French, before quickly noticing his colleagues' looks of concern and repeating more quietly, 'German?'

'Yes, your worships, he's a German national. The deception offences he has been charged with today result, it is alleged, from numerous thefts in mainland Europe by the defendant or accomplices. He is also accused of the thefts of chequebooks from hotels around the United Kingdom.'

Mortimer glared at Gunter and said bitterly, 'Is he now?' which left no one in the court in any doubt of the outcome of the hearing. The unfortunate Gunter, who spoke not a word of English, smiled gamely at Mortimer. Mortimer's right eye began to twitch wildly at this display of Teutonic arrogance. He was about to rise from his chair and physically assault the despicable Hun when he felt the restraining hand of his female colleague on his forearm. She had seen the twitch kick in and astutely predicted what might follow. Like most of the Handstead magistrates, she was in awe of Mortimer and recognised that the reputation they all revelled in as arse-kickers was entirely down to him. She had no wish to see him come unstuck.

'Steady, Colonel, steady,' she whispered into his hairy ear. 'More than one way to skin a cat.'

Snapping out of his rage, Mortimer took a moment to compose himself before addressing the court.

'Thank you, Mr Drake. Who is representing the prisoner?'

'I am, sir,' said a dishevelled little man, getting to his feet alongside the police inspector who would present the case for the prosecution.

Mortimer and his two colleagues glared at the man as if he was something they had stepped in.

'And who exactly are you?' asked Mrs Humphreys, Mortimer's saviour a few moments ago. She didn't add the phrase, 'you little piece of shit', but her tone certainly suggested it.

'Your worships, Tony Morrison from Palmer and

Tomkinson. I represent the defendant Joachim Gunter and on his instruction would oppose any application to remand him in custody. He is a respectable businessman from—'

'Yes, yes, Mr Morrison.' He was interrupted by Colonel Mortimer. 'Your client can tell us all about himself when he gets the opportunity.'

'Quite so, sir,' responded the brief, who was not going to allow himself to be bullied. His company took on lots of legal aid work and specialised in representing no-hoper cases. He was used to dealing with aggressive and biased benches.

'If the interpreter is ready, I call Mr Joachim Gunter,' said Morrison.

'Where's the interpreter?' asked Mortimer testily, keen to get Herman the German banged up quickly.

'Inspector, where's the interpreter?' queried the clerk.

'John, where's the interpreter?' hissed the court inspector to DC Benson, sitting behind him in the body of the court.

'Fuck,' replied Benson, acknowledging that he'd completely forgotten to book one.

'You twat,' growled the inspector before getting to his feet and addressing the bench.

'Your worships, I have liaised with the officer in charge of this investigation, who informs me that shortly before the court convened this morning, he received a telephone call from the interpreter stating that because of a family crisis he would not be able to attend court this morning. Despite his best efforts, the officer has not yet been able to secure the services of a substitute. Your worships, please be assured that we will be bringing this unacceptable state of affairs to the attention of senior officers for the appropriate action to be taken. I can give the court an assurance that this will not happen again and ask for a brief adjournment so the officer in the case can take steps to bring an interpreter to court as quickly as possible.'

Mortimer looked suspiciously at the inspector. 'We can't delay this unnecessarily. Surely we can find an interpreter somewhere. Is there anyone in the court who could assist – someone who might speak German?' His colleagues nodded their agreement.

'Is there anyone in the court who speaks German who could help with a basic interpretation?' asked the clerk, getting to his feet. There were no takers, so the clerk asked again, this time directing his question towards the public gallery and the press benches where a few pensioners had gathered to save the cost of heating their own homes for the day as the library was closed. All stone deaf, they smiled at the nice man in the gown who appeared to be asking them if they were comfortable before resuming their crocheting.

'Does anyone speak German?' shouted the clerk.

Inspiration had struck, and Psycho had spotted the opportunity quickly. Getting to his feet alongside the dock, he announced dramatically, 'I may be able to help your worships. I speak a little German.' He felt those present in the court gaze at him with new-found respect. Jesus, a copper who spoke German, what next?

'Oh no, stop him, for fuck's sake,' hissed Benson urgently to the court inspector, but before the inspector could get to his feet, the clerk had taken matters into his own hands.

'Thank you, Constable.' He smiled at Psycho. 'Please ask the prisoner to confirm his name and date of birth for the court.'

Clearing his throat loudly, Psycho turned to Gunter and said in his best Colditz guard accent, 'Vot ist your name?'

Benson and the court inspector dropped their heads on to the desks in front of them as an incredulous Colonel Mortimer bellowed, 'What did you say?'

Psycho repeated himself to the still beaming Gunter, at which Mortimer exploded, 'Get him to the cells!' and pandemonium ensued. Unsure whether Mortimer's instruction related to Gunter or Psycho, Benson quickly moved to the dock area and took them both down the stairs to the underground calls whilst Mortimer ranted and raved from his seat and the court inspector tried to calm him.

'What the fuck is the matter with you, Psycho?' asked Benson as he locked Gunter up again. 'Why the fuck would you pull a stunt like that? You'll be lucky if Mortimer doesn't bang you up for contempt of court.'

'Nah, I'll be fine,' Psycho assured him. 'Don't worry about Mortimer, he'll get over it soon enough.' Inside, he was glowing. He'd added another chapter to the myth of Psycho.

Upstairs in the court, an irate Colonel Mortimer had eventually been placated by the offer of a long lunch at Handstead nick bar, during which time an interpreter would be located.

The Manchester Crown Court trial would require all Benson and Clarke's expertise. Long before the days of witness protection programmes, witnesses were left very much to their own devices and often endured days of misery in the corridors outside the courts subjected to threats, ridicule and intimidation from the families of those they were giving evidence against. Like many career detectives and years ahead of their time, Benson and Clarke cared for their witnesses like mother hens. A week before the trial they had moved their star witness, the pub landlord who had been viciously attacked by the Park Royal Mafia, out of his flat and into a hotel owned by a mate of theirs. Once the trial started, he and the other witnesses were kept during the day at Bootle Street police station and only called over to the court, escorted by two enormous Greater Manchester uniformed officers, when required to give evidence. The two huge coppers remained at the court door, barring entrance to any but officials, before escorting the witnesses back to Bootle Street. At the end of each day, the witnesses were driven back to their homes or safe houses by circuitous routes to ensure they had not been followed. The reverse happened each morning. At the weekends, all the witnesses were contacted every couple of hours by telephone and could phone either Benson or Clarke at home at any time if they had concerns. The detectives were absolutely determined to get their convictions.

The jury, however, could not be wrapped in cotton wool. Benson had spotted two well-known Mafia staring from the public gallery at a young female jury member. She had spotted them too, and Benson had seen the colour drain from her face as she realised she was being targeted. One afternoon after the court had broken for lunch, Benson had followed her down to Bridge Street, where she had gone into the Golden Egg café. He had slid into the seat opposite her, causing her to look up, initially startled but relaxing a little when she recognised the officer leading the investigation.

'Don't worry, I've seen them too,' he said quietly.

'Seen who?'

Benson smiled. 'I won't be telling anyone about this chat, and neither should you. But don't lose any sleep over the two pricks who've been giving you the silent treatment from the gallery. They've decided not to come to court again.'

'Are you sure?'

'Yeah, they won't be back after this afternoon, trust me. Just do the right thing and don't worry,' he said, easing his huge frame out from behind the table and walking out of the packed café.

That afternoon was indeed the last time the two threatening Mafia members attended the Crown Court. As they left, shortly after five p.m., and walked back along Crown Square towards Bridge Street, two very large men, previously seen wearing immaculate Greater Manchester Police uniforms, slipped out of a side door and followed them. As the two Mafia walked past an alleyway, they were aware of suddenly being whipped effortlessly off their feet and taken very quickly and efficiently out of sight to the rear of a derelict pub. There, without any discussion, the two large men began chanting, 'I will not come back to court again,' each word delivered to the accompaniment of the Mafia men's heads hitting the wall. The message was received. The Old Bill were fighting fire with fire.

Three weeks after the trial had started, the judge, His Honour Marcus Carter-Smith, turned to the jury in Number One Court to address them.

'Members of the jury, my role is a simple one, in that all I am required to do is to direct your attention towards the relevant evidence that has been presented to you. You will have digested that evidence and accepted or rejected it, just as you have assessed the integrity of the witnesses delivering that evidence. And the integrity of the witnesses in this case is, I would suggest to you, paramount. The police officers who have given evidence so professionally have done so, in my view, in the face of a cynical and shabby effort by several of the defence team to denigrate and belittle them. That those police officers remain above such slurs is to their enormous credit, and their evidence is, I would consider, enhanced because of it.'

At this, two members of the defence team looked at each other aghast, whilst the Crown's counsel, Mr Russell Pengelly QC, sat back and contemplated the high ceiling and its ornate architecture. The defendants, all intellectually incapable of understanding the implications of such a biased summing-up, remained slack-jawed in the dock as the legal juggernaut thundered towards them with the one-eyed Judge Carter-Smith at the wheel.

'Allow me to take you through the sequence of events leading to the arrest of the defendants,' continued Carter-Smith. 'Under the malevolent influence of an individual who does not appear with them, the defendants entered a public house in Handstead, where the relief landlord received a beating that nearly resulted in his death. The pub was then looted. The victim has courageously given evidence to this court and unequivocally identified the defendants he says attacked him. Forensic evidence offered by the Crown corroborates his version of events. The landlord owes his life to the prompt medical attention he received from some of the officers who arrived shortly afterwards.

'Some of the defendants were arrested at the scene; the others escaped to a flat owned by the defendant Alan Baker. Sometime over the next few hours, Myra Baldwin, the sole female member of the group, was subjected to a horrific sexual attack by two men. Forensic evidence identifies one of the offenders to be an individual who does not appear before you. The Crown states, and the defence does not refute, that the forensic evidence identifies the second man as the defendant Alan Baker. He has, however, offered a defence that the sexual activity was consensual. You must decide if you believe it likely that a vulnerable young woman would submit willingly to a brutal sodomy by Mr Baker as she had consensual sex with another man. The evidence of that vicious assault has been corroborated with sound forensic evidence post-mortem.

'Local police officers then entered Mr Baker's flat to detain the defendants who had escaped from the public house. PCs Baines and Petty went to a bedroom where they found the unfortunate Myra Baldwin. She was now in possession of a handgun that forensic evidence showed had at some time previously been in the hands of the defendant Alan Baker and another person. Indeed, Mr Baker's fingerprints were found on the empty cartridges recovered from the weapon. The Crown's thoroughly reasonable case is that Alan Baker supplied Myra Baldwin with that handgun in the certain knowledge that she would use it to kill or injure someone. Which is exactly what happened. Myra Baldwin shot PC Baines in the chest before shooting herself in the head. Both she and PC Baines died at the scene. PC Petty gave this court an extraordinary account of those final fatal moments despite outrageous attempts by the defence to denigrate his testimony overall.

'Let us consider the evidence given to this court by the defendants,' continued the judge, almost laughing out loud as he spoke, 'particularly the monotonous litany of claims of police malpractice. Allegations of torture to extract confessions, fabricated interviews and statements, planting of evidence to implicate the defendants and so on. Members of the jury, you have had three weeks to observe and listen, to make your own informed decisions and judgements, and so I ask you one final question. Who do you believe? If you believe the thin tissue of lies and half-truths offered as a defence, then you must acquit. For example, do you really believe that Mr Baker's fingerprints found on the handgun and cartridges were planted there by police officers? If on the other, more likely, hand you believe the version of events proposed by the Crown, then you must find the defendants guilty.

'I would ask you now, dear members of the jury, to retire to consider your verdict, which I would expect to be unanimous. I do not anticipate you will have much difficulty in reaching a decision, but you may of course come back into court for further advice, direction or guidance. I am confident, though, that the Crown has presented you with some very compelling evidence,' he finished, smiling over his half-moon glasses, gimlet eyes sparkling.

He gave the jury a long, hard look as they filed quietly out before turning his gaze to the motley collection in the dock. That animal Baker was chewing gum again and staring around with his usual arrogance and lack of respect. Carter-Smith promised himself he'd add an extra year when the jury came back with their guilty verdict. He yearned for the days when he had first sat on the bench, just after the war. He was one of the few remaining judges on the northern circuit who had actually sentenced a defendant to death. He still had his square of black silk, which he kept as a memento in his pocket and rolled through his fingers when he became particularly irate with a defendant or, more usually, their counsel.

Once the jury had retired, Carter-Smith spoke again, this time to Baker in the dock.

'Mr Baker, are you chewing gum again?'

Baker grinned at him and continued to chew like a cow grinding grass. Carter-Smith's face tightened with rage and Baker's counsel, noticing the danger signs, gesticulated wildly at his client from his seat on the bench. Sourly, and very reluctantly, Baker removed the large wad of chewing gum and rolled it between the fingers of his right hand. Then he flicked it into the well of the court. There was an audible gasp from the assembled ushers, police officers, lawyers, stenographers and members of the public. All eyes turned to Carter-Smith. His face was a mask as he looked unblinking at Baker. Then he smiled like a wolf, revealing sharp, perfectly white teeth – and winked.

'Members of the jury, have you reached a verdict?' asked the clerk to the Court an hour and a half later.

The young girl Benson had followed into the Bridge Street café got to her feet and glanced over at the two DCs sitting at the back of the court, giving them the briefest of smiles.

'We have,' she said loudly.

'Very well, for the defendant Daniel Morgan, on count one of attempted murder, do you find the defendant guilty or not guilty?'

'Guilty.'

A gasp went through the crowded court like a wind through a cornfield. Morgan slumped back in his seat, staring into the middle distance, his young life over. The youngest of the Park Royal Mafia, arrested for the attack on the relief landlord, he had also made a statement implicating the other members of the gang. He had, however, been encouraged to do so by Detectives Clarke and Benson with the aid of large elastic packing bands. His guilt was not in question, just the means by which it had been proved beyond a reasonable doubt.

'On count two, robbery, do you find the defendant guilty or not guilty?'

'Guilty.'

'For the defendant Alan Baker, on count one, conspiracy to murder, how do you find the defendant, guilty or not guilty?'

'Guilty.'

A louder gasp went through the court. The colour drained from Baker's face and he glanced at Carter-Smith, who had fixed him with his piercing eyes and was almost licking his lips.

'You cunts!' screamed Baker. 'They fitted me up,' he continued, pointing at the policemen sitting at the back of the court, all of whom were pointedly looking elsewhere. Baker was restrained from vaulting the dock by two prison officers, who remained holding his shaking arms as the clerk continued.

'On count two, unlawful possession of a Section 1 firearm with intent to commit an indictable offence, do you find the defendant guilty or not guilty?'

'Guilty.'

'Fucking hell!' exploded Baker, and the prison officers increased their grip on him.

'On count three, buggery, do you find the defendant guilty or not guilty?'

'Guilty.'

'On count four, assault with intent to inflict grievous bodily harm, do you find the defendant guilty or not guilty?'

'Guilty.'

'On count five, robbery, do you find the defendant guilty or not guilty?'

'Guilty.'

Carter-Smith was almost beside himself with glee and nearly pulled out his black silk square and put it on over his powdered wig. Instead he contented himself with some thoughtful stroking of his chin as he calculated Baker's sentence.

And so it went on, with every one of the defendants receiving guilty verdicts on every indictment. A few muted protests from friends and family in the public gallery were quickly stamped on by the numerous uniformed officers placed up there.

The court fell silent as it caught its breath after the jury's verdicts and waited eagerly for Carter-Smith to administer the coup de grace.

'Alan Baker, you are a deeply unpleasant and violent young thug,' began Judge Carter-Smith, 'whose reign of terror has at last, and not before time, been brought to an end. You stand before me convicted quite properly of extremely serious offences, not least an appalling sexual assault on a young woman who subsequently murdered a police officer before taking her own life. Who knows how your assault unbalanced her and led to the chain of events and consequences that followed. The murder of Constable Baines is, I believe, firmly in your area of responsibility, in that the court accepts that you provided Anna Baldwin with the firearm she used to murder the officer and then kill herself. Your malevolent influence and aura is all over this case, Mr Baker, and I have a duty to protect the public from individuals like you. For the offence of conspiracy to murder I sentence you to twenty years in prison; for the offence of buggery you will go to prison for ten years; for the offence of robbery you will also serve ten years; for the offence of assault with intent to commit grievous bodily harm you will go to prison for fifteen years, and for the firearms offence you will serve five years' imprisonment.'

He noticed the defence counsel trying desperately to tot up the total sentence given before he added reluctantly, 'These sentences will run concurrently.'

Baker neither moved nor reacted to Carter-Smith's words. He was going away for twenty years. Still, it was better than the life sentence Carter-Smith had handed out to Danny Morgan. Morgan had collapsed when he heard the verdict and had to be carried from the dock. Whichever way you looked at it, the hard-core Mafia were well out of play for a long time, though Baker knew he would be able to exercise a degree of control over one or two of the older survivors back in Handstead. That was due more to lack of intellect than to misguided loyalty, but it would not yet be true to say that the King was dead, long live the King. Whilst changes at the top of the Mafia were inevitable now, it would not be a straightforward process.

Chapter Three

PC Bob Young and his partner Alfie had been cruising a division north of Handstead since midnight, whiling away the time with idle chit-chat and argument, waiting for a call. Nothing had yet merited a visit from them and they were becoming bored and restless.

'Fuck me, it's quiet,' sighed Young, more as an observation to himself than a direct comment to his partner. Young was a thirty-year-old ex-RAF grease monkey, medium height, skinny, with a full head of blond hair left deliberately long just below his ears, kept in a huge side parting and complemented by impressive butcher's grips. He suffered from short-sightedness, which he corrected with a pair of tinted aviator-style spectacles, but his pride and joy was his handlebar moustache, which he kept neatly trimmed and again, just a bit longer than regulations allowed. He was universally known by his nickname of 'Ooh Yah', or to give him his full title, 'Ooh yah, pumpen harder', after his uncanny resemblance to a number of the German porn stars he and many of the other cops at Handstead had sat and watched in poor quality 8mm for many an hour. 'Ooh Yah' Young was privately delighted with the resemblance but regrettably the similarity did not extend to the meat and two veg department, where he was distinctly average. Still, he cultivated the image as much as he could and had even been seen off duty wearing the obligatory porn star's uniform of a tan linen safari suit with a silk scarf. The suit became the stuff of legend for all the wrong reasons and was swiftly discarded when he discovered that the tan linen very unsympathetically highlighted the stains in the front of the trousers from his leaky downstairs tap.

Young didn't expect any response to his remark, and certainly not the response he did get – a bite to his left ear.

Alfie was a hugely unpleasant, aggressive individual. He was feared by everyone who knew him because of his habit of attacking them physically. His only social contact was with Young, with whom he lived. He was extremely fond of Young, not least because he pandered to pretty much all of his whims. Of course there was a down side to a relationship of that nature, with Young insisting on keeping Alfie in a locked shed when they weren't out and about in their van. Their neighbours loathed the pair of them, regularly complaining about the fighting in the small hours as Alfie was locked in his shed. Sometimes they commented on his apparent ill treatment. One winter, Alfie had persuaded Young to let him sleep in the garden overnight. The following morning, horrified neighbours noticed a mound of snow in the back garden move and reveal Alfie, who had been covered by an overnight fall of about six inches.

'You bastard!' yelled Young, instinctively putting a hand up to his injured ear before backhanding his partner across the face. 'You bastard,' he repeated, gingerly rubbing his throbbing ear. 'You do that again and you're in the back.'

Alfie glared at him before turning disdainfully away to stare out of the window at the occasional passing traffic.

'Fuck me,' grumbled Young, continuing to stroke his throbbing ear, 'save it for the villains, will you?' He glanced over at his partner as he spoke and saw that he had his penis out, with a huge dewdrop hanging from the end that soon dripped on to the cloth seat.

'For crying out loud!' shouted Young. 'Put your knob away, will you, it's disgusting.'

Alfie turned to look at him again but said nothing, preferring to show how he felt by curling his top lip to reveal his huge slimy teeth.

'Put it away!' bellowed Young. 'Put it away or you're in the cage, you smelly bastard.'

Alfie knew Young meant what he was threatening, so reluctantly, and very slowly, he settled down into the passenger seat and his erection became hidden from view. Young was about to continue to berate his repulsive partner when the radio burst into life, instructing him to change to Channel One and speak to the operator there. Excited, Young did as he'd been told and gave his Delta One call sign. Alfie clocked his excitement and sat up again as they listened to the message that was being passed.

'Delta One, Hotel Alpha units have suspects disturbed at the Handstead Marshes Social Club. Officers have suspects adrift on the marshes and have requested a dog van. Can you assist? Do you need directions?'

'On our way, Control, know the club well. ETA is about fifteen minutes,' replied Young, before shouting at his partner, 'Hold tight, shithead, we've got a job,' hitting the blue lights and two-tones and flooring the accelerator.

In the front passenger seat, Police Dog Alfie heard the two-tone sirens and went berserk, trying to climb out of the slightly open window to attack a group of youths walking on the pavement. He had grown accustomed to the siren being a direct prelude to the treat of getting to savage someone. The youths were transfixed in horror. The police van that hurtled past them with twos and blues on contained what appeared to be a foaming yeti trying to get out of the passenger window, and most disturbingly, the beast appeared to have its beady, glowing copper eyes fixed directly on them. Its huge, crocodile-like jaws were apparently hinged at its neck and when fully open looked capable of swallowing a small child. Even at speed, the group could discern huge sprays of slobber pouring from the gaping jaws, and they stared open mouthed, praying the window held up to the struggle and the monster remained caged.

Alfie was a huge jet-black German Shepherd, weighing nearly eight stones, with a heavy shaggy coat and deep-set, menacing piggy eyes in a bison-like head. He was a superb tracker, but his real forte was man work. He had excelled at this during his training and he now had a reputation for it the length and breadth of the county. Whereas most police dogs adhered to their training and generally went for a running man's trailing arm, Alfie preferred to overtake his prey and then charge to deliver a full-on body smash followed by an attack to the head. Surprisingly, though, he had not taken naturally to savaging people at first. There was no disputing that he had a fantastic nose, but during his training he had initially shown a reluctance to bite. Searching vast buildings, he would invariably find his hidden instructor, but then instead of nailing him or barking to raise the alarm, he would run off to find his handler. That had been remedied by an instructor who had stepped out of a cupboard and given the dog a crack over the head with a piece of two-by-two. Now Alfie bit first and asked questions later.

Unfortunately, the unwelcome side effect of the instructor's action was that Alfie associated anyone wearing a dark three-quarter-length coat with a length of wood about to land between his ears. The first victim of that association had been an elderly pensioner on her way home from the shops in a dark mackintosh, shortly after Alfie and Young had got back to the force. Alfie had waited patiently for her to get into range before launching an attack on her head and upper body. Luckily Young had felt the dog tense prior to the attack and had a good grip on his lead, but couldn't prevent Alfie flooring the unfortunate old girl. Her subsequent complaint had been quietly filed and put down to Alfie's inexperience. He had bitten and savaged his way across the county, unable to differentiate between cops and robbers. He had disgraced himself in the past taking out police officers in pub fights, but plumbed new depths by putting a young constable through a shop window when he joined in a foot chase through a shopping precinct. His arrival at any scene would prompt urgent returns to police vehicles as the cry went up: 'Fuck me, it's Alfie!' But whilst they were terrified of him, officers who saw him arrive at pub fights and the like knew they would be in for a display of primeval savagery when he got to grips with someone, preferably one of the bad guys. It was awesome viewing, made all the more enjoyable when someone else was on the receiving end.

As they raced along the dual carriageway towards Handstead, Alfie's efforts to leave the van became more and more frenzied, prompting Young to reach over, grab him by the back of the neck and manhandle him down into the footwell. As the dog continued to try to break free, Young steered Delta One one-handed at speed towards the social club, occasionally giving Alfie a left-hand jab to the head to encourage him to remain where he was. He knew Alfie well and was confident that once he released him from the van, someone was going to be in a world of shit.

'Hotel Alpha units at the Handstead Marshes Social Club, be advised Delta One is en route to you, ETA about ten minutes,' reported the Channel One main set operator.

'Delta One?' repeated H, looking at Jim. 'That's Alfie, isn't it?'

'Bloody right,' replied Jim. 'Back in the car before he gets here. Back in the cars!' he repeated louder for the benefit of Ally and Piggy. 'Alfie's on his way.'

'Alfie?' shrieked Ally, who had had a very scary near-miss with him six months previously. 'Fuck that,' and he leapt back into Bravo Two One and locked the door. Piggy followed suit and the two nervous crews sat silently in the darkness of the social club car park, awaiting the arrival of the legendary beast.

Out in the pitch black of the marshes, Brian Jones had become separated from his companion in crime, Patrick Allen. They had been disturbed leaving the rear of the social club they had just burgled and had taken advantage of the police officers' delay in getting out of their car to disappear on to the marshes. Neither Jones nor Allen had given a thought to the other's welfare, and now Jones found himself quite alone in a fringe of saplings alongside a soggy meadow, soaked to the skin and gasping for breath after his panicked dash. He stared anxiously in the direction he had come, both for a sign of his mate and more importantly for the police officers who he was sure would be in close pursuit. With mixed feelings, he realised that neither was coming. Recovering his breath, he took stock of his surroundings and spun slowly through three hundred and sixty degrees. Other than some distant streetlights, he was in total darkness and very lost. The moon was almost totally hidden by thick, leaden clouds and he quickly became despondent. He squatted forlornly on his haunches, devoid of any idea as to how to remedy his situation. Behind the fringe of saplings was a dark and uninviting wood, which he resolved to avoid like the plague. Slowly he got to his feet and began to walk cautiously back the way he had come, gathering his courage. He hoped to get back to the vicinity of the social club, from where he had an idea of how to get back to the Park Royal estate.

Delta One careered to a halt behind Yankee One, sliding across the loose gravel. Even above the crashing of the tyres, the officers in the stationary vehicles could hear the prehistoric roaring from within the van that announced Alfie's arrival.

'Check your door,' cautioned Jim anxiously, locking his. He watched Bob Young in his rearview mirror as Young left Delta One, raining punches on an enraged Alfie to keep him in the vehicle. With some difficulty he got his door shut, sauntered over to Yankee One and tapped on Jim's window.

'All right, boys?' he began brightly. 'What you got for us?'

'All right, Bob, how's things?' replied Jim, winding his window down a fraction, continuing to watch Delta One in his rearview mirror. The van was rocking violently from side to side as Alfie attempted to smash his way free. 'Two had it away from the back window as we pulled into the car park. They've legged it on to the marshes – reckon you'll get much in this weather?'

Bob Young glanced up at the darkening sky and shut his eyes against the light drizzle before replying with a smile, 'Oh yes, no worries on that score. He'll free-track on air scent alone. So long as they haven't kept going or found themselves a motor, we'll get a result.'

He returned to Delta One, gingerly opened his door and reached in to grab Alfie by his thick leather collar. Then he snapped a short lead on to the steel ring and pulled him out of the vehicle. On his hind legs, Alfie was almost as tall as Young. He continued to struggle violently to free himself. Then Young threw back his head and from deep within his diaphragm, and at an ear-shattering pitch, began to shout to the heavens. At once Alfie stopped his struggling.

'Police officer with a dog!' bawled Young into the night. 'Stand still or I'll send the dog.' Alfie dropped to all fours and stood rigid with the hackles on his neck raised, staring into the dark distance. He had completely stopped his frenzied efforts to escape Young's control and now waited for the magic words followed by the click as his lead was released. The crews of Yankee One and Bravo Two One also knew what was coming and sat enthralled in their vehicles, grateful to be well out of the way.

'Arthur Scargill!' bellowed Young slowly, dwelling on and lengthening the words, which seemed to well up from his very soul. 'Arthur Scargill!' he repeated, before bending slightly to hiss into Alfie's pricked ear, 'Kill him!' At the same time, he released the sprung lead grip.

Alfie leapt slightly as he was freed, like a horse leaving the stalls, and then began to gallop out on to the marshes, accelerating quickly. Before he reached full speed, and whilst still within view of the enthralled spectators, he raised his head slightly, opened his crocodile-like jaws and emitted a blood-curdling howl. Then he vanished into the inky wet darkness.

Safe in his seat in Yankee One, Jim shook his head. 'God help anyone he finds,' he muttered. 'I know they deserve it, but can you imagine being caught by that thing out there?' H didn't reply – there was really no need.

As they watched, Young slung the lead over his shoulder, turned to wave to the two car crews and jogged off after Alfie.

'I'll give you a shout if we get anything,' he called.

Half a mile away, Brian Jones had also heard Alfie's howl, which had brought him to an immediate standstill, heart thumping as he peered in the general direction of the awful sound.

'What the fuck was that?' he whispered to himself, straining his eyes and listening intently. He heard a shout, from some distance away, but it was definitely a man's voice. He stepped back into the edge of the dark wood and continued to peer and listen. Then he heard the voice again, slightly closer, and he was able to make out what it was saying.

'Go on, son, where is he? Find him, find him. Kill him, kill him.'

Jones's heart froze and his stomach reared into his throat.

'Oh no, a fucking p-police dog,' he stammered.

The voice was even closer now. 'Find him, big fella, find him. Kill him, kill him.'

Jones panicked, turned into the wood he had been desperate to avoid and began to flee through the undergrowth and ferns, crashing into trees, spinning round, running desperately into the dark, thorns grabbing at his body, tearing at his clothes. He fell to the ground hard against a large tree root, shins grazed and bruised. Regaining his feet, he continued his flight through the dark wood until he crashed past a small fir tree and found himself in short grass by a fast-flowing stream with high steep banks. It was about twenty feet wide. Looking left and right, and panting almost uncontrollably, Jones quickly concluded that his best chance of escape lay on the far bank. As he steeled himself to jump, he heard the man shouting again, very close behind him in the wood, and what sounded like an elephant smashing its way through the undergrowth.

Jones surfaced in shoulder-high water and looked back towards the wood in time to see a huge dog break cover and begin to search desperately for its prey. Its mean, copper-coloured eyes glowed in its jet-black head as it dashed desperately from side to side seeking an air scent, occasionally dropping its nose to the ground for the telltale smell of recent passing footsteps. Jones gave a shudder unconnected with being in freezing water.

'Where is he, big fella?' shouted Young, also breaking through the trees. 'Where is he?' He remained at the edge of the wood, nonchalantly swinging the lead as Alfie frantically free-tracked around the river bank trying to get his prey's scent. He stopped twice at one particular spot, but turned away unsure and continued elsewhere.

Mid-river, Jones had dropped below the surface, leaving only his eyes and nose above water. The current was relatively gentle, but its flow was sufficient for it to occasionally get into his nostrils. Desperately he fought the urge to lunge out of the water to breathe properly. Somehow he regained his composure and remained submerged, managing to keep one eye on the dog, which had not moved far away and continued to cast in circles, looking for a scent. It kept returning to the spot where Jones had gone into the water.

Young had seen Alfie returning to the same place and called out again, 'Where is he, big fella? Crossed over, has he?' Alfie ignored him and continued to gallop around.

The current was strong enough to move Jones slightly round in his watery hide, and disconcertingly, he now lost sight of the dog, which was directly behind him. He could still hear the awful noise it was making, but not to be able to see it was dreadful. He considered trying to move himself back round but was afraid the current would bowl him over completely and alert the dog and its handler. He decided to remain where he was.

Young saw Alfie come to a screeching halt at the same spot he had stopped at three times before, legs stiff as pokers, hackles raised, head dropped into an attack posture, staring intently into the river.

'What you got, big fella, where is he?' hissed Young, sensing the monster had found his man and advancing quickly to his side, though he was careful not to touch him and distract him. He followed Alfie's gaze into the river and quickly spotted the back of Jones's head, just visible above the water's surface. A smile spread across his face as he patted Alfie on his bulging shoulders. 'You fucking beauty,' he whispered. 'He's all yours, just let me get him going for you.'

Alfie knew there was something in the river but couldn't work out what. He had picked up the familiar air scent at the spot at which he had located ground scent previously, but without an obvious source for it had become confused. Young intended to make things clear for him. He quickly found a large stone nearby and returned to stand alongside Alfie, who had not moved a muscle or taken his eyes off the river. Taking careful aim, Young hurled the stone at the head in the water, catching it a heavy glancing blow. The stone ricocheted up into the air before splashing into the river nearby and the head disappeared briefly under water.

A split second later, Jones emerged screaming and choking from the depths, turning as he did so to face his nemesis, one hand clutching his injured head. The dog's eyes had grown to the size of saucers and its jaws opened slightly at the scene in front of it. Jones saw the jaws open and screamed even louder – no words, just a blood-curdling scream from the soles of his freezing feet. With a roar, the dog launched itself into the air like an Olympic freestyle swimmer, briefly silhouetted by the moon as it broke free from behind the scudding clouds. All four legs were fully extended, the massive jaws wide open and those evil copper eyes fixed on him, and Jones knew his hour had come.

The dog hit Jones full on, attempting to swallow his head whole, inflicting deep cuts to his scalp and forcing him back under water. As he thrashed about at the bottom of the river, Jones caught a glimpse of his nightmare looking at him. The eyes were as dead as a Great White Shark's and Jones was now quite sure he was going to die. He broke surface again and began to wade frantically towards the bank. Behind him, he could hear the dog swimming after him. He felt searing pain as teeth sank into his right shoulder, then the animal put its front legs on to his head, forcing him under again. He surfaced gasping for air, thrashed behind him to push the dog away and realised he was within touching distance of the bank.

'Help me!' he screamed at the handler. 'Help me!'

Young remained where he was, roaring with laughter, whilst Jones scrambled up the steep muddy bank. Alfie could see his prey escaping and hurried after him, snapping at his heels as they disappeared over the top of the bank.

Jones was trying to crawl away towards the now-welcoming dark wood when he again heard that awful roaring. He looked desperately over his shoulder to see the monster shaking itself in a huge shower of water that covered several square yards before again setting its gaze on its prey, dropping its head into an attack posture and starting to stalk him.

'No!' pleaded Jones as he rolled on to his back and began

to scramble away, keeping the dog in sight. 'No,' he repeated, looking to the handler for salvation. 'Please stop him!'

Young looked at him and smiled. He barked out the single command, 'Stay!' at which Alfie stopped in his tracks and fixed Jones with an unflinching stare.

'Stop him? Why should I stop him?' asked Young conversationally. 'It's what he gets paid to do,' he added.

'For fuck's sake, please stop him. I'll do whatever you want me to, just stop him!' cried Jones.

'You've got fuck all to offer me, son,' said Young. 'A piece of shit like you deserves everything you get. What you got to give me, then?'

'I can get money if you want!' shouted Jones, not taking his eyes off the dog.

'I don't want your fucking money, you arsehole. Get ready to bleed slowly to death.'

'No, no, wait, wait!' Jones yelled desperately. 'I'll work for you, I can get you information any time you like.'

'What information?' queried Young, interested now.

'Anything you like. I know what's going on.'

'Who you running with then?'

'Andy Travers, Hugh Briggs and a few others.'

Young knew of Travers and Briggs – a couple of hard nuts who had filled the vacuum left by Driscoll and Baker. The original Park Royal Mafia had begun to disintegrate the day Baker had gone down, but Travers and Briggs had stepped up and moved things on, and had quickly become a problem locally as the new Mafia began to flex its muscles.

'Sounds promising. What sort of information are you talking about? Better be decent or the boy's going to have you.'

'I know what they've got lined up.'

'Like what?' scoffed Young.

'You going to call him off?' said Jones, relaxing slightly.

'Come!' barked Young. Slowly and extremely reluctantly, without taking his eyes off Jones, Alfie padded over to Young and positioned himself by his left leg. Reaching down, Young quickly clipped the lead to Alfie's collar. 'I'm all ears,' he said.

'Blaggings and that,' offered Jones.

'Blaggings and that?' roared Young. 'Fuck off, you'll have to do better than that,' and he reached down to Alfie's collar again.

'No, no, don't! I know what they've got planned, and when.'

'You fucking better had,' said Young. He put Alfie in the down position and walked over to Jones, unravelling the thirty-foot tracking line he had slung round his shoulders. Hauling Jones to his feet, Young trussed him like a chicken before marching him back through the woods and across the marshes with Alfie nipping at his heels and circling him like a sheep dog shepherding a flock. During the journey Jones spilled his guts to Young, who made a mental note to visit DCs Clarke and Benson in their office at Handstead. The new Handstead Mafia had been infiltrated and was now very vulnerable.

Brian Jones had waited nearly half an hour alongside Bob Young to be booked in at the Handstead cell block. Two violent drunks were ahead of them and the delay was worsened when both kicked off and had to be forcibly restrained by their arresting officers. The night-duty station officer, Sergeant Paul Costin, was an unflappable ten-year veteran, but even he was starting to feel the pressure. The booking-in area consisted of a single beaten-up wooden table secured to the floor by huge bolts and a single plastic chair for the station sergeant. Lit by a pair of flickering fluorescent strip lights, the nicotine-yellow gloss walls were covered in notices informing prisoners of their various, usually denied, rights and entitlements. The only natural source of light came from a large chequerboard window of opaque armoured glass.

Costin wearily instructed the arresting officers to get their drunks down to the cells, pulled another self-carbonated A3 custody record sheet from a drawer alongside his desk and looked up at his next customer. He recognised Bob Young, who regularly brought prisoners into Handstead.

'Hi, Ooh Yah, what you got for me?' he asked, trying to

ignore the screaming and shouting coming from the passage behind him.

'One for burglary at the social club, Sarge,' replied Young. 'Tracked him away from the back of the club and nicked him about a mile away in a river.'

Costin nodded, not now needing to ask why the prisoner was soaked to the skin and shaking like a leaf with the cold. He quickly ran through the time and location of the arrest with Young before turning his attention to Jones.

'What's your name, mate?'

'I want to complain about him. He set his fucking dog on me out there – look at the state I'm in,' Jones replied, dropping his head forward to show the still-weeping bite marks in his scalp. 'I've got more on my back,' he added.

'Shut your fucking mouth,' snarled Costin, who had had more than enough of bolshie prisoners for one night. 'I want your name, address and date of birth. I'm not interested in anything else, clear?'

To reinforce Costin's message, Young then cracked Jones across the back of the head with the lead he had brought in with him.

'Button it, otherwise the dog'll be dealing with you again,' he whispered.

'Fucking hell,' was all Jones could manage as he rubbed the back of his head and wondered how much worse things could get. Although a regular visitor to the cells at Handstead, he could testify to the fact that no one ever got complacent about being banged up there. It had a hard-earned reputation as being the worst place in the county to get nicked, with various stories in circulation amongst the villains about brutality and other abuses. He quickly provided the information Costin had demanded and stood sullenly as it was recorded longhand.

'Anything on him at all, Bob?' asked Costin as he turned the page to record property brought into custody with the prisoner. Jones knew he'd had nothing on him when he was nicked, so he was more than a little surprised to hear Young reply, 'Just this jemmy tucked down the back of his trousers, Sarge,' and a loud metallic clang as Young dropped a small jemmy on to Costin's desk.

'What's that?' shouted Jones.

'Found it down the back of your trousers,' said Young innocently.

'Did you fuck! He's fitting me up, the bastard,' yelled Jones.

'Keep it down, arsehole,' interrupted Costin. 'You'll get your say later,' and he slipped the jemmy into a plastic evidence bag before recording it on the property record.

'I've never seen the thing before – he's fucking planted it,' persisted Jones.

'Yeah, yeah, they all say that. Here, just sign this record for me,' said Costin, pushing the custody record across the desk to him.

'I'm signing fuck all. He's planted that. I'm getting fitted up here is what's happening.'

Costin shrugged his shoulders and pulled the record back. 'Stick him in number seven. Don't bother with a change of clothes, he'll dry off soon enough,' he said to his gaoler, who grabbed Jones unceremoniously by the shoulder and carted him off to the cells. His continued protests were soon lost in the cacophony of noise from the cell area.

Costin reached down to the drawer beside him and pulled out another plastic evidence bag containing an identical jemmy to the one Young had dropped on the desk.

'Got a job lot of these, have you, Bob?' he asked the grinning Young.

'Always come in handy, Sarge, you know how it is.'

'Bob, use your imagination a bit, will you? This is the third jemmy you've brought in to us this month that I'm aware of. Fuck me, a bit of variation wouldn't go amiss, you know – the odd screwdriver or wire-cutter.'

Young continued to smile. Actually, he'd brought in five prisoners with identical jemmies, all part of a set of ten he'd found in his father's garage.

'Point taken, Sarge,' he said finally. 'We all right with this one?'

'Last one, Bob. Now fuck off and I don't expect to see any more of 'em, OK?'

'No problems, Sarge, see you later,' he called as he left the custody area in search of Clarke and Benson.

*   *   *

He found the two detectives sitting, feet up, in the CID office enjoying a quiet glass or two of Scotch. They knew the cells were filling up quickly and that they were in for an absolute ball-breaker of a night. They had dealt with Young in the past and had got some good results from him, so they pulled him out a chair, poured him a polystyrene cup and listened intently to what he had to say. When he'd finished, they asked him to let them have a copy of his arrest notes, and when he'd gone, they discussed their plan of action.

'D'you know Jones?' asked Clarke.

'Heard of him, that's all. Definitely Mafia, though.'

'Think we can get into him?'

'Yeah, we should do. Got plenty to be going on with, haven't we?'

'Yeah, suppose so. We can threaten to start letting all the wrong people think he's grassing them up. That always seems to work.'

'We've got him bang to rights on the break-in at the social club, and of course there's always Ooh Yah's jemmy – a bit of leverage there, I think.'

'I reckon this could be a job for the good Dr Kirk St Moritz,' said Clarke with a knowing smile.

'Like it, Bob, like it very much. I'll give him a call. I'm sure he's working tonight,' said Benson, reaching for his desk phone.

* * *

Two hours later, having spent the last hour in the dark of the prisoners' cupboard in the CID office on the first floor, Jones found himself facing DCs Clarke and Benson in an interview room on the same floor. The room was identical to the cell-block interview rooms, devoid of any distractions. Lit by a harsh fluorescent strip light, the off-white walls were totally blank – Jones had nothing to look at except the detectives. As Clarke and Benson took their seats and arranged some papers on the table in front of them – more for show than to actually use during the interview – Jones opened proceedings.

'I want a brief,' he announced boldly.

Clarke smiled benevolently at him like a patient father.

'You silly boy.'

'I'm saying fuck all until I get a brief.'

'No one knows you're here, you twat. You're not having a brief. Besides, you don't need one; you've already put your hands up to the burglary and you're bang to rights with the jemmy. What we want to talk about is what you know.'

'That fucking dog-handler planted that jemmy,' shouted Jones. 'I've never seen the fucking thing before.'

'Maybe, maybe,' mused Benson. 'Still, would have been useful getting into the social club.'

'Didn't need a jemmy . . .' began Jones before he realised where he was being led and clammed up.

Clarke smiled at him and leant back in his chair, hands behind his head.

'Listen, Brian, we've got everything we need to charge you with the burglary and the jemmy. We can come to some arrangement with you, catch my drift?'

'Arrangement? What the fuck are you on about?'

'Fucking hell, Brian, you had a long chat with the uniform who nicked you. You flapped your gums like a ninety-year-old wing-walker. Tell us what you told him.'

'Bollocks, I made that up to get his fucking dog off me. I don't know fuck all.'

'Wrong again, Brian, you're well in with Travers and Briggs. We knew that anyway, but what we want to know is just how well in you are. We can come to some arrangement about the burglary and the jemmy when you've told us.'

Jones remained silent, head down and arms folded as he desperately considered what he was hearing. They were offering him a clean bill of health for the burglary and the planted jemmy, but they wanted something on the Mafia in return. The silence was only disturbed by faint screaming and swearing somewhere off in the distance.

'He planted that jemmy,' he said finally.

'May well have done,' acknowledged Clarke, leaning forward, 'but it's his word against yours, isn't it? He tracks you away from the scene of a burglary, finds you holed up in a river, searches you and finds a jemmy hidden down the back of your trousers. Who's going to believe he planted it?'

Jones's shake of the head answered that question as he accepted bitterly that he was well fucked.

'But there's a happy ending to the story,' said Benson cheerily, getting to his feet and moving alongside Jones, resting a hand on his shoulder. 'You tell us what you know about Travers and Briggs, what they're up to, what they've got planned, who they're talking to, all that sort of stuff, and we'll see you all right. OK, Brian?'

'What, fucking grass, you mean,' protested Jones.

'Grass is such an unpleasant term,' continued Benson quietly. 'No, no, not grass, merely keep us up to date on things on the Park Royal. You get to keep out of nick, you'll get a few bob for the work you do and no one will ever know – couldn't be cleaner or simpler.'

'I'm not fucking grassing anyone up,' said Jones defiantly, folding his arms again. 'Fucking charge me if you can.'

'I was expecting better of you, Brian,' said Clarke, shaking his head. 'This is very disappointing but we realised it might happen, which is why we arranged for the police doctor to come along.'

'Police doctor?'

'Yes, Dr St Moritz is here to help you,' replied Clarke, getting to his feet and opening the door. He leant out into the corridor and called, 'Dr St Moritz?'

A few seconds later, a man limped into the room.

'Dr St Moritz, good of you to come. This is Brian Jones,

who needs your help,' said Clarke by way of introduction.

To his horror, Jones noted that the white-haired doctor was staring at the wall to his left through the thickest milk-bottle glasses he had ever seen. His white coat appeared to be covered in dried bloodstains and resembled an energetic and inefficient butcher's apron.

'Over here, Doctor,' said Clarke gently, getting hold of his shoulders and turning him to face Jones, who could now see that his eyes were magnified to incredible proportions.

'Good evening,' drooled the doctor in a heavy French accent through the most appalling set of Billy Bob teeth.

'Who the fuck are you? I don't need any help from any-one,' said Jones, getting to his feet and taking a step back.

'Dr Kirk St Moritz, police surgeon,' came the reply as the doctor offered a handshake in Benson's direction.

'Over here, Doctor,' said Benson, taking hold of his arm and moving it towards Jones.

Swallowing hard, Jones took the offered hand and was surprised at its strength. Gripping him hard, the doctor pulled Jones close to him and hissed into his ear, 'Soon we have the truth, yes?'

Recoiling from his breath, which smelt like he gargled dog shit, and roughly shaking himself free from the handshake, Jones took another step back and shouted, 'Truth? What the fuck are you on about?'

'Truth serum, my dear boy. Now, where's my bag?' said the doctor, beginning to look around at the floor.

Clarke retrieved the doctor's large black Gladstone bag from the corridor outside and thumped it down on the desk. Dr St Moritz began to rummage about in its depths whilst Jones stood desperately against the far wall, looking aghast at the implements coming out of the bag. A small handsaw, pliers, a chisel and a pair of wire-cutters had been laid on the table before the doctor exclaimed triumphantly and produced the largest syringe Jones had ever seen, with a needle easily twelve inches long. It contained what appeared to be about a pint of a milky white liquid, some of which the doctor squirted dramatically into the air. Then he flicked the side of the syringe with his finger.

'Truth serum,' he repeated menacingly, fixing his massive eyes on Jones and giving him the full force of his snaggle-toothed smile.

'What the fuck is he on about?' Jones screeched at Clarke and Benson.

'Dr St Moritz is going to administer a shot to make sure you're telling the truth, Brian. Nothing to worry about, he does this all the time.'

'Fuck off!' yelled Jones, turning to see the doctor limping towards him waving the syringe vaguely in his general direction. As he got closer, Jones noticed that the syringe, which was big enough to inseminate cattle, had what appeared to be bloodstains along its length.

'Fuck off, you old cunt,' screamed Jones, backing against

the wall as the optically challenged doctor began to lunge at him like a demented fencer.

'Just give him your arm, for fuck's sake, Brian,' said Benson irritably. 'It's always worse when he has to fight and goes through an artery. Remember the last one, Bob?'

'Fuck me, yeah, claret everywhere. Stains are still on the ceiling.'

Glancing quickly upwards and then back at the nightmare still limping after him as he moved around the interview-room walls, Jones screamed again. 'Fucking hell, stop the mad bastard!'

'Can't do that, Brian, we need some information from you, and Dr St Moritz's truth serum is the only way we're going to get it.'

Jones had momentarily taken his eyes off the circling, menacing, vulture-like doctor, who suddenly lunged at him and grabbed one of his arms. St Moritz was immensely strong and quickly dragged the squealing Jones to the table, where he slammed the arm on to the tabletop with Jones desperately pummelling his back, screeching, 'No, no, stop him!'

As the deranged doctor examined the restrained arm very closely through his milk-bottle glasses, looking for a vein to ram his syringe into, Jones became hysterical.

'Stop him, for fuck's sake, stop him, I'll tell you anything you want. Fucking hell, stop him!' he sobbed, tears of pure terror running down his ashen cheeks.

'Can't hear you, Brian,' said Clarke, cupping an ear.

'Stop him, I'll tell you anything you want, please stop him,' cried Jones.

Clarke and Benson stepped forward and took hold of Dr St Moritz.

'That'll do, Doctor, I don't think we need any truth serum now. Brian's going to tell us what we want without it.'

'Oh no, please,' drooled the doctor. 'Just a little injection, please.'

'Sorry, Doctor, not today, maybe next time,' said Benson, leading the doctor towards the door as the sobbing, shaking Jones fell to the floor, wrapping his arms around himself and curling into a foetal ball.

'Just a tiny one,' continued the doctor, trying to break free from Benson to get back to Jones.

'No, no, Doctor,' said Benson firmly, opening the door and shoving the doctor out into the corridor. He passed his bag out to him and then slammed the door shut. With his back against the door, he looked down at Jones on the floor.

'Fucking hell, Brian, thought he was going to have to stick you then.'

From outside in the corridor the doctor could be heard calling, 'Please, just a little injection,' and knocking on the door.

'Hold on here, Bob,' said Benson. 'I'll just get rid of the doctor. I'm sure he's due back in the secure unit by now.'

'Secure unit?' called Jones from the floor.

'Don't ask,' replied Clarke as Benson left, closing the door behind him.

Outside in the corridor, Benson offered a handshake to Dr St Moritz.

'Fucking quality performance again, Darren,' he laughed.

As he removed his white wig, milk-bottle glasses and Billy Bob teeth, Detective Sergeant Darren Vaughen returned the handshake.

'No worries, John, works every fucking time, doesn't it?' he laughed.

'Yeah, the worry is that one day you're going to end up having to jab one of them. Jones got pretty close, didn't he?'

'No, not really, he just spun it out a little longer than most,' said Vaughen. 'Give us a ring if you need me again.'

Benson returned to the interview room, where Clarke had heaved Jones back into his chair.

'Well, Brian,' he sighed heavily as he retook his own chair, 'tell us what Travers and Briggs are up to.'

Over the next forty-five minutes, Jones gave them chapter and verse on the make-up of the new Park Royal Mafia, what they had done to date, and most importantly, an undertaking that any information about upcoming jobs would be passed on. Clarke ensured that a warranty was in place for the sale.

'Brian, anything happens involving that lot that you've

forgotten to tell us about, we're going to chop your fucking legs off, understand?'

'What you on about?'

'You keep us up to date with everything or we'll spread the word that you're an eighteen-carat snout. Keep things ticking over and you'll earn a good few bob, understood?'

'You pair of bastards.'

'Yeah, but do you understand? We want to know everything, always.'

'Yeah, yeah, OK,' snapped Jones irritably.

Benson's response was a resounding slap across the back of Jones's head which sent him flying back on to the filthy floor. Wide eyed, he looked up at Benson, who stood looming over him.

'You need to fully understand the nature of this relationship we're going to have, you little prick. The tail doesn't wag this dog, OK? You bring us information, we give you a few bob, we let you live your crappy little life pretty much as before, but you fuck up just once and you're finished. D'you understand?'

'Yeah,' said Jones flatly, now totally broken and subdued, 'I understand, but what about the burglary?'

'And the jemmy,' Clarke reminded him. 'Don't worry too much about those. We'll bail you out whilst we continue inquiries. You come up with the goods, those inquiries can go on for ever.'

Twenty minutes later, Jones left the station with his bail

notice tucked in his back pocket, very reminiscent in fact of his own position, tucked in the back pockets of DCs Benson and Clarke. It was now the early hours of the morning and still drizzling. He stood under a bus shelter in the forlorn hope that the drizzle would cease and scanned the deserted, glistening streets. Nothing moved and the rain got heavier. He walked dejectedly back to the Park Royal estate, getting drenched in the process, his mood as foul as the weather by the time he slammed his front door shut. Leaving his soaked clothes in a pile by his bed, he lay for a while under the covers trying to rest his spinning brain. But sleep would not come to him as he considered the awful predicament he now found himself in – on the end of a very short leash held by two of Handstead's finest.

Chapter Four

Sercan Ozdemir was the thirty-five-year-old director of a haulage business based just outside Handstead. The business was booming on the face of it, with thirty liveried HGVs carrying freight to and from the Continent seven days a week. The success of the company appeared to mirror the decline of the national rail network's ability to move freight efficiently, but in fact it was due in no small part to the smuggling operation that Ozdemir was involved in as part of a serious organised-crime syndicate.

A Turk from the Mediterranean port city of Antalya, he had been born into the fringes of a large crime family. His branch of the family had been moved over to Manchester in 1950 to support a burgeoning global crime syndicate operation, and young Sercan cut his criminal teeth on the murky streets of Moss Side. His marriage in 1965 to the daughter of one of the main players cemented his place in the crime family, and he rose to a position of influence, albeit one resented by many of his contemporaries, who rightly suspected nepotism at work. He was a handsome, charming six-footer with a mop of curly dark hair that he tried to tame with copious use of brilliantine, a flashing smile and smouldering brown eyes – but he harboured dangerous visions of grandeur. In 1968 he had been instructed to create his haulage company in order to satisfy the family's desire to get a serious piece of the developing illegal drugs market. He had located the perfect premises outside Handstead, which was only a short drive from the family stronghold in north Manchester, and paid cash for a brand-new fleet of lorries which were soon a regular sight on cross-Channel ferries and continental motorways. In his first two years of operations, Sercan Ozdemir smuggled over three tonnes of heroin and cannabis into the United Kingdom, along with millions of cigarettes and countless gallons of alcohol, making thousands of pounds of profit for the family. He was careful to carry plenty of legitimate cargoes, and in the eyes of Customs and Excise officers at the ports was one of the few reputable haulage operators. His vehicles were immaculate and well maintained, his drivers smart and polite and the paperwork always, but always, spot on. It was a fabulous operation that aroused virtually no suspicion and provided him with an opulent lifestyle he could only have dreamt about – but he wanted more.

He deeply resented the fact that he was at the beck and

call of his uncle in Manchester, that he could never operate independently of the family. Everything had to be OK'd by them first and he had begun to feel like little more than the hired help. For some time he had had ambitions to pull off a real coup by bringing in a cargo so large that the family could not fail to be impressed. And then one day the opportunity fell into his lap. A reliable contact had put him in touch with a friend in Amsterdam who represented a Burmese warlord operating in the Golden Triangle who was also looking for a lucrative sideline away from his usual business sources. Sercan Ozdemir had been offered ten tonnes of high-grade heroin, but first he had to find the money. He had pondered his options for some time. He needed significant sums of cash, and the obvious source was banks and security vans. He directed his attentions that way and was soon convinced that he needed to rob half a dozen properly selected vans to finance his new business enterprise. He would also need some muscle to undertake the job, and that was when his smouldering brown eyes fell on what remained of the Mafia.

In common with most of the residents of the area, his knowledge of them was gleaned from following the TV and newspaper reports of the trial following the murder of PC Dave Baines and the subsequent convictions of most of the senior players. He had read a follow-up piece in a Sunday magazine and was intrigued to learn that despite having its head cut off, this particular snake still had life left in it. It occurred to him that hiring some hooligans from the Mafia would fit the bill very nicely, and so long as he kept them at arm's length he could keep his own nose clean when, almost inevitably he felt, the Old Bill rolled them all up again.

He made his move one evening accompanied by two of his own huge Turkish minders wearing identical dark suits and raincoats, breezing into the saloon bar of the Park Royal pub, home of the remaining Mafia. Andy Travers and Hugh Briggs were playing pool as the doors opened with a bang and Ozdemir and his minders made their grand entrance. Ozdemir was dressed to kill and looked every inch the criminal godfather he longed to be. Looking round the pub, he spotted Travers and Briggs and walked slowly over to them.

'I'm looking for what remains of the Park Royal Mafia,' he said in his still heavily accented English.

'Who the fuck are you?' responded Briggs menacingly, picking up his pool cue again. Before he had got it six inches off the table, one of Ozdemir's minders had moved like greased lightning and in a single movement shoved the barrel of a Magnum .45 Colt under his nose and thumbed back the hammer.

'Drop it,' he hissed.

Bug eyed, Briggs let the cue drop back on to the table and spread both his arms wide in submission. Travers stood open mouthed alongside him, also spreading his arms wide to be on the safe side. The other drinkers in the bar, all

Mafia, waited and watched with their hearts in their mouths. The tension in the air was electric, sparking around the room, almost tangible.

Smiling benevolently, Sercan stepped forward and laid a hand on his unblinking minder's shoulder.

'OK, Ahmet, relax, let him go, he understands now.'

The minder took a deep breath and very slowly removed the gun from under the trembling Briggs's nose. Then he took a step back, keeping the weapon levelled at Briggs's forehead.

'Ahmet, it's OK,' insisted Ozdemir. 'Everything's OK now, put it down.'

Ahmet dropped the gun to his side, took another step back and then slowly released the hammer before slipping the gun into his trouser waistband and pulling his double-breasted jacket across to conceal the handle.

'Gentlemen, allow me to introduce myself,' Ozdemir continued as though nothing had happened and flashing a 1000-megawatt smile. 'My name is Sercan Ozdemir. You may have heard of me,' and he offered a handshake to the still-shaking Travers and Briggs. They had indeed both heard of him and some of the rumours that had begun to circulate in the criminal fraternity about his connections with organised crime in Manchester. They both took the offered hand and glanced warily at the two minders, one of whom was staring unsmiling at them, while the other, with his back to them, was watching the rest of the pub.

'And you two are?' pressed Ozdemir.

'I'm Andy Travers; this is Hugh Briggs.'

Precisely the pair he had set out to find, after some rudimentary research by his staff had identified them as the new top dogs. It couldn't have worked out better. Something about them as he walked in had told him that they were the ones who had moved into the vacancies left by Driscoll and Baker. And he had been right.

'Guys, we need to speak. I have a business proposition for you. But not here, I think. Can you be at my office first thing tomorrow morning?'

Both men nodded, and Ozdemir gave them the address they were to come to. Then he and his minders turned on their heels and were gone as quickly as they had arrived.

'What the fuck was all that about?' asked Travers.

'Fuck knows. We'll find out tomorrow. Fucking hell . . .' Briggs's voice trailed off. He was still very shaken from his encounter with the gun up his nose. The pair decided to abandon their game of pool and took themselves off to a corner table, where they discussed what had happened and what Ozdemir might have in store for them tomorrow. They agreed that any business proposition from a man like that would be one they probably wouldn't refuse. By the end of the evening they were discussing Ozdemir in terms that would have massaged his criminal ego handsomely.

The following morning they met Ozdemir as arranged in

his large office above his transport premises. His stunning secretary, wearing a micro-miniskirt, delivered coffee to the group, convincing Travers and Briggs that they were in the company of the real deal. Ozdemir for his part was appalled to note that the duo were wearing their filthy clothes from the previous evening and that neither appeared to have had a wash.

The business proposition was a simple one, as it needed to be with Travers and Briggs. Ozdemir needed the Mafia to take out some security vans, preferably all on the same day. Travers and Briggs would get ten per cent of what the vans contained, to distribute as they saw fit. Ozdemir's team would take care of all the planning and logistics – the Mafia would be briefed as and when needed, and would then go out and do the job as ruthlessly as they liked. Travers and Briggs looked at each other and smiled. They were going to be very rich young men.

'Don't sound too difficult, Mr Ozdemir. We'll run it past Alan Baker and get back to you.'

'Baker? What's he got to say about anything?'

'He runs things really, since Bobby Driscoll got it.'

'He's doing twenty years.'

'Yeah, we know, but he's still running things from inside.'

'Don't you worry about Mr Baker,' laughed Ozdemir. 'Consider him history. I'm dealing with you two from now on.'

He indicated over his shoulder to one of his goons, who

leant forward. Ozdemir whispered into his ear, and the goon nodded and quickly left the office.

'Guys, you're going to need weapons for this enterprise. Do you have access to any firearms?' continued Ozdemir.

'No. Alan had a shooter, but we've never had any.'

'Can't do this without them – you need to get hold of some pretty quickly.'

The silence from the other side of the table confirmed that he was dealing with a pair of cretins.

'Guys, you're going to have to speculate to accumulate. Do I make myself clear?'

Their continued silence answered the question.

'Guns beget guns,' continued Ozdemir patiently. 'You need to start small and get big. For example, I would start by burgling one of the houses out in the countryside here. They all go shooting, and every home will usually have at least one shotgun in it. I'll adapt the guns you steal and then you go big.'

'Go big?' queried Travers.

'Very big. You do the gunsmith's in Tamworth and stock up with everything you need for the operation you're going to embark on. Clear?'

'Right!' exclaimed Travers and Briggs, the fog clearing.

'So tomorrow night, perhaps, you get your boys out to lay their hands on a couple of shotguns. My guys will adapt them for you and then plan the job at Tamworth. All you have to do is turn up.'

'Right,' chorused Travers and Briggs enthusiastically, and Ozdemir rolled his eyes to the ceiling. There was a real risk getting involved with these idiots, but on reflection, it was well worth it. He estimated that six good hits on properly selected security vans would net him something in the region of £3 million. The ten tonnes of heroin was costed at £1.5 million; even with ten per cent going to the Mafia, and other as yet unidentified overheads, there'd still be a tidy profit. And that was before he started selling the gear on the street. If Travers and Briggs proved too much of a problem in the future, he'd simply remove them from the face of the earth. He'd done it before.

'OK, guys, you come back to us by ringing this number when you've got guns that need taking care of,' he said, writing a number on a piece of paper and pushing it across the table. Briggs picked it up and looked quizzically at him.

'We won't be seeing each other again,' explained Ozdemir. 'You deal with the person on the end of the phone. We don't know each other, understood?'

Briggs tapped the side of his nose and Ozdemir groaned inside. They were a huge risk, but where else could he go to get help? And anyway, the stupider the help, the better. The Mafia ticked all the right boxes – violent, thick and malleable.

Ozdemir got to his feet to signify that their meeting was at an end and offered both men a handshake before the remaining minder escorted them out of the office and off the premises. Alone in his office, he continued to ponder on what he was embarking on. If he succeeded, he calculated that the family would move him rapidly onwards and upwards, recognising his latent talent for great things. Fuck it up and he would be fed to the pigs kept by his aunt near the M6. They were used to eating human flesh, and nothing had ever been left.

He closed his eyes and laid his head back into his large leather armchair. His contemplations were disturbed by his desk phone ringing. He listened intently before replacing the receiver without saying a word. Things were moving quickly and were already past the point of no return.

Nature abhors a vacuum, and vacuums had been filled at Handstead nick too, albeit by the original material in some cases. Inspector Hilary Bott had spent a couple of months off sick before returning determined to make her mark again. She had fallen foul of PC Sean Pearce, who had begun a psychological war against her which included using her senior officers' toilet and not flushing it. On the last occasion he had left her a present, Bott had staggered away from the toilet and knocked herself out on the door. The officers who had found her had mistakenly assumed she had fainted after passing the enormous stool and had called an ambulance crew, who had sedated her before whisking her unceremoniously off to hospital. Unfortunately, she had now developed a stress-related stammer, which her number two nemesis, Sergeant Tucker, had quickly seized on, addressing her whenever possible as 'm-m-m-m-m-ma'am', which she hated but didn't have the balls to take him to task for. She was also unsure whether he actually had a stutter himself, and despite everything, didn't want to risk offending him.

Acting Chief Inspector Curtis was still in full-time residence at Handstead. Formerly Chief Constable Daniels's staff officer, he had been in the wrong place at the wrong time when the chief inspector's position at Horse's Arse fell vacant, after C.I. Pat Gillard's attempt to smear Bott had gone horribly wrong. He was desperate to get the rank, but failed miserably to appreciate that going to Handstead was only ever going to be grief. He was feeling the pressure both professionally and personally. Shortly after his temporary promotion in the field, his fickle and ambitious wife had left him for a bearded mature student who'd never done a day's work in his life whom she met at her Open University summer campus. Curtis had developed a nervous twitch that manifested itself in a huge jerk of the head, mouth screwed up at the same time. Meetings that involved Curtis and Bott had become must-see events for other senior officers, who moved heaven and earth to get a glimpse of the pair of them twitching and stammering as they were put under pressure. Curtis's mental-health decline had become something of a concern, but nothing had been done to help him. Handstead continued to be the septic boil on the Force's backside. There was no way any other divisional commander was going to agree to sending any of his management team to disappear into the maelstrom that was Horse's Arse.

Chapter Five

DCI Harrison had been at their regular rural pub for over half an hour and was very seriously pissed off. Unusually, Simon Edwardes had phoned Harrison in his office and asked to meet him urgently. Harrison had tried to fob him off, but Edwardes had been insistent and reluctantly the DCI had left for the meeting immediately. Now he'd been kept hanging around; he didn't fancy a pint that early in the afternoon and his miniature cigars tasted foul. He drank the remainder of his pint of Coke, looked at his watch and was about to leave when he glanced out of the lead-light window and saw Edwardes's Triumph Stag swing into the car park. Harrison was uneasy at yet another ostentatious arrival in a flash motor that he felt only drew attention to him. It was the last thing he wanted, and he checked around the pub to see if anyone else had noticed the new arrival in the car park. Satisfied that no one had, he resolved to bring it up again with Edwardes first thing.

The fat solicitor walked past the window, waved at Harrison, who didn't respond, and shortly afterwards heaved his flabby frame through the low pub entrance. From there he asked with his eyes and a hand movement whether Harrison wanted a drink. Angrily Harrison indicated 'no' and motioned him over to his table.

'Will you stop turning up like a twat,' he barked.

'What d'you mean?'

'Fucking hell, Simon, squealing tyres, roaring engine, gravel flying everywhere – why not fit a loudspeaker to the motor and announce, "Bent solicitor arriving to speak to a detective"?'

'Hold on, less of the bent solicitor, Mr Harrison. You're not so squeaky clean yourself, you know.'

'Point taken, Simon, but stop being so fucking flash, especially when we're meeting up. People are going to notice you and I don't need anyone seeing us together. Fair enough?'

'OK, you've made your point very forcibly, as usual.'

'What's so urgent that you needed to see me? Not in the shit, are you?' the DCI asked, settling back into his chair.

'Nothing like that, Mr Harrison, but I do have some information that could be very, very useful to you.'

Harrison waited but said nothing, knowing that few people could ignore a pregnant silence without feeling they had to carry on talking.

'Well,' continued Edwardes without prompting, 'you

84

may be aware that I continue to act for a number of the so-called Park Royal Mafia.'

'Still?' queried Harrison. 'They're a done deal now, Simon. Why you wasting your time with them?'

'True, they're not the force they used to be in their own right, but did you know that they're now muscle for Sercan Ozdemir?'

Harrison was now as alert as a racehorse in the starting gate. He knew Ozdemir very well. The Turk's interest in the Mafia was extremely worrying.

'Ozdemir and the Mafia?' he said, feigning disinterest. 'Why would a serious career criminal like Ozdemir tie up with a bunch of loose cannons – doesn't make sense, does it?'

'You're the detective, Mr Harrison, you make of it what you will, but it's happening.'

'Ozdemir and the Mafia?' repeated the detective. 'OK, thanks for that, Simon, I'll have a look at it when I get a moment,' he said, resolving to make it a priority. He began to get to his feet to bring their meeting to a close, but Edwardes didn't move.

'There's a bit more,' he said coyly, with a slight smile. Harrison dropped back into his chair and eyed Edwardes with scarcely disguised anger.

'Go on,' he said, brooking no argument.

'Ozdemir called me to a meeting in his office yesterday. He knew about what I've done for the Mafia in the past and that I'm acting for Danny Morgan.'

'And?'

'He's worried about Alan Baker.'

'Worried, why?'

'Baker still pulls strings with the Mafia; he's very influential in Handstead.'

'He's doing twenty years.'

'I know, but people are still scared of him and he can get things done in town even now.'

'So why's Ozdemir worried about him?'

'He wants a clean slate, no outside influence, things done his way.'

'So where do you fit into his plan?'

'He wants a message sent into Strangeways.'

'What message?'

'Baker's going to have a nasty accident.'

'Is that right? What sort of accident?'

'Things are going to get broken, that sort of thing.'

'Who's going to do that? Not the other Mafia, surely?'

'No, but he wants them to understand that Baker is history. My tame prison officer will pass his instructions to some of Ozdemir's boys – they'll do Baker, and the other Mafia will know why.'

'Fucking hell,' mused Harrison, rubbing his cheeks with both hands as he thought furiously. 'What a set-up.' He paused for a few moments as he pondered his options. 'Tell you what, Simon, be fucking useful if a different message went in,' he said finally.

'Different message?'

'Yeah, be a right result if Ozdemir wanted Baker dead, wouldn't it?'

'Dead? Are you serious, Mr Harrison?'

'Fucking right I am, Simon. Time for a change of plan. When you go to the prison, the message is that Ozdemir wants Baker topped, understood?'

'Topped? I can't do that – where does that leave me?'

'Richer than before, Simon, much richer.'

'How much?'

'At least five hundred, maybe a grand – depends if I can go elsewhere for the cash.'

'I don't know, Mr Harrison. Topping Baker is pretty extreme.'

'Doesn't really get more extreme, does it, but look at the pluses. Baker gets topped; one nasty problem for the future is removed, and I know that Ozdemir ordered the hit. Very useful for the future, having that sort of hold over someone.'

'Ozdemir hasn't ordered a hit.'

'Got lost in translation, things went wrong. These things happen when you go down this sort of road. Whatever, you take that message into the prison and I've got a hand round Ozdemir's balls for as long as I want. Fancy a beer?'

Edwardes's mouth was as dry as a desert as Harrison went to the bar, returning shortly after with two pints of lager.

The DCI lit himself a celebratory cigar, and eyed

Edwardes through the smoke as he lit the cigarette in the solicitor's trembling fingers.

'Relax, Simon, there's no comeback for either of us. Baker gets topped, and if Ozdemir asks how or why, the answer is that things must have got out of hand – it was a nasty accident, happens all the time in prison, doesn't it? I won't be making anyone any the wiser, and I'm sure you won't either.'

'I don't know, what about the prison officer?' said Edwardes hesitantly.

'He'll keep quiet, don't you worry,' said Harrison. 'What's he going to do, tell everyone he passed on instructions to top a prisoner in his care? Not a chance. Just get the message in and we win all ways, OK?'

'Topping him, though . . .'

'You're not doing it; Ozdemir's scum in there will do it. Baker would probably have got it soon anyway – we're just bringing the date forward.'

Edwardes continued to stall, caressing his chin thoughtfully. Finally he took a momentous decision.

'OK, I'll take the message in, but I need to know you're going to stay onside with me.'

'Simon, some twat from your profession could always claim we were guilty of serious criminal offences. We need each other.'

'Conspiracy to murder, you mean?'

'Whoa, steady on,' laughed Harrison. He took a long

pull on his cigar and smiled grimly. If this all went to plan, he could see a very rosy future in law enforcement and crime detection for his CID office at Handstead. He was well aware of the significant infiltration into the Mafia that Benson and Clarke had made with Jones, but to have Ozdemir's balls in a vice too would be very handy – even if it meant throwing Edwardes to the wolves.

They finished their pints without further conversation and parted, with Harrison merely saying, 'Ring me when you've been to the prison. Tell me when the message goes in.' Edwardes nodded quietly and left ahead of Harrison, exiting the car park in a much more sedate fashion.

Following him a few minutes later, Harrison mused ruefully on his relationship with Simon Edwardes. It had proved enormously beneficial to him as the head of CID at Handstead. Not many DCIs could boast of having a tame solicitor on the books, particularly one like Edwardes with good connections with local villainy – and now apparently more serious villains like Sercan Ozdemir. But he loathed Simon Edwardes the person. A flabby, unkempt man who still lived at home with his parents, the solicitor was an unctuous, hand-wringing creep who generated feelings of revulsion in everyone who met him. But he remained part of Harrison's plans for the foreseeable future as he plotted to smash the Mafia and get his hands round Ozdemir's nuts.

Chapter Six

In late June 1976, the heatwave was starting to really take hold, and in common with the rest of the country, Handstead sizzled and sweated like a turd on a bonfire. During the last few days it had got as hot as ninety-two degrees, and some newly tarmacked roads had melted like liquorice strips. Despite the incredible heat, Headquarters had refused to budge from their standing instruction that ties were to be worn at all times. With not a breath of wind, and a blazing sun in cloudless blue skies for over twelve hours a day, Handstead began to bake solid.

As the temperature rose, so did tension on the Park Royal estate, where the Mafia and those of a similar persuasion took comfort in filling themselves up at every opportunity with pints of cold lager. There had been a couple of attacks on police officers the previous night as the drunken, befuddled hordes had scurried out of their rat-hole pubs and clubs at the end of an evening's hard drinking. The tension in the town was a living entity, threatening to devour everything. What was needed was a good downpour, or a serious blood-letting up on the Park Royal. No one was in much doubt as to how the pressure was likely to be relieved.

At the back of the untidy muster room, an elderly stand fan battled vainly at full speed to move the thick, sticky air around as D Group wandered in ones and twos into the room.

Despite the early hour, the temperature had quickly hit seventy degrees, and the officers' shirts were already stuck to their bodies. Overnight the temperature had remained at around sixty-five degrees, rendering sleep almost impossible, and everyone bore the obvious signs of a restless night. The windows were open on to the rear yard, but it made no difference, and the cheap threadbare curtains hung motionless in the still, early-morning air, which smelt strongly of exhaust fumes.

Returning to duty after two days' leave following a week of late turn, the group were still suffering from the heavy drinking session that had ensued at the conclusion of the shift – PC Ally Stewart especially, who now sported two black eyes, a split lip and a large white sticking plaster over his obviously broken nose. The pint-sized, ginger-haired Scotsman with appalling 'small-man syndrome', sat alone, arms folded and face set in a permanent scowl, occasionally glancing over at the rest of the group and muttering threats to no one in particular.

The group had travelled into central Manchester to drink until the early hours in a private members' drinking club run by an ex-professional footballer who had had the misfortune to be stopped in his car by PC Sean 'Psycho' Pearce in Handstead one night whilst well over the drink-drive limit. Psycho had as usual looked at the bigger picture, and had taken his keys off him and driven him to Handstead railway station. Though hugely grateful at his escape, the ex-pro had never expected to see Psycho again, despite the offer of free drinks for him and any of his mates, and he had been a little miffed when Psycho had appeared a week later and disposed of around fifty quid's worth of booze. He was, however, mortified when Psycho turned up with most of D Group and proceeded to pour well over two hundred pounds' worth of drink down their necks, and began to think that maybe it would have been cheaper to have been nicked.

Being the tight Jock that he was, once Ally had realised that he wouldn't have to pay for anything, he'd poured three quarters of a bottle of Johnnie Walker Black Label whisky down his throat before passing out in a corner booth. The rest of the group had subsequently had a discussion about how best to take advantage of his drunken stupor, with suggestions ranging from shaving his head to blacking his face up or stripping him off and tying him to the railings outside in the street. However, they all agreed that the Brothers had come up with an absolute belter. The Brothers,

Henry Walsh and Jim Docherty, crewed the area car with the call sign Bravo Two Yankee One. They were the complete opposite of each other, which was probably why they got on so well. Henry, known simply as H, was an ex-public schoolboy, whilst Jim was a former paratrooper who had seen shots fired in anger in Ulster. On paper they had nothing in common, but in reality they possessed almost extra-sensory powers of communication, knowing instinctively when the other would unleash a punch on the scumbag they were dealing with. They both had a penchant for violence which proved very handy in a shithole like Horse's Arse but which was something of an Achilles heel as they never had a Plan B. They were hated by the locals of Handstead and regarded warily by their own colleagues. Violence was their calling card.

The Brothers were the reason Ally Stewart came to wake up with a jolt in a linen cupboard on the London express as it pulled out of Manchester Piccadilly station at six a.m. Falling out of the cupboard and staggering into the corridor, Ally quickly sobered up as he saw the station signs begin to slip slowly past the window in front of him. 'Bastards!' he roared, and ran to the nearby door, slamming down the window and reaching for the handle. Alerted by the swearing, a steward appeared from the nearby restaurant car and began to remonstrate with, and attempt to restrain, an apparently deranged passenger. 'Come along, sir, you can't leave the train whilst it's in motion,' he said reasonably as he pulled at Ally's arm. 'Watch me!' shouted Ally, head-butting the steward in the classic Sauchiehall Street style. As the steward collapsed in a heap, Ally got the door open, said triumphantly, 'Fuck you, arsehole,' and stepped out of the still slowly moving train on to the platform and straight into a large metal sign, shattering his nose, splitting his upper lip and knocking himself cold. An hour later, he had recovered sufficiently to shuffle off the platform covered in dried blood and stinking like an old wino. Early-morning commuters gave a wide berth to the muttering, bloodstained tramp as they hurried for their trains.

Now Ally sat in the muster room swearing vengeance on those responsible for his mishap. But no one was saying anything. All they would tell him was that they had forgotten to wake him when they had left the club and had no idea what had happened to him. Only Psycho, unable to contain himself, had threatened to let the cat out of the bag by making train noises as Ally had entered the muster room.

Finally Sergeant Andy Collins and Inspector Jeff Greaves walked in, and Collins commenced his briefing, assigning D Group to their beats for the day and going over the events of the two days they had been on leave.

'Who's got the Ashbridge estate this morning?' he asked.

'We have,' replied Piggy Malone, holding up the keys to Bravo Two Two, which he was due to crew with the simmering Ally. The news that he had once again been crewed with Piggy had not gone down well. PC Ray 'Piggy'

Malone was the shortest of the short straws, and Ally seemed to get lumbered with him more than most. Piggy was a flatulent, porky eating machine who did as little as possible except where food was concerned. If it was free, he'd eat it – regardless of its age or origin. He'd been spotted looking longingly at road kill.

'More of the same with Mr Hayward and his car, I'm afraid, boys. Nip up there after muster and sort him out, will you?'

All of D Group knew about the problems Mr Hayward had with his car. He was an extremely old coffin-dodger who lived with his similarly ancient one-armed wife in a bungalow on the Ashbridge estate. Their preferred mode of transport was a green Reliant Robin three-wheeler, which the local yobs had discovered was extremely light. On a fairly regular basis old Mr Hayward would go out to his car in the morning to find that it had very carefully and quietly been turned on to its roof overnight. Handstead cops regularly rolled it back on to its wheels and had a cup of tea with Mr Hayward and his wife, listening to them bemoan the lack of respect old folk got from the youth of today. Mrs Hayward had lost her left arm in an industrial accident some years earlier and displayed her stump as a red badge of courage; red literally, because the stump was always covered in livid, weeping, cracked sores. It was a gruesome sight and visiting cops didn't stay long. Another factor in curtailing their visits was the Haywards' Jack Russell, Patch, which attacked anything that moved, specialising in the ankles of anyone sitting on the smelly, hair-covered sofas in the living room. The Haywards had become targets for the local hooligans shortly after Mrs Hayward's accident, enduring years of harassment including fireworks through the letter box and the infamous burning bag of shit trick. They had both fallen foul of that one in quick succession. Mrs Hayward had been the first to answer the ring on the doorbell to find a large paper bag ablaze on the doorstep which she stamped out, only to return indoors and find her left shoe and leg covered in dog shit. Mr Hayward fell victim the day after, adding insult to injury by not noticing the mess on his shoes and wandering around the bungalow for a couple of hours before his wife commented that he smelt worse than usual. His car had been overturned again and the old couple now sat patiently in their living room waiting for a nice policeman to roll it back over before they could go shoplifting again.

'Psycho, you and Pizza have got Two One. And don't forget, Psycho, you've got an appointment with Mr Grainger at Complaints. Nine a.m., his office,' continued Collins. The group exploded with laughter.

'You should fucking laugh,' complained Psycho. 'Fuck me, I could put the lot of you away,' he finished with a broad smile. Very true, but they all knew he wouldn't, not if he wanted to retain his reputation within the group as the stunt mastermind.

'Drop Pizza off before you go,' added Collins. 'Pizza, you and I will do a foot patrol on the Park Royal whilst Psycho's with the head-hunters, OK?'

PC Alan 'Pizza Face' Petty nodded in agreement. Collins's words were another unequivocal confirmation of his full membership of the group. His acceptance by his colleagues had been fast-tracked by the fact that he had been with Dave Baines when he was shot. Pizza was the copper who had survived.

'When are we getting a replacement for Bovril?' asked Psycho suddenly.

The room fell silent for a second. Dave Baines's death still reverberated around the group and the mention of his name generated bitter memories. It was getting easier, but it still hurt.

'Mr Curtis told me that we should get someone either next week or the week after,' replied Collins.

'Fresh meat?'

'Probably not. Transferee, I think.'

The group exchanged glances. A transferee meant only one thing – someone in the shit and on their way to the penal colony. Collins in particular was anxious about who the new recruit might be.

'Any ideas who?'

'Heard a couple of names: fellow called Ferguson from Central, and a bloke called Andy Malcolm from West Darrick.'

Psycho sat bolt upright in his chair, eyes wide open in excitement.

'Not Malcy the Mong Fucker?' he asked.

'Malcy who?'

'Malcy the Mong Fucker,' repeated Psycho. 'He got busted a couple of months ago. Had a thing about humping mental defectives in a home near his nick. I heard they didn't have enough to charge him – explains why he's on his way to us.'

'*If* it's him,' said Collins, deeply concerned at the prospect of another serious head banger arriving on the group. Collins was starting to become very concerned with the direction D Group was going. They were all cutting too many corners, taking too many risks and going just a little too far with their excesses. He was going to have to take action soon, but he was unsure when or how. The difference between them and the bad guys was diminishing daily.

He glanced at Inspector Greaves, who had wandered over to the Police Federation noticeboard and was quietly reading the notices aloud to himself. Greaves was continuing with his cunning plan to get himself pensioned out of the job as a complete nutter, broken by his time at Handstead. There was absolutely nothing wrong with him that a good punch wouldn't put right, but his return to uniform from the CID in disgrace had hurt him financially. Now he was set on getting his pension early.

Collins shook his head in despair.

'If it is him,' he repeated.

'Fucking hope so,' shouted Psycho. 'He's a legend. Malcy the Mong Fucker coming to Horse's Arse,' he mused happily. 'Who'd have thought it.'

'Sounds like a cunt,' said Pizza bitterly. He harboured aspirations to become a legend himself and was pretty pissed off at the prospect of a true original arriving on the group. 'Shagging a few retards hardly qualifies for legend status, does it?'

'Wind your neck in, Pizza,' snapped Psycho. 'You'll learn when you grow up.'

Pizza was about to argue back when he noticed the Brothers glaring at him and decided against it.

'He'll be company for you, Ally,' went on Psycho. 'He's another sweaty sock, someone for you to moan together with.'

'Aye, he is,' replied Ally sourly; he knew Andy Malcolm but had been unaware of his impending move to Horse's Arse. 'He's a good lad.'

Psycho spotted the opportunity for a bit of sport at Ally's expense.

'I heard that during the inquiry, Complaints discovered that Malcy was operating with an accomplice, another jock, but he was so fucking useless with women he had to chloroform the mongs before shagging them. Malcy never grassed him up apparently,' he lied.

As the group digested this piece of gratuitous fiction, Ally's brow furrowed as he considered the implied connection. Then very stupidly he blurted out, 'Well, it wasn't me.'

The group dissolved into a cacophony of cat calls, hilarity and insults as Ally desperately tried to dig himself out of his home-made cesspit.

'Fucking sex case,' muttered H as he followed Collins, who had given up on his muster, out of the room.

'It wasn't me,' protested Ally vehemently, arms spread wide.

'You would say that, wouldn't you?' hissed Jim as he pushed past him. 'Pervert.'

'Fucking hell!' shouted Ally. 'It wasn't me!'

Psycho winked knowingly at him as he passed and Ally clutched at the straw.

'There, there, he fucking winked at me, he's fucking made it all up!' he shouted. His protests were ignored by the group as they made their way along the corridor to collect their car keys and radios from the group's only WPC, Amanda 'Blood Blister' Wheeler, Ally constantly pleading his innocence.

'I hope it is Malcy,' said Psycho as he waited in line for the perspiring Blister to exchange his laminated blue and yellow tickets for a radio transmitter and receiver.

'Sounds like bad news,' replied Pizza, who had decided that he needed a quality stunt pretty soon to eclipse the newcomer's arrival. 'Probably all a load of old bollocks anyway.'

'We'll see, we'll see,' mused Psycho, who had previously been quite happy to team up with Pizza as his sorcerer's apprentice but was now contemplating partnering up with a true monster in his campaign against Inspector Bott and anyone else in authority.

'I've got an idea for Curtis this morning if you're interested,' said Pizza as they shuffled forward behind the Brothers. The backs of the Brothers' shirts were both heavily sweat stained between the shoulder blades. It was getting hotter.

'Oh yeah? Tell me about it.'

'It'll be a good one, don't you worry. Tell you about it in the car.'

Psycho raised his eyebrows and pursed his lips in response, nodding his agreement. Pizza definitely had potential, he had to admit. Shaving half of Jason Middleton's head had been inspirational, earning him some serious respect. Jason Middleton was the hated son of Chief Superintendent 'Mengele' Middleton who commanded neighbouring C Division. He had been on an unofficial list circulating at Horse's Arse – if you see him, nick the little shit – after his father had pulled all sorts of strokes to get him off a drunkenness charge at Handstead some months earlier. Pizza had got to him and shaved half his head bald as an egg whilst he was unconscious in the cells. Psycho was very interested to hear what he had in mind for the twitching nervous wreck currently occupying the Chief Inspector's office on the first floor.

The Brothers had not hung around after the muster. After a cursory handover, Jim had grabbed the keys and driven them quickly up to Pinehurst Gardens on the Park Royal estate and the crumbling end-of-terrace house occupied by John Patrick O'Neil and his fiery wife. The Brothers had picked up a court warrant for O'Neil's arrest and had been after him now for nearly eight weeks. Warrants like this were really low-grade stuff, something to be dealt with quickly. To have one hanging around for eight weeks was unheard of and becoming extremely embarrassing for them. Sergeant Collins had heaped further shame on them at muster when he'd run through D Group's list of outstanding cases.

'Fucking hell, boys,' he'd said loudly, 'haven't you nicked JP yet? You've had the warrant ages, need some help with it?'

'It's in hand,' replied H flatly as he and Jim glared at the others, who were thoroughly enjoying themselves at their expense.

'Listen, fellas, we're going nights in a few days' time. Get it sorted out before the end of nights or I'll have to reassign it. Fucking hell, nearly two months for a warrant, what you been up to?'

The Brothers were steaming. Actually they'd been very busy, but JP O'Neil was not offering himself up for arrest and his wife was an active and willing accomplice. A friend of theirs had been in court when the warrant had been issued and they knew it wasn't backed for bail. JP would need to come up with over £600 in unpaid traffic fines or spend twenty-eight days in prison. Hence when the Brothers came calling, lying to Mrs O'Neil that the warrant *was* backed for bail and he'd be home soon, she had lied right back at them. JP was never home, they'd just missed him, he'd be back in half an hour, he was working away this week, he'd left her for another woman, he'd gone on holiday with his mates – her list of excuses was endless and inspired, and JP remained concealed in the cupboard under the stairs until the Brothers had gone. Now, however, the pair had come to the end of their tether. They were in no mood to listen to her bullshit any more and had resolved to search the house despite the fact that they had no power to do so.

They parked a short distance from JP's house and H went quietly along the service road to the back of the terrace and through the gate to the rear of JP's home. Exactly three minutes after they had parted company, Jim knocked loudly on the front door and kept knocking until an irate Mrs O'Neil threw the door open. She was a lump of a woman, shaped like a pile of sand, who hated the police more than most of the residents on the Park Royal estate. Both her brothers and an uncle were serving long prison sentences for a series of violent tie-up burglaries, and her husband, JP, was constantly falling foul of the Old Bill. His offences were fairly low key, mostly traffic related, but he had served time in the past and his wife blamed the Old Bill for the troubles visited upon her extended family. It would never have crossed her mind that they were actually the architects of their own misfortune; it was a lot easier to blame the police, which she did regularly and very loudly.

'What the fucking hell do you want?' she shrieked in her broad southern Irish accent.

'Out of the way, you lying bitch,' snarled Jim in his equally broad Geordie accent, and pushed her hard with both palms against her upper chest. She staggered back in a heap to the foot of the stairs as Jim strode past her into the kitchen, where he let H in through the back door.

'You bastards, get the fuck out of here!' screamed Mrs O'Neil, getting to her feet and facing up to the Brothers, who now stood over her in the hallway.

'Where's JP?' growled Jim.

'Go fuck yourself!'

Jim grabbed the front of her dressing gown in his fist and slammed her against the wall.

'Where is he?'

His aggression had knocked the wind out of her sails and she replied meekly, 'Not here.'

'Missed him again, did we? I fucking doubt it, so we're going to have a good look round.'

'You got a warrant to do that?'

'Don't need one. You just gave us permission.'

'Did I fuck, you bastards!' she shouted, getting all brave again. 'Get out of here.'

Jim didn't release his grip on her dressing gown, but dragged her into the living room, where he threw her on to the floor. As she landed, her dressing gown fell open and gave the Brothers a full display of her wildly unkempt horse's collar. She saw them looking and grin at each other. She blushed deeply and started screaming.

'See enough did you, you pair of perverts? Get a kick out of that, did you?'

'Hardly, you withered old witch. Looked like a fucking clown's sleeve,' said H nonchalantly.

'You cunt!' she screamed at the top of her voice, but she kept her distance.

'Not pleasant at all,' continued H. Jim cackled insanely as Mrs O'Neil went totally apeshit and subjected them to a barrage of profanities, much of which had the Brothers nodding their heads in admiration as they mentally logged it away for their own future use. During the tirade, they were joined by two scruffy children who had wandered downstairs from their bedroom as the bedlam increased in the living room. Mrs O'Neil pulled them protectively to her but continued to berate the Brothers. Jim turned to his partner.

'Have a good look around upstairs, H. I'll keep this monster caged.'

H nodded and jogged upstairs. He searched everywhere, including the attic, before returning empty handed to the ground floor. He then searched downstairs, including under the stairs, but JP was not home. He returned to the living room.

'Nothing. Did the attic as well.'

'I told you he wasn't here, didn't I?' said Mrs O'Neil triumphantly. 'Now fuck off and die.'

'So where is he?'

'Find him yourselves, you pair of bastards.'

'Lovely children you got there,' said H pleasantly. 'They twins?'

'Twins?' she sneered. 'How stupid are you? One's two years old with ginger hair and the other's seven with black hair. What the fuck's wrong with you?' Even Jim looked over at H, wondering what the hell was wrong with him.

'Just couldn't believe more than one person would want to fuck you,' continued H in the same calm, pleasant voice. As she realised what he had said to her, Mrs O'Neil was rendered temporarily speechless before she went completely berserk. As she ranted at them, H had begun to leaf through a heap of letters and bills piled on top of a garish orange record player in the corner of the room. As he flicked through what were mostly final demands from the utilities companies, he came across a document that caught his eye. It was a log book for a blue Mini Cooper, still in the name of a female owner from south Manchester, but now probably in the hands of JP O'Neil. He quickly made a mental note of the registration number and slipped the book back into the pile.

'What are you doing going through our mail?' shouted the irate Mrs O'Neil.

'You should pay your bills, maybe cut down on the mail you get.'

'Fuck off!' she screamed, pulling her dressing gown tight and covering the Brothers in spittle. The two children, now bored with yet another screaming match involving their mother and a strange man, trotted past the Brothers and made their way back upstairs to play.

'Come on, Jim, we'll be back again soon to get the little shit,' said H, tapping his partner on the shoulder. Jim glanced at him, a little surprised at the suggestion that they should leave the house, but the look on H's face told him that he'd found something significant

'Don't get comfortable, will you?' he snarled at Mrs O'Neil. 'We're going to keep coming back, early and late, until we find him and lock him up.'

'Up your fucking arse, you squaddie bastard,' she shrieked.

It may just have been a lucky guess, but she had correctly identified Jim as an ex-soldier, and that really pissed him off. Enough was enough. He took a half-step back and then dropped her with a straight-arm jab to the jaw as quick as a lightning strike. She collapsed like a deck of cards on to the grubby carpet.

'Fucking hell, Jim,' said H, kneeling beside her and checking for a pulse.

'Forget her,' snapped Jim. 'Have you found something? You were keen to move out.'

'Yeah, have a look at this,' he replied, getting to his feet and leafing through the pile of post again until he found the Mini Cooper's log book, which he passed to Jim.

'Hmm . . . reckon he's out and about in it?'

'Well, it's something for us to have a look at, isn't it, rather than keep calling round here every day?'

'You're right. Keep an eye out for this motor, I reckon we'll find him behind the wheel. Keep it to ourselves, though, H. Don't want anyone else bagging the little shit.'

'No worries. He's ours, just a question of finding the motor. Get hold of her legs, Jim, and give me a hand getting her up on the sofa.'

The Brothers manhandled the bulky Mrs O'Neil on to the threadbare sofa and doused her with a couple of glasses of water. Then they left her lying in state and quickly left the house to continue their hunt for JP O'Neil.

Chapter Seven

Standing further back in the shadow of the recessed doorway and shielding his eyes from the high summer sun, PC Phil Eldrett reminded himself for the umpteenth time that generally people were completely switched off and unaware of others around them. And that they were creatures of habit – herd-like – walking the same routes at the same times as far as humanly possible. Standing on the same spot on the pavement to catch the same bus home every night. The same side of the bus, the same seat, back towards the driver if that was their preference. They made his job very easy, which was just as well. Standing at well over six feet and with a shock of distinctive, prematurely white hair, Eldrett should have stood out. But he didn't, because people didn't pay attention.

Eldrett was one of many Horse's Arse officers in the part-time employment of Inspector Greaves's brother, Ian, who ran a hugely successful private investigations business in the area. Eldrett was on a group currently on two leave days after seven late turns. In common with many cops with days off during the week, when his wife and anyone else with a normal life would be at work and the kids at school, he had tired of constantly going on the piss and had been looking round for another source of income when Jeff Greaves had given him a discreet pull. Some cops drove buses, utilising their advanced and PSV driving qualifications; others worked as car mechanics; and the ones who loved fighting moonlighted on the doors of clubs outside Handstead. Greaves had quickly identified Eldrett, a highly qualified former surveillance officer, as perfect for many of the follows that came into the office, and subsequently Eldrett had found himself working most of his leave days for the Greaves firm. Not that he minded at all. He was bouncing off the walls at home, bored shitless, restless to get back to Horse's Arse, and the cash came in very handy. His wife had never bothered to ask where it was all coming from, preferring to live in ignorance of what she suspected was petty crime.

Of course, all these moonlighting cops operated under assumed identities and only worked for cash. As an ex-cop himself, Ian Greaves knew that serving officers would not only be hungry for the extra pay, but would also be the best qualified to undertake the jobs he had coming out of his ears. His brother Jeff, despite still being a serving inspector, was now to all intents and purposes his chief recruiter and job coordinator. Pretty much anything that Ian felt would be best done by a cop, with access to all the necessary information, would be passed to Jeff, who would find the right man for the job and keep 20 per cent of the fee Ian offered. As Ian had already skimmed off 75 per cent from the original client fee, it left precious little for the foot soldiers, but it was still good money and being on the Greaveses' books was considered a real perk.

If the information Jeff Greaves had given him was accurate, Eldrett could expect Mr John Woodcock to leave the offices of ERL Ltd in Shortlands Gardens, Handstead, any time between five and five thirty p.m. He had been watching the only door to the company since four thirty, and as he glanced up at the clock in the centre of Seven Dials, his interest increased. It was now five and he expected his target at any moment. He had got to Shortlands Gardens around three and given himself time to establish that ERL Ltd had only the one door, controlled by a buzzer and intercom system. As the Market Square bus and tram station was near by, and anticipating that Woodcock was likely to use it, he had spent time walking the surrounding streets and alleyways to familiarise himself fully with the geography and street names. He had then gone to the Red Lion on the corner of Shortlands Gardens and Seven Dials and had a pint as he again read over his description of John Woodcock. White male, early fifties but looked younger, about five foot eleven, slim build, should be wearing a suit, wore glasses to read, smoker, probably carrying some sort of rucksack or holdall. Recently been on holiday somewhere in North Africa, drove a blue Mark One Ford Escort. What a discarded Mrs Woodcock wanted to know was where he was now living with his new, much younger, girlfriend. What she was sure of was that it wasn't with his elderly mother in Bandley as his solicitors were advising. Hence Eldrett's contract.

At 5.05 p.m. he saw the door open and a man stepped out into Shortlands Gardens, blinked in the still blistering sunshine, and turned left, towards Eldrett. The man glanced neither left nor right but stared squint eyed ahead to infinity. Eldrett quickly compared him with the description he had. He liked what he saw. A very good bet. Woodcock passed within two feet of Eldrett in the doorway without so much as a glance, and Eldrett slipped quickly into the torrent of like-minded office workers who now poured down Shortlands Gardens, fixing his eyes on the back of Woodcock's head as he battled his way through the crowds. Keeping about twenty feet behind him, he followed him into Painters' Alley, across Long Mile and into the Market Square bus and tram station. There, as Woodcock queued at a ticket window, Eldrett was two places behind him and close enough to hear him ask for a single to Manchester Central. Eldrett eased out of the queue and stood anonymously in the crowd as Woodcock bought a copy of the *Manchester Evening News* from a vendor in the ticket hall. Rolling the paper under his arm, he walked to the stairs and jogged down to the westbound bus stops. Eldrett was never less than six feet from him, never in his eye line, and he took up a position slightly behind him on the raised bus stop, nicely concealed amongst other passengers.

They didn't have to wait long, and soon both Woodcock and Eldrett were seated on a westbound bus rumbling through the town towards the bright lights of Manchester Central. Woodcock had got a seat near the rear door, and Eldrett had settled in five down from him. From here he could safely keep an eye on him without standing out. Woodcock rummaged around in his rucksack for a pair of glasses, which he put on, and then buried himself in his paper, whilst Eldrett wrote up his notes in a small pocket notebook in preparation for the full report he'd need to submit before he got paid.

The bus swayed and rocked along the streets, stopping regularly, emptying and filling with passengers, but Woodcock remained glued to his newspaper. Eventually it emerged into the centre of Manchester and Eldrett relaxed back into his seat and contemplated the situation. He had some sympathy with Woodcock, who was obviously attempting to conceal assets from his embittered wife, but needs must and the money he got for this job would come in handy to take his own wife and their two children down to a static caravan park on the coast later that summer.

Something didn't seem quite right, though, when he thought it through. Here he was, a police officer with twenty-five years' experience, desperately trying to make ends meet by moonlighting. He'd tried it all. Garden maintenance, a bit of driving, bar work, and now he'd decided to put some of his training to good use and thrown his hand in with Jeff Greaves's brother. He'd done a few jobs for him now. All fairly routine, non-confrontational follows.

He was very good at following people about. It was something he'd excelled at on his many surveillance courses, and it had earned him his nickname of 'The Shadow'. He'd been assigned a person, taken at random from the phone book, and given a week to prepare as full a profile on that individual as possible. He'd done the best job his instructors had ever seen, but wisely they didn't ask how.

That first morning, watching the house revealed that a smartly dressed man aged in his late twenties lived there alone and drove a black, two-year-old Ford Capri 3-litre Sport to a road near the station, from where he caught a train into Manchester. Day two established that the man walked from Victoria station to the Midland Bank in Oxford Street, where he used a lift in the lobby marked 'For Staff Use Only'. Eldrett didn't see him leave the bank again until 5.30 p.m., when he reversed his route exactly, even down to crossing roads at the same places. Wonderful things, routines. Day three was when Eldrett really went after him. He followed the Capri to its usual parking place alongside a post-box and then followed his man to the station. Once he was sure he was safely on his way to work in Manchester, he walked back to the quiet street where his, and a thousand another commuters' cars were parked. The street was deserted and quiet now, and the well-kept houses in it were set back from the road. Satisfied he was not himself being watched, Eldrett pulled a flat, steel slimjim from the inside pocket of his jacket and pushed it quickly down the side of the driver's window. With practised ease he felt for the central lock and eased it up. Without causing a scratch, Eldrett opened the door, slipped into the driver's seat and shut the door quietly. He waited for a few seconds, looking round for signs of interest in him, but there was none so he began to search. He found the house keys very quickly, thrown casually into the driver's door map pocket with half a dozen long-forgotten cassette tapes. So many people did it, he mused, never gave it a moment's thought.

He left the Capri as quickly and quietly as he had entered it, returned to his own car parked a short way away and drove back to the vicinity of his target's home. He parked up two streets away, walked briskly to the house, up to the front door and let himself in using the Yale key. The deadlock in the door had not been used. Once inside he again waited and peered through the round bull's-eye glass in the door for any sign that he had been seen. Satisfied that he had not alerted any of the neighbours, he spun the house for information on his profile target. An hour later, armed with every piece of personal information available, he left the house and walked quickly back to his car. He drove back to the Capri, replaced the house keys, secured the vehicle and drove away. In a little under three days, he had learnt everything there was to know about Peter Clarke of the Midland Bank. And Peter Clarke would never have a clue.

Greaves's brother paid cash, no questions asked. It really was money for old rope, but deep down, Eldrett resented having to do it to keep the wolf from the door. Christ, he did a difficult, hugely responsible job as it was, and he considered his pay should reflect that – but it didn't.

He occasionally glanced over at Woodcock's reflection in the window opposite and found himself considering his plight. He was going to be taken to the cleaners by his wife, no mistake about that. Wherever he was living now, if he had a share in even 1 per cent of it, she would have it off him. Poor bastard. Eldrett felt a pang of guilt over his role in Woodcock's impending disaster but soon dismissed it with an inward shrug of the shoulders. He needed the work. Closing his eyes, he tried to relax and enjoy the journey, occasionally opening them briefly to check that Woodcock was still in place. He hadn't moved and was clearly a man who believed in getting value for money out of a newspaper.

As the bus pulled in to Manchester Central, other passengers began to get to their feet and move towards the doors, but Woodcock remained behind his paper. Had he clocked Eldrett? Was he waiting to dash off the bus at the last second, forcing him to show out? Or was he simply engrossed in what he was reading? Eldrett decided to make a move. He stood up and joined the passengers waiting to leave the bus. As it came to a halt and the doors opened, he was relieved to see Woodcock glance over his paper and panic as he realised where he was. Eldrett wandered to the far side of the stand, from where he watched as a flustered Woodcock left the bus with his *Manchester Evening News* falling to pieces around him on the pavement. Ignoring the pages now being spread around the station by the breeze, Woodcock threw his rucksack over his shoulder, put his glasses into the inside pocket of his suit jacket and marched purposefully, and still seemingly unaware of his shadow, towards the exit. He passed through the ticket hall and turned right out of sight. Eldrett waited thirty seconds before following him out, and when he did so he saw him about fifty yards ahead, striding at a good pace along Hampton Road and the edge of Hampton Park.

Having been concealed amongst anonymous crowds so far, Eldrett was now somewhat surprised to find that he and Woodcock were the only people on the footpath. He had expected there to be plenty of other pedestrians about at this

Charlie Owen

time of day, but there weren't, so he'd have to act accordingly. He crossed the road and stayed about fifty yards behind and well out of range of Woodcock's casual glance. Now Woodcock would have to turn through a hundred and eighty degrees to see him. On they walked, with Woodcock maintaining the same pace and always looking ahead. After ten minutes he suddenly paused, stepped to the kerb and looked right towards the oncoming traffic. He was going to cross the road, and Eldrett guessed that the journey was nearly at an end. Woodcock was directly opposite a large, new and very expensive six-storey block of flats. The road traffic was as light as the pedestrian traffic and he crossed quickly and walked into the drive serving the flats. Eldrett rapidly made up the distance between them and was only a few feet behind him as Woodcock put a key into the front door of the block. As he pushed it open, he turned to see Eldrett trotting towards him with his own house keys in his hand.

'Coming in?' asked Woodcock pleasantly.

'I am, thanks very much,' replied Eldrett, putting his keys back in his pocket, reaching above Woodcock to hold the door open, and allowing him to step into the entrance hall ahead of him.

'Thanks,' said Woodcock, moving into the lobby area and walking to the stairs. Eldrett shut the door and followed, and Woodcock glanced behind and gave him a friendly smile.

120

'Amazing weather we're having,' he said. 'Makes me cross listening to people complain about it.'

'Yes, shame it won't last,' replied Eldrett. 'Best we make the most of it.'

They strolled along the first-floor corridor chatting as newly acquainted neighbours about the extraordinary heatwave before Woodcock stopped outside a flat door and put a key into the lock.

'Well, this is me,' he said affably. 'Good night.'

Without slowing, Eldrett smiled at him and continued on along the corridor. 'Good night,' he called over his shoulder, not looking back until he heard the key turning in the lock and the door open and shut. Glancing back to check the corridor was empty, he retraced his steps past the door Woodcock had opened – Flat 133 – then hurried down the stairs to the lobby, where he had noticed a rack of post-boxes for the occupants of the flats. There was no name on Flat 133's box so he decided to have a look around to see if he could find Woodcock's car. It didn't take long. At the rear of the flats was a large private car park where Woodcock had very obligingly parked his blue Ford Escort. Eldrett was now absolutely sure he had him housed properly, and walked back to Hampton Road, heading back towards the bus station. Outside the station he used a public phone box to let Greaves know that he'd had a result.

'Nice one, Phil. Cash as usual?'

'Yes please,' replied Eldrett. 'I'll pick it up at the weekend if that's OK.'

'Fine. By the way, I've just taken on another divorce job if you're interested.'

'Always interested. Give me the details when I see you,' Eldrett said before hanging up and hurrying to catch a bus back into Handstead.

A crumbling reminder of Handstead's former, more glorious past was the huge Chapman's department store, which stood just outside the town's ring road. Its heyday had been in the 1920s and 30s, and more recently it had been the second largest employer in the town after the now-departed petro-chemical industry. These days it perfectly reflected the decline of the once-prosperous town. The building still bore testament to its magnificent past, and if the casual passer-by were to look closely beyond the decades of grime and neglect, its classic Art Deco architecture would become apparent.

The store had remained in a time warp as shopping habits evolved, retaining a millinery department that was usually as busy as Santa's grotto in midsummer. It insisted that the staff in the menswear department wore suits and ties, and steadfastly refused to embrace any technological advances. Even electronic tills were shunned, with all purchases being recorded on hand-written bills of sale. Subsequently Chapman's went to the wall very quickly as other more aggressive and progressive chain stores moved into the area and undercut every facet of its core business infrastructure. Regularly raped by the legions of local shoplifters, who had quickly identified the wounded giant as a ready source of income, the store haemorrhaged what little profit it made until the geriatric family board members decided to embrace the future and bring in a store detective. This heralded the arrival of the formidable Rita Walker.

Walker was a former major in the Royal Army Medical Corps who had made her career her only interest in life. She had never married, finding all that 'unpleasant men's business' quite unnecessary. On retirement she had resigned herself to an anonymous, lonely decline, until on a whim she had wandered into Chapman's one winter afternoon to escape the bitter cold. There in the store pharmacy, she had encountered two of Handstead's junkies busily stealing razor blades and paracetamol tablets. Carol and Eddie Jenkins were a pair of prolific shoplifters with huge heroin habits to support, and were regular visitors to Chapman's, where they would steal anything they could sell on the street. But on that particular afternoon they crossed paths with Rita Walker.

'What on earth do you think you're doing?' thundered Rita as she turned in to an aisle and found them on their haunches shovelling packets of razor blades and boxes of tablets into their pockets. Eddie looked casually over his shoulder at her, then sneered and turned back to the shelf he was clearing.

'Fuck off, Grandma,' he drawled.

Carol Jenkins sniggered and also continued to load up her pockets. With their backs to Rita, they did not notice her step to one side and pick up something from another shelf before returning to them.

'On your feet, you pair of rodents,' she snapped.

Wearily, Eddie and Carol got to their feet and turned to face her, fully intending to kick the living shit out of her.

'Listen, you fucking old witch—' started Eddie, before taking the full blast of a can of Ralgex muscle spray in the eyes. As Carol began to scream abuse, Rita directed the jet into her toothless mouth. Screaming and choking and clawing at their faces, the Jenkinses collapsed to the floor.

The commotion soon drew an audience, including the pharmacy floor manager, who called the police. Eddie and Carol Jenkins were locked up, and the following day Rita was offered the post of store detective at Chapman's. She had a purpose in life again and soon had a reputation with the town's thieves as an opponent to reckon with. But she also became a huge pain in the arse for the cops at Handstead. She would regularly be on the phone to them several times a day, warning them of suspicious characters in her store, and was not averse to actually fitting up the occasional scumbag. The cops didn't really have a problem with that, but what they did take exception to was the role she had played in locking up the wife of one of the Handstead cops whom she had nailed walking out of the store with a packet of nail files. The woman was suffering badly from post-natal depression, but that had cut no ice with the dried-up old Rita Walker. The irate cop husband had subsequently confronted Walker and berated her about her treatment of his wife, in response to which, Rita had made a formal complaint about him. She had appeared inordinately keen to help Complaints and Discipline nail him, even making a statement claiming that he had threatened to snap her scrawny old neck. The uniformed cops were deeply suspicious of her, but what really irked them was her constant contact with DCI Harrison. It was not uncommon for him to assign uniforms to Chapman's as a result of her calling him direct. Some of the uniforms were convinced he was boning the old crone, but the more reasonable gave him the benefit of the doubt. You really wouldn't – ever.

Chapter Eight

At the end of a late-turn shift, D Group had adjourned en masse to the bar on the top floor of the nick. There, as usual, they had got hammered before making their bleary way home in the small hours of the following morning. They all drove home in that state, sometimes waking in their own beds the following day with no recollection of how they had got home and being pleasantly surprised to find their cars parked, undamaged, outside. However, there was the odd occasion when the journey home was extremely eventful, ending up with vehicles abandoned in ditches, against trees or through damaged walls and long walks home across country. What none of them ever did was wait for the police to show up, especially the traffic police. Loathed by most of humankind, traffic cops took a particular delight in locking up their own, and the Handstead cops knew they could expect no quarter from the traffic officers who patrolled the roads on their way home. Few of them lived in Handstead itself, so they had a few miles to cover to get home and the traffic cops knew it. They also knew of the heavy drinking culture that existed at Handstead and that there was a better than average chance of catching a drink-driver if they stopped a Handstead copper on his way home. So the traffic cops plotted themselves up around the arterial roads out of the town like bears waiting for spawning salmon, and occasionally bagged a pissed copper. The D Group officers had so far escaped any brushes with Traffic and all had resolved there was no way they would roll over and die if they saw blue lights in the rearview mirror – no fucking way. Hence at the first sign of trouble, the rule was to bail out and get running.

PC Sean 'Psycho' Pearce had enjoyed more than his fair share of incidents getting home whilst hammered, and to ensure it didn't happen again, this particular night his new partner in crime, Pizza, had relieved him of his car keys, lifting them from his bomber jacket inside pocket as Psycho drank himself to a standstill and leaving them behind the bar with Julie, the resident barmaid and confessional. Come going-home time, Psycho went berserk when he couldn't find his keys. Because no one else fancied having him in their car in that state (he was a notorious projectile vomiter), he found himself abandoned without a lift home.

'Fuck it, I'll walk – I could do with the exercise,' he bellowed at passing traffic outside the nick, and lurched off on the six-mile hike back to his flat. He had gone barely half a mile when he decided he urgently needed a piss and staggered across the road towards a park, straight into the path of a speeding car. The car was being driven by a disqualified driver who had consumed at least as much alcohol as Psycho had, along with half a dozen spliffs, and barely noticed Psycho lurch out in front of him. For his part, Psycho hardly registered the headlights bearing down on him, and subsequently was totally relaxed when the car hit him square on and flipped him clear over the roof. He landed hard on his back, knocking himself out, but apart from a few cuts and bruises was otherwise uninjured.

The driver of the car slowed and then stopped as he realised what he had hit. He could see the body in the road behind him in his rearview mirror. It wasn't moving and he assumed, not unsurprisingly, that it was dead. Quickly he glanced around him and was relieved to see that he was alone and totally unobserved. For a moment his conscience told him to check the body, just in case, but soon survival instincts took over and he drove off with a squeal of tyres.

Psycho lay by the verge for about half an hour. Eventually he was found by two passing night-duty officers, Tracey Burton and Anne Roland, who recognised Psycho and called an ambulance. They were a couple of station beauties, much desired and pursued by all and sundry. However, both preferred to pick and choose their partners and subsequently had acquired reputations as ice maidens, and even the scurrilous accusation that they were lesbians. True, they shared digs together, but they were most definitely heterosexual.

Now the girls knelt alongside Psycho, stroking his head.

'Fucking hell, he stinks,' said Tracey to Anne as she bent closer to his face to try to detect some sign of breathing. 'Drunk as a fucking skunk,' she finished, getting to her feet and fanning the smell away from her face, leaving Anne stroking his grimy hair.

Anne was a member of the Christian Police Association and one of life's carers. Now she looked compassionately at Psycho's battered face and whispered gently to him until he began to stir and eventually opened his eyes. The last thing he remembered was the headlights coming at him, and now he found himself looking into the face of an angel. Was he dead?

'Praise the Lord,' whispered Anne as Psycho regained consciousness.

'Praise the fucking Lord,' echoed the delighted Psycho, who was quite looking forward to being dead in such company. He reached down to squeeze his swelling genitals, which was always a sure sign that he was in rude health, before starting to try to get to his feet so he could get to grips with this beautiful blonde angel.

'You stay where you are, Sean,' said Anne gently, pushing him back on to the road surface. 'We've called for an ambulance.'

How did the angel know his name? pondered Psycho, resting his head back on the blanket they had placed behind him. No matter, he was in heaven and things were going to be great, especially if all the angels looked like these two.

After treatment for his cuts and bruises at Handstead General Hospital, the girls ran Psycho home. He was now determined to screw Anne and had quickly identified her membership of the Christian Police Association as a route into her knickers. He became a born-again Christian that morning, and soon after, a religious zealot. He was prone to suddenly shouting, 'Praise the Lord!' or 'Hallelujah!' as pieces of positive news were read from the General Occurrence Book, and muttering, 'He moves in mysterious ways,' or 'As you sow, so shall you reap,' to the less positive stuff. Sergeant Mick Jones, who had recently arrived at Horse's Arse after screwing the wife of a colleague at a rural nick, was already a gibbering wreck, and his nerves were shot to pieces by Psycho's religious outbursts.

Worse, Psycho had become a fully paid-up member of the Christian Police Association in his pursuit of Anne's cherry and began attending all their meetings. He usually had a good drink first and would sit at the back of the hall bellowing hymns out of tune or snoring loudly whilst drooling like a bulldog. He finally went too far when he arrived for a meeting bearing gifts for his new friends. At his own expense, he claimed (in fact he had called in a favour), he had produced T-shirts for the Association. Ripping open one of the plastic bags he was carrying, he opened up the white T-shirt inside for the apprehensive audience in front of him. They were pleasantly relieved to see quite a professionally produced lithograph of Jesus Christ with His arms outstretched and bathed in heavenly light. Unfortunately he was wearing a police officer's helmet, and around his feet were the words 'Christian Police Association' and the Force crest. Underneath all that were the bold black words 'Jesus Loves You . . .' One or two of the members present actually began to applaud, more out of relief than anything, but they were soon screaming with horror as Psycho reversed the T-shirt to reveal the legend, '. . . But Everyone Else Thinks You're A Cunt'.

Psycho's membership of the Christian Police Association soon became a hot political potato. Senior members of the CPA began to actively encourage him to explore Catholicism and join the Catholic Police Guild, until the Deputy Chief Constable, himself a serious son of Rome, got wind of it and forbade the transfer.

Following the early-turn muster, Piggy and Ally had travelled in frosty silence to the Ashbridge estate to render assistance to Mr and Mrs Hayward. Ally parked at the end of the concrete driveway on which the green Reliant Robin lay on its roof like an overturned beetle. Piggy went to the front door and rang the bell as Ally ruefully examined the vehicle and rocked it back and forth.

'Morning, boys,' chorused the Haywards delightedly as they opened the door. The combined smell of cigarettes, dog, fish, urine, ointment, liniment and bandages immediately punched Piggy in the face.

'Fucking hell.' He gagged involuntarily, taking a step back into the fresh air.

'Morning, boys,' they chorused again, following Piggy out to their vehicle, where Ally stood with his elbow on one of the rear wheels.

'Little bastards,' spat the rancid Mrs Hayward, almost losing her false teeth as she vented her spleen against the local hooligans. 'Got no respect is the trouble,' she continued, top plate rattling about in her mouth, making her sound as though she was gargling marbles.

'Fucking hell,' said Piggy again. 'Let's get this done, can we, Ally?'

It was not often that the pair agreed on anything, but now they did, and they quickly got the Robin back on to its wheels.

'There you go,' said Ally, wiping his hands together to get the dirt and dust off. 'Give us a ring if you need anything else,' he called as he headed quickly back towards Bravo Two Two.

'You pair of angels,' said Mrs Hayward. 'You got time for

a bit of breakfast? Fancy a bacon buttie or something?'

Not as long as I've got a hole in my arse, you old witch, thought Ally, who was then horrified to hear Piggy say, 'Breakfast, hmm, sounds good. I could murder a bacon buttie. Come on, Ally.'

'You twat!' hissed Ally across the roof of the car. 'Are you mad? Look at the state of them. Fuck knows what the inside of the house looks like. She'll poison us.'

'Never known anyone whine like you, Ally,' replied Piggy cheerfully. 'Wind your neck in and be sociable. They probably don't get much company. Come and do your police public relations thing – try and feel good about yourself for a bit.'

'Don't get much company?' fumed Ally. 'Of course they don't get any fucking company, because they stink. They're rotting away from the inside and you want to *eat* with them?'

Piggy was already halfway into the bungalow, leaving Ally little choice but to trudge bitterly after him. As he walked into the hallway, he immediately recoiled from the smell.

'Fucking hell!' he said. 'Where's the body?'

Neither of the Haywards appeared to register the insult, and Ally was ushered into the front living room, where Piggy was already waiting expectantly. The room had a worn brown carpet, two battered cloth sofas covered in white dog hairs and suspicious stains, threadbare curtains and nicotine-stained walls and ceiling. The entire house stank, partly of its two occupants and their dog, but mostly of their sixty-a-day cigarette habit. The interior of the house was stained yellow. A few minutes inside left any visitors needing a good shower and a change of clothing.

Ally and Piggy took stock of their surroundings.

'Look at the state of the place,' whispered Piggy, glancing over at the open door. 'Think the old witch ever does any cleaning?'

'Fifty years ago maybe, and you wanted to eat here, you fat bastard,' said Ally, getting to his feet and walking over to the fireplace to look at some framed sepia photographs.

'I wish you'd stop calling me a fat bastard,' complained Piggy. 'It's my slow metabolism.'

'Yeah, and a fast pie arm, you fat bastard.' Ally moved a small vase to one side and saw for the first time the original colour of the wood in the round mark in the dust. 'Jesus Christ, this dust must be an inch thick.'

'They say that after a while it doesn't get any thicker.'

'That's a great comfort.'

At that moment Ally heard a growl and turned to see Patch the Jack Russell glaring at him from the doorway, baring his teeth. The animal was as yellow as the decor and looked demonic.

'Fuck off, you little bastard,' growled Ally as Piggy drew his legs up on to the sofa like a woman avoiding a mouse.

Patch's response was to launch himself like a yellow missile across the room at Ally's ankles. Ally was expecting the attack, and had adjusted his weight and stance accordingly, and as the yellow peril got within range, he kicked it as hard as he could in the ribs.

'There ye go, ye wee shite,' he shouted as Patch flew backwards over the ducking Piggy and crashed with a loud yelp against the wall before disappearing in a cloud of dust behind the sofa.

'Fucking hell, Ally, you've killed it,' said Piggy, getting to his feet and peering behind the sofa where Patch was howling for all he was worth.

'What's up?' asked Mr Hayward, who had appeared at the door.

'Little fella slid off the back of the sofa,' said Ally, smiling benevolently. He pulled the sofa away from the wall, revealing a perfect white outline against the yellow surface. 'Come on, little lad,' he called through clenched teeth, flaring his eyes and nostrils at the howling dog still trapped in the space. The sight of his nemesis approaching spurred the animal into drastic action, and it wrenched itself free and fled from the room.

'What happened?' asked Mr Hayward again, suspiciously.

'He was walking along the back of the sofa and slipped off, didn't he, Piggy?'

'Yeah, yeah, that's right, he slipped down the back,' Piggy repeated, not altogether very convincingly and looking daggers at Ally.

Old Mr Hayward shrugged his shoulders and went in

search of Patch, whilst Piggy sat down again in a cloud of dust and Ally thrust his hands into his pockets and had a mooch about.

'Behave yourself, Ally,' pleaded Piggy.

'What is she doing out there?' replied Ally. 'We're going to be stuck here all day.' Without waiting for a response, he walked out of the living room and into the hall, from where he could hear and smell Mrs Hayward frying bacon in the small kitchen at the back of the house. As he walked towards her he could see her holding a frying pan in her hand, and a thought framed itself in his head – how does she cook with only one arm?

As he got closer, the answer became obvious. Wrapped around her stump were two rashers of bacon waiting to go into her frying pan.

'Jesus fucking Christ,' he gasped, making her turn round, startled.

'Hello, darling.' She smiled at him, showing him her stained upper plate. 'Can't wait for your breakfast, eh?'

'Oh Christ,' started Ally before he suddenly blurted out, 'I didn't appreciate you were doing bacon. I can't eat it because of my religion. I should have told you.'

'Religion, darling, what are you on about?'

'I'm an . . . Arctic Rollertologist,' stammered Ally.

'What?' said Mrs Hayward, raising her voice. 'What's that, some sort of Jock thing?'

'Yeah, yeah, that's it. Anyway, I can't touch bacon or any

meat, actually, so I'll have to give it a miss, I'm afraid. My mate's OK with it, though; he can have mine if it's all the same to you.'

'All right, darling, whatever you say,' she replied, and putting down the frying pan, she unwrapped the two rashers of bacon from her stump – which Ally gleefully noted was weeping badly – and threw them into the pan along with a plaster that had detached itself from one of the sores. He stood alongside the old crone making polite small talk to ensure that she didn't notice the plaster and remove it, and once the bacon had fried, volunteered to take the sandwiches through to Piggy.

'He likes a drop of sauce if you've got any,' he said.

'Tomato sauce OK?' she said, going to a cupboard and handing him a bottle that would not have looked out of place in a museum. The dried black crust around the cap would have tested an oxyacetylene torch, but eventually Ally wrenched it free and dumped some of the strangely coloured liquid inside on to the bacon, taking particular care to cover the crispy fried plaster. He then strolled back into the living room and handed Piggy a plate containing two rounds of bacon sandwiches.

'You not eating?' asked Piggy greedily as he ploughed into the first sandwich without even a glance at its contents.

'Nah, didn't fancy it. I'll get something when we're back at the nick,' replied Ally, watching keenly to satisfy himself that everything was consumed.

'Suit yourself,' said Piggy, cheeks bulging as he raced through both sandwiches without dropping a crumb. Once he had finished, he wiped his mouth with the back of his hand and addressed Mr and Mrs Hayward, who had watched in some admiration as he apparently inhaled the two bacon sandwiches.

'That was lovely, darling,' he said, belching quietly into his fist. 'We'd love to stay a bit longer but we need to shoot off. Maybe another time, eh?'

'That'd be lovely, officers,' said Mrs Hayward, smiling broadly at Piggy. He reminded her of her eldest son, Duncan, who never visited or wrote any more, probably on account of the ten-year stretch he was serving down south somewhere. Her leathery old face creased up like a brown paper bag. Unfortunately the dehydrated skin, ruined by decades of heavy smoking, remained in position for some time afterwards, only gradually assuming its original state and making almost as much noise as a brown paper bag. It gave the impression that her face was permanently, but slowly, on the move.

As Ally and Piggy said their goodbyes and went to leave the bungalow, they paused at the front door, where Patch was thrashing about on the doormat in the throes of a fit, blood foaming from his nose. The pair glanced at each other before hurrying out and almost running back to Bravo Two Two, gulping in the welcome fresh air on the way.

'Fuck me, you could smoke a mackerel in that place,' Ally observed as Piggy got himself comfortable.

'Quick, quick!' shouted Piggy. 'Get the fuck out of here, he's coming over.'

Old Mr Hayward limped towards the police car with his arm raised. Patch appeared to be getting worse, and he intended asking the nice officers if they could get him to a vet on the twos and blues. He was somewhat perplexed to see the car career away, tyres smoking and engine screaming before he could say anything.

'Perhaps something important came up,' he called to his wife, who stood at the front door dabbing at her weeping stump with a drying-up cloth, occasionally glancing down at the writhing animal at her feet.

Chapter Nine

Psycho and Pizza had a quick spin round their ground in Bravo Two One, but the beat was quiet and subdued in the early-morning heat. It was as if everyone knew the day would be another hot, sticky and unpleasant one and had no wish to start it any earlier than absolutely necessary. They chatted briefly about Pizza's future plans for Chief Inspector Curtis, which Psycho had to admit were superb. He dropped Pizza off at Handstead to pair up with Sergeant Collins, giving himself plenty of time to negotiate the rush-hour traffic and get to Headquarters for his date with Superintendent Grainger.

As he eased Bravo Two One out into the increasingly heavy traffic, he pondered his latest, and some would say best to date, complaint. Although the rest of the group had been willing and active participants in the stunt, only he had been named and summoned to be served with yet another Regulation 9 discipline notice. Grainger had attended

Horse's Arse himself to make the appointment. Eighteen months earlier, he had been responsible for the procedural cock-up that had let Psycho off the hook over the toilet fairy incident, and now it was personal between them, with Grainger determined to get Psycho out of the job one day, one way or another, and every subsequent complaint against him had been dealt with by Grainger. All the Regulation 9 notices had been accompanied by a whispered, 'Got you this time, you mad cunt,' and were all followed by the same outcome – no case to answer. It was driving Grainger nuts and starting to dominate every waking hour of his life and quite a few sleeping ones.

Psycho shook his head ruefully as he reflected on the stunt to sort out a gobshite probationer that had worked better than any of them had dared hope. Maybe too well. PC Adam Courtenay had arrived on the group not long after Bovril's funeral, straight from training school, where he had quickly gained a reputation as an opinionated smartarse. The inspector at the school who was responsible for all postings back to the Force had taken inordinate delight in pencilling him in for Horse's Arse.

Should sort the little shit out, he thought happily to himself as he pinned up the postings list on a notice board outside the canteen. And he was absolutely right.

At his first muster, Courtenay had taken up a position at the back of the room where the Brothers always, but always, sat alone. Initially he had politely declined to move, and only a very serious threat to tear him a new arsehole had persuaded him to sit at the front, where he tried to ingratiate himself with Psycho.

'Fuck off, you cunt,' bellowed Psycho as Courtenay opened his mouth to speak to him. The Blister had simply ignored him and blown a large cloud of smoke in his direction, whilst Ally and Piggy were too busy arguing to pay him any attention, and only Pizza, who recognised what Courtenay was being subjected to, offered him any advice. Pizza was a made man now, having played such a significant role in the downfall of the Mafia. With nearly a year's service under his belt, he was now operating independently of a tutor and was on the list for a Standard Driving Course in early autumn. Relatively young in service, his early exposure to an experience that most police officers would never encounter had made him something special in the eyes of his peers. He had survived a shooting despite losing his colleague, Bovril. Importantly, no one had ever questioned whether he could have done anything to stop the shooting or save Bovril. He was simply the copper who had survived. He had been to the very edge of the abyss, looked over and then come away. Pizza had endured three days in the box at Manchester Crown Court giving evidence in the trials of the Mafia and he had withstood a real battering at the hands of desperate defence counsel. His evidence of the crucial find of the gang's clothing in the underground garages had secured him a place in local police folklore. But what had really sealed his place within the group was his vivid imagination when it came to stunts.

'Wind your fucking neck in,' he whispered. 'Just shut the fuck up and listen, OK?'

Sage advice from someone who knew and had endured the rites of passage. But Adam Courtenay wasn't the type to take advice. He was a bright lad who harboured aspirations of senior rank within the Force, but he wasn't nearly as clever as he thought he was, and he was unable to recognise that his presence on the group was causing problems. It was unfortunate that he had been brought in so soon after Bovril's murder, but someone more streetwise would have seen that the secret to long-term survival lay in an initial period of anonymity. Not Courtenay, though. Sergeant Jones had taken the muster and briefly introduced Courtenay to the group, who greeted his presence with bored indifference. Courtenay, however, had got to his feet and began a short speech expressing his excitement at being there.

'Sit down and shut the fuck up!' shouted Psycho. Then he winked at the rest of the group and announced, 'As you sow, so shall you reap,' which they all understood to mean that young Courtenay was in deep shit. And so it came to pass, as Psycho persuaded him to come in on a stunt to scare the living shit out of Pizza. Keen to fit in with the religious maniac, Courtenay agreed, and it was arranged that during the next set of night duty, the two of them would call on the services of a friendly mortuary worker to give Pizza the fright of his life.

On the night in question, Psycho and Courtenay drove to Handstead General Hospital and parked up at the rear of the mortuary annexe. As they waited for the night attendant to answer the doorbell, Psycho giggled insanely.

'This is going to be fucking great. He'll shit himself.'

'Yeah,' agreed Courtenay uncertainly. He was becoming increasingly unsure of what was planned, having never set eyes on a dead body before.

The door was soon opened by a pale, ghoulish attendant who obviously knew Psycho well, and they exchanged banter and pleasantries as he led the way down a dimly lit corridor into the main mortuary. It was garishly lit by harsh blue strip lights and tiled in white from floor to high ceiling, adding to the chill of the room. The only natural light would have been provided by the four frosted-glass windows at the highest point of the wall where it met the gloss-white ceiling. The terracotta-coloured floor was highly polished and the room smelt strongly of industrial-strength disinfectant. In the middle of the room stood a large gleaming aluminium wheeled trolley with a scissor jack hydraulic system, which much to Courtenay's relief was empty. At the back of the room were four large refrigerators standing eight feet tall with polished steel doors, each with a small chalkboard with space for six names. Clearly there were some residents in tonight.

'You don't need me, do you, Sean?' asked the attendant, who scuttled back into the dark corridor like a large spider when Psycho replied in the negative.

'You ready then, Adam?'

'Not sure about this, Sean,' replied Courtenay nervously. 'Not sure at all.'

'Don't be a soft twat,' scoffed Psycho dismissively. 'We've all had a go at this, it's fucking brilliant, I promise you.' He put a large hand into the small of Courtenay's back and guided him towards the refrigerators.

'Here it is, number four,' he said loudly, releasing the handle and pulling open the heavy door, which made a loud sucking noise as the rubber seals parted. As the billowing clouds of icy steam cleared, inside they could see a six-tiered rack. The top two trays contained covered corpses, which were clearly very deeply frozen.

'Not this one, these must be the long-stayers,' remarked Psycho casually, slamming the door shut and opening fridge number three. Inside it was identical in design but only chilled to about four degrees as opposed to the minus eighteen in fridge four. This fridge had only one occupant, concealed under a shroud on the second rack. On the floor at the front was a pint of milk and a small Tupperware box containing the mortuary assistant's evening snack.

'Fucking hell, I don't know about this,' said Courtenay again, looking from the corpse to Psycho and back again, and chewing his bottom lip.

'Don't be a twat,' Psycho repeated. 'You'll only be in there for a couple of minutes, then Pizza will come in to identify the body from the fatal RTA he's dealing with, and you sit up making *whoo* noises. He'll shit his pants, job done. Couldn't be easier. Now get yourself on that tray and pull the cover over you, he'll be here in a moment,' he finished, forcing Courtenay down towards the lower corpse tray, which he had helpfully pulled out for him.

Very reluctantly, Courtenay lowered himself on to the tray, shuddering as he felt the cold aluminium through his trousers, and pulled the cover up to his chin. It smelt strongly of dead things and embalming fluid.

'Over your head,' commanded Psycho. 'I'll be right back with Pizza,' and with that he slid the tray back into the fridge, nearly hitting Courtenay's head on the tray above, and shut the door with a resounding bang, rendering further argument useless.

'Oh Jesus,' said Courtenay to himself in the inky, chemical darkness. 'I don't know about this.' He tried to comfort himself with the image of Pizza screaming the place down as his 'corpse' came to life, and the rest of the group patting him on the back for a gutsy performance. 'Nice one, Courtenay,' they'd be saying, 'that took real balls.'

He had only been there for maybe thirty seconds when he became acutely aware of the intense cold. It was absolutely fucking freezing, but then, he reasoned, it obviously needed to be. They were, after all, storing dead bodies in here. Dead bodies, one of which was directly above him. Fucking hell, Pizza, hurry up.

After a couple of minutes he was beginning to shake with the cold and let out an involuntary gasp, his teeth literally chattering. That was when the corpse on the tray above him said, 'Fucking cold in here, isn't it?'

The screaming from the mortuary alerted the rest of the group gathered outside in the car park, and they rushed back inside to get him out of the fridge. His frenzied kicking had actually smashed the sprung handle and opened the door, and he was freeing himself from his icy tomb as they entered the room. He looked deranged, with eyes like black saucers, and fled past them without seeming to notice them. A smiling Pizza pulled back the cover from over his face up on the second tray.

'I thought he was never going to feel the cold,' he said as Psycho helped him down and patted him on the back. 'Where's he gone anyway?'

'Fuck knows,' replied Psycho.

They began searching for Courtenay, but he was nowhere to be found. He had not made his way back to the nick or to his lodgings, and as the night wore on, the group began to realise that they might have to consider reporting him as a missing person and admit to their supervisors what had taken place. They were spared that when, in the early hours of the morning, Inspector Greaves received an irate phone call from Courtenay's father, who had found his son in full uniform hammering on the front door of the family home some five miles from Handstead. He had run all the way home, and eventually managed to tell his astonished parents some of what had happened to him. 'Says he was locked in a mortuary fridge with a dead body that came to life. What the hell is going on there, Inspector?'

Greaves had responded by quoting the final verse of 'Stopping By Woods On A Snowy Evening' by his favourite poet, Robert Frost, which Courtenay's father had listened to in astonished silence before hanging up. Clearly the lunatics had taken over this particular asylum and he resolved that his gibbering son would be looking for alternative employment as soon as he learnt to control his bladder again. The phone call had been followed up by a formal written complaint, which was passed to Superintendent Grainger, who could barely conceal his joy when he saw Psycho's name amongst the list of suspects to be interviewed. The summons to Headquarters to be served with another Regulation 9 notice and be interviewed had followed within a week. Grainger would, however, have been disappointed at Psycho's reaction to the summons. If he imagined that Psycho feared such an event, he was sadly mistaken. In fact, he relished his clashes with Complaints and Discipline and was positively straining at the leash to get to Headquarters and lock horns with Grainger.

* * *

In his office on the fifth floor at Headquarters, Super-intendent Grainger glanced at his watch as he prepared himself for his latest clash with the dangerous psychopath PC Sean Pearce. He picked up his desk phone and dialled his PA in the adjoining office, drumming his fingers impatiently as he waited for her to answer.

At her desk, Dawn Masters glanced at the flashing red light, muttered, 'Bollocks,' and resumed her vigorous nail filing. Her contracted hours of work were from nine to five, but Grainger had insisted on an earlier start because he had a nine o'clock appointment and wanted to make an impression by having her in place to direct whoever it was to wait until summoned. Prick, he can fucking wait, she thought viciously. She left him fuming for a couple of minutes before she answered cheerily: 'Morning, Mr Grainger, how can I help you?'

'Bring me the Pearce file,' bellowed Grainger imperiously and slammed the phone down.

Dawn made him wait again before walking into his office and placing a large manila folder on his desk.

'Will you knock instead of just barging in, in future, please, Dawn?' he growled.

'Why, were you expecting someone else?' she replied innocently.

'I could have been with someone. You need to knock before coming in,' he said testily.

'I knew you were on your own; you were picking your nose when I came in.'

'Just fucking knock next time,' he snapped, and dismissed her from his presence with an arrogant wave of his hand and not so much as a glance at her.

She turned on her heel and left without closing his door, walking straight out of her office and down towards the drinks machine on the third floor.

'Door!' shouted Grainger from his desk. 'Shut the fucking door,' he screamed before getting to his feet, storming over and slamming his office door shut. At times like this he wondered why he kept her on, she was so insolent and disrespectful – but he still harboured the ambition to get her huge hooters out and have a play with them. 'Maybe at next year's Christmas Party,' he smiled to himself – then he'd sack her.

He began to leaf through Psycho's discipline folder, tutting and shaking his head as he did so and pursing his lips when he came to the fiasco he had supervised eighteen months ago. 'Not this time, Pearce, not this time,' he promised himself. Grainger had decided to load the dice in his favour this time, and had called in reinforcements in the shape of Detective Inspector Paul Chislehurst. Chislehurst and Grainger could have hatched from the same egg, in that neither had ever got their hands dirty doing any real police work and they had both identified a career in Complaints and Discipline, which no self-respecting cop would consider, as a relatively pain-free route up the slippery promotion ladder. Fortunately for the real cops, their incompetence, born of a lack of experience, rendered them pretty ineffectual – more of an irritant than a threat – but they managed one or two successes a year. Chislehurst's greatest asset in Grainger's eyes was his close ties to the Deputy Chief Constable, who was his uncle. DCC Chislehurst had also made a career out of trying to lock up other cops, and supported his slimy nephew's chosen career path wholeheartedly. Ergo, he similarly supported Grainger. The three of them would occasionally meet socially to discuss current investigations and career aspirations and had become known throughout the Force as The Three Thrushes in that they were irritating cunts. Their pathetic success rate was only tolerated by Chief Daniels because he had no time for his inherited DCC and despised Grainger and Chislehurst as a pair of obnoxious, untalented arseholes. But it suited him to have them somewhere where they caused the minimum of damage.

Grainger picked up his desk phone again and dialled Chislehurst, who answered immediately from his office down the hall.

'Morning, Paul,' said Grainger. 'You about ready? Pearce is due at nine.'

'Morning, boss,' squealed the effete Chislehurst. 'Ready and raring to go,' he added, causing the seriously homophobic Grainger to cough and splutter at the thought of the slim plucked chicken, white-skinned confirmed bachelor ready and raring to go.

'Get yourself down here,' barked Grainger, who only tolerated the little ponce because of his uncle, before turning back to the Pearce file and the statements in front of him concerning the mortuary stunt.

Despite the fact that of the officers on D Group, only the supervisors had been unaware of the mortuary stunt, so far only Psycho had been identified, and Grainger was relying more than he wished on someone rolling over to implicate others. Holding his breath whilst he waited for that to happen would not have been a good idea. The rest of the group were quite confident that Psycho would never drop any of them in the shit, not because he was some kind of saint, but because the unwritten code said it would never happen. Street cops simply did not put their colleagues away unless they were prepared for dire consequences. Cops who had committed the cardinal sin soon found themselves totally ostracised. Any subsequent calls for assistance would always go unanswered, and they generally decided their futures lay in non-operational roles. It was not a job in which you could afford to have your back unguarded or be unsupported for long. Transferring to another nick wasn't an option either. The grapevine information system preceded any in-Force transfer, and all mistakes and certainly any snitching followed them around. There was simply no escape from your past. Psycho could be guaranteed not to blot his copybook. The code was as strong as anything the criminal fraternity adhered to, perhaps stronger, and it was something that every Complaints and Discipline department around the country failed miserably to overcome.

Psycho pulled into the huge car park at Headquarters, parked adjacent to the radio workshops and booked off with the main Force control room.

'Hello, Delta Hotel, show Bravo Two One off air, inquiries Hotel Quebec extension 2110,' he said. Everyone in the Force knew what a visit to extension 2110 meant, and a few unidentified catcalls followed.

'Thank you, Bravo Two One, extension 2110 it is – good luck,' responded the main set operator.

Psycho hit the off button on the tin main set box slung below the overflowing ashtray and made his way sullenly across the car park, around the side of the new Force operations room and through the large smoked-glass double doors emblazoned with the Force crest. The main foyer was busy with numerous pencil necks and desk warriors making their way to what passed for work, and Psycho wandered over to the main reception desk. It was surrounded by glass cabinets full of huge silver sports trophies, historical items and curios of absolutely no interest to anyone except the Force museum curator. The receptionist who doubled as a telephonist until nine a.m. was busy pushing and pulling plugs into and out of the ancient switchboard and glanced up as Psycho loomed over the counter. She recognised him from his many past visits and before he could open his mouth to speak said simply, 'Room 520, fifth floor . . . Force Headquarters, how can I help you?' as she went back to the calls on her switchboard, which was lit up like a Christmas tree.

Psycho turned away with a wry smile and took one of the four lifts to the fifth floor. On arrival he was faced by a frosted-glass door with a huge sign on it that announced 'Complaints and Discipline Department'. All it lacked was the famous old sign at Dartmoor Prison that warned arrivals, 'Abandon Hope All Ye That Enter Here'. He pushed through the door and into the reception area, where Dawn Masters had resumed furiously filing her nails as she waited for her cup of coffee to cool. She looked up as the door opened and both recognised the other immediately. Psycho happily recognised a previous, very willing recipient of one of Dr Sean's internal spine supports and protein pick me ups, whilst she recognised one of the ugliest buggers she'd ever shagged, but also one of the most well endowed.

Their paths had crossed at a retirement party at Alpha Tango about six months ago, where Dawn had got herself blitzed on a Watney's Party Seven and a bottle of Thunderbird, and despite the best efforts of her concerned girlfriends, had staggered back to Psycho's filthy flat with him. Gentleman that he was, he had later regaled the group with his exploits, telling them how he'd 'fucked her till her eyes bugged out and her head fell off'. It was hard for another man to understand, but there was something about Psycho, something inherently dangerous that women found immensely attractive. Subsequently he was never short of female company, often from very dubious sources, but as Dawn would willingly testify, he was probably worth the risk.

'Morning, Sean, didn't realise it was you first up today,' she said smiling.

'Yeah, 'fraid so,' he replied, returning the smile and wondering whether she'd be up for a return visit. 'How long you been working here?' he continued, glancing around the sparsely furnished reception area before he slumped down on to a low faux-leather sofa in front of a beechwood table. Bizarrely, considering that most of the likely readers were going to be cops in the shit, the table was littered with ancient and well-thumbed copies of the teenage girls' magazine, *Bunty*.

'What the fuck . . . ?' he queried, picking up a copy and quickly throwing it back on to the table.

Dawn smiled and answered both his questions. 'About a year, and they're down to TCG,' she said.

'TCG?'

'That cunt Grainger,' she explained. 'All part of his cunning plan to confuse you lot and get you so fucked up, you get your ridiculous cock-and-bull stories all wrong when he interviews you. Got to admit, learning how to make your own tassel handbag or how to apply cobalt-blue eye shadow could put you off your stride a bit.'

'Jesus,' replied Psycho, shaking his head mournfully. There really were no depths Complaints and Discipline wouldn't plumb to put coppers away.

'He's brought in some help for your interview,' Dawn said quietly, glancing towards Grainger's office in case he suddenly appeared.

'Help?'

'Yeah, Inspector Chislehurst, know him?'

'No,' replied Psycho. 'Name's familiar, but don't think I've met him. Who is he?'

'DCC Chislehurst's nephew. Eighteen-carat shit looking to make a name for himself in Complaints and Discipline,' she continued in a whisper, constantly looking over her shoulder. 'Never done a day's police work in his life but knows his way round the Discipline regulations and loves bagging coppers – little poof,' she concluded vehemently.

'Poof?' queried Psycho.

'Reckon so. Camp as a Boy Scouts' jamboree,' she went on. 'Call it woman's intuition, but my money's on him being a fudge packer.'

'Pitcher or catcher?'

'Too frail to pitch, got to be a catcher.'

'Hmm,' mused Psycho, a germ of a plan of action forming. 'Thanks, Dawn, could be a big help. Forewarned is forearmed and all that.'

'Good, hope it's of some use,' she said doubtfully. 'Those two deserve everything they get.'

'Maybe, maybe,' said Psycho. Absent-mindedly, he picked up a copy of *Bunty* and leafed, unseeing, through it.

Dawn returned to filing her nails to a talon-like sharpness. She was interrupted by her phone. The red light told her that it was Grainger again, so she let it ring for a while before answering it sweetly, 'How can I help you, Mr Grainger?'

'Has Pearce arrived?' he barked.

'Been here a while.'

'Then why the fuck didn't you tell me?' shouted Grainger. Jesus, big hooters or not, the girl had a brain the size of a walnut – she'd have to go.

'His appointment is for nine,' replied Dawn, who had four A levels and was temping before going up to Oxford. 'I thought you'd need every minute you've got to get ready for his interview,' she finished insolently.

'Send him in,' screamed Grainger, slamming the phone back on its cradle and then smiling weakly at Chislehurst, who had a very odd expression on his face. He couldn't afford for Chislehurst to report that little outburst back to his uncle, he mused as he wiped spittle from around his mouth. 'Bloody woman's incompetent,' he said limply.

Chislehurst nodded in reply but said nothing. He had his eye on Grainger's job and was keeping his counsel and his powder dry. Whilst there was little honour amongst thieves, there was absolutely none amongst the lizards and back-stabbers that inhabited the Complaints and Discipline world.

Dawn showed Psycho into the main office, where he found Grainger seated behind his desk and Chislehurst to one side, notebook in his lap, pen poised like a prissy secretary. Psycho glared menacingly at him, causing Chislehurst to swallow hard and glance nervously over at Grainger.

'Sit down, Pearce,' snarled Grainger, not looking up from the paper he was pretending to read and indicating with a wave of his hand the chair opposite.

'You know why you're here, Pearce, so let's not fuck about,' he began aggressively. 'This is DI Chislehurst, who's going to be assisting me with the interview,' he added dismissively.

Psycho spotted the slightest gesture of irritation from Chislehurst and quickly identified the first flaw in Grainger's cunning plan.

'Assisting you? Why assisting, sir?'

'What do you mean?' asked Grainger, looking up for the first time since Psycho had entered the room. 'He's assisting, that's all.'

'Oh, right, a bit of moral support, you mean.'

'Moral support?' hissed Grainger. 'I don't need any fucking moral support to interview a piece of fucking shit like . . .' He trailed off as he became aware that both Pearce and Chislehurst were looking at him very strangely.

'Go on,' encouraged Psycho, beaming at him as he unravelled in front of them.

Grainger quickly pulled himself together and coughed loudly as he bunched the file between his hands.

'Right, let's get on with this, shall we,' he started. 'Mr Chislehurst will take some notes as we go along so there's no dispute later about what we've said, OK?'

'Good idea, sir. Don't want any more fuck-ups, do you?'

Grainger coloured up at the reminder of his faux pas eighteen months ago and glanced at Chislehurst, who was clearly looking for a reaction. He managed to hold himself in check and continued.

'I need to speak to you regarding an allegation of gross misconduct that's been made against you by the family of Constable Adam Courtenay. The allegation is that on—'

'It's all a carve-up,' interrupted Psycho.

'A carve-up?'

'Fucking right. This has got fuck all to do with anything that may have happened to Courtenay. This is just victimisation and you know it.'

'Victimisation?' asked Chislehurst.

'Fucking right, this is plain victimisation because I'm a homosexual, got fuck all to do with Courtenay.'

'Homosexual?' bellowed Grainger.

'Homosexual?' echoed a delighted Chislehurst, who could see a cause célèbre developing in front of him. 'How are you being victimised?'

'Been happening for years,' lied Psycho, who was now on a roll and prepared to say or do anything in his campaign to take on Grainger. 'My career's been thwarted at every turn, and people like *him* take every opportunity to make my life a misery.'

'Oh come on,' laughed Chislehurst. 'It can't have been that bad, surely? I've never found that my homosexuality has held me back in my career,' he added, totally ignoring the fact that his uncle was the Deputy Chief Constable.

Grainger had listened to the exchange with open-mouthed astonishment and now allowed his rabid bigotry to bubble to the surface. 'You're a fucking shit-stabber?' he blurted out loudly.

'That's outrageous!' shouted Psycho, getting to his feet and holding his arms out imploringly to Chislehurst.

'That's outrageous!' shouted Chislehurst at the same time, also getting to his feet and approaching Psycho on the other side of the desk.

'This is what I have to put up with from him all the time, praise the good Lord,' said Psycho, getting hold of Chislehurst's scrawny arm and pulling him close. 'He hates pooftas . . . I mean homosexuals,' he corrected himself.

Chislehurst had missed the slip and continued to shout, 'That's outrageous!' in an increasingly hysterical voice. 'You poor man.'

Grainger stared resignedly at them as they berated him from the other side of his desk. Psycho had escaped his clutches once again. His humiliation was complete when Dawn put her head round the door to enquire if everything was all right.

'Fine, thank you, Dawn,' said Grainger.

'Didn't sound fine, lots of shouting . . .'

'Fuck off, you stupid cow!' screamed Grainger.

'That's outrageous!' squealed Psycho and Chislehurst in unison, arms locked together in a display of solidarity.

'Get the fuck out of here, Pearce,' shouted Grainger above the din as Dawn added her two bobs' worth to the shambles his interview had quickly become. 'I'll notify you of the new interview date in due course.'

'How can I ever get a fair hearing? He hates me because I'm a Christian and homosexual,' Psycho told his new ally.

'A Christian as well? That's truly outrageous!' screamed Chislehurst at the top of his voice. He was close to wigging out completely.

'Thank goodness you were here to see what he's like, Mr Chislehurst,' whispered Psycho into his ear, hammering the last nail into Grainger's professional coffin.

As he left the office, leaving Chislehurst screeching, 'That's outrageous!' at Grainger like a scratched record, Psycho took hold of Dawn and walked out into the corridor with her.

'Fucking brilliant,' he beamed. 'That little tip you gave me about Chislehurst came in handy.'

'Glad I could help, Sean.'

'What you doing later?' he continued.

'Not much, why?'

'You are going to get loads,' he answered, smiling broadly. 'Call you later, OK?'

'Sure,' she replied with an equally broad smile as he left the office with a triumphant punch of the air.

Grainger's day got worse. After Psycho had left, he spent some considerable time calming the hysterical Chislehurst before sending him home to recover. He needed to get out of the office, and leafing through the complaint file, he noticed that a statement still needed to be taken from the mortuary assistant who had facilitated Psycho's stunt. After a quick phone call he arrived as arranged, bang on eleven, to interview the assistant, only to find he had been double-booked.

'So sorry, Mr Grainger,' said Crispin Jennings in his best Vincent Price voice, rolling his bulbous black eyes to the ceiling. 'Just got a quick viewing to get out of the way and then I'm all yours. I've had an absolute bastard of a morning. Got two families trying to get in to pay their respects and both want the deceased in their favourite Sunday best. Fucked if I can remember who should be wearing what.'

Shuddering, Grainger sat down on a hard bench to allow a grieving family in for their last view of a dearly departed in the adjacent Chapel of Rest. A sniffling group swept past him, guided by Jennings, who left them to it and returned to the waiting room. Grainger was about to start quizzing him when they heard the sound of loud wailing from inside the chapel. The door then opened and an angry red-faced man stuck his head out.

'He's in a fucking blue safari suit and we specifically asked for him to be in his favourite brown three-piece Burton's suit,' he complained loudly. 'Why isn't he in his brown suit, why?'

'Excuse me, Mr Grainger, this won't take me long,' whispered Jennings, causing Grainger to gag on his poisonous breath. 'Please wait outside, ladies and gentlemen, I'll take care of things,' and he scuttled back into the chapel as the family filed sullenly out and waited in the anteroom with Grainger.

Grainger's awkwardness in their silent, grief-stricken company was alleviated when Jennings sprang back through the door thirty seconds later to announce, 'All done, ladies and gentlemen, please come in.' The family filed silently back into the chapel, where their beloved now lay resplendent in his favourite brown suit, and Jennings quietly closed the door behind them and rejoined Grainger.

'I'm impressed, Mr Jennings,' said Grainger. 'How did you manage to change him into his brown suit so quickly? Dead bodies weigh a ton.'

'Easy, Mr Grainger. I just wheeled the one in the brown

suit in and swapped the heads round,' he announced to the horrified cop-catcher. Grainger sat back in his seat, genuinely fearful of this creepy little man with breath that could stun a horse and who was now offering for a handshake a suspiciously manicured white hand that had very recently been tucking severed heads into shirt collars.

'Holy fucking shit, I've just remembered I should be somewhere else,' Grainger said loudly, ignoring the handshake and dashing for the door. 'I'll be sending someone else to see you very soon,' he finished, resolving to assign Chislehurst to deal with him.

He was back in his car within a minute, and screeched away from the car park, occasionally glancing in his rearview mirror, expecting to see Jennings chasing after him holding a dripping severed head in each hand.

Chapter Ten

The Grosvenor Park car park was deserted as Yankee One came to a standstill alongside the single-storey, white-washed, graffiti-covered changing room and toilet block. Smack bang in the middle of the six-hundred-acre park and only accessible by vehicle via the one badly rutted road, the car park was usually deserted except at weekends, when local football teams kicked lumps out of each other on the muddy pitches ranged as far as the eye could see. Until, that is, the toilet block complex caught the eyes of first the local and then the regional homosexual community. Remote and virtually unknown to the local police, it had quickly become a big draw on the cottaging circuit, pulling in players from all round the north-east of the country.

Unfortunately, the secret had been inadvertently disclosed to the Brothers one evening when they had stopped a succession of vehicles leaving the park. All had contained rampant queens returning from 'nature rambles' in the park. The Brothers had quickly worked out that they had stumbled on a cottaging venue, but what had really intrigued them were the occupations of the men they had stopped. Two were local social workers, one a solicitor from Manchester, and a fourth a shady car dealer from Liverpool. He was the one who had really interested them, because cursory inquiries revealed that he moved on the periphery of major crime in Liverpool and was known to associate with some big-hitters. What if some of them harboured similar dark secrets? reasoned the Brothers. What an opportunity to use a little blackmail to get them working for the Old Bill.

With that in mind, the Brothers had begun an occasional war against organised gay criminals, staking out the Grosvenor Park toilets with a view to capturing a Mr Big indulging in a little stench trench action and threatening to reveal all to his family and associates unless he played ball with the police. They had not had much success so far – the only highlight had been a journalist they'd captured having a solo wank in the absence of any trade – but they had decided to persevere. They were nothing if not persistent and had devised another cunning facet to their plan by drilling a glory hole between two cubicles. Now they took it in turns to sit in one of the cubicles waiting for a patron to poke his old man through from the other side. No joy there so far, but they had resolved to play a long game.

'Not a fucking sausage,' remarked H, glancing around the car park. They sat briefly in silence looking at the parched brown playing fields that stretched out to the horizon, a heat haze shimmering in the distance.

'Fuck me, it's hot,' remarked Jim, pushing his cap back on to the crown of his head and wiping a finger across his sweaty brow. 'Come on, H, your turn today.'

H wriggled uncomfortably in his seat, his back stuck to the cloth cover, and looked across at Jim, who had briefly closed his eyes.

'Fucking hell, Jim, it's as dead as a dead thing, we aren't going to get any trade today,' he pleaded. He turned his eyes forward again through the insect-spattered windscreen and watched the living heat devour Grosvenor Park.

'Give it half an hour, we'll get something soon. The harder we try, the luckier we'll get,' replied Jim, grateful that it wasn't his turn to sit in the stinking toilet cubicle waiting for an erect penis to come through the wall. 'Besides, it'll be cooler in there.'

'Marvellous,' sighed H, opening his door and stepping out into the searing white light, which fried his eyes immediately. He adjusted his heavy serge uniform trousers and looked back into Yankee One, where Jim sat grinning at him.

'Half an hour and that's it, right?'

'Half an hour,' agreed Jim. 'I'll monitor the main set, you switch to Channel Two, and anything comes your way I'll call you, OK?'

H didn't reply, but stood away from the vehicle as Jim

started back up Yankee One and stood watching as he drove slowly away from the car park to hide in a nearby cul-de-sac, which afforded a perfect view of the only vehicle entrance into the park. The Brothers had experimented with the range of their radios, and whoever was driving now acted as spotter for the other. H watched as Yankee One was swallowed in the heat haze, and paused in the scorching silence of the vast park, listening to the heat. He sighed deeply and then walked towards the toilet block. The smell of industrial-strength disinfectant, failing miserably to counteract the stench of human excrement, assailed his nostrils yards from the entrance. He stopped in the gloomy doorway to allow his eyes to adjust from the nuclear blast whiteness outside before stepping into the pungent interior. The only light was provided by half a dozen wire-glass windows high in the walls above the six broken urinals and a similar number above the three toilet cubicles at the far end of the block. A solitary wrecked sink hung off the near wall and a pool of stagnant water had accumulated under it on the rough, unfinished concrete floor. Above the sink, a single sheet of scarred, scratched galvanised steel acted as a mirror, reflecting the graffiti-covered peeling white emulsion walls. The three toilet cubicles incredibly still had their doors and partitions, though the locks had been nicked years ago. The smell in the block was simply indescribable, and not for the first time H found himself wondering what possessed otherwise respectable men to come to a place like this for sexual gratification. It was a little piece of hell on earth, though as Jim had predicted, it was cooler than outside. After checking that the three cubicles were empty, H began to pace slowly around the block, keeping in the shadows as he occasionally glanced out into the shimmering car park.

He didn't have to wait long before his radio hissed into life and Jim's voice blurted out, 'Bingo, one on the way.' Peering quickly out, H saw a vehicle floating towards him through the heat haze, and then went quickly to the far cubicle and shut the door behind him.

As he approached the toilet block in his Volkswagen convertible, Justin Byrd felt the mounting anticipation inside him grow tenfold. A prolific cottager, he had discovered the Grosvenor Park toilets six months ago and had never failed to score on every visit he had made since. He had left his Georgian townhouse in Manchester city centre on a whim three hours earlier and had trawled a couple of his regular haunts unsuccessfully before deciding on a trip out to Handstead. Justin ran a hugely profitable private dental surgery in the city centre that had trebled its turnover when he had embraced the new fad of cosmetic surgery, which had mushroomed in the United States and then made its way across the Atlantic. The trend had predictably proved popular in London, and Justin had seen an opportunity for him in Manchester. He was the first practitioner in the north and had made his own personal fortune sorting out the dodgy teeth of a number of soap stars and professional footballers, sporting his own set of flashing ivories as a walking testament to his business acumen. His huge wealth allowed him to indulge pretty much all his whims and fancies, and when it came to his favourite indulgence of young Oriental boys, his money came in very handy.

Unfortunately, though, he had a very serious Achilles heel – a wife and small children. He had married young when still unsure of his sexual preferences, fathered two children, and then, too late, realised that he batted for the other side. He had managed to keep his secret from his wife, who harboured a few suspicions but who had taken a pragmatic approach to the change in their relationship – that what she didn't know couldn't hurt her and the kids, nor of course, the affluent lifestyle they all enjoyed. She had, however, let him know in no uncertain terms that if he ever decided to change the status quo, she'd rob him blind in the divorce courts.

But despite all his wealth and privilege, he just couldn't help himself when it came to a bit of rough trade, and he regularly visited public toilets around the Manchester area in search of it. Jason was in his early forties, medium height, with pale jowly cheeks and expensively salon-dyed collar-length black hair. He fought a constant battle with his weight, and had a penchant for dressing in the style of the TV star, Jason King, in a crushed velvet lilac jacket and frilly-fronted high-collared shirt. Justin was confident he'd score at Grosvenor Park and was not in the least bit bothered at the absence of parked vehicles outside the toilet block. He knew there could well be plenty of walk-in trade.

From his cubicle H heard the car stop and the engine die, and then a door open and shut and footsteps approach the doorway of the toilet block.

Justin paused to allow his eyes to adjust to the gloom of the block before he stepped inside. To his joy he noticed the closed door on the far cubicle.

'Hello?' he called. There was a cough in reply and he hurried to the adjacent cubicle. Twenty seconds later, he had eased his erection into the glory hole that the Brothers had helpfully installed.

As Justin's penis hove into view, H grinned broadly, reached into his pocket and pulled out an enormous bulldog clip, which he deftly clamped over the helmet, securing it inside his cubicle. On the other side of the filthy partition wall, Justin screamed at the excruciating pain and continued to scream as there was no let-up.

Jim had allowed a couple of minutes to pass before he had followed Justin's vehicle up to the toilets, and he could hear him screaming before he had parked up. He jogged into the toilet block, and as his eyes grew used to the gloom he saw H leaning nonchalantly against the cubicles at the far end. The screaming had not diminished as Jim approached H to examine his handiwork.

'Look what I've caught,' H laughed, indicating Justin with a nod of his head. Jim looked over at Justin, who stood on tiptoe against the partition wall, facing the Brothers, trousers around his ankles, tears of pain and humiliation coursing down his cheeks.

'Have a look at this, will you,' mused Jim. 'What have we got here, then? What's your name, pal?'

'Jesus fucking Christ!' screamed Justin. 'Get it off me.'

'You've caught the main man apparently, H,' mocked Jim, going into the cubicle recently occupied by H. There the blackened end of Justin's cock caused him to gasp out loud in shock.

'Fucking hell, H,' he hissed. 'Look at the state of it! Looks like the fucking thing's about to fall off.'

'Not pleasant, is it? Teach him to stick his dick through a wall, though.'

'Know who he is?'

'Not spoken to him yet – who are you, mate?'

'Justin Byrd . . . get me out, please.'

'What do you do for a living?'

'Fucking hell, I'm a dentist. Just get me out, please, just get me out, will you?'

'A dentist?' repeated H disgustedly. 'Fuck me, Jim, we've caught the tooth fairy.'

'A lot of fucking good that's going to be to us,' grumbled

Jim. 'Of all the luck. Can you believe it, a fucking tooth fairy? Got any ID on you?' and without waiting for an answer, he began to rummage through the inside pockets of Justin's now sweat-drenched velvet jacket and patted down his Farrah slacks until he located his wallet in the back pocket. As Justin continued to squeal in agony, the Brothers spun his wallet, the contents of which soon confirmed his identity and profession.

'Bollocks,' swore H. 'Get his picture, Jim, and I'll cut the bastard free.'

Jim hurried back out to Yankee One, returning shortly with the brand spanking new Polaroid camera the Brothers had invested in. He quickly took two photographs of Justin's horrific situation, one of him spread-eagled against the wall on tiptoe, trousers round his ankles, the other of his blackened, bulldogged cock. As he stood waving the photos in the air to dry them, H walked back into the cubicle and wrenched the bulldog clip away. Justin's screams hit new heights as he collapsed on to the floor clutching his throbbing manhood, sobbing in pain and humiliation.

H had kept hold of the man's wallet and now found something of real interest to him.

'Who's this?' he asked, holding up the colour photograph he had found sandwiched between two credit cards.

From the floor Justin glanced up, and both the Brothers spotted the flash of fear as he looked at the photograph.

'Well?' pushed H. 'Who are they?'

175

The dentist kept quiet.

'The wife and kids? I take it Mrs Byrd knows fuck all about your nasty little habit?'

Justin shook his head but still said nothing. He could see where this was going.

'Take it you'd like to keep it that way?'

The man nodded briefly.

'Get yourself sorted out, fella,' said H benevolently. 'We'll get this squared away and you can take yourself off home – to your family,' he finished caustically.

Justin rose unsteadily to his feet, feeling physically sick from the pain at the end of his knob, but mostly from the threat now presented to his future financial well-being. Pulling a silk handkerchief out of his jacket pocket which he held gingerly to his pulsating cock, he turned to face his grinning tormentors.

'What exactly did you have in mind?'

Justin had been rolled by the police before and paid off uniforms more than once when he'd been found in compromising situations, but the response he got now completely floored him.

'Always fancied a decent set of choppers myself. How about you, Jim?'

'Fucking right. I assume those ones you're flashing about are all your own work?'

'Of course, but these things cost a fortune,' the dentist protested.

'And?' demanded H. 'What doesn't cost a fortune is the stamp on the letter addressed to Mrs Byrd with these photos inside,' he said as Jim held the two Polaroids aloft to reinforce the demand.

The man caved in immediately.

'OK, OK, there's no need for anyone else to know about this, is there? I'll gladly sort your teeth out in return.'

'We don't want any fucking fillings, just sparkling white teeth like one of them film stars.'

'I may have to do some remedial work, but yes, you'll get a set like mine.'

'What d'you reckon, H?' asked Jim, looking long and hard at the trembling Justin.

'You fuck us about, mate, those photos are going everywhere, and I mean everywhere. Understood?'

'Yes, understood,' he replied meekly.

'When's a good time for us to visit you?'

'Well, maybe you could ring me tomorrow to arrange an appointment?'

'Fucking ring you to arrange an appointment. You're having a laugh!' shouted Jim. 'Tell you what, we'll be round after closing tomorrow, shall we say seven?'

'Yes, that's fine,' said Justin resignedly. 'When do I get the photos?'

'You don't,' said H abruptly, throwing the man's wallet to the floor.

The Brothers turned quickly and left Justin in the semi-gloom gingerly dressing himself, his shaking hands struggling to pull up his fly and fasten his belt. By the time he got back to the car park, Yankee One was disappearing into the heat haze. He opened his car and retracted the roof to allow the heat inside to dissipate as he pondered his fate. There was nothing he wouldn't do to keep those photos away from his wife, and he was resigned to throwing away thousands on the coppers' teeth to achieve that.

After a few minutes he eased himself painfully into the car and drove slowly home, conjuring up an explanation for his injuries.

Two days later the Brothers appeared for early-turn muster sporting amazing Hollywood smiles that they refused to account for. D Group were agreed that it was the first time any of them had seen the pair smile so much when they weren't kicking the shit out of someone. The teeth actually looked extremely sinister, set as they were perfectly symmetrically in their pale, sinister faces. The Brothers looked like a pair of vampires. But very slick vampires. They had always taken great care with their appearance and were immaculately turned out. Jim brought his military background and training into play and had creases in his tunics and trousers that could cut paper. H was not far behind him in the pressing stakes. Their blue uniform shirts were always clean and the collars carefully starched, and they preferred to wear proper ties rather than the issue clip-on ones, despite the obvious risks. They had both stitched down the epaulettes on their tunics to stop them bulging, and the buttons and numbers gleamed like the sun. Their brushed caps had smartly slashed peaks (Jim's influence again) and their shoes were always polished to a glass finish. It was not uncommon to find them carefully cleaning their shoes after they had given a villain a good kicking. With their new teeth, they were the dog's bollocks – and they knew it.

Chapter Eleven

Acting Chief Inspector Curtis replaced the phone on his desk and ran his trembling hands through his rapidly thinning hair. It was coming out in clumps, and several strands wrapped themselves around his sweaty fingers. The double windows in his first-floor office were wide open to try to catch any breeze that might come along, but in common with every other room in the nick, the curtains remained absolutely still in the unrelenting heat. Outside he could hear the constant roar from the heavy traffic on St Helens Road East which belched vast amounts of poisonous petrol and diesel fumes into the porridge-like atmosphere that now hung over the whole town.

Curtis was in extremely poor shape, both physically and mentally, especially since the unwelcome departure of his ambitious wife. Whilst their relationship could never have been described as anything other than convenient from her point of view, he had actually harboured quite deep affection for her and had done all he could to please her. She had marked him out for a career as a high-flyer in the police service, especially armed with his degree, and his admission on to the accelerated promotion course and quick elevation to inspector without much effort at all had convinced her he could go a long way. Maybe even to the highest echelons; anything was possible in her eyes. But everything had changed when she had enrolled on an Open University sociology course, where she had fallen under the spell of another mature student. His influence, coupled with her husband's move to the Chief Constable's staff officer role, had convinced her that she had made a terrible mistake. When her idiot husband had jubilantly told her about his move to Handstead, which even she knew was tantamount to a death sentence for his career, she realised that their relationship had come to an end. She ruthlessly ended their marriage, packed her bags and left, emptying the joint account and leaving Curtis with nothing but bills to pay.

Her departure had devastated him, and if he was honest, he had not dealt with it well. He had begun to drink at home on his own, stopped eating properly and rarely slept. He looked like shit as the weight dropped off his frame and dandruff littered his thin shoulders. Working at Handstead only exacerbated his depression, as he quickly became the whipping boy for Chief Superintendent B Division, who was under pressure to put things right following Chief Inspector Gillard's sudden departure. He found working with Hilary Bott almost impossible because her stammer rendered her unintelligible when under pressure. He really needed an ally, but she was proving as much use as tits on a bull. He pined for his runaway bride who, if only he knew it, was now also regretting her change of partner almost as much. The euphoria of a secret lover quickly diminished as they lived under the same roof of a rundown, one-bedroomed flat in the Bigg Market area of Newcastle. As neither she nor the new Mr Right had ever worked, they relied solely on state benefits and their standard of living dwindled to rock bottom once the contents of the pilfered joint account had been frittered away. She often found herself thinking about what might have been as the bearded one snorted into her ear through irritating nostril hair as he gamely pounded away on top of her in their 'love nest'.

The phone call had been from the Chief Super, berating him for another unacceptable outbreak of public disorder on the Park Royal estate the previous night. A WPC had been lured into the Park Royal pub by a series of bogus 999 calls, trapped inside and badly injured by a volley of pool balls hurled at her by members of the Mafia. Officers backing her up had smashed their way in after her and had only narrowly prevented a serious indecent assault. Word on the estate, which had got back to the police, was that the Mafia intended to capture a female officer and rape her. Curtis had just been furiously warned to take steps to ensure that never happened. As he rubbed his red, puffy eyes, his stomach churned and boiled. His new gastric ulcer was giving him gyp, and he felt the telltale signs of uncontrollable diarrhoea again.

He hurried into his private toilet, locked the door and settled himself in for what he knew was likely to be a lengthy session. He leant forward with his elbows on his knees and rested his head in his hands. Closing his eyes, he relaxed in the one place on earth he felt truly safe. He had been sitting like that for a few minutes when he heard his office door open and footsteps cross the floor to the washroom door, which he had left ajar. That door creaked open as the caller cautiously pushed against it. Then he heard a falsetto male voice with an exaggerated Irish accent call out, 'Hello there, Mr Curtis – you in there taking a dump, are you?'

Curtis knew he was in trouble. The accent was deliberately disguised, he was sure of that, but he prayed his rank would get him out of the shit, so to speak.

'How dare you!' he shouted in his best outraged senior officer's voice. 'This is a private convenience and you have no right to be here. Get out immediately and wait for me in the corridor outside the office. How dare you stroll in here like you own the place.'

'Blow it out your arse, you English bastard. This should help your constipation,' interrupted the Irish voice. 'Enjoy, man.'

Curtis heard what he suspected was a Zippo lighter click

open and fire up, followed by a loud hissing sound. A split second later, a fizzing package shot under his raised toilet door, past his feet, and lodged behind the toilet pan. Leaping to his feet, he saw that the package appeared to consist of half a dozen red sticks of dynamite strapped together with a single fuse that had almost reached its end.

'NO!' he screamed, panicking as he realised he didn't have time to retrieve the package and throw it back under the door, or to open the door to escape. Slamming the lid shut, he jumped awkwardly on to the toilet with his trousers and pants around his ankles as the thunder flashes exploded.

The detonation actually shook the whole nick. Upstairs in the canteen on the fourth floor, the lights flickered and dust showered from the ceiling. Viewed from outside, the building appeared to shrug its shoulders as a dull thud lifted it from its foundations. In other offices, cups of tea and coffee and glasses of water shivered and heads looked towards the sound of the explosion as dust descended through shafts of sunlight.

In the stairwell between the first and second floors, Psycho and Pizza looked at each other and simultaneously said, 'Fuck!' before racing upstairs, Psycho trousering his Zippo lighter.

Still standing on the toilet, Curtis opened his eyes to see that the door to the cubicle had been blown off its hinges by the blast and the cistern behind him had cracked and was now steadily leaking water. The single window in the washroom had shattered but what Curtis could not see was that his face was covered in black soot and his hair was gently smoking where embers had landed.

'Fucking hell!' he shouted in delayed fright. He remained standing where he was, smoke rising from his head as the explosion echoed around him.

Hilary Bott and DI Barry Evans were first into the office, alerted by the huge blast, to be greeted by the sight of a trouserless, blackened and smoking Curtis standing shaking on his toilet, clutching his manhood. Bott and Evans stood temporarily speechless as they viewed the extraordinary spectacle.

'What the fuck is wrong with you woodentops?' Evans finally gasped. 'Fucking hell, you can't take a shit without something going wrong,' he added, looking sidelong at Bott. She ignored his barbed reference to her own toilet troubles and continued to stare at Curtis, who appeared to have turned to stone.

'For fuck's sake!' bellowed Evans, striding into the cubicle, where he grabbed Curtis by the upper arms and pulled him off the ruined toilet. 'Get your trousers up,' he instructed. 'You've been well stitched up,' he continued, looking behind the toilet at what little remained of the thunder flashes.

Bott continued to stare, open mouthed, at the smoking and trembling Curtis.

'For fuck's sake, Hilary, if that's the best you've got to

offer, bugger off back to your own office and carry on with your raffia baskets or whatever it is you do in there,' snapped Evans. She nodded and backed out of the washroom like an automaton. Evans kicked the door shut and put an arm round Curtis's shaking shoulders. He knew better than most what a state the other man had been in before this latest episode.

'You OK?' he asked.

Wide eyed, Curtis nodded.

'You need to get yourself home. Is your motor here?'

Again Curtis nodded.

'Pull your trousers up and get yourself home. Take the rest of the day off, I'll cover for you. Have a bath, have a good drink, get absolutely fucking blitzed, but don't come back for a couple of days. Sort yourself out first, all right?'

Curtis nodded again but didn't move.

'Trousers!' shouted Evans.

Slowly Curtis pulled his charred underpants and trousers up and secured his belt.

'Get yourself off home,' said Evans again. 'I'll tidy things up here and we'll see you when we see you. No rush now.'

Curtis shuffled out of the washroom into the main office, where his jacket hung from a peg behind the door. With trembling fingers he took it down and put it on, and walked slowly out along the corridor lined with gawping spectators and down the stairs to the ground floor. As he crossed the yard towards the garages where his car was parked he could hear mocking laughter from the building behind him, but he didn't look back. He had had enough. His wife, Chief Superintendent B Division, the Chief Constable, Psycho and Pizza had all broken him. He was done. He knew where he now needed to go, and quickly. Somewhere they'd understand what he was going through, somewhere they'd be able to help: Handstead General Hospital Psychiatric Wing – or as it was known by the locals, Fuckwit Farm.

Unfortunately for him, his ordeal was not yet quite over. Psycho and Pizza had spent the first two hours of their early-turn shift rounding up a pair of stray mongrel dogs, which they had brought back into the nick. In the garage block, they had quickly located Curtis's Austin Allegro, which very foolishly he had not locked. Not that locking it would have thwarted their scheme for long. They had thrown the raging strays into the vehicle, chucked in four bars of Ex-lax chocolate and slammed the doors shut. The ravenous dogs had devoured even the paper wrappers, and half an hour later begun to aerosol shit inside the car. Soon the entire vehicle was covered in a film of stinking dog shit.

Curtis turned in to the garage block and walked towards his car. In the semi-darkness he did not register that the windows appeared to have had a tint applied since he last used it. As he pulled the driver's door open, the two demented dogs went for him, biting him viciously around the head and body before fleeing through the open garage doors and escaping through the back yard. Unmoved, Curtis got into his stinking, shit-covered car, cleared the dripping windscreen with his hands and drove sedately to Fuckwit Farm. There he presented himself at the desk, hair still smoking, covered in dog shit and claiming to be a police officer wishing to commit himself voluntarily under the Mental Health Act. Even when he had showed the dubious staff his police warrant card, they insisted on phoning Handstead nick to confirm the identity of the strange, twitching man standing in their reception.

News of Curtis's voluntary committal at the Farm quickly spread around the station and then out into the Force. The causes of his predicament heard the news as they booked off duty with Sergeant Collins at the end of their shift.

'Where's Mr Curtis?' asked Pizza conversationally. 'He's usually here to make sure we're not screwing the job for a couple of minutes.'

'Haven't you heard?'

'Heard what?'

'He's committed himself. Someone blew him up in his toilet and filled his motor with dog shit. He's turned himself in at the Farm, just after lunch apparently.'

'Fucking hell,' said Psycho jubilantly to Pizza once they were out of earshot of anyone who might ask questions. 'Fucking sectioned himself, what a result.'

Pizza was nowhere near as jubilant. He actually felt quite concerned about Curtis and not a little guilty about his role in his downfall.

'Tonight we'll really finish him off,' continued the beaming Psycho.

'Finish him off? What the fuck are you on about? He sounds finished as it is.'

'Nah,' said Psycho dismissively. 'He needs to be sorted out properly. Don't you start getting all soft on me now, Pizza. I'll pick you up about half nine, once it's properly dark, and we'll get it done.'

'Get what done?'

'You wait and see. Just be ready about half nine and I'll sort everything else out.'

It had been dark about half an hour, and Curtis snuggled his head comfortably into the freshly laundered pillows and surveyed his new, albeit temporary, surroundings. He had been placed in a ground-floor secure unit with views through a pair of locked French doors out on to landscaped grounds. Although sparsely furnished and strictly functional, it was cool and comfortable and, most importantly, wonderfully quiet. The room was lit by a small lamp on the table, which Curtis had switched on after he had watched a magnificent sunset from the sanctuary of his bed. He felt calmer than he had for months, and, after a fabulous hot shower, cleaner. His filthy uniform had been cut from his shaking body by the sympathetic Fuckwit Farm staff before being incinerated, and he was now wearing a pristine pair of blue-striped hospital pyjamas. He sighed deeply and closed his eyes. His once-racing mind was now ticking over more slowly, due in no small part to the huge sedative he had been given on arrival. He began to feel welcome sleep approaching, promising to wrap him up deep and warm for ever.

He had nearly gone under when he heard the tapping. Maybe he was dreaming. But the noise continued and he reluctantly forced open his heavy eyelids. There was no one in the room with him, but still the tapping went on. He raised himself up on to his elbows and looked around, but he could see nothing that could be responsible for the now very irritating sound. He was about to try to relax back into his warm pillows when he discovered the source. Standing outside the French doors in the dark, waving frantically at him, were two large yellow bananas. Their faces were vaguely familiar, but in his distressed psychotic state, Curtis was unlikely to trouble his memory bank for long. As his screams rent the heavens, Psycho and Pizza hurried away across the manicured lawns as fast as their pantomime costumes would allow. They were crying with laughter, barely able to speak as they waddled back to where Psycho had parked his Ford Cortina. As quickly as they could in their state of near-hysteria, they rolled out of the borrowed costumes, which they threw into the boot of the car before speeding off to the nearest pub to celebrate. Pizza's initial concerns for Curtis's mental health had swiftly disappeared as the mischievous benefits of what was planned became apparent.

Back at Fuckwit Farm, Curtis was further sedated as he screamed to the concerned staff about the two bananas that had come to visit him.

'Poor bloke's a complete hatstand,' said the large male nurse struggling to hold Curtis still so his colleague could jab him into oblivion. As he leant across to restrain him fully, his mate saw his opportunity and swiftly fired a huge dose into the patient, who immediately ceased struggling and shouting and was tied back on to his bed as he dreamed of talking bananas in lalaland.

The following day, the Force received the not so good news about Acting Chief Inspector Curtis's breakdown, and arrangements were quickly made to appoint his replacement. The same chief inspectors around the county who had previously toasted Curtis's temporary promotion now ran for cover as the horror of a move to Horse's Arse again became a dreadful possibility for one of them. Headquarters let it be known that a decision on Curtis's replacement would be made the following Monday, and the Force held its breath.

Chapter Twelve

Back at Horse's Arse, the early-turn gaoler had moved his overnight prisoners down the connecting passage to the magistrates' court cells. The six prisoners included the notorious violent drunk Oliver Charles. He'd been nicked by half a dozen night-duty officers at the railway station, where he'd knocked out a ticket inspector who'd challenged him for a fare into Manchester city centre. Charles was a former professional boxer who had fallen by the wayside when it became obvious that he was never going to be a real contender. He'd found he was a better drunk than a boxer, and when he got pissed, as he did regularly, he could be a real handful. But even his battered brain was still sharp enough to recognise that laying out coppers was not a good idea, so he usually contented himself with a bit of pushing and shoving, perhaps a wild swing or two, before one of the police generally laid him out with a sly shot to the back of his head. Which was exactly what had happened last night.

The gobby ticket inspector took a round house to the exit button which knocked him out for a couple of hours, whilst the cops had a bit of pushing and shoving and loud threats of dreadful violence before one of them put Charles's lights out with a baseball bat he had thoughtfully brought along in his panda car.

As Charles had lain in his cell sleeping off the effects of a dozen cans of Tennants Extra and a home run hit, he had an early-morning visit from Pizza. Pizza had made cell stunts his forte. Overnight prisoners regularly left the nick with a trouser leg removed, a heel missing from a shoe or wearing women's make-up. His pièce de résistance was the half-shaved head, a style he had famously applied to the hated Chief Superintendent Middleton's son. Any dreadful haircut was now referred to as a 'Middleton' in tribute to Pizza's expertise with a pair of scissors. Charles now sat in his cell nursing an horrific hangover and a lump the size of a grapefruit on the back of his head, blissfully unaware of how he looked to the rest of the world.

As was the custom, the court heard the overnight remand cases before they ploughed through their list for the day. Colonel Mortimer and his two timid colleagues had filed into number two court on the dot of ten and the clerk called the court to order. Mortimer took his seat ahead of his colleagues, who waited deferentially for him to get comfortable before doing likewise. He smiled at the court over his half-moon spectacles, nodded at the court inspector who would prosecute the coming cases, and glared at the court-appointed duty defence solicitor. Qualified for only three months, the poor youth had not set foot in Handstead before and had little idea of what to expect.

'Shall we make a start, Mr Hannah?' he asked his skinny clerk, who got to his feet and, reading from his list of overnight remand prisoners, called out loudly to the court, 'Bring up Oliver Charles.'

Two minutes later, the dishevelled Charles stood unsteadily between two court constables at the front of the large, oak-panelled dock, blinking in the unwelcome sunshine streaming into the room. He glared at Mortimer and then at the court. His appearance had prompted howls of laughter from the press and public benches.

'What are you lot laughing at? I'll fucking do the lot of you!' he shouted, prompting the two officers to lay restraining hands on his shoulders. He had still not noticed that the denim shirt he had been wearing when he was arrested had been replaced by a pink chiffon blouse at least four sizes too small for him, and that an indelible red marker pen had been used to write in large letters across his forehead the single word 'CUNT'.

He was not the first prisoner to appear before Colonel Mortimer in such a state, and with a wry smile the magistrate resolved to have an informal word with the court inspector about it. But not today. As his two colleagues stifled laughs, Mortimer again addressed his clerk.

'What's the charge, Mr Hannah?'

'Assault, and threatening and abusive words and behaviour, your worships. The defendant was arrested at Handstead railway station after an altercation with a ticket inspector.'

'How do you plead, Mr Charles?'

'Guilty,' shouted Charles, and then, 'Shut the fuck up, you lot,' to the still giggling public gallery.

'That will do, Mr Charles. Another outburst like that and I'll jail you for contempt of court.'

'Fuck off!' bellowed Charles, who was close to going over the front of the dock into the well of the court. The two cops now had a firm hold on him.

'Last warning, Mr Charles,' hissed Mortimer.

'Arse.'

'What did you say?'

'Arse,' repeated Charles.

'Like you, Mr Charles, I am a man of few words,' smiled Colonel Mortimer. 'Fourteen days. Take him down, please, officers.'

'Fucking hell!' shouted Charles.

'Twenty-eight days,' amended Mortimer quietly.

'You twat.'

'Five weeks.'

'Your worship, if I may . . .' started the young whippersnapper defence solicitor, who felt he needed to step in and do his duty.

'Six weeks,' said Mortimer dreamily, gazing at the ceiling.

'Shut up, you cunt!' screamed Charles.

'Seven weeks,' murmured Mortimer.

'Not you, *that* cunt,' emphasised Charles, indicating the open-mouthed solicitor, who had remained on his feet, barely able to comprehend what was going on around him.

'Fair enough, six weeks.'

'Your worship,' protested the solicitor again, throwing his arms wide in exasperation.

'You, you, yes, you, you cunt!' roared Charles, pointing wildly at the defence solicitor. 'Shut the fuck up,' before he pushed past the court officers to get back down the stairs to the cells before the dick of a solicitor got his sentence added to again.

Back at Handstead nick, in the CID office on the first floor, DC Benson dropped the phone on to its cradle and drummed his fingers on his desktop. He looked over to a group of detectives gathered around a desk by the window, still laughing about the earlier explosion in Acting Chief Inspector Curtis's office. Bob Clarke was amongst them.

'Bob,' called Benson, indicating with his head that he should join him.

'What's up?' Clarke said, perching himself on the edge of Benson's desk.

'Just had a call from Brian Jones.'

Clarke's raised eyebrows and nod prompted him to continue.

'He's come in for us but wants a meet. He's after some cash.'

'What's he got for us?'

'They're going out on a job tonight. He says it's the first stage of a big one but he wants to see us to hand it all over.'

'What d'you reckon?'

'Well, he sounded very nervous, shitting himself actually, but he's confident we'll shell out to get the goodies.'

'Hmm, what did you say to him?'

'Just strung him along, no promises, but d'you reckon we should run it past the DCI, get some cash just in case?'

'Too early. We'll bung him a sweetener if it sounds good and get him some more later. We need to check out what he's got first. Could all be bollocks.'

'Yeah, I know, but he sounded genuine, really spooked, whispering into his hand sort of thing.'

'Where was he calling from?'

'The railway station. I said we'd meet him in the marshalling yards in fifteen minutes.'

'OK. How much cash you got on you?'

Benson pulled his wallet from his jacket pocket and quickly flicked through it.

'Five quid,' he replied.

'Got a tenner,' said Clarke, putting his own wallet back into his rear trouser pocket. 'I'll get a motor.'

Ten minutes later they were parked up behind a large steel skip, sitting on the bonnet of the unmarked Ford Escort to get some respite from the unrelenting heat. They didn't have to wait long. Brian Jones slunk into the yard looking furtively over his shoulder very soon after and hurried over to the two detectives. Neither moved from his perch on the bonnet, both looking impassively at the nervous youth, who was continually glancing back to where he had just come from.

'This had better be quality, Brian,' said Benson after a pause. 'We're busy men, you know.'

'Yeah, well this is eighteen carat and it's going to cost you,' replied Jones without looking at him.

Benson sighed deeply, shook his head and slid off the bonnet before strolling over towards Jones. Had Jones been looking, he would have clocked Benson taking off his watch and carefully tucking it away in his trouser pocket.

'You haven't understood our arrangement at all, have you?' he snarled before punching Jones hard in the back of the head. Jones nosedived into the dust of the rutted yard and rolled over on to his back, looking up at Benson, who was shaking his hand in mock pain.

'You bastard,' he finally gasped, rubbing the back of his aching head. 'What was that for?'

'What is it, are you a bit slow or just trying to piss us off?' asked Benson, advancing threateningly. 'You don't start telling us things are going to cost us. What you do is give us what you've got and if it's any good we might chuck you a bit of a sweetener. Or if it isn't, we let the Park Royal scumbags know you've been snouting for us. Simple, isn't it? We pull your chain, not the other way round. Now, what you got for us?'

'Fucking hell, this is all bollocks.'

'Listen, son, it's fucking hot, I'm really, really tired and pissed off, and if you don't tell me something very soon that makes my day, I'm going to smash your head against that skip until there's a big red smear on it. So what have you got for us?'

Jones swallowed hard and glanced over at Clarke, who had now leant back against the windscreen and had his hands behind his head, catching some serious rays. Benson pulled at his already loosened tie and took another menacing step towards Jones.

'OK, OK, leave it out. I got a call to Briggs's flat this morning to see him and Travers.'

'Briggs and Travers?' repeated Benson.

'Yeah, yeah. They're putting a team together for a job tonight and I'm part of it.'

'What's the job?'

'We're doing an old house out at Tamworth.'

'Nothing special about that, Brian, but could be useful, I suppose.'

'We're just after the shooters in the house.'

'The shooters?'

'Yeah, apparently the old boy who lives there has a couple of shotguns. We're going to take them and nothing else.'

'What the fuck do Briggs and Travers want with a pair of shotguns?'

'Dunno, didn't say.'

'They must have said something, even to a thick cunt like you. Surely you asked?'

'Course I did. All they said was the break tonight was part one of the big job.'

'The big job?'

'That's what they said.'

'What did they mean?'

'Fuck knows.'

'What d'you think they meant?'

'Fuck knows.'

Benson shook his head again. 'What happens to the shotguns once you've got them?'

'What d'you mean?'

'Where do they go? You're not going to wander about the fucking town with them, are you?'

'No, no, they go back to Briggs's place. He said he's taking them somewhere to be adapted.'

'Adapted?'

'That's what he said.'

'What's he talking about?'

'Cutting them down, I guess.'

'Is that what he said?'

'No, but what else could he mean?'

'Fuck me, the Park Royal Mafia with a pair of sawn-off shotguns,' said Clarke nonchalantly from the bonnet of the car without moving or opening his eyes. Jones and Benson turned to look at him.

'What do they want with a pair of sawn-offs?' he went on.

'Fuck knows, but something big probably,' Jones said. 'The team doing the break tonight is the same for the next one.'

'The big one?'

'Yeah, the big one,' laughed Jones nervously, again glancing over at the entrance to the marshalling yards.

'Who's on the team tonight with you?'

'They didn't say and it's not the sort of question you ask, is it? I was told to meet round the back of the pub at closing time tonight.'

'But they did tell you the team is going to be the same?'

'Yeah.'

'When d'you get to know about the next one, the big one?'

'Don't know. You're interested, then? Got to be worth a few bob, hasn't it?'

'We'll see. It's a good start, that's for sure. But listen up, son, there's a few rules you need to be clear about. We want to know who does the job with you tonight, where the shooters end up and who adapts them. And finally, under no circumstances is anything to happen to the old boy and his family. And I mean absolutely fucking nothing. Anybody lays a finger on them, you're all in as quick as you like for a tidy fitting, understood? You might be on to something here, so screw your loaf, OK?'

'Yeah, yeah, but this has got to be worth something now. Fucking hell, I'm seriously on offer here, give me a break.'

'He's right, John,' said Clarke, rolling himself off the bonnet and walking stiffly over to Benson and Jones. He fished his wallet out and quickly pulled out a ten-pound note, which he folded and slipped into Jones's shirt pocket.

'This is just a taster, Brian. Keep us up to speed on this little escapade and there's more where that came from, OK? You accidentally forget to tell us something and we'll shit down your neck. Keep cool, go along with what's planned and keep talking to us, understood?'

'Fucking hell, ten quid, is that it?'

'For the time being. Now fuck off and give us a ring when you know what comes next.'

Muttering to himself, Jones crept cautiously out of the marshalling yards, and the two detectives returned to their car. They sat in their searing plastic-covered seats giving themselves a decent gap before following Jones out.

'Robbery,' said Clarke simply.

Benson nodded in agreement as he stared at nothing through the dusty windscreen.

'Nasty one, as well.'

'He didn't mention Ozdemir.'

'Obviously knows fuck all about the tie-up.'

'The Mafia with a pair of sawn-offs? Fuck me, that's a step up for these boys. Ozdemir's got to be behind it. We'll have to speak to the DCI, get a team on this.'

'Yeah, reckon you're right,' said Clarke, firing up the engine.

Back at Handstead, Benson and Clarke knocked on DCI Harrison's office door, which as usual was shut to give Harrison time to hide the bottle of whiskey and have a quick squirt of Gold Spot before calling out, 'Come in.'

'Guv, we need a quick word,' said Clarke, putting his head around the door and sniffing the tell-tale smell of Bushmills in the air. Harrison waved them into the drab office and motioned to a pair of battered armless chairs in front of his desk.

'We've just had a meet with Brian Jones.'

'Brian Jones?' queried Harrison vaguely.

'Our Park Royal snout.'

'Oh yeah, yeah, what about him?'

'We reckon the tie-up with Ozdemir just got serious.'

'How?'

'Jones and a few other low-level muscle are off to screw a house out at Tamworth tonight.'

'And?'

'The shopping list is a small one. Just a pair of shotguns.'

Harrison didn't reply immediately but looked closely at the two detectives.

'Shotguns? What the fuck for?'

'Not sure. All he was told was that the shooters are needed for a bigger job.'

'Any idea what that will be?'

'Not a clue yet, but it's not going to be pretty if they want shotguns.'

'Adapted shotguns,' offered Benson.

'Sawn off?'

'Yeah. Once they've been nicked, Briggs is taking them somewhere to be done properly.'

'Any idea where?'

'No.'

Harrison remained silent as he pondered what he knew of Ozdemir's interest in the Mafia, what awaited Baker languishing in Strangeways and what he had just been told.

'What d'you want to do, guv?' pressed Clarke.

'Let them run, Bob,' he replied finally. 'Let them run, but keep Jones fucking close, and I mean like a second skin. This has got Ozdemir's greasy hands all over it but I need to be sure. Keep pushing Jones. I want to know what those shotguns are going to be used for, OK?'

'OK, guv,' chorused the two detectives. They turned and left Harrison to his many thoughts, shutting the door as they went and walking in silence along the linoed corridor towards the main CID office. Once they were sure they were out of earshot, Benson turned to Clarke and smiled.

'He'd had a little snifter.'

'As always. Thought the tight old bastard might have offered us one. He's got some balls, though, got to give him that. I know a few guv'nors who'd have shit their pants at that sort of information, but he's happy to let it develop. Quality, that's what he is.'

Benson nodded in grim agreement.

'We need to keep the uniforms away from Tamworth tonight, Bob.'

'I'll have a word with Alex Williams in the collator's office and get something on to the night-duty briefing board. Doubt they get out there much, but best make sure.'

Alone in his office again, Harrison opened his bottom drawer and pulled out the bottle of Bushmills, which, ever the optimist, he happily noted was still a quarter full. He poured himself a large one into his cut-crystal tumbler (he refused to use polystyrene cups, which he viewed as tantamount to a mortal sin with a good whiskey) and settled back into his chair. He took a slug and cast a glance around his shabby office, which was a replica of every DCI's office anywhere in the country. The walls were covered with framed black and white group photographs from every course he had attended in his twenty-five-year career, as well as a number of commendations he'd picked up along the way. A glass-fronted bookcase was filled to overflowing with copy bundles of cases awaiting a crown court trial date. His jacket hung on a wire hanger on the back of the brown gloss-painted door. His desk was a riot of paper amongst which was a battered green telephone, and on the wall to his right was a Police Federation 1976 wall calendar, which hung at an odd angle from its damaged spring hinge.

The only personal touch was the framed photograph of his daughters on the windowsill behind him, taken many years ago when the girls were still at school and he was still at home. His marriage had finally foundered four years ago as he and his wife grew apart and he pursued his childhood dream to be a detective. He paid a heavy price to achieve it. His marriage and two children and the detached three-bedroomed house just outside Handstead were all sacrificed on the altar of his career. He could have rescued all of it at any time, but his focus was total, and one morning he woke up in his rented studio flat, and wondered where the fuck it had all gone.

Harrison had taken to CID work like a duck to water, particularly the seedier, darker side. His particular skill had always been running informants and all the skulduggery that entailed. He had pulled off some spectacular coups using informants, but by a distance his most productive had been the bent solicitor, Simon Edwardes. The information Edwardes had fed him had raised him to the rank of DCI, and he harboured great hopes of another promotion in the not too distant future. Now he had taken something of a step into the unknown with the instruction to Edwardes to send the altered message dooming Baker to an untimely death. Still, he mused, Baker's death was a both-ways winner from his perspective: the old Mafia leadership gone and Ozdemir's balls in his hand.

He eased his portly six-foot frame from his chair and strolled over to the large sash window, where he stood and watched the heavy traffic below crawling along St Helens Road East. He harboured a few doubts about what he was embarking on, but nothing that would prompt him to call it off. He was absolutely certain that Edwardes would never put him away – he had just as much to lose. Yes, he told himself again, all in all, things were going pretty well. The new Mafia was nicely infiltrated, and now so was Ozdemir's enterprise. He strode back to his desk and dialled Edwardes's number. As he waited for the phone to be answered, there was a loud bang and the nick was plunged into semi-darkness.

The process office for the subdivision was situated on the fifth floor of the nick and was run by the flamboyant Sergeant Paul Rice and his staff of six civilian support staff. They were responsible for bringing to court all of the traffic and crime cases generated by the officers at Horse's Arse, and they were very busy. Rice had enjoyed an almost exclusively office-based career, making sergeant without ever breaking sweat. He was smart enough to realise that he had landed a cushy job and he had made it his personal, exclusive domain. He knew his role inside out and had become extremely proficient at it. He was a fount of all knowledge in matters of procedure, and his advice and guidance were sought by officers of all ranks.

His off-duty hours were spent indulging his passion for amateur dramatics. He was an active member of the Handstead Amateur Dramatic Society, which put on two or three productions a year, in which he usually secured a leading role. Until two years ago, the society had been based at the magnificent but crumbling local theatre, but a suspicious fire had reduced them to the status of a touring company. They now moved around the county and neighbouring towns putting on their productions, which always included a pantomime in December and January. The panto was Rice's pride and joy, and he excelled in any role that required him to dress as a woman, which had led to his nickname of 'Dame'. The company had been on the verge of abandoning pantomimes until the fire forced their hand. The behaviour of the panto audiences had been getting worse and worse, culminating in a performance of *Mother Goose* where Rice had played the lead role. The audience finally overstepped the mark when Mother Goose felled the villain and called out to the simmering mob,

'What shall I do with him, children?' The frenzied, eye-bulging screams of 'Kill the fucking bastard!' convinced Rice and his colleagues that they were wasting their time with the ignorant, unwashed youth of Handstead and they resolved to concentrate their efforts on their adult audience. And then some of those cretinous youths broke into the theatre and burnt it to the ground, forcing the company onto the road. It was another example of the residents of Handstead shitting on their own doorstep as yet another facility disappeared.

Rice adored the theatre and had adopted a 'lovey' persona, speaking in a rounded, plummy voice in the style of Kenneth Williams. He was in the habit of turning up for work in a black fedora and cape, aping his hero, Orson Welles, and had arrived at Hanstead late this morning after meetings at Headquarters in his usual style, flouncing through the front doors, cape billowing. As he arrived at the lift lobby, he saw the appalling Poisonous Pat hoovering inside the lift itself.

Poisonous Pat had earned her nickname: she was truly foul. A forty-five-year-old widow from the Park Royal estate (it was rumoured her husband had willed himself to death to escape her), Pat was a bigot and a racist who hated coppers and regularly abused anyone who crossed her path in the nick. Everyone was terrified of her and tried to avoid any contact with her, but this morning Rice decided he could soft-soap her.

'Patricia, my darling,' he oozed, 'how are you this wonderful morning?' He walked into the lift behind her and hit the button for the fifth floor. Pat scowled at the fat, poofy copper in the stupid hat and cap and continued to slam her ancient Hoover against the sides of the lift as it began to travel upwards. As she crashed it into Rice's ankles, causing him to hop about like a line dancer, a thought fluttered into his theatrical brain: how the fuck was the old witch's Hoover still working?

His question was answered immediately by a huge explosion as the plug in the wall on the ground floor ripped out the entire socket, the main fusebox shorted and the nick was plunged into gloom. The lift shuddered to a halt in total darkness between the second and third floors, leaving the nervous Rice trapped with Poisonous Pat in their metal coffin. For a few brief moments they both contemplated their predicament before Pat let forth with a few observations.

'You cunt!' she screamed, inches from Rice's terrified face. 'You fucking stupid cunt!'

And so she continued for the next forty-five minutes until the lift was winched up to the third floor by the fire brigade and the doors forced open. An ashen-faced Rice made his way out of the door, his fedora battered shapeless, closely followed by the Hoover, which crashed against the opposite wall. As Poisonous Pat continued her tirade, the firemen dashed for cover and any nearby cops all found reasons to leave the nick quickly.

The story quickly passed into station legend, suitably embellished to include the fallacy that Pat had shoved the Hoover pipe up Rice's arse. The building manager soon replaced the blown fuse and replastered the wall, and Horse's Arse prepared itself for another day in paradise.

Chapter Thirteen

Holes get filled, gaps close. It's the way of things. The vacancy at the top of the Park Royal Mafia after the death of Bobby Driscoll and the demise of Alan Baker was filled by a duo who had previously only operated on the periphery. Andy Travers and Hugh Briggs had never been part of Driscoll and Baker's world, and whilst they had never run together they had not fallen out. They had been on nodding terms but that was it, despite having been to school together and frequenting the same pubs and clubs. If it was possible, they were also as thick as Baker and Driscoll with a combined IQ equal to that of a ring doughnut. Whilst they had never been an integral part of the Park Royal Mafia they had still pursued extensive criminal careers from an early age. Born and bred on the Park Royal, they had the usual impressive range of convictions as juveniles and latterly as adults, but what made them stand out from other potential successors to the Mafia empire was their propensity for gratuitous violence. Of the two, Briggs was probably the more violent. His recent meeting with Sercan Ozdemir had been a good example of how he usually operated. Had he not had a shooter stuck up his nose, he had fully intended to smash Ozdemir's face to a pulp with the pool cue. His first response to any perceived slight or challenge was to attack – and to attack with such savagery that there could be no response from the victim. He had recently been released after serving a three-year sentence for glassing a young lad in a Handstead town centre club. The boy had made the mistake of accidentally nudging Briggs's arm as he supped from a pint glass, spilling some of the drink on to his hand but missing his clothes. He had immediately apologised, 'Sorry, pal,' to which Briggs had snarled, 'I ain't your pal,' and driven his glass rim-first into the lad's face. As the glass disintegrated, the jagged shards of glass narrowly missed penetrating both his eyes but he suffered appalling injuries that required hundreds of stitches and months of recovery. Briggs had then left the club and his subsequent arrest and conviction had depended solely on forensic identification. Despite the assault taking place in a crowded club, not one person had come forward to tell police they had witnessed the attack. Only the actions of some really switched on uniform coppers who were first on scene and recovered the remains of Briggs's glass, secured his most serious conviction to date.

Briggs was a man of contradictions. About six feet tall,

well built, with dark, swept-back hair, he was extremely handsome, but his eyes kept everyone at arm's length. They were dead, like a shark's, and could quite literally look through you, betraying no emotion. His good looks initially drew women to him, but those eyes, coupled with his low intellect, ensured that he usually ended his nights out on his own.

He had lost his virginity with a tom at the railway sidings because sex was not available elsewhere. The tom had initially been rather confused, asking herself why such a good-looking lad was in need of a ten-pound whore – until she glanced into his eyes. He confirmed all her worst fears when he beat her up after he had finished with her and stole all the money she had earned that night. She had not reported the attack to the police, who were notoriously reluctant to take seriously any crime against street girls, but among the local whores Briggs was well known and avoided like the plague. Now he was forced to travel further afield, often into Manchester or Leeds, to slake his sexual desires.

Andy Travers was of similar build but favoured a full-on skinhead haircut, T-shirts to accentuate his toned upper body, and jeans and braces with brown Dr Marten twelve-lace boots. He looked threatening and backed up the permanent implied threat with regular, unprovoked alcohol-fuelled attacks, usually on complete strangers. He had done plenty of time inside, nothing serious, but he had a reputation he thrived on, and as a pair he and Briggs posed quite a threat. But they were so thick it was sad. Both were semi-literate, barely able to read or write their own names. That was something the Old Bill never failed to capitalise on whenever they got nicked, abusing them for their stupidity at every opportunity. Travers and Briggs subsequently loathed all police officers, but particularly those stationed at Handstead, and were forever promising themselves that one day they'd get some serious revenge. They had been behind all the recent trouble on the Park Royal, particularly the attack on the WPC at the Park Royal pub, but had been careful to make sure they were elsewhere at the time, putting an idea into the tiny minds of their followers and then sitting back to watch it happen.

Their elevation to the top tier of the Mafia had been quite accidental. Over a period of time, the remainder of the Mafia had simply gravitated into their sphere of influence. There had been no discussion or debate or sales pitch; it had just evolved. An ugly wart morphed into a cancerous scab. Travers's and Briggs's animal cunning told them that their association with Sercan Ozdemir could be a real coup. They recognised they would be playing second fiddle to him, but if they sold it right to the Mafia they would be viewed as the dog's bollocks, eighteen-carat criminals. Without any real idea of what Ozdemir had in mind for them, they were confident they could pull it off. After all, violence was what they knew best.

Whilst the cops at Horse's Arse went about their business, so too did Travers and Briggs, the latest source of most of their problems, current and future. The pair now shared a flat a few minutes' walk from the Park Royal pub, which they used virtually as their office, a base from which to direct operations. They avoided using public telephones to do business as they were avid fans of *Mission: Impossible*, which had convinced them that all forms of communication were constantly being tapped, and preferred to use a system of runners to send out their orders. Reminiscent of the trench messengers of the First World War, young Park Royal Mafia wannabes spent their days taking messages to and from the pub, always verbal, nothing written down, which was great in principle but prone to regular breakdown because the messengers had memories like sieves and the attention spans of goldfish.

After their meeting with Ozdemir, Travers and Briggs had spent a little time picking their team for the burglary and then sent out summonses for a meet. Brian Jones and Patrick Allen, the Handstead Marshes Social Club burglars, and Dave Martin and Ian Chance, the unwitting killers of Bobby Driscoll, the former leader of the Park Royal Mafia, all found themselves recruited for the burglary out at Tamworth. Had they tried, Travers and Briggs could not have selected a worse team. Brian Jones was now working hard, albeit reluctantly, for the CID at Handstead, and Martin and Chance were still terrified that one day the fact they had been driving the car that killed Bobby Driscoll would get out. Whilst he had no dark secrets to keep from his bosses, Patrick Allen was still a huge liability because he made all the others look like rocket scientists. His escape from the social club had been pure luck. Alfie had immediately picked up two strong scents and opted to go left rather than right. Allen had made his way home in a couple of hours untroubled by the police, only learning later that Brian Jones had been captured. What Jones left out of his subsequent tale of woe was his turning to the dark side at the hands of the infamous Dr St Moritz. It was a huge embarrassment to him that he had been captured while the moronic Allen had trotted home and gone to sleep without a moment's thought about his partner in crime. Some of the other Mafia had begun to take the piss out of him as well, referring to him as the Village Idiot's Idiot Brother. Jones really needed to make a success of something, and in his current predicament he couldn't see where that success could possibly come from.

As the Park Royal Mafia flexed its muscles for stage one of their graduation into the big time, Chief Constable Daniels had arranged to address his senior management team around the large oval rosewood table in the meeting room adjacent to his office on the fifth floor at Headquarters. The Deputy and Assistant Chief Constables looked worried enough, but the eight divisional commanders looked like men awaiting root-canal surgery. They all knew why they had been summoned – to discuss, or rather be told, who the new chief inspector at Handstead would be. Some of them had considered preparing dossiers to make a case for hanging on to their own favoured chief inspectors, but had quickly dismissed the idea as pointless. Now they all sat, paperless and propless, waiting to hear who had drawn the short straw, and eyed each other like Western gunslingers waiting for the man at the end of the dusty street to crack. The jugs of coffee and plates of custard cream biscuits remained untouched.

'You offered anyone up?' queried Chief Superintendent 'Mengele' Middleton to his neighbour Jock Hathorn, the commander of F Division in the west of the county.

'Have I fuck,' growled Hathorn under his breath. 'I need all my chiefs as it is. No way I'm offering up any of mine, especially not to Horse's Arse.'

'Me too,' hissed Mengele, catching the eye of the A Division commander, Barry Murphy, on the other side of the table. Murphy had seen Middleton and Hathorn begin to whisper, and knowing they were both active Freemasons, immediately jumped to the conclusion that the Brotherhood was planning a carve-up.

'Look at that pair of scheming bastards,' he muttered venomously to his nearest neighbour, who had also spotted the whisper and was saying exactly the same thing to the divisional commander to his right. Soon they were all at it, desperately backstabbing and besmirching each other's characters until it seemed likely that open hostilities were about to break out. The peace was only preserved by Daniels's arrival, closely followed by his new staff officer.

'Morning, gentlemen,' he boomed as they rose to greet him.

'So, Handstead,' he began simply, eyeing each of them in turn. No one returned his gaze. After a pregnant pause he continued, 'I asked all of you to have a good look at your management teams and, in the best interests of the Force, come up with a strong chief inspector to take on the problems at Handstead. The purpose of this morning's meeting is to see who you've identified. So, let's go round the table, shall we? Mr Middleton, we'll start with you.'

Mengele was temporarily stunned – he was sitting nowhere near the Chief, who had clearly singled him out deliberately. Quick as a flash he recovered and launched into an obviously rehearsed speech about why C Division could not afford to lose any of its chief inspectors. To an objective and uninformed observer, Mengele's expression of regret at being unable to help out sounded genuine and heartfelt, but everyone at the table knew exactly where he was coming from. Their own parochial needs would always take precedence over every Force tasking requirement, and any request to the spokes to help the centre of the wheel would be met with a negative response or at best the transfer of troublesome or incompetent staff. Mengele droned on for what seemed an eternity before Daniels interrupted him impatiently.

'That'll be no, will it, Mr Middleton . . . again?'

'Sorry, Chief, just can't see a way to help out on this occasion.'

Daniels glared at him and then turned his attention to Chief Superintendent Randall, who ran E Division in the north of the county. Mengele had begun to relax, his ordeal successfully navigated, when Daniels suddenly turned back to face him, holding his hand aloft to forestall Randall's reply.

'What about Chief Inspector Stevenson, Mr Middleton?' asked the Chief triumphantly. There was an audible gasp of 'Yes!' from around the table and Mengele's jaw dropped. He glanced at his hateful colleagues and then looked at the Chief.

'Stevenson?'

'Yes, Chief Inspector Peter Stevenson,' said Daniels cheerfully. 'What's he doing currently?'

'Doing?' replied Mengele, desperately trying to buy himself time. 'Doing?' he repeated.

'Yes, doing, Mr Middleton. Is your hearing giving you problems? What exactly is Chief Inspector Stevenson doing under your command at the moment?' pushed the Chief, determined not to allow Middeton time to clear his head.

'What's he doing? Well, right now he's ... hmmm, he's ... he's engaged in looking at a number of important initiatives for the division aimed at—'

'As I thought, he's doing fuck all of any use,' interrupted Daniels, who knew that Mengele had a real down on Stevenson and was persecuting him mercilessly and keeping him from any real work.

While it would have been easy for Mengele to offer up Stevenson for sacrifice at Handstead, he preferred to hang on to him and twist the knife all day, every day. Stevenson was the sort of cop Mengele absolutely detested – a good one with a proven track record at every rank. He had a real knack for the job and was beginning to rise through the ranks without getting up his own arse or stabbing his peers in the back. He was enormously popular with the street cops he came into contact with, who all quickly recognised his pedigree as one of them come good. He was everything Mengele could never be, and without any effort or intent had made him look the incompetent, overpromoted twat he was – and everyone knew it. Stevenson had gone to C Division on promotion to chief inspector and Mengele had set out to break him, little realising he was dealing with a man of iron will and resolve. Descended from a clan that claimed kinship with Bonnie Prince Charlie, Stevenson was a formidable manager who drove his staff hard but himself harder. As a divisional inspector he had led from the front, locking up prisoners as regularly as his other duties allowed, and had continued to do the same at C Division until Mengele had confined him to station duties. Locked indoors, he had set out to install his work ethic in the civilian support staff working for him. They were in awe of him and stories now circulated about how effective his motivational skills were. Passing the typing pool one bitterly cold winter morning, Stevenson had overheard a typist bitching about how cold she was and how she didn't think she would be able to carry on working unless she warmed up soon.

'Work harder,' bellowed Stevenson in his glorious Highland brogue, his blood-red face and ginger hair highlighted by his white uniform shirt.

He was a massive man with enormous presence who had generated his own legend over the years, with stories being repeated faithfully over and over again. As a constable on the patrol group he had attended a basic firearms course where the only rudimentary psychological profiling of the candidates was in the form of the question, 'Do you think you could shoot someone?'

Stevenson's response had been simple. 'I've nearly beaten a man to death with my bare hands. I'm pretty sure I could shoot one.'

Too frightened of him to fail him for that clearly homicidal reply, the firearms instructor, Sergeant 'Sundance' Samuels, who liked to strut about at all times with a handgun strapped to his hip, had allowed him to take the course, which of course he excelled at. Samuels had complained bitterly to Stevenson about his habit of bellowing 'Yes!' every time he loosed off a shot with either handgun or shotgun, but as every round was going dead centre there was little he could do about it. Stevenson had qualified top of his course and enjoyed a spectacular two-year attachment to the patrol group. To his eternal regret, he was never presented with the opportunity to shoot someone, and then he discovered ambition and the Accelerated Promotion Course.

Stevenson was a highly intelligent man as well as an outstanding cop, and the combination had been spotted by his chief superintendent on the patrol group, who had convinced him he could go a long way. His lack of a degree was no obstacle to inclusion on the course, and so with the appropriate sponsorship he had embarked on the Bramshill Flyer, as it was scathingly referred to by everyone not on it. Which was how he came to attend an extended interview in front of the Deputy Chief Constable of South Yorkshire, a Home Office principal and a shadowy individual from the security services. The interview had taken place after a busy two days of written and practical tests at the training centre of a neighbouring force. Stevenson had taken advantage of the overnight stay by getting hammered at the bar at the end of day one and had suffered badly during day two. By the time of his interview he was feeling decidedly jaded. The interview had been a lengthy affair, nearly fifty minutes, and Stevenson had remained still as he had been coached, with one leg crossed over the other for the entire time as he dealt with the various questions fired at him. He had coped pretty well considering how hungover he was, politely declined to ask any questions of the panel at the end and got to his feet thanking them for their time. Unfortunately, his crossed leg had cramped and was completely numb, and as he placed his foot on the floor his leg collapsed and he hit the ground like a demolished house. As he thrashed about on the floor rubbing furiously at his calf and apologising profusely to the panel, who were peering over their desk at him, the security services officer had come round to assist.

'Can I help?' he asked.

'Fucking cramp,' groaned Stevenson, forgetting etiquette for a moment.

'No worries,' said the spy, grabbing the troublesome leg, pulling it straight and beginning to bend the foot back to relieve the cramp. Ever the tight Jock, Stevenson was wearing a pair of shoes with soles the thickness of tracing paper. The spy's thumbs broke easily through the sole and touched sock. Bug-eyed, he looked at his hands and then at Stevenson on the floor, who said calmly, 'I suppose that's me fucked then?'

His assessment of the situation was spot on – he didn't get on to the Accelerated Promotion Course, but instead began his rise through the ranks like the majority of police officers: the hard way. But he could justifiably boast that he was worth every promotion he had achieved so far.

'He's very busy,' blustered Mengele now, prompting one or two of his colleagues who knew about the situation to laugh out loud. Glaring at their insubordination, Daniels continued.

'He's *going* to be very busy, Mr Middleton. He starts at Handstead nine a.m. sharp tomorrow morning with my backing and blessing. You can give him the good news when you get back. He's just what Handstead needs. I understand Mr Curtis is undergoing a psychiatric evaluation right now, but he was only ever going to be temporary until I found the right person for the job. Now Hilary Bott's back on the case, I'm confident she and Mr Stevenson will sort things out. Any questions?' he finished, leaving them in no doubt that he didn't expect any.

As the other divisional commanders sat back in their chairs and contemplated the good news, Mengele took off his round wire-framed spectacles, which had started to steam up. Polishing them furiously on his handkerchief, he fumed quietly that the Chief had humiliated him in front of the others and resolved to find out who had fed him the information about what he was doing to Stevenson.

'Make sure you let Mr Stevenson know yourself, won't you, Mr Middleton?' called the Chief as he swept out of the room followed by his nervous staff officer. 'I don't expect you to delegate this to your deputy.'

'Very good, sir,' hissed Mengele, glaring at Barry Murphy on the other side of the table who was grinning so hard it had to hurt. Alongside Murphy was Chief Superintendent Phillip 'The Fist' Findlay of B Division, who would be the main beneficiary of Stevenson's move to Handstead. Findlay was an ineffectual intellectual snob who, like Mengele, owed his exalted status to his membership of the Freemasons. Junior to Mengele in the trouser-rolling club, and in the same police-dominated lodge, he was unsure how he should react to the news that would soon be sweeping across the Force, so he opted for what he did best: he looked blank and sat there with his mouth open. It was how he ran his division, trying to ignore the chaos at Handstead, praying that he'd get a move soon to another post that didn't involve even having to pretend that he was a police officer. An ex Royal Naval junior rating, Findlay was another of those senior officers whose progress through the ranks gave rise to the question, 'How the fuck did that happen?' You would have been hard pushed to find a single officer of any rank who had a kind word for him. He was universally referred to as 'that wanker Findlay'. He, as so many people like him do, failed to pick up the vibes and fondly believed that his nickname, 'The Fist', had something to do with being tough on criminals on his patch. The reality was that it was derived from an old matelot nickname that had followed him into the police service, namely the Electric Throbbing Sailor's Fist, generally shortened to just 'The Fist' or to 'The Fister' by people who really hated him.

As his fate for the immediate future was being decided at Headquarters, Chief Inspector Peter Stevenson busied himself in the found property store at Tubbenden Road nick, C Division's divisional headquarters better known around the Force as Mengele's lab. Along with alcohol and women, property was the third most likely source of trouble for a cop, and in the half-hour Stevenson had been in the store, he had uncovered half a dozen potential career-busters.

Right at the back of the store, on the only windowsill, he had found ten foot-high cannabis plants that were pretty obviously being very well cared for. The property register informed Stevenson that the plants had been seized by the patrol group a few weeks earlier as mere seedlings. Rather than have them photographed and then allow them to die naturally or destroy them after laboratory analysis, the idiot property officer had been carefully tending them with regular watering and the occasional shot of Baby Bio. The unmistakable suffocating smell filled the room, and Stevenson had begun to feel light-headed before he had opened the windows to air the place.

Shaking his head, he had quickly fired off a memo to the PC in charge of the store, pointing out the criminal offence of cultivating a controlled drug and instructing him to get rid of the plants yesterday. Then he sat quietly at the desk in the otherwise deserted property store and ruefully pondered his predicament. He had been so close to moving into the higher echelons years ago, but if he was honest with himself he knew he would never have fitted in, or enjoyed himself, at Bramshill College. Instead he took great pride in the fact that he had got where he had by sheer hard work and results. But ending up with Mengele had been a disaster. Mengele had made his feelings about him clear on his first day, describing him as 'a PC with pips'. Not the worst thing in the world to be called, but in the rarefied world of senior police officers it was a career death sentence. Stevenson had continued to infuriate the Chief Super by going out alone on foot patrol and bringing in his own prisoners.

'Fucking prisoners?' screamed Mengele when Stevenson was summoned to his cold, characterless office. 'You're a senior officer, not a copper,' which pretty much summed up everything that was wrong with the hierarchy in Stevenson's eyes.

'Just keeping my hand in, sir. Always useful to know how things are going on the ground,' Stevenson had responded gamely.

'Not any more you won't,' snapped Mengele. 'You can start the long-overdue audit on the property store; that should keep you out of trouble for a while.'

Property stores were never audited, and for one very

good reason – they were an absolute chaotic shambles, without exception, and anyone foolish enough to start an audit on one could expect to encounter a task as difficult as that facing a one-legged man at a kick-in-the-arse party. Stevenson knew exactly what that bastard Mengele was up to and genuinely feared that his career had come to a gruesome halt. Little did he know that twenty miles away, Mengele was getting a massive kick in the nuts from Chief Daniels which would lead to his escape from the purgatory at Tubbenden Road nick. He would ultimately welcome the move, as would all the other chief inspectors around the Force who went out on the piss again to celebrate their second escapes from a posting to Handstead. Stevenson, on the other hand, took a different view of it. His choice was the ultimate dilemma question. Mengele or Horse's Arse? Stabbed in the back or in the chest? In fact, Stevenson recognised the ray of salvation. Chief Daniels's decision to move Stevenson to Handstead was inspired. He was just what Horse's Arse needed – a lunatic in charge of the asylum.

As Stevenson sat and pondered his fate, Pizza was doing exactly the same as he waited in the police room at the magistrates' court to give evidence in a traffic case. He could scarcely comprehend how his life continued to change, not by slight degrees like most people, but huge, life-shaping changes that kept leaving him reeling like a boxer on the end of a serious hammering. Joining the job straight from school had been significant enough. Watching Bovril being shot by Anna Baldwin and having him bleed to death in his arms had put hairs on his chest. His role in the downfall of the original Mafia had established him with his peers. He had grown up in three months of intense living. And now there was Lisa. Very definitely, now there was Lisa, and he sat with his head spinning, her name bouncing off the sides of his skull just as it had in Bovril's last moments.

At the end of the Mafia trial, Lisa and Pizza had wandered slowly into Manchester city centre, hand in hand like old, comfortable lovers. Despite his total inexperience with women, Pizza felt no awkwardness with Lisa, who seemed genuinely interested in him and what he had endured. Their relationship was strictly platonic, the hand-holding little more than two desperately lonely people craving intimate personal contact. Her pregnancy was of no consequence to him. All that mattered was that she was as alone as he was. At that point of course he was blissfully unaware of the scale of her loss, a loss she was unable and unwilling to share with anyone. No one knew that she was carrying Bovril's child. Not her waster of an ex-partner, whose departure from their shared home she had engineered soon after Bovril's murder and before her pregnancy showed. Nor her girlfriends, who assumed the child was her ex-boyfriend's and that he had baled out when he had found out. And not Pizza, who had held Bovril close as he died.

Pizza's presence during Bovril's final seconds had elevated him to an exalted status in Lisa's eyes. There was probably a valid and complicated psychological explanation for how she felt about him, but the simple fact was that Pizza had become very special to her. As she had watched him give evidence for nearly two days at the Crown Court, her admiration for him had flourished. She observed a pale, spotty, slightly built young boy endure fierce cross-examination from the defence counsel with the aplomb and skill of a twenty-year veteran. Quietly and with dignity, Pizza had dismantled the allegations made against him and the others. His calm, concise and businesslike description of Bovril's last moments had reduced the court to complete silence. Two female members of the jury were observed weeping. From the public gallery Lisa had swelled with a pride she didn't really understand as Pizza dominated the court. It was his humility and lack of any pretension that shone through, and as he left the box at the end of his cross-examination he had glanced up at her and given her a brief, shy smile. Something had clicked inside her then.

They strolled into a quiet back-street pub and chatted amiably like old friends about the sentences just handed down by Judge Carter-Smith, skirting round the issues they both wanted to address. After a drink they had caught a tram back to Handstead and went their separate ways, having exchanged phone numbers. Pizza had looked at her number scrawled on the back of a book of matches a dozen times a day since then. He had even begun to dial it a few times before hurriedly replacing the receiver as his nerve failed him. Lisa was made of sterner stuff and had phoned Pizza's lodgings three times. He had not been in, and the phone had been answered on each occasion by his appalling old witch of a landlady, Mrs Wood. She had lodged young coppers from Handstead for years because they were an easy source of income. Because she only served meals to suit herself, her charges were rarely fed properly, and none ever stayed long, but the police were desperate for accommodation for their young single officers, and she was guaranteed business despite her obvious shortcomings.

Mrs Wood was a cold, puritan widow who was incapable of offering any kind of affection to her young charges, even to the extent of refusing to address them by their Christian names. Hence Pizza was always addressed as 'PC Petty' around the house. He had been presented with a long list of rules and regulations on his arrival, which included such gems as no drinking in his room, no coming into the house under the influence of alcohol, no entertaining of women, no television or modern popular music after ten p.m., and only two baths a week and then only when booked with Mrs Wood in advance. His early months in the job had been an absolute misery. Desperately unhappy and isolated at work as he endured the usual rite of passage, he would return to his lodgings and sink into dark despair. He tried to get home to his parents on his days off, but as he couldn't drive, that entailed an arduous three-hour bus journey involving two changes. Things were improving for him at work, but he knew he would have to do something about his living arrangements before he lost it with Mrs Wood and knocked her out.

Despite Lisa asking Mrs Wood to tell Pizza that she had phoned, the sour old mare had decided not to. After he and Psycho had finished celebrating the attack on Curtis, Pizza had been dropped off and gone straight to bed before Mrs Wood smelt the booze on his breath. She heard him come in and trot up to his room as she was stretched out in front of the television watching a Clint Eastwood film. Ten minutes later the phone in the hallway rang. It was now after eleven and she very grumpily stalked out into the hall, grabbed the receiver and barked, 'Yes?'

'Can I speak to Alan, please. I'm sorry it's so late,' said Lisa pleasantly.

'Is this a personal call?'

'Well of course it is, just like the others.'

'This phone isn't meant for my lodgers to receive personal calls.'

'What sort of calls do you expect them to get?'

'I think he's asleep anyway.'

'I really need to speak to him. Would you call him, please?'

'What about? It's very late.'

'I just need to discuss with him the extraordinary skills of the Navaho Indian trackers who navigated their way across thousands of miles of uncharted desert in the Wild West with their foreskins pulled over their heads, relying totally on the changing surface beneath their feet to stay on course.'

'Did you call last week?'

'Yes, I did. Now please get him to the phone,' said Lisa firmly.

Sighing deeply, the old crone put the receiver down on the shelf and went to the foot of the stairs before shrieking loudly, 'PC Petty, PC Petty!'

Pizza appeared on the landing in his pants, rubbing his eyes.

'What's up?'

Dramatically shielding her eyes, Mrs Wood pointed at the phone.

'It's for you. I can't believe someone is ringing you at this ungodly hour. I've told you before, I don't pay line rental for you to take personal calls.'

Shaking his head, Pizza came downstairs, pushed past her and picked up the receiver.

'Hello?' he said sleepily.

'Alan?'

'Yes, who's this?'

'It's Lisa. I'm sorry it's so late, but I'm not sure you've been getting my messages.'

'Messages?'

'Thought not. I've phoned a few times.'

'No, not a thing,' said Pizza, staring at his landlady, who had remained in the hallway to earwig his conversation. 'No messages passed on.'

'*Is* that a personal call?' blustered Mrs Wood, unfolding her flabby arms and fussing with her nylon apron, which she wore all day.

'Yes, it fucking is,' hissed Pizza menacingly, 'and if you don't crawl back into your coffin, I'm going to shove this phone up your arse, you old witch.' As he glared at her, Mrs Wood realised she had never seen him behave like this before. He was different somehow, older.

'How dare you speak to me like that,' she sniffed before hurriedly returning to her front room as Pizza moved aggressively towards her with the receiver raised in his hand.

'And fucking stay there,' he shouted before returning his attention to Lisa.

'Sorry about that,' he said.

'I heard all that,' she laughed. 'I reckon you'll be packing your bags in the morning.'

'Bollocks to her. I've had enough of it here anyway, I was thinking of moving out soon.'

There was a long, awkward pause before Lisa spoke.

'Why don't you pack tonight and come over here? Sleep on things and see what you want to do in the morning. Are you working tomorrow?'

Shaken, Pizza took a moment to reply.

'I'm at court,' he finally said quietly. 'Are you sure, about me coming over, I mean?'

'Yes, if you'd like to, I'd love you to come over. No strings – that OK with you?'

'Jesus, yes. What's your address?' said Pizza joyously. 'You never gave me it.'

Lisa gave him the details, and Pizza scribbled them down on a page ripped from the telephone book.

'I heard that,' shouted Mrs Wood from the living room. 'Those phone books cost money, you know.'

'I'll pack and get a taxi over. Give me half an hour,' said Pizza to Lisa before slamming the phone down and striding into the front room, where Mrs Wood sat simmering on the sofa.

'I'm off now, you old witch. I'm all up to date with my rent so I'll bid you a not very fond farewell.'

'Don't think you can just go like that. You need to give me a month's notice,' she snapped.

'Tell you what,' Pizza replied. 'You push it, I'm going to tell my bosses you've been trying to get into my room at night to give me a blow job. We'll just call it quits, shall we?'

As her jaw hit the floor in astonishment, he turned and walked to the door.

'It's your phone – get me a taxi, now,' he demanded, pointing a finger at her.

Two minutes later he was back in the hallway with his case and two suit carriers containing his uniforms.

'Where's my taxi?' he bellowed.

'Five minutes,' grumbled his ex-landlady, now bitterly calculating the loss of an income that she had only ever done the bare minimum to earn. As she paused, a car hooted from the street and Pizza grinned broadly at her.

'That'll be for me then. Wish I could say it has been a pleasure, but it's been more like open-heart surgery without anaesthetic. I'm going to make sure you never get another copper as a lodger ever again. Bye.'

He strode purposefully out of his former lodgings a changed man, in pursuit of the next chapter in his extraordinary life.

Having given the taxi driver Lisa's address, he settled back in the rear seat, closed his eyes and pondered on recent dramatic events. Of all of them, the phone call he had just had with Lisa had the potential to be the most significant. It was quite clear even to Pizza, the most gauche of virgins, that she wanted him, and he found himself enormously attracted to her despite, or maybe because of, her pregnancy. She positively glowed, radiating health and huge sexual promise. Pizza wondered often what she would look like naked and how her bursting breasts would feel in his hands. As his taxi hurried through the deserted town centre and past the looming Grant Flowers tower blocks, which stretched up to the dark sky like badly lit Christmas trees, he slipped into the dream he had been having regularly for the last couple of weeks.

He was in a crowded room, probably a party, so cramped that he could barely lift his arms from his sides, and the noise of the crowd laughing and talking was deafening. Looking around, he realised he didn't recognise anyone near him and that he had no idea why he was there. None of the hundreds of conversations taking place around him were intelligible and he began to peer into the throng for the bar, or even better, a familiar face. And then he saw one. Standing at the far side of the room, just visible above the heaving crowd, in an immaculate uniform, was Bovril. He was looking directly at Pizza and smiling. Pizza could see his lips moving and knew he was calling to him, but he could not hear a word above the din. Desperately he began to push his way through the dense crowd, physically shoving people to either side with both arms like a man wading through a ripening crop of corn cobs. As he fought his way towards Bovril, he could still see his lips moving, sometimes in close-up, but he couldn't interpret the words and he still heard nothing. As he burst through the crowd to within a few feet of his smiling friend, he woke up, as he always did. The frustration was immense, causing him to shout, kick at furniture and punch the walls of his room at his lodgings. Now he contented himself with a long sigh of disap-pointment. He didn't try to analyse the dream – it was pretty obvious. Bovril needed to tell him something, and Pizza needed to get to him quicker, but his failure so far was leaving him angry and unfulfilled beyond description.

As he failed to hear Bovril for the umpteenth time and drifted back into consciousness, Pizza glanced back towards the Grant Flowers tower block through the taxi's rear window. The place still made him shudder, and he had not been back there since Bovril's murder despite numerous opportunities. He had absented himself from a couple of disturbance calls and a suicide, and it would be some time before he felt able to venture inside the flats.

'That'll be three quid, mate,' said the taxi driver, shaking him roughly back into the real world.

'Huh?'

'We're there, mate, that'll be three quid,' repeated the driver, indicating a nearby house with a nod of his head.

Pizza settled his fare and stood motionless on the pavement in the dark as the taxi drove off. As the sound of the engine died away completely, he listened intently to the sultry, humid night. In the distance a dog barked, and far away he could hear a train racing into silence, but otherwise the hot night was still and welcoming. As he bent down to lift his suitcase, he heard a door open and looked up to see Lisa standing in a lit doorway, smiling at him. She leant back against the door frame with her arms folded.

'You coming in?'

'Got here as quick as I could,' replied Pizza, hurrying up the path and craning his neck to give her a friendly kiss on the cheek. She was intent on more, however, and took his face in both her hands, kissing him long and passionately full on the lips. He melted into her, arms by his sides, case and suit carriers clattering to the floor as he surrendered totally. Without breaking the kiss, Lisa manoeuvred him into the hallway and pushed the door shut with her foot.

Chapter Fourteen

Andy Travers and Hugh Briggs pulled their team of breakers into the toilets of the Park Royal pub. Brian Jones, Patrick Allen, Dave Martin and Ian Chance stood quietly in the graffiti-covered gents' listening intently as stage one of the master plan to elevate the Mafia into the big time was outlined.

'You're going out to Tamworth, boys,' began Travers. 'We've found a big house with a couple of shotguns you're going to bring back for us.'

'Shotguns?' queried Allen.

'Shotguns,' confirmed Briggs. 'They're in a cupboard under the stairs in the main hallway. There's ammo in there as well, so take as many boxes as you can carry.'

'How do you know they've got shotguns?' continued Allen, who, thick as he was, could see an inherent fault in the plan.

'Bloke that wired up the light under the stairs last month

saw them,' replied Travers impatiently. 'Now, enough of the fucking stupid questions. You get in, get the shooters and get them back here. We'll take care of them and let you know when we need you for part two.'

'Part two?'

'Fucking hell, Pat,' shouted Briggs, punching the side of the battered contraceptive machine on the wall and advancing menacingly on him. 'Shut the fuck up, get the shooters and we'll be in touch.'

Allen furrowed his brow in bemusement but wisely kept quiet – he had no idea what part two would entail.

'How do we get out to Tamworth?' asked Ian Chance, glancing nervously across at Dave Martin. They had suffered a dreadful experience at the hands of Psycho and his air rifle soon after they had accidentally run over and killed Bobby Driscoll. Escaping from the chasing police officers, they had blundered into Psycho's line of fire as he shot up an illegal gypsy camp. Assuming they too were occupants of the site, he had shot both of them in the head. It was still a horribly vivid memory and both still bore the livid scars of their meeting.

'There's a motor outside, round the back of the pub,' replied Briggs, showing him a single key. 'Blue Allegro. Get rid of it afterwards.'

Chance nodded before continuing, 'Address?'

'Gunnels Wood House. Just stay on the Tamworth road out of town and it's on the left as you go through a crossroads and before a sharp left-hand bend. Fuck all else out there, can't miss it. Pair of old fuckers live there so shouldn't be a problem.'

Brian Jones thought about the very clear instructions he had received from Benson and Clarke about no harm coming to the occupants of the house.

'How old?' he asked.

'Fuck knows, ancient, who gives a fuck?' snapped Briggs.

'Just wondered, that's all.'

'Well fucking don't. Get in, get the shooters, get out. Those old fuckers get in the way, stretch them out. Fuck me, it's not exactly rocket science.'

As the others giggled, Jones realised he would have his work cut out to keep the elderly occupants safe, and cursed the predicament he found himself in.

'Who wants to drive?' asked Briggs, dangling the single key on a piece of string above his head. 'Dave?' he queried, glancing over in the direction of Martin and Chance.

'Hah, not me, can't drive, Hugh,' lied Martin, determined never to give any information that could connect him to Bobby Driscoll's death.

'Nah, nor me,' echoed Chance with similar aspirations to self-preservation.

'I'll drive,' offered Jones, who now saw the driving role as his opportunity to stay on the periphery of what he felt was the almost inevitable violence.

'OK, all yours. There's a bottle of petrol under the driver's seat,' said Briggs, tossing the key at him. He caught it deftly, one handed, in front of his face.

'Blue Allegro round the back of the pub,' repeated Briggs.

Jones nodded his understanding and stepped away from the grimy wall he had been leaning against.

'No point hanging about,' he said to the others. 'Let's get on with it.'

Very unenthusiastically the rest of the team filed out of the toilet block behind Jones and into the deserted pub car park. It was a dark, moonless night, perfect for a bit of crime, but still unforgivably hot, and they were all sweating freely. Jones slipped into the plastic-covered driver's seat, shoved the key into the ignition and fired up the Allegro, which roared unhappily on only three cylinders and belched acrid smoke into the faces of the others gathered at the rear. Coughing and spluttering, they all piled in, Allen in the front passenger seat, and Jones coaxed the clapped-out old rust bucket out of the car park and into Broadwater Gardens. One of the vehicle's headlights was out, and Jones realised he was driving a motor virtually guaranteed to be pulled by the Old Bill. As if on cue, as he approached the outskirts of Handstead on the Tamworth Road, he glanced in the skewed rearview mirror and spotted a police vehicle behind him.

'Bollocks, coppers,' he hissed loudly. With the precision

of a synchronised swim team, all three passengers turned to look out of the rear window.

'Don't fucking look,' he shouted. 'Fucking hell, we're on offer enough as it is.' He was absolutely right. Four scumbags in a clapped-out Allegro, coming off the Park Royal estate and headed for the sticks, would attract the interest of the thickest copper.

'What d'you reckon?' said PC Dave Rogers, operator on the night-duty Yankee One, to his driver, PC Geoff Machin.

'It's got "Stop Me" written all over it,' replied Machin. 'Headed for Tamworth, though,' he continued, mindful of the briefing they had been given at the start of their tour of duty.

'Fucking hell, Geoff, there's four prisoners in there with our names on them,' moaned Rogers.

'PNC it,' instructed Machin. Rogers quickly conducted a moving vehicle check with the operator on the main set Channel Two. The response was quick.

'Yankee One, you've got a lost or stolen from Park View, Handstead, since May this year. Your location, please.'

Machin grabbed the handset and spoke quickly before the Channel Two operator linked with the main operating Channel One.

'Thanks, Oscar One Zero, we won't be stopping this one. Believe it's part of an ongoing CID operation. Just log this as intelligence-gathering for now. I'll ring you with details when we close for refs.'

'Understood, Yankee One,' replied the PNC operator, who most definitely did *not* understand why a crew in the busiest area car in the county was not going to stop a stolen vehicle. 'Speak to you later,' and cleared the air for the next caller.

Machin replaced the handset and looked at Rogers.

'Put money on it that's involved in the CID job out at Tamworth. We can't stop it.'

'I hope you're right,' said Rogers, who was massively unconvinced but respected his senior colleague's nose for a wrong 'un and his ability to usually do the right thing.

'Me too,' mused Machin, 'but everything's right about it. Mob handed, off the Park Royal and headed for Tamworth. Fingers crossed, eh?'

'Fucking hell, let's at least get past them and have a quick look at who's on board.'

Machin laughed. 'Yeah, we can scare the shit out of them if nothing else. Put some music on.'

Rogers pulled the blues and twos button and the dark road was immediately lit up by the spinning blue light and resounding to the ear-splitting twin air horns on the roof of Yankee One. As Machin dropped into second gear and sped past the Allegro, he and Rogers glanced at the four pale, apprehensive faces inside before disappearing quickly from view.

* * *

'Fucking hell!' shouted Jones. 'What a fucking result. They must have got a call. Thought we were bagged then.'

The others were also gleefully celebrating their close shave, but as his racing heart began to slow, Jones found himself wishing that the police had actually stopped them and locked them all up. He continued out towards Tamworth, continually checking behind him, but the stolen Allegro was now the only vehicle on the lonely road. As they travelled further and further from the lights of the town, the countryside got darker and darker. To the four city boys, all products of the shallow gene pool that was Handstead, the countryside was a complete mystery. They knew absolutely nothing about it and, typically of the uneducated, they feared the unknown. The darkness seemed impenetrable and hid a thousand terrors for them as they drove deeper into its threatening arms.

Jones drove slowly through a quiet crossroads before, through some trees on the left, he caught sight of the target for the night. A large, whitewashed detached Victorian house, set at the end of an unmade private road, Gunnels Wood House enjoyed an elevated position on the slope of a hill looking out over wonderful countryside towards the heaving cesspit of Handstead. On many an evening, the elderly occupants had sat on their veranda at the front of the house watching the nicked cars or overturned police vehicles burning, thanking their lucky stars that they lived where they did. However, even in a rural idyll like Tamworth, you had need of life's essentials, like an electrician. They had been unfortunate enough to call out an emergency electrician to their home who augmented his salary by selling on details of his clients' various assets to his criminal contacts who included Briggs and Travers. Whilst replacing a blown fuse at Gunnels Wood House, for which he had charged a fortune, he had spotted the pair of superb Purdey double-barrelled shotguns wrapped in hessian sacking, stashed at the back of the cupboard under the stairs. He knew he'd have no shortage of takers for that kind of information and Briggs and Travers had jumped at it. What they hadn't done though was pay for the information. The transaction had merely been an agreement not to break his legs in exchange.

Killing the sole headlight, Jones brought the Allegro to a grinding, screeching stop against the grass verge and switched off the engine. He glanced up at the rearview mirror and addressed the others.

'Off you go, boys, I'll hang on here.'

'You not coming, Brian?' asked his erstwhile partner in crime, Patrick Allen.

'No, I'll hang on here for a quick getaway.'

'What you fucking on about?' snarled Ian Chance. 'I thought we were all going in. Hugh and Andy said fuck all about you waiting outside.'

'I'm the fucking wheelman. The wheelman always waits outside to get everyone away safely. Christ, everyone knows that.'

'Wheelman? What the fuck are you talking about? We're not robbing a bank.'

'Just get out of the fucking car and get those shooters, will you? I'll be waiting with the engine running.'

Deeply suspicious, and in their single-cell minds imagining that they were being abandoned in the terrifying countryside, the others slowly left the vehicle and stood glaring at Jones.

'You better be fucking waiting here for us when we get back,' said Allen, speaking for Chance and Martin as well. 'Otherwise I'll fucking kill you.'

'There's a queue,' said Martin menacingly.

'I'll be here. Now fuck off, will you,' hissed Jones urgently.

Scowling, the others turned away and walked nervously up the unmade road towards Gunnels Wood House, allowing their eyes to adjust to the threatening dark. To a man they continued to glance back, just waiting for the engine to burst into life so they could run back and lynch Jones. But the car remained quiet, and soon it was lost to sight completely as the dark swallowed them all up.

Jones had no intention of abandoning them, but he was quite determined that his prints would not be found anywhere in the house. None of the cretins currently approaching it had thought to bring gloves or masks, and he intended to be as far away as possible when the inevitable police round-up began in about a week's time.

He had been waiting quietly in the hot darkness, sitting bolt upright, listening to the strange nocturnal noises of the countryside, for about ten minutes. The screams of the foxes and night birds had him twitching like a puppet on a string. Then he heard a sound he definitely recognised, a muffled gunshot from the direction of Gunnels Wood House, followed by shouting.

'Fucking hell, get the fucking car started!' shouted a distant voice he recognised as Patrick Allen's. He could hear other raised and panicked voices getting closer and almost immediately he made out running figures coming down the road towards him. Sitting up even straighter, he quickly turned the key in the ignition. The lights came on, the engine turned once, and then silence.

'Oh no, not now,' he said desperately to himself, turning the key urgently back and forth and pumping the accelerator. The engine refused to turn over.

'Fucking hell!' screamed Jones as Allen wrenched open the passenger door, threw a large hessian-wrapped package on to the back seat and dived in.

'Move it, for fuck's sake!' shouted Allen.

'Fucking engine's dead.'

'You cunt, all you had to do was drive.'

'It's not my fucking fault,' bellowed Jones. 'Get out and push.'

Chance and Martin had also arrived panting at the car and began to throw themselves through the open windows on to the back seat and the parcel Allen had flung there.

'Quick, the old cunt's got a gun!' panted Chance.

'Gun?' yelped Jones. 'Get out and push, the engine's fucked.'

'Fucking hell!' screeched Chance and Martin in unison, scrambling out of the car and racing to the rear, where Allen had already begun to push whilst looking desperately back towards Gunnels Wood House. They heard another shot and the three at the rear of the car threw themselves to the ground whilst Jones ducked down behind the steering wheel. Anxiously popping up again like a meerkat, he looked back up the access road and could just make out a figure moving slowly towards them.

'Fucking push!' he again urged his accomplices. The three of them got to their feet again and began to push as if their lives depended on it, which of course they did. The car quickly gathered pace and Jones switched on the ignition again and selected second gear. The three pushers were sprinting, heads down, hands planted on the boot of the car, when the third shot boomed out around them, echoing through the surrounding trees and sending unseen birds flapping up into the dark.

'Fucking hell, Brian!' yelled Allen. 'Get the fucking engine started, will you!'

Jones needed no second bidding, and with the car now

doing a good panic-fuelled twenty-five miles an hour, he let the clutch out. The effect was immediate. The engine roared into life and Allen pitched forward violently on to the boot, smashing his face into the bottom of the rear window. As Chance and Martin again dived through the rear windows, Allen scrambled back into the passenger seat.

'You cunt!' he bellowed.

Jones glanced at him and quickly noted that his nose was probably broken and most of his front teeth were missing. Fair payback for legging it away from the social club and leaving me to cop it all, he thought to himself as he got the Allegro going as fast as its three functioning cylinders would allow. Eventually he put the single headlight on and glanced at his colleagues, who were still panting with fright and the exertion of propelling a three-quarters of a ton car to twenty-five miles an hour. They were all bathed in sweat.

'Well, what the fuck happened?' Jones asked eventually.

Allen glared at him, touched his damaged nose and mouth and said nothing.

'Well?' persisted Jones, looking at Chance and Martin in the rearview mirror. Between gasps for breath, Chance answered.

'Got in fine, found the shooters no problem, just leaving and the old bastard appears at the top of the stairs. He's only got another shotgun up there, hasn't he? Lets one go at us in the house so we get the fuck out of it but he comes after us.

Fucking hell, I thought we'd had it, fuck this for a game of soldiers.'

The shooting in the dark outside the gypsy camp still haunted Chance and Martin. To be shot at again in the dark by some deranged old-age pensioner seemed certain to condemn them to sleepless nights for years to come. They had quickly discovered the down side to a life of crime. Sometimes it jumped up and bit you firmly in the arse.

Martin and Allen remained silent as Chance babbled for the duration of the journey back to the Park Royal estate. All the windows were down, allowing the slightly cooler night air to rush over them and dry the sweat that covered their faces and had soaked their clothes. Back on the Park Royal, unhindered on their return by any nosy Old Bill, Jones drove to a street near the flat occupied by Briggs and Travers, where the others got out with their parcel.

'I'll go and torch this. Be with you in ten minutes,' said Jones quietly to Allen, who was looking at him grimly, dried blood covering his face and the front of his grey Fred Perry shirt.

'Course you fucking will. Come on,' he growled to the others, then turned to hurry to the flat to deliver their hard-won booty to their masters.

Jones drove quickly to a nearby school playing field. There he emptied the contents of the lemonade bottle thoughtfully provided by Briggs over the interior of the vehicle. Throwing a lit match in, he trotted away and retreated to the shadows of the school building to watch the blaze take hold. A dull thud told him the petrol tank had ignited, so he began to make his way back towards the flat. As he ran, the flames began to light up the surrounding streets and a few lights came on in upstairs windows. He was back at the flat in five minutes, unsure of the reception he would receive.

He need not have worried. The two master criminals were on the same wavelength as him and had given Allen a slap for moaning about Jones remaining in the car.

'He's the fucking wheelman. The wheelman always, always stays with the motor, every fucker knows that,' shouted Briggs impatiently, giving Allen another kick in the shins as he sat sulking on the black faux-leather sofa.

'The car wouldn't start anyway,' he whined.

'Can't afford for that to happen again, Brian,' warned Travers, carefully unwrapping the hessian package in the middle of the living-room floor and gazing at the pair of immaculate Purdey shotguns.

'Fucking beauties,' he purred quietly. 'Good, got some ammo as well.' He put the two boxes of slugs to one side and began to squint down the barrels of one of the guns.

'Seems a shame to chop them up, don't it?' he said absently.

'Got to be cut down, mate, can't go out on a blag without a sawn-off,' observed Briggs sagely as he began to line up the cowering Chance and Martin through the sights of the other shotgun.

'I'll get them over to Mr Ozdemir first thing. Brian, we'll need a decent motor in a couple of days, nothing like that piece of shit you had tonight, OK? Something newer and quick as fuck.'

'I had fuck all to do with getting that Allegro,' protested Jones. 'What are you taking the shooters to Mr Ozdemir for?'

'I know, I know,' replied Briggs impatiently. 'Just get us something decent, OK? And never you mind about Mr Ozdemir,' he continued smugly.

Things were spiralling out of control quicker than Jones had anticipated. A couple of days to get a decent motor? His car-stealing had always been limited to heaps of rubbish. Where the fuck would he lay hands on a decent one? He'd have to speak to DCs Benson and Clarke in the morning.

'Give Ozdemir's man a ring now,' said Travers, drawing down on Chance, who had curled into a ball on the sofa.

'Yeah, why not?' replied Briggs, grabbing his leather jacket from the back of an armchair. 'I'll do it.'

He hurried to a public telephone box not far from the Park Royal pub. There he pulled out the slip of paper Ozdemir had given him and carefully dialled the number on it. It rang for about a minute before an irritated male voice with a distinct foreign accent answered abruptly. Briggs pushed a ten-pence piece into the slot.

'*Efendim*,' said the voice.

'Huh?'

'*Efendim*!' repeated the voice.

'What the fuck are you on about? This is Hugh Briggs with a message for Mr Ozdemir . . .' he started.

The voice responded loudly with something unintelligible.

'Huh?'

'In the morning. Fuck off!' screamed the voice before the phone was slammed down.

Briggs listened for a second to the buzzing dial tone on the phone before replacing the receiver with a puzzled frown on his face. Why had Mr Ozdemir's man told him to fuck off? Surely he'd want to know that part one of the mission had been a success? He resolved to ring the bloke again first thing and request another meeting with Mr Ozdemir to discuss the next steps. He hurried back to the flat and threw his jacket back over the chair.

'How'd it go?' asked Travers.

'Fine, wants me to ring him back in the morning to give him the details, but he sounded well pleased.'

'Did you mention the old bastard shooting at them?'

'Nah, didn't seem any point. He doesn't need to know about it, does he?'

'Suppose not. OK, you lot can fuck off, get yourselves home to bed and we'll see you in the pub tomorrow evening.'

The four of them got quickly to their feet and made for the door. Chance and Martin's motivation for their haste was simple self-preservation. Neither had any faith in Travers's declaration that the shotgun he had been aiming at them for the last twenty minutes was actually empty. Brian Jones, on the other hand, was desperate to get to a phone and contact his CID handlers. Suddenly the whole escapade had entered a new dimension, and he desperately needed to distance himself from the approaching shit storm he could see darkening his horizon. They hurried out of the flat, into the humid, graffiti-scarred stairwell and down to the street. Patrick Allen, however, was not prepared to let things go. As they got ready to head their separate ways, he grabbed Jones by the shoulder.

'This ain't fucking over, Brian,' he growled menacingly.

'How's that then?' replied Jones coolly, turning to look at him and taking a step towards him. He was lots of things but he was not a coward, and he recognised a challenge when he heard one.

'You fucking sold us up the river out there,' said Allen, going nose to nose with him.

'What the fuck are you on about?'

'You fucking bottled it. You know it, I know it, and so do the others.'

'You mean those two fuckwits, do you?' said Jones dismissively, indicating with his head towards Chance and Martin, who were disappearing into a gloomy adjacent alleyway. 'They know jack shit, like you, Pat. I was driving, I stay with the vehicle. Billy basics, you thick twat. Ask Hugh and Andy what they think – no, don't bother. You already did that, didn't you, and got a slap for it.'

'A lot of good you were. The fucking car wouldn't even start.'

'Not my fault, was it? I had fuck all to do with laying hands on that pile of shit. That's down to whoever nicked the fucking thing.'

Allen's lack of a response to that explanation prompted Jones to continue quickly.

'Wasn't you, was it, Pat? Wasn't you that laid on that pile of fucking junk, was it?'

Allen stayed quiet, pursed his lips and looked away towards where Chance and Martin had gone.

'Fucking hell,' exploded Jones, 'it was you, you bastard. Shooting your mouth off and all along it was down to you – the whole fucking thing was down to you.'

'Fuck off,' snarled Allen, turning away and jogging off in the direction of the alleyway. He turned back to throw a 'V' sign at Jones, who smiled and responded with a 'wanker' gesture before he began to walk slowly in the other direction, back towards his home.

As he passed under an orange streetlight and ran a hand through his sweat-drenched hair, he didn't even glance at the battered dark green ex-Post Office van parked opposite the entrance to the flats complex. It had been there for thirty-six hours without attracting any attention. The rear windows were blacked out and a large sheet of plywood behind the bench seat divided the front from the back. Sitting in the suffocating dark heat in the rear in only his underpants, with sweat literally running off him on to the slimy floor, was PC Phil Eldrett – The Shadow.

Through one of the six observation holes drilled into the side panels of the van, he watched Jones walk away, waiting until the street outside was again completely silent and deserted. Then, satisfied that his hideout was still undiscovered, he leant back against the ten-gallon water barrel alongside him and blew upwards on to his steaming face. Quickly he flipped on a small gunmetal-grey torch, and by its weak light recorded what he had just seen. He had been watching as the team returned from Tamworth with the shotguns, and had seen the telltale package go into the flats and all four members leave. He had identified Jones from one of the photographs taped to the walls of the van and knew Patrick Allen from his own dealings with him. Chance and Martin had not come on to his radar before, but he had seen enough to record good descriptions of them for future reference.

Eldrett had been plotted up outside the flat for nearly two days at the request of DCI Harrison, who had used him before and knew his expertise. He had remained quietly in the blistering heat, night and day, recording the comings and goings to and from Travers and Briggs's flat, and now he felt sure he had hit the jackpot. Something big had either just gone down or was about to. The nose-to-nose confrontation between Allen and Jones intrigued him and led him to surmise there was more to come.

Eldrett had established himself as one of the most resourceful and enterprising of the Force's surveillance-trained officers. He had previously spent happy days concealed in hedges and undergrowth, and once an entire night in a full rainwater butt. He was regularly in demand all round the county, but truly in his element at Horse's Arse, where DCI Harrison protected him like the Crown Jewels.

Satisfied that he had seen enough for now, Eldrett prepared the pre-arranged signal that would alert a passing CID vehicle that he was ready to be pulled out. Edging gingerly past the numerous plastic bottles full of stinking piss, he carefully pushed out the rear offside light cluster so that it hung clearly visible from the rear of the van by its wires. He then covered the light cavity from inside with another small piece of plywood. A CID vehicle passed his hideout every two hours throughout his vigil and was due again in forty minutes. The signal would be clocked, and shortly afterwards a dark-clothed figure would walk swiftly to the van from the rear, enter with a spare key and the van would disappear into the night. If the light cluster had been replaced, the walker would keep going. Eldrett had his own key for dire emergencies, such as his cover being blown, but he preferred to be driven to and from his plots by colleagues who could be observed leaving and subsequently returning to the vehicle. It made it less suspicious. It wouldn't do for an apparently unoccupied vehicle to suddenly start itself and drive away, and he had no desire to have to replace the van, which blended perfectly into the surroundings he so often worked in.

Eldrett operated under enormous strain, with no means of communication with his colleagues. Other than the two-hourly drive-by, sometimes extended to four-hourly, he was completely on his own. It took a unique form of courage to do what he did.

As Eldrett waited for his extraction from the war zone, PCs Rogers and Machin pulled into the rear yard at Handstead nick. It was a little after one a.m. and they hoped to get at least a short refreshment break off the streets. They went off air with the main force control room on a 'listening watch', which meant they would be grabbing a sandwich near the main set radio in the station. There they listened to the night-duty radio traffic increase as the violent, drunken town went into meltdown. As they ate, passing occasional comment between themselves and the front desk PC, Dave Rogers filled out a collator's intelligence form detailing the earlier incident involving the stolen Allegro.

'I clocked Brian Jones driving,' he remarked casually.

'Me too. The two little scrotes in the back were familiar as well. Sure I've dealt with them as juveniles. Ian somebody . . . they run as a pair, I'm sure. I need to go back over my collator's slips.'

Machin got up and walked down the corridor to the collator's office, leaving Rogers to carry on with the paperwork. As the junior partner and the car operator, that was his clearly understood role. Less than five minutes later, Machin returned looking jubilant, holding a collator's bulletin sheet.

'Bingo!' he exclaimed happily. 'Nicked the pair of them as juveniles in September 1974 in a stolen motor. Ian Chance and Dave Martin, both off the Park Royal, obviously moved into the full-time Mafia. No surprises there, then.' He dropped the sheet in front of Rogers to finish off tonight's report and chatted quietly to the front-office PC, who was making them all a cup of tea in the teleprinter room.

'You about done, Dave?' Machin asked a few minutes later as he listened anxiously to the radio. 'It's warming up nicely out there.'

'Yeah, all done,' replied Rogers, getting to his feet. 'Do me a favour, Alan, stick this in the collator's box for me, will you?' he asked the front-office PC, pushing his intelligence form across the desk to him. Two minutes later, Yankee One was back out on the hot, treacly streets of Horse's Arse.

Just after ten a.m. that morning, DCI Harrison would be

poring over their intelligence report, a burglary concerning Gunnels Wood House, and Phil Eldrett's surveillance document. Things were coming together nicely, he mused happily to himself as he picked up his phone to call Benson and Clarke into his office.

Chapter Fifteen

As Pizza sat waiting to give evidence at Handstead Magistrates' Court and DCI Harrison slotted another piece into his devious and deadly jigsaw, Simon Edwardes embarked on perhaps the deadliest leg of the plan. He had presented himself at the visitors' gate at Strangeways Prison just after ten a.m. for an arranged legal visit with his desolate client, Danny Morgan. Still reeling from the shock of his life sentence, Morgan clung desperately to Edwardes in the forlorn belief that he could either free him on some obscure legal technicality or at least get his sentence reduced. He was, of course, blissfully unaware that Edwardes was working closely with DCI Harrison. Serving his sentence in solitary confinement because of his coerced statement against Baker and the others, and abandoned by his fickle family, Morgan's only contact with the outside world was through the flabby, corrupt solicitor. Edwardes, on the other hand, maintained their ostensibly professional relationship only in order to facilitate his access into the prison to carry messages to and from the other Mafia, and more importantly to nurture his well-placed man inside, Prison Officer Pete McCutcheon.

Edwardes had defended McCutcheon on an assault charge, brought after a remand prisoner had gone the distance with a complaint against him. McCutcheon had walked free and a sinister business arrangement had developed between the two men. Now McCutcheon passed messages to and from the prisoners inside Strangeways, and did some low-level smuggling of tobacco, rolling papers and cannabis to supplement his income. His arrangement with Edwardes was strictly cash on delivery.

Edwardes had passed unsearched as usual through the visitors' gate and was escorted deeper into the echoing bowels of the prison by a guard he didn't know but who certainly recognised him.

'You're back again soon, Mr Edwardes,' remarked the young screw pleasantly, walking ahead to unlock another barred wicket gate.

'You know how it is, no peace for the wicked,' laughed Edwardes, turning slightly to get his fat frame through the opening. He stood listening to the prison, the distant echoing, muffled shouts and calls, machinery humming, metal on metal, doors slamming, as the screw locked the gate behind them. 'I wonder if I could have a word with Mr McCutcheon this morning after I've spoken with my client?' he continued.

The screw didn't appear surprised by the question. 'No problems. Mr McCutcheon mentioned you'd be in this morning, said he wanted to catch up with you. Once you've finished with Morgan, I'll bring him over if you like.'

'That'd be great, thanks,' replied Edwardes, who was keen to get rid of the two pounds of Old Holborn rolling tobacco in his briefcase as quickly as he could.

He was shown into his usual interview room, just off the prison main wing, and settled down in a plastic seat opposite the door and lit a cigarette as he waited for Danny Morgan to be ushered in. Ten minutes later, echoing footsteps arrived outside the door, and with a perfunctory knock the young screw opened it and ushered Morgan in. Edwardes immediately noticed the deterioration in the young man's physical condition in the two weeks since they had last met. Bleached pale under the relentless fluorescent lighting, his gaunt face showed deep black rings around the eyes as a result of virtually no sleep since his incarceration nearly six months ago. His prison uniform of grey trousers and a T-shirt hung off his sparse frame, and as he swallowed, his now pronounced Adam's apple bobbed up and down his skinny neck like a bag of marbles.

'Hello, Mr Edwardes, it's good to see you,' he said nervously, smiling and showing teeth now heavily stained and yellowed from smoking almost nonstop twenty-four hours a day. The greeting was genuine: he really was pleased to see Edwardes, because it meant that for the next hour he didn't have to keep glancing over his shoulder in anticipation of the next attack by another con looking to make a name for himself. Despite being in solitary confinement, he had still been attacked twice – once on his way to a visit from Edwardes as he was escorted through the main remand wing, and again in the prison hospital as he was treated for the injuries. Now the screws always walked him the long way round to avoid the general prison population, only ever going through the main wing during a period of lockdown. Even they seemed to hate him, and he now relished the time with someone who didn't appear to want to cut his throat.

'How's my appeal going, Mr Edwardes?' he began, pulling up the seat opposite and then flinching as the young screw slammed the door behind him as he left.

'We're working on it, Danny,' lied Edwardes, mentally noting that all Morgan's arrogance had been hammered out of him by his new environment. 'We're still looking to show that your statement and confession were coerced and also that the judge's summing-up was so biased as to warrant a retrial.'

'Could I get bail if I got a retrial?'

'Well, that's always a possibility, but a retrial, even if you got one, could be a few years away. There's no point in getting your hopes up just yet. How are you doing in here now?'

He had seen Morgan's thin shoulders slump at the

prospect of further time inside without any hope and felt a pang of sympathy for the boy. But it was only brief, as he reminded himself of the appalling attack he had carried out on the pub landlord.

The remainder of the hour-long legal visit was a muted affair, with Morgan, as usual, far away in his private hell, not hearing any of Edwardes's inane platitudes or encouragement. Glancing at his watch and seeing that their time was up, the solicitor pushed his packet of Benson and Hedges across the table.

'Time's up, Danny. Here, you hang on to this packet; I've got another. I'll see you in a couple of weeks, OK? Hopefully I'll have some better news for you then.'

Morgan looked at him and smiled grimly. His once cornflower-blue eyes were now grey and haunted, and clearly indicated that he knew Edwardes was talking through his arse – but he needed to hear it. Months ago, sitting in his cell at Handstead nick in a paper suit, he had recognised he was fucked, but until recently he had never really appreciated how much.

Edwardes got to his feet, walked to the door and knocked twice, loudly. The young screw opened it and peered in.

'All done?' he asked.

'Yes, thanks. Mr Morgan can go back now,' said Edwardes, putting his hands on Morgan's bony shoulders to encourage him to move. 'Come on, Danny, time to go,' he said quietly.

Very reluctantly, Morgan got to his feet, offered Edwardes a cold handshake and without a word followed the screw out of the interview room. Edwardes lit another cigarette and sat back in his chair, blowing the smoke towards the ceiling, listening to the echoing footsteps move away and then disappear amongst the maelstrom of background prison noise. He was grinding the stub into the floor with his shoe when another knock at the door announced the arrival of Prison Officer McCutcheon.

McCutcheon was a tall man in his late thirties who had driven a lorry for years before tiring of life on the road and opting for a more secure career in the prison service. He had continued his sideline as a smuggler without a break, though he now had to confine himself to smaller contraband cargoes.

'Morning, Simon,' he said brightly, offering a handshake, then removing his cap and running a hand over his glistening bald pate and the brilliantined remains of his hair. 'Fuck me, it's hot,' he continued, slumping down into the chair recently vacated by Morgan and gratefully accepting the cigarette offered to him. As he pulled hard on it, he eyed Edwardes through the smoke. The solicitor had still to say a word.

'You're very quiet this morning,' McCutcheon observed. 'Everything OK?'

'Yeah, I'm fine, just a little worried about young Morgan. He's unravelling very quickly.'

'Don't worry about him,' snapped McCutcheon dismissively. 'All the lifers struggle to come to terms with their sentences initially. Can't get their heads round the fact that that's it for the rest of their life; well, most of it anyway.'

'That's what's worrying me. This is the most dangerous time for him – when he's got no hope.'

'When he might top himself, you mean? Don't bother yourself, we'll be watching him closely for the next few months just to make sure he settles down and doesn't do anything daft. Now, you got something for me?'

Nodding, Edwardes reached down and picked up his battered brown leather briefcase from under his chair. He released the two leather and brass buckles, reached inside and then placed a white paper bag on the table in front of McCutcheon. The prison officer quickly glanced in the bag and smiled.

'Perfect, better than cash. No Golden Virgins, then?'

'No, best rate I could get was on that stuff. Same deal as before?'

'Yeah, no worries, seventy–thirty is fine with me.'

'Actually I've got a little job that needs taking care of. You can keep the whole lot and earn a few quid as well.'

'Go on,' said McCutcheon, now all ears.

'I need a message taken in to the Turks.'

'The Turks?'

'Mr Ozdemir's boys.'

273

'I know who you mean. What I meant was, why the fuck do you want a message sent to those head-bangers?'

'Are they trouble?'

'Not to us, but they run their bit of the prison, and anyone steps out of line they get well hammered. They don't have a lot to do with the rest of the cons.'

'Mr Ozdemir's got a message for them.'

'You work for him now?'

'Only on a consultancy basis, a one-off thing,' replied Edwardes smoothly.

'What's the message?'

'Alan Baker's got to have a bad accident.'

'Alan Baker?' sneered McCutcheon. 'What's he done to upset the great Mr Ozdemir?'

'That doesn't matter. His accident is to be very, very serious. Understood?'

'Very, very serious? What you on about?'

'I mean he doesn't recover from it.'

'Fuck me, you mean they top him?'

'Nicely put, yes, they top him.'

'You're fucking joking!' exclaimed McCutcheon. 'I can't take in a message like that. Topping the little bastard is way out of line.'

'Yes, you can, and there's a little bit more. Once Baker has gone, you're to tell the other Mafia who ordered it. No need to explain why, because you don't know, but you tell them Ozdemir ordered the hit.'

'This is fucking bollocks, Simon. Running a bit of baccy and blow into the prison is one thing, but getting someone topped is bang out of order.'

'We're talking about Alan Baker here, scum of the earth, Pete,' soothed Edwardes, 'not Mother Teresa. No one's going to miss him, no one's going to enquire too closely about what happened. Not the police, that's for sure,' he added with some certainty.

'Not the police? Are you fucking mad?'

'Relax. Baker helped kill one of their own, so any inquiry will be very low-key, trust me. These things happen in prison, don't they? I understand sex offenders meet with terrible accidents all the time.'

'That's different,' protested McCutcheon indignantly. 'They deserve everything they get, but Baker's just a scumbag. Topping him is fucking serious stuff.'

'It'll be a good earner, Pete. There's no risk to you at all. You merely pass the message to the Turks, tell the Mafia boys who ordered it, and you get a decent drink out of it.'

'How decent?' replied McCutcheon, starting to warm to the idea.

'Three hundred?' offered Edwardes, keen not to part with too much of the cash offered by DCI Harrison, which he had yet to see.

'Three hundred?' whistled McCutcheon, who was now quickly persuading himself that Baker would be no great loss to anyone. That would get the increasingly aggressive bookies off his back and still leave him with some spending money.

'OK,' he said finally, standing up and offering Edwardes his hand, as though a handshake between two such dubious individuals meant a thing. 'I'll do it for three hundred. When does he want the message to go in?'

'Today's as good as any.'

'And what about his nasty accident?'

'Today will be fine, why not?'

'Fucking hell. Yeah, why not? OK,' said McCutcheon, straightening his remaining strands of hair and replacing his cap. 'You'll hear about it soon enough, I don't doubt,' he continued with a grim laugh as he picked up the white paper bag and left.

Edwardes allowed him a few minutes before stepping out of the interview room, to be greeted again by the young screw, who had returned after binning Morgan.

'Everything OK, Mr Edwardes?' he asked as he escorted him back to the exit gates.

'Couldn't be better, thanks. By the way, I don't know your name, young man.'

'Darren McClune,' offered the screw, extending a hand.

'Good to meet you, Darren. Maybe we should have a drink sometime, talk about some business I could put your way, if you know what I mean?' said Edwardes. He was taking a bit of a risk, but he needn't have worried – it was exactly what the screw was looking for.

Leaving him one of his home-made business cards with a couple of contact numbers on, Edwardes bade McClune a cheery farewell at the prison gates and strolled off towards the main road to find a taxi. Having two screws on the inside would be a real coup, though he'd have to be careful they never found out about each other. That would be even more dangerous than having two women on the go, or so he had heard.

McCutcheon didn't hang about. As Edwardes dozed on a train back to Handstead, he pulled one of the Turks, Kazim Murat, into a TV room on their wing. The well-muscled man, wearing only prison shorts and a vest, looked at McCutcheon defensively.

'Why you do this? What I do?' he asked.

'Shut the fuck up,' snarled McCutcheon. 'I got a message from your boss, Mr Ozdemir.'

Murat raised his eyebrows. 'What message?'

'D'you know that piece of shit Alan Baker?'

Murat nodded.

'Ozdemir wants him dead, today.'

Murat remained expressionless.

'D'you hear me? He wants him topped today.'

'Why would he want him dead? How you know this?'

'Don't know why, couldn't give a fuck. He's got a bent brief working for him who brought the message in. Best you get on with it, boy,' growled McCutcheon as he turned and left.

Murat breathed slowly, weighing up what he'd been told. He had killed two men on behalf of Mr Ozdemir before. One of them was the reason he was currently locked up in Strangeways. This would be the first he had done in prison, though he suspected it would not be the last. After a pause he left the TV room and returned to his cell, where he called a hasty meeting with ten other Turkish-origin prisoners. All the other Turks inside with him had been born and bred in and around the Manchester area, with close ties to the Ozdemir crime family and associates, but only Murat could claim direct kinship. He too had been born in the port city of Antalya and had grown up with Ozdemir's first cousins in their cramped apartments overlooking the Mediterranean Sea. Their families were related by blood spilled together, and once he had followed the Ozdemir exodus to Manchester, albeit some years later, he had quickly gone on to the payroll as a very efficient enforcer. Now serving life for cutting the throat of a car dealer who had defaulted on payment for large quantities of smuggled stolen luxury cars from Europe, he remained an integral part of the family, which continued to support his wife and three children whilst he was banged up. He took care of things in prison and could not, would not, dare ignore such an instruction from Ozdemir. He quickly outlined to the others his plans to dispose of Alan Baker that afternoon.

* * *

Chief Inspector Pete Stevenson dropped his bags and suit carriers on to the desk in his new office at Handstead nick. Despite the fresh coat of paint the walls had been given, the room still smelt strongly of the cordite and smoke from the thunderflash attack on Curtis. The wrecked toilet door had been replaced but there were vivid scorch marks around the base of the toilet, and the window still bore a crack along its width from the blast. He opened the main office window to try to reduce the foul mix of smells and was hanging his suit carriers on the pegs behind the door when it was flung open, narrowly missing cracking him full in the face. Hilary Bott peered round at him.

'Oops, sorry about that,' she stammered with a nervous grin as the enormous red-faced Stevenson glared at her.

'Who are you?' he bellowed.

'Hilary Bott,' she spluttered, offering him a handshake, which he ignored. Striding behind his desk, he slammed his hands on the surface, sat down in his chair and glared at Bott.

'What do you want?' he asked, more pleasantly this time.

'Well, I thought I'd introduce myself as I'm your deputy,' she stuttered, 'and I thought you'd like to have a look at this.' She handed him a bulky manila folder, which he took from her as though she was offering him a turd.

'What's this, then?'

'My initial inquiry into the attack on Mr Curtis in his toilet. I assumed you'd probably want to take it over, now that you're here.'

Stevenson had already had enough of her. What his predecessor had tolerated for nearly a year had already become too onerous for him.

'Plenty of time for introductions later, Hilary,' he said firmly, dropping the folder into the bin at the side of his desk. Then he got to his feet, took firm hold of one of her arms and led her to the door. 'Now is the time for working, not talking, so off you go, and don't ever walk into my office again without knocking in case I'm having a wank. I have a very high sex drive and need regular relief.'

She stared at him open mouthed. 'Having a wank?' she repeated slowly and without any trace of her troublesome stammer. 'Having a wank?' she continued even louder, causing a passing typist to look at her in disgust and tut loudly.

'Two or three times a day, darling,' whispered Stevenson, before slamming his door shut and slapping both hands over his mouth to stifle his laughter. He was going to enjoy himself here, he decided.

'Having a wank?' shouted Bott from outside in the corridor, causing DI Barry Evans to come out of his office.

'What are you doing, Hilary? You OK?' he called wearily. 'Come on, back in your office and have a couple of aspirin. Maybe you should go home?' he fussed as he marched her back to her office and shut her inside. He then knocked on Stevenson's door.

'Come in!' shouted Stevenson. He smiled at Evans as he entered and shook his hand warmly. 'Pete Stevenson,' he offered. 'Just got here from Mengele's lab.'

'Barry Evans, DI. Good to meet you, boss. You've met Colonel Klebb, then?'

Stevenson laughed. 'What's wrong with her, for fuck's sake?' he asked.

'Mad as a fucking fish,' said Evans. 'The uniforms make her life hell. She spent some time in the nuthouse after her last run-in with them. She's had that stammer ever since.'

'What, her and Curtis both been in hospital?'

'Yep. Curtis is a total basket case now since they blew him up in his toilet. She's not a lot better. You'd better go softly with her.'

'Shit, I've just told her I'm a compulsive pud-puller to keep her out of my office.'

Evans smiled broadly. 'That should do it, boss, but be careful. Chief Daniels put her in here to support your predecessor, Pat Gillard, so she's got a powerful ally. Glad you're here, though. The uniforms need a firm hand.'

Once Evans had left, Stevenson pondered on what he'd been told. Things were clearly totally out of control. No matter how big a twat Curtis had been, blowing him up in his toilet was a step too far. He resolved to take the bull by the horns and make a mark on every officer at Handstead.

First, though, he needed to know the scale of his problem, so he picked up the phone and rang a good mate of his in the personnel office at Headquarters.

Fifteen minutes later, he replaced the receiver and sat back in his chair as he digested the detailed background information he had just received.

'Oh shit,' he said quietly to himself.

Chapter Sixteen

'I need you and Clarke in my office now,' barked DCI Harrison, before slamming down the receiver.

Clarke was not in the office, but Benson soon found him at the Xerox machine at the end of the corridor, busily putting together another committal file.

'Boss wants us,' he said flatly.

Sighing heavily, Clarke boxed what he had completed and strolled down the corridor with his partner to Harrison's office. As usual the door was closed, so Benson knocked lightly. Inside, the telltale smell of Bushmills again hung in the air, but to the detectives' delight, this time there were three cut-glass tumblers on Harrison's desk alongside the bottle.

'Come in, boys,' Harrison called cheerfully as he rummaged about in his bottom drawer. 'Have a drink with me. Got lots to tell you.'

Benson and Clarke poured themselves a two-fingered

shot each and settled into the two armchairs in front of the low table in the middle of the office.

'Cheers, fellas,' said Harrison, pouring himself a large one and raising his glass in salute. The two detectives returned the gesture and took a slug of their drinks.

'There's been a bit of activity on the Ozdemir front,' began Harrison, looking through the papers on his untidy desk. 'Quite a bit, actually. First up, the night-duty area car clocks a lost or stolen driven by your man Brian Jones on its way out to Tamworth.' He glanced up to see Benson and Clarke nod at each other but say nothing.

'Also in the car are Ian Chance and Dave Martin, new Mafia apparently. There's also a fourth, unidentified person in the vehicle. An hour or so later, three scumbags break into Gunnels Wood House at Tamworth and pinch two Purdey shotguns. The owner shoots at them – that's all taken care of, by the way – but the little scrotes get away. Half an hour later the same team arrives at Briggs and Travers's flat with a shotgun-shaped package. The fourth member of the team is identified as Patrick Allen, also Park Royal Mafia.' He paused to let the information sink in.

'Guys, you need to get to Jones again, and fucking quickly. Something big is just round the corner. How soon can you get hold of him?'

'This morning probably, or after lunch for definite,' replied Clarke. 'We've got the phone calls lined up on a daily basis.'

Like all detectives running informants, Clarke and Benson had a list of the number and location of every public phone box in Handstead and an arrangement with Jones. They would phone the first box on the list every day at eleven a.m. If it was engaged or someone else answered, they would phone again at half past the hour and every half-hour after that if necessary. The box would change every week, or if they or the informant felt it was getting risky.

'We're due to call him in ten minutes,' added Benson.

'Good. Find out what's happening. I've got a feeling in my water this is very close.'

'Will do, boss,' chorused the detectives, draining their glasses before hurrying back to their office to make their first call of the day.

Brian Jones answered the phone box at the junction of Birchwood Road and Primrose Gardens immediately.

'Hello?' he shouted.

'Is that the Wickham Green garden centre?' asked Benson, using the pre-arranged greeting.

'Thank fuck it's you,' said Jones urgently. 'Can we meet soon? Got some blinding stuff for you.'

'Railway sidings in five minutes,' replied Benson simply before grabbing the keys to an unmarked vehicle and jogging down the stairs to the back yard, followed closely by Clarke.

Jones had run the short distance from the phone box and was waiting for the two detectives when they arrived in a cloud of dust. He was sheltering against a large skip bin, as much to stay out of the searing heat as to keep himself out of sight. He remained in the cool shadows as the sweaty detectives parked up and walked over to him.

'What you got for us, Brian?' asked Benson, feigning indifference. Jones hit the ground running.

'Fuck me, what a night. The team got pulled together by Hugh and Andy and we met up at the Park Royal . . .'

'Who's in the team?'

'Me, Pat Allen, Ian Chance and Dave Martin. Anyway, Hugh gives us the address of a big place out at Tamworth where he says there's a pair of shotguns under the stairs. I'm the driver, so we bimble out there and I park up and stay with the motor while the others do the house. Only been gone a few minutes and I hear a shot. The old boy's only got himself another shooter upstairs. Anyway, he chases the boys out, shooting at them, and the fucking car won't start so they end up pushing it with the mad old bastard blasting away at us. We take the shooters round to Hugh and Andy and I'm told to get a quality motor for the next job. Fuck me, where am I going to get a decent motor from?'

'Don't worry about that, Brian,' soothed Clarke. 'Where are the shooters now?'

'Probably still round at the flat.'

'Didn't they go off to be adapted?'

'Not straight away, probably later today, and you'll never guess where they're going: only to Mr Ozdemir.'

'Ozdemir, is that right? Who's taking them?'

'Hugh, probably. I reckon Ozdemir's putting something their way.'

'What's the next job?'

'They still haven't said, but it's got to be grief if they've brought shotguns in for it.'

'Maybe. Anything happen to the old boy or his wife?'

'Not a thing. They didn't need to go upstairs, thank God. Fucking old bastard just loosed off without a please or thank you,' he whined.

'You were screwing his house, Brian,' reminded Clarke. 'Not altogether unreasonable under the circumstances.'

'Fuck me, thought we'd had it,' continued Jones, shaking his head.

'No one got hurt, then?'

'No, we were fucking lucky. It was like the Wild West out there, the old bastard just loosing off all over the place.'

'When does the next job go off, then?'

'They still haven't said, but I've got to get a decent motor or I'm fucked. What am I gonna do? I'm no car thief, am I?'

'I told you, don't worry about that,' said Clarke again. 'We'll sort it out for you, but we need to know when it's going off or you really are fucked.'

Jones was starting to sound desperate. 'They've told us fuck all. I'm not even sure *they* know where and when yet. Maybe it's something they'll be told by Ozdemir when they drop the shooters off.'

'Get yourself back to wherever it is you hang about all day and ring us in the office if anything comes up, OK? Otherwise we'll ring you same time tomorrow. Keep on top of this, Brian, we need to know what's going on. Fuck it up and you're in deep, deep shit, understood?'

'Fucking hell, you're a pair of bastards, you know that, don't you? I'm really on offer here. Anyone finds out what I'm doing, if Hugh and Andy don't do me, I'm fucking sure Ozdemir will.'

Benson smiled at the unintended compliment. 'You don't have a choice, remember?' he said coldly. 'Keep on top of it and we'll see you all right. Now fuck off and keep in touch.'

'That it then?' asked Jones forlornly, arms outstretched as the two detectives turned away from him towards their car. Despite his awkward predicament, he was still going to claim his few quid if it killed him – which it very likely would.

The detectives turned back and smiled at him, then rummaged about in their trousers for their wallets. Eventually he was presented with a crumpled ball of notes, which he flattened out greedily against the side of the skip.

'Thirteen quid?' he complained. 'Fuck me, I'm giving you quality information and you're giving me shit.' He still hadn't learnt. The response was a fierce punch in the side of the head from Benson that sent him crashing to the hard, dusty ground.

'Pull this off, Brian, and you'll be on a very nice earner,' promised Clarke, looking mournfully down at him before turning away.

Jones remained lying in the dust at the side of the skip, watching as Clarke and Benson drove away. Eventually he got to his feet and stepped out into the dazzling white heat of the late morning, heading for the Park Royal estate to wait for the summons back to Travers and Briggs's flat. His was now the classic quandary, literally caught between a rock and a hard place. He was completely at the mercy of Benson and Clarke, who could throw him to the wolves as and when they chose. He had no choice but to do as he was told and hope they cut him free once they had achieved whatever it was they were aiming for.

As he trudged back along the sticky, strength-sapping pavements, avoiding the numerous deposits of white dog shit, Andy Travers and Hugh Briggs had found themselves with a bit of a problem. Briggs had again called Ozdemir's contact who, after shouting at him again in Turkish, had instructed him to bring the stolen shotguns to a lorry park in the north of the town. Their problem was that their only form of transport was now smouldering in the nearby school playing fields whilst the irate headmaster berated the switchboard operator at Handstead Town Hall to get it removed. Their hen-brained solution to the problem was to get a taxi to the meet, complete with the shotgun-shaped parcel under Briggs's arm.

'Fuck off, please tell me you're joking,' gasped an incredulous Sercan Ozdemir as he stood examining the shotguns on his desk and listened to his two minders.

'They arrived in a taxi, boss,' repeated Ahmet nervously.

'What did you do?'

'Fucked off pretty quick soon as we saw them, gave it a couple of minutes before we went back. The two idiots were wandering around the trailers with these under their arms when we found them,' he said, indicating the shotguns.

'Good work, boys. Fucking hell, then what?'

'Took them off them and told them to ring again at two, as agreed.'

'Sure no one saw you?'

'Absolutely, quiet as a graveyard. It's too hot to be out and about. No tractor units in the park, only trailers. We're clear, boss, trust me.'

'Those two idiots are a fucking liability. I want our business relationship to be kept as brief as possible, so let's bring the planning forward. You've done the recce on the gunsmith's, haven't you? We're OK doing it pretty much when we want?'

His minders nodded in the affirmative.

'Right, they can do it next week. When they ring at two, get them picked up by our people and brought here. I'll brief them, and then I want them as far away from me as possible. Ahmet, get these shotguns cut down as quickly as you can. I want them ready for the fuckwits when they leave,' he said, pushing the hessian package across the deeply polished mahogany desktop.

As Ahmet and the other minder left the office with the shotguns, Ozdemir slumped back into his deeply cushioned black leather chair and sipped from a small china cup of strong black Turkish coffee. The instant caffeine hit helped clear his buzzing mind, and he concentrated on the job he was going to get the Park Royal Mafia to do on his behalf. He was getting very worried about his association with the Mafia. If Travers and Briggs were the brains behind the operation, then God only knew how stupid the others must be. It had seemed such a simple solution to his problem at first, but now he harboured serious doubts. The imminent hit on the gunsmith's was only going to equip the teams for the series of armed hits on wages vans. He was no longer sure of the Mafia being able to perform the simplest of tasks. Had he known of the débâcle at Gunnels Wood House, he would have cancelled everything immediately and settled for a quiet life running things for the family.

Glancing again at the notes he had made as he spoke to his mate in the personnel office at Headquarters, Chief Inspector Pete Stevenson decided that now was as good a time as any to start meeting the troops. He strolled downstairs to the corridor that ran along the length of the nick and was pleasantly surprised to find it deserted. Obviously all out and about, he thought happily. He could hear voices coming from the front office and the sergeants' office, so he made his way up there, but was again surprised to find both offices empty. The voices he had heard came from the irate throng crammed into the front office waiting to be seen. The phone in the sergeants' office was ringing off the hook. Puzzled, he continued on into the teleprinter room. The ancient old machine was clattering away at full tilt at a deafening level. It was impossible to hear anything above it, which was why Sergeant Mick Jones and Belinda 'the Blister' Wheeler were blissfully unaware of Stevenson standing bug eyed behind them. The Blister was a fifteen-stone lump with a puce face that had earned her her nickname. She had not had any sort of real relationship during her entire twenty-five years of service. The nearest she had come was a period fifteen years ago when she'd been the secret other half of a married DI. She had also been five stone lighter. Now she was on her haunches in front of Jones, whose trousers and underwear were in a roll around his ankles, busily sucking his plums dry as he leant against the wall, eyes shut in abandon.

Jones and the Blister had become an item following the late-turn binge that ended up with Ally Stewart unconscious on the platform at Manchester Piccadilly station. Both deep in the arms of Bacchus, they had found themselves talking dirty to each other in a corner booth of the club, and as lust overtook them both, they made their excuses and left. They had spent the rest of the night in a seedy nearby bed and breakfast, humping each other senseless, until they had fallen into a deep, drunken, sated sleep. Jones woke in the early hours with the sun streaming through the open curtains to find himself in bed in a strange room next to a beached whale. The whale was lying on its side on his left arm, and as he gingerly moved over to identify it, it farted against his leg and rolled over to reveal itself.

'Oh no, please, Jesus, no,' whispered Jones to himself, 'not the Blister, please no.'

The Blister began to snore loudly as she settled on her back, quivering like a large jelly and crushing his trapped arm deeper into the cheap thin pillow. As he debated how long it would take him to gnaw his arm off to avoid waking the human blob, she opened an eye and stared at Jones. Then she opened both eyes wide in horror and screamed.

'Jesus, not you?' she shrieked. 'What are you doing in my bed?'

'Your bed? We're in a bed and breakfast.'

'You and me? We came back here and ... you and me ... we did it?' said the Blister with a look of revulsion on her face.

'You've got some front,' shouted Jones, rolling out of bed and starting to search furiously for his clothes. 'Fuck me, you're no catch yourself, darling, trust me.'

'You shrivelled up old cunt,' riposted the Blister, also rolling out of bed but holding the eiderdown around her to protect her already compromised dignity. 'How did you get me into this rat hole? Bet you drugged me or something.'

'Drugged you?' protested Jones. 'You dragged me in here by the balls. Trust me, if anyone needed drugging, it was me.'

'What little I can remember, you were all over me like a rash. Don't make me laugh, you horny old billy goat, you were up for it big time. You'd fuck a hole in the wall if you had to.'

'It was the drink,' huffed Jones, pulling up and belting his crumpled trousers. 'Though it was pretty good as far as I can remember,' he added with a smile.

'For a wrinkled old fart you had a few good moves too, as I recall,' answered the Blister, returning the smile from the other side of the bed. A few seconds later they were thrashing about again on the ancient bed, which was barely coping with the unequal struggle.

Their relationship, exclusively physical, had continued from there, but they had crossed into new territory with this workplace blow job. First time out at work and they had been captured by the fire-eating Chief Inspector Stevenson.

'What the fuck do you think you're doing?' bellowed Stevenson rather pointlessly above the incessant clatter of the teleprinter. Jones opened his eyes, saw Stevenson and panicked, nearly driving his knob through the back of the Blister's head. She gagged and her eyes bulged before she desperately rammed her index finger up Jones's arsehole. He screamed with pain and leapt into the air as the Blister fell backwards in a wobbling, coughing heap at Stevenson's feet.

'Jesus Christ,' continued Stevenson, watching incredulously as Jones frantically pulled his trousers up. 'What's your name, Sergeant?'

'Mick Jones. Sir, I'm really sorry about this. I can explain if you'll let me.'

'What exactly is there to explain, Sergeant? My first morning here and I find you getting a blow job in the front office.'

'Teleprinter room,' corrected the pedant Jones, tucking his shirt into his trousers.

'My office!' bellowed Stevenson, grabbing Jones and frogmarching him towards the stairs.

As he slunk away in disgrace, Jones consoled himself that at least only Stevenson knew his sordid secret. He found himself unable to resist the mountainous pile of lard that was the Blister. Clearly all his life he had harboured a thing for fat ugly birds with florid red faces, and shagging the Blister had let all these unnatural feelings flood out. As he hurried up the stairs to Stevenson's office to have a distress flare fired up his arse (a poor substitute for the Blister's finger) he felt himself hardening and he imagined himself disappearing into the folds of her stomach as he sought out the object of his desire, her flabby bingo wings slapping against his ears as she pushed him deeper. His bollocking rendered him speechless, such was the ferocity and obscenity of it, and delivered at such a volume that his penchant for the Blister was no longer a secret. He eventually crept downstairs to hide in the sergeants' office before, wonder of wonders, he put on his dusty uniform patrol cap and took the supervisor's unmarked Morris Marina out on patrol.

While Jones had his eyebrows singed by Stevenson, a flushed and unsteady Blister began to deal with the large crowd of irate members of the public who had been waiting to speak to a police officer. At the front of the queue was the elaborately coiffured and dandy Neil Hamilton. Hamilton was a solicitor from south Manchester who was on a permanent retainer to a team of robbers living in the Wirral. Two of them had recently been arrested by the Regional Crime Squad as they had attacked a wages van. They had subsequently disappeared into the custody system, as armed robbers invariably did, being moved quietly from nick to nick without any record of their presence. Any inquiries from friends and family, or more importantly, solicitors, would be batted away fairly truthfully with replies such as 'never heard of him, mate', or 'not here, try somewhere else'. Hamilton had spent the last twenty-four hours scouring

nicks across the north of England for his clients. He had
located one at Alpha Tango but had fallen foul of the Crime
Squad DCI there. At the end of a long day of 'no comment'
interviews, he had haughtily left instructions that no one
was to speak to his client without him being present. A little
after one that morning, the Alpha Tango custody officer had
telephoned him at home.

'Squad need to talk to your client,' he said to the sleepy
Hamilton.

'No one talks to him until I get there,' roared the
arrogant Hamilton, diving out of bed.

Two hours later, he was sitting alongside his client in an
interview room opposite the DCI and a DS from the
Regional Crime Squad.

'Shall we proceed, gentlemen?' he smirked, glancing at
his client for approval.

'Sure thing, Mr Hamilton,' said the DCI, leaning
forward to address his client. 'How many sugars do you
have in your tea, Dave?'

'Three,' mumbled the armed robber.

'Black or white?'

'White.'

'What the hell is going on?' demanded Hamilton.

'Asking your client some questions, Mr Hamilton. You
said you wanted to be here whenever we had anything to ask
him,' replied the DCI innocently.

'You know fucking well what I meant,' shouted

Hamilton. 'You've completely wasted my time, dragging me out of bed in the middle of the night.'

'Just a misunderstanding, Mr Hamilton,' soothed the DS, getting to his feet and opening the interview room door for him. 'We thought you meant any question. How'd that happen, guv?' he asked his DCI as Hamilton flounced out of the room in a gust of expensive aftershave. Hamilton received another phone call just after four in the morning from the duty inspector to confirm it was OK to ask his client if he wanted his cell light turned off, before he took his phone off the hook and resolved to make a formal complaint later that day.

Having dealt with one client at Alpha Tango, Hamilton had been sent to Hotel Alpha to look for the other one. He was tired, irate and in the mood for a real row, having been kept waiting in the front office reception area surrounded by the *Untermenschen* of Handstead. Hamilton was a slippery forty-five year old who wore his greying hair to collar length with a centre parting which he fondly imagined took years off him. He actually resembled an unctuous old lounge lizard, but with his expensive suits, which hid his middle-age spread, and his cruelly handsome features, which were just beginning to sag, he cut a bit of a dash with ladies of a certain era. But not with the Blister, who was rubbing her jaw which ached from her pink oboe-playing session with Sergeant Jones. Crashing the sliding-glass window to one side, she glared at the simmering Hamilton.

'Yes?' she said rudely.

'I'm here to see my client—' began Hamilton loudly.

'He's not here,' interrupted the Blister, rooting about in her mouth and removing what looked suspiciously like a fuse wire.

'Who's not here?' demanded Hamilton incredulously.

'Your client.'

'You don't even know his name,' exploded Hamilton.

'Try Tubbenden Road, he's not here,' said the Blister disinterestedly, looking past him at the crowd behind. 'Who's next?'

Hamilton went berserk. 'Just a minute,' he roared. 'I want to see my client. I demand to speak to someone in charge. Get me the organ grinder, I've had enough of the monkey,' he spat.

'You want the organ grinder, you can fucking have the organ grinder,' hissed the Blister, picking up the desk telephone and dialling the sergeants' report room at the far end of the corridor. 'Sarge, could you pop up the front for a moment? I've got some arsehole here won't speak to the monkey, wants the organ grinder.'

Over the phone, Sergeant Tucker heard an irate voice shout, 'Who are you calling an arsehole?' before he answered: 'Where's Sergeant Jones? He's duty sergeant, isn't he?'

'Upstairs with the new chief inspector. Can you help me, he's becoming quite abusive,' continued the Blister, putting on her little-girl-lost voice.

Tucker replaced the receiver without replying and strode out of his office and along the polished lino corridor at a Guards regulation hundred and twenty paces a minute, humming a few bars of 'The British Grenadiers' as he went. Seconds later he arrived at the front office, threw open the doors into the milling throng and barked, 'What's going on here?'

Hamilton, hearing the authoritative shout behind him, turned away from the glass window and forced his way through the crowd to where Tucker stood, ramrod straight.

'You in charge?' he yelled, looking the immaculate Tucker up and down.

'That's me, lardarse,' replied Tucker, cocking a threatening eyebrow at him.

'I want to speak to someone in charge, you insolent oaf,' bellowed Hamilton.

'You're not listening, chubby. It's me. What the fuck do you want?'

'You're in charge here?'

Tucker stared at him, wide eyed and demented. 'Oh yes, the lunatics have taken over this asylum,' he laughed, spittle forming at the corners of his mouth as he warmed to his task.

'You're as fucking useless as that bag of shit over there,' shouted Hamilton, pointing behind him at the Blister, who was now busy filling out a document production form. She glanced up to see Hamilton lifted off his feet and frogmarched into the nick, the front door banging behind him. Life in the front office continued as though he had never been there.

Hamilton found himself being rushed down to the cell block, past Sergeant Collins, who glanced up as he and Tucker went by.

'Everything all right, Graham?' he asked.

'Gobshite solicitor, that's all, Andy,' called Tucker as the speechless Hamilton disappeared into the gloomy cell corridor. Collins turned back to the spotty youth in front of him, who had watched the exchange wide eyed in astonishment.

'Name, son?' said Collins nonchalantly, picking up his pen.

Hamilton was thrown into a cell at the far end of the corridor and stood in the gloom listening to Tucker march away. He peered anxiously through the open inspection hatch, which afforded him a view along the entire length of the corridor. The walls were devoid of all decoration except chalk boards outside each cell and two framed fire regulation notices on either side. He watched in appalled fascination as Tucker marched halfway up the corridor and then with a loud shout of 'Mark time, ina', he began to mark time on the spot. After a few seconds he resumed his marching. Tucker was back on the drill square at his beloved Pirbright on his All Arms Drill Wing course, listening to his instructor bellowing instructions. As he approached the fire regulation notices, he began to call out, 'Up, two, three, four, five, down, swing,' as he snapped up a perfect salute to the right on the march before ripping his arm violently back down to his side as his instructor had shown him – 'like ripping a nigger off your sister, son.' Ah, Pirbright, the Grenadier Guards, the old days, thought Tucker to himself as he swung out of the cell passage with the same swagger he had displayed as he marched into Rome with his battalion all those years ago. A veteran of World War Two who had seen action at Anzio and Casino before he had got to Rome, Sergeant Tucker had completed thirty years' service with the Police but now found himself drifting back to the old, simpler days of his youth on a regular basis. His marching around the nick whilst mimicking an army band was the stuff of legend around the Division. Even 'The Fist' Findlay had heard of it and had ventured over to Handstead to see it for himself. Unfortunately, Tucker had seen him first and took him upstairs to the canteen where he berated him for half an hour about the ills afflicting the modern police force. The Fist was eventually rescued by his driver and resolved never to set foot in Handstead again. By all accounts, Tucker was one of the less dangerous inmates.

Hamilton realised he was dealing with a maniac and wondered what to do next. Five minutes later he timidly called out, 'Hello?' but his echoing voice went unanswered. He spent the rest of that day, and the evening, tearfully arguing with the other officers who came down the cell corridor, but they were as unsympathetic as Tucker. He spent a cold, dark, lonely night in the cell before Tucker appeared shortly after six the following morning. Hamilton was subdued and broken as Tucker stood grinning at him from the doorway, hands on his hips.

'I'm going to release you now, fat boy, for good behaviour and time served. On your way, and mind your fucking language next time you walk into a police station. Have a bit of respect in future. Go on, fuck off.'

He escorted Hamilton back to the front doors and pushed him out into the now-empty front office. Hamilton made his way to his car parked outside in the slip road to find that Tucker had thoughtfully had it ticketed. He drove sullenly home and fell into bed absolutely exhausted.

There was no complaint. Hamilton recognised the futility of that course of action. There was no paperwork concerning his time in the cells, no record of his visit. Like his client, he had vanished, albeit temporarily, into the custody system.

Alan Baker swaggered arrogantly into the carpentry shop, stopped and surveyed the sight in front of him. The large room smelt strongly of cut wood and glue and the walls were covered with poster diagrams of woodworking tools and examples of screwless joints. He had never been to the shop before, his usual assignment being in the prison

laundry, but the change in his duty by Prison Officer Pete
McCutcheon had barely merited a response from him. He
was used to the screws trying to fuck him about. Every time
they reckoned he had settled into a routine or role, they
would move him to another, equally monotonous, task. No
doubt the carpentry shop would be as pointless and aimless
as every other prison job. Fuck them, he mused, no way was
he going to react to their provocation. Whatever they threw
at him, he'd deal with it.

He glanced around the busy shop, noticing idly that the
other occupants all appeared to be dark, olive-skinned men,
busily engaged in cutting and sawing planks for fencing
panels. The screeching from the large circular saw in the
centre of the shop was ear-splitting, and Baker picked out a
set of battered black ear protectors from a cardboard box by
the side of the door and pulled them down on to his aching
ears. The respite from the noise was instant, and with a
bored sigh Baker glanced around the room to find the screw
who would give him his pointless assignment for the day.
Had he paid a little more attention, he would have noticed
the carpentry shop duty screw disappear from the room as
soon as he entered, summoned by McCutcheon, who had
remained in the corridor outside after escorting Baker from
his wing.

As Baker strolled further into the room to take in his new
surroundings, a figure moved stealthily behind him from
the rear of a large free-standing double-doored equipment

cupboard. It was one of the Turks, carrying a large sock filled with wet sand. He moved behind Baker, swinging the sock quickly around his head several times before felling the other man with a shot to the back of the head. Baker felt the impact, which oddly didn't hurt, and saw stars as he pitched forward on to the sawdust-covered floor. He lay on his front, still conscious but stunned, head swimming. His ear protectors had fallen off as he nose-dived on to the ground and his spinning brain was again filled with the manic scream of the circular saw, totally disorientating him.

He was aware of hard, rough hands grabbing his upper arms and his legs, and of being lifted, still face down, into the air. The noise of the saw got louder until it resembled the roar of a jet engine, and he was thrown heavily on to a bench. He felt his wrists being grabbed and pulled firmly away from his body until his arms were stretched out, and he shook his head desperately to try to clear it. Something serious was happening and his animal instinct was kicking in, urging him to act and survive. He had no chance. The six Turks restraining him had all spent time in the prison gym honing their physiques until their muscles resembled coiled cable, and now they held him virtually motionless as he began to squirm and try to break away from them.

It was then that he felt the breeze from the spinning, screaming saw, and his mind cleared immediately as he realised what was coming. His arms had been pulled across the steel track of the saw, which was being slowly propelled towards him by one of the grinning Turks. Baker's eyes widened, and then he screamed as loudly as he could. The single word, 'No!' was hardly audible above the noise of the saw, and then totally lost as the spinning two-foot-high serrated blade began to cut into his right arm, halfway up the forearm. A spray of blood flew on to the far wall, and the tone of the saw changed to a lower whine as it began to chew through the arm, fragments of bone and lumps of bloody tissue splattering on to the wall along with the bloody spray. Baker was screaming and struggling as violently as he could, racked with excruciating pain, his facial skin stretched to breaking point across his skull, eyes popping and bloodshot with the effort.

'Quickly!' shouted one of the two Turks wrestling with Baker's arms. Murat, who was wielding the saw, seemed to be dwelling on the task in hand. The smell of burning flesh and bone, reminiscent of the smell in a dentist's chair, filled the room, and Murat pushed the spinning blade all the way through both arms. The men holding Baker's wrists staggered backwards as the arms were severed, and the four holding his hips and legs dragged him off the bench and allowed him to crash to the floor. The blood continued to spurt from the severed veins in his arms and he jammed the stumps on to the filthy floor and tried to lift himself. The awful pain as the blade first tore through his forearm had completely gone, replaced by a terrible numbness, but he continued to scream as his world began to darken. The severed hands were tossed to the side of the bench, and Murat and his gang left quickly and quietly, as Baker slumped back on to the floor, his life blood gushing over the rough boards, his head a few feet from his severed hands. The bleeding continued for a few minutes until he slipped into unconsciousness and then a coma. He was dead within five minutes, his last conscious image being of his own, cold, lifeless hands lying in an ever-increasing pool of blood.

Prison Officer Pete McCutcheon was the first to come across the gruesome scene. A doctor arrived and pronounced Baker dead. As the instigators of the plot had hoped, the investigation into his death was at best rudimentary. It was quickly ruled to be a tragic industrial accident caused by Baker's unfamiliarity with the machinery in the carpentry shop. The cons, though, knew different, and McCutcheon made sure that the stunned Mafia inmates learnt who had called the hit in. The old guard was now definitely a thing of the past – the Park Royal Mafia was under new management.

Simon Edwardes received a brief phone call from McCutcheon. DCI Harrison's phone rang shortly afterwards.

'It's done,' said Edwardes simply.

'Fucking hell,' breathed Harrison. 'They didn't hang about, did they? We're talking about the real deal, I trust?'

'Absolutely. I guess the police in Manchester will contact you in due course as part of their *investigation*.' Edwardes emphasised the word with some mirth.

'Suppose so. Does Ozdemir know yet?'

'Don't know. I'm not sure how effective his lines of communication into and out of the prison are.'

'Not that good, I reckon; that's why you were told to take the message in. Listen, why don't you give him the good news? Let me know how he takes it.'

'Yeah, OK. He's not going to be happy.'

'Fuck him. Accidents happen when you go down this route. Can't see him losing too much sleep over it just yet, but once he knows that I think he ordered the hit, he'll have something to sweat about. Let me know, OK, Simon?'

'Will do,' replied Edwardes. He paused for a moment to collect his thoughts before telephoning Ozdemir. He was unsure how the wannabe crime godfather would react to the news of Baker's death. He'd either be furious that his instructions had not been carried out properly, or else quite unconcerned, because there would be no negative impact on his plans for the future of the Park Royal Mafia.

Ozdemir took the latter view as he listened to Edwardes pass on the news from the prison.

'How did that happen?' he asked quietly once the solicitor had finished.

'Sounds like they took things a bit far, Mr Ozdemir. Going to take his fingers off but took his hands, maybe?'

'Maybe, Simon,' said Ozdemir. 'What message did you pass to my guys?'

'I didn't pass it directly, obviously. It went in via a highly placed source there. Just as you asked, Mr Ozdemir, Baker was to have a very serious accident so that the Mafia got to know who's in charge now.'

'Well, these things happen, don't they? Dead or alive, Baker's history as far as the Mafia are concerned. I've got those fucking cretins Briggs and Travers running things for me for the time being. Are you able to find out where the investigation into Baker's unfortunate accident is going?'

'What do you mean?'

'I need to know if any of my guys are in the frame, understood?'

'Oh yeah, I should be able to keep an eye on that. I'll let you know, OK?'

'You be sure you do, Simon,' said Ozdemir. 'I'd hate to see you meet with an unfortunate domestic accident. Or your parents,' he added ominously.

He replaced the phone without waiting for a response, and Edwardes swallowed hard. His role as DCI Harrison's well-placed double agent was becoming increasingly risky. Though Harrison knew of his contact with Ozdemir, the reverse was obviously not true. Whereas Harrison would likely get very unpleasant if he didn't come up with the goods, Ozdemir's response would undoubtedly prove to be fatal.

* * *

'As soon as those idiots ring, I want them brought here,' Ozdemir instructed his aides. 'They can do the gunsmith's at Tamworth on Monday morning.'

'Doesn't give them long, boss,' observed Ahmet.

'To do what? You've done all the donkey work. All they've got to do is go and get the guns. The last thing I want is those morons to have time to fuck everything up. Let me know when they get here,' he finished as he indicated with a nod of his head that he wanted them out of his office.

Once they had gone, he settled back in his chair and rested his chin on the tips of his fingers as he considered his situation. Across town, DCI Harrison adopted a similar pose as he considered a future with Ozdemir's balls gripped firmly in both his hands. Ozdemir had briefly considered pulling the plug on his plans to bring the Mafia under his wing as he reached for new criminal heights. He quickly reasoned, however, that it was extremely unlikely that any investigation into Baker's death would be particularly vigorous, and that there was almost no chance it would ever be connected to him. DCI Harrison, on the other hand, knew different. As Ozdemir chewed his bottom lip nervously, considering the family's likely response when they became aware of his plans to move into the big time independently of them, DCI Harrison got his bottle of Bushmills out. Pouring himself a generous shot, he swilled the honeyed elixir around his mouth. Then he swallowed and stared out of the office window without seeing anything. The enterprise had passed the point of no return, and he was determined the outcome would be in his favour.

Travers and Briggs returned to their shabby flat after their very brief meeting with Ozdemir and immediately sent out runners to summon the Gunnels Wood House breaking team to get details of the next step on the road to criminal greatness.

'Monday morning, we're doing the gunsmith's at Tamworth,' announced Travers to his sullen audience. 'Or rather *you* are.'

'A fucking gun shop?' asked Chance, whose recent experiences at the hands of gun-wielding maniacs had pushed him to the brink of a nervous breakdown.

'That's right, Ian, a piece of piss. The shotguns you nicked have been adapted, the job's been planned; all you've got to do is go in, scare the shit out of the staff and nick all the shooters you can carry.'

'What the fuck do we want more shooters for?' continued Chance.

'Stop asking fucking stupid questions. Brian, you've got to lay your hands on a decent motor with a bit of poke. You'll be doing the shop about half ten, so it's up to you when you nick it and where you keep it, but we want you here about nine thirty. Don't be late, will you?' Travers said threateningly.

'Monday?' exclaimed Jones. 'Fucking hell, Andy, it don't leave me a lot of time, does it? Fuck me, it's Friday already.'

'Best you don't delay then.'

'Fucking hell,' said Jones again. He could see it all going horribly wrong. 'Where the fuck am I going to get a decent motor from?'

'Just get one, Brian. You put yourself up as the driver, remember? You want to drive while the others get their hands really dirty, then you come up with the fucking motor.'

'Fucking right,' chimed in the beaming Patrick Allen, rubbing self-consciously at his broken nose. He would never forgive Jones for the débâcle at Gunnels Wood House and now looked like a panda as both eyes had blackened up. Coupled with his broken and bloody teeth resembling a series of ancient tombstones he looked truly horrific.

'Yeah, fucking right,' chorused Chance and Martin, who both saw Jones's likely failure to secure a decent motor as their only source of salvation. No wheels, no job, they reasoned.

'Got something for you two to do,' said Hugh Briggs, eyeing them fiercely. 'You're going to need some boiler suits for the job. Get yourself down to Chapman's and get four boiler suits with hoods.'

'What for?' asked the despondent Chance.

'And some balaclavas.'

'Why?'

'Stop you being identified of course, you idiot,' shouted Briggs, who hated being questioned by people he considered to be inferiors. 'Just fucking get them.'

'I suggest you lot get cracking,' advised Travers. 'Chapman's closes in an hour. And Brian, you need to sort that motor out swiftly.'

'What about him?' asked Jones sourly, pointing at Allen.

'Looks to me like he did the most last time out,' growled Briggs. 'Never mind what Pat's doing. You fuck off and lay your sweaty hands on a nice motor, why don't you?'

Sweaty hands was about right, and as he and Allen, Chance and Martin hurried out of the flat to take care of business, Jones checked his watch. It was four fifty; DCs Clarke and Benson would be phoning the Birchwood Road phone box at five, so he resolved to head in that direction as soon as he could. He was praying they would come up with a solution, otherwise he was a dead man. He kept quiet as the others continued to discuss what would be needed to hit the gun shop at Tamworth. Chance and Martin also fell silent as they contemplated having to negotiate the fearsome Rita Walker, who knew both of them well. If the old witch clocked them, she'd have them both thrown out of the store as part of their lifetime ban. Neither had mentioned the potential problem to Travers and Briggs, preferring to take their chances. Their simple task was already beginning to appear as difficult as polishing a turd.

A minute later, the four would-be armed robbers found themselves outside in the street in the blistering heat of the late afternoon.

'How come you didn't get anything to do?' complained Jones to Allen, shielding his eyes from the searing sun, which had not lost any of its intensity as the day drew on.

'Like they just said, because I fucking copped for this lot last time,' snapped Allen, indicating his panda eyes and wrecked nose and teeth. 'Time you got your fucking hands dirty, Brian. Just make sure you don't fuck things up again, won't you?' he added dismissively as he turned away from the others and began to make his way home. He too was secretly hoping that Jones would fail miserably in his task and the robbery would be called off, or at the very least turn out to be an abject failure. He had served a few months' gaol time in the past, and whilst he would prefer not to go back to prison, getting an early capture on this job was a much better option than actually carrying out the robbery. Even in his small mind it had disaster written all over it. Telling Travers and Briggs that was not an option at all, not unless he wanted to take his food through a straw for a while. Having said that, he was not far off doing that anyway at the moment, so sore were his broken teeth and split lips.

'Fuck off,' called Jones to Allen's back as he began to

make his way to the Birchwood Road phone box for the five p.m. call with Clarke and Benson.

Chance and Martin trotted away down the alleyway opposite towards Chapman's, about a ten-minute walk away. If they hurried they would get there before it shut, but they still had to negotiate the formidable Rita Walker. They arrived at the store's ornate and majestic front doors shortly after five fifteen, panting and bathed in sweat. The white-hot pavements had baked their feet, and they paused briefly to rest on the cool shady steps outside the store.

'Christ, I hope she's not here,' gasped Martin, hands on his knees, sweat dripping off his sunburnt nose like a leaky tap.

'Let's get it over with,' panted Chance. 'Quick in and out, no fucking about. What floor is hardware on?'

'How the fuck do I know? We'll have to ask someone, or maybe they've got one of those boards at the front showing you where everything is,' snapped Martin irritably.

The pair hurried up the steps and through the large revolving doors into the cool, cathedral-like main foyer of the store. The respite from the all-consuming heat was immediate, and they paused and relished the moment. The store appeared to be empty of customers, as was the norm, and the only sign of life was a bored salesgirl filing her nails on the perfume counter visible through a double set of monogrammed glass doors. The lifts were directly in front of them, and to the right was a marble staircase. Over on the left was a more basic set of stairs marked as a fire escape. There was, however, no information board to tell them on which floor hardware could be found.

'Go and ask that bird,' hissed Chance. Shaking his head in irritation, Martin pulled the double doors open and strode up to the perfume counter.

'Which floor's hardware on?'

The girl paused briefly and looked up at the spotty toe-rag in front of her with scarcely concealed contempt. She frowned, then replied, 'Third,' before resuming her labours, mentally ticking off the seconds before the store bell announced the end of the day's sales, or rather lack of them. Martin returned to Chance and punched the lift button.

'Third,' he said tersely as they waited impatiently for the ancient lift to make its way to the ground floor. After what seemed an age, Chance and Martin pulled open the metal lattice doors, stepped into the ornate wood-panelled interior and pushed the button for the third floor.

The hardware department was as deserted as the cosmetics department on the ground floor. They glanced left and right for an indication as to where they might find boiler suits, but nothing presented itself. Salvation then fluttered into view in the form of James Sutton, the effeminate department floor manager, who could scarcely believe his luck. Five twenty on a hot Friday afternoon, not a sale all day and then two real rough trade present themselves to him. Joy of joys.

'Gentlemen,' he twittered joyously, 'how can I help you? Your wish is my command,' he added hopefully.

Chance and Martin took a step back and glared at him. Resisting the urge to flatten the camp little fairy, Chance growled, 'Where can we find boiler suits?'

'Boiler suits? Oh, how wonderful, boiler suits,' trilled Sutton. 'Walk this way, gentlemen,' he said, before mincing off with Chance and Martin following, vowing never to walk that way. 'What size, gentlemen?' he continued, glancing coyly over his shoulder at the appalled duo, who were trying to keep a safe distance from the little queen. 'Let me guess,' he laughed. 'Large?'

'Fucking hell,' exploded Martin, who had quickly run out of patience. 'Just show us where the fucking boiler suits are, will you?'

'In a rush, are we?' simpered Sutton, who had decided to go out on a limb with these two on the off chance they might be in play. It was his experience that the rougher they were, the better the chance. 'Here we are, gentlemen,' he continued in the same light, camp style, indicating a stack of boiler suits wrapped in polythene bags. 'With or without hoods?' he queried, beginning to sort through the stack.

'With,' shouted Chance, keen to be on his way.

'Large or medium?' continued Sutton, casting a knowing eye up and down Chance.

'Large.'

'One each?'

317

'Four,' shouted Chance, grabbing the bag that the assistant offered him.

'Got some friends, have you?' enquired Sutton, flaring his eyes at Chance.

'Just fucking give them to me,' snarled Chance, grabbing the other packages Sutton was holding.

'Do you want them wrapped, gentlemen, or will you wear them out?' laughed Sutton.

'Wrap this, you poofta,' hissed Chance, stepping forward and head-butting the assistant, who collapsed like a dynamited block of flats into the display cabinet, blood gushing from his broken nose.

As Martin and Chance turned to leave, they were horrified to see Rita Walker standing at the far end of the aisle, hands on hips, glaring at them. 'Oh fuck,' they gasped in wide-eyed horror.

'Stand still, you rodents,' she bellowed, with such intensity that it momentarily stunned them. 'Stand still,' she thundered again as she began to march towards them. Chance and Martin grew wings and flew in the opposite direction. With her dreadful voice resonating in their ears as she pursued them across the hardware department, they searched desperately for a way out.

For an old woman, Rita was still fairly fit, and kept them in view as she chased them up and down the aisles, continuing to shriek for assistance at the top of her voice. With no customers to come to her aid, she had to rely on the ineffectual help of a seventy-year-old cleaner who, alerted by the din, inadvertently stepped into the path of the fleeing duo and was flattened by them almost without pause.

Chance and Martin then spotted some fire doors at the far side of the floor. Hitting the crash bar at speed, they hurtled out and flew down the concrete steps five at a time until they crashed through another set of fire doors and emerged gasping in the ground-floor reception area. Quickly getting their bearings, they hared through the revolving doors, which spun like a food processor, and out into the hot late afternoon.

Rita had given up the chase once the pair had entered the fire escape and had gone back to speak to the cleaner and to James Sutton, who was getting painfully to his feet holding his still-bleeding nose. None of her medical training was brought to bear as she regarded the pitiful specimen in front of her who confirmed the decision she had taken years ago to forgo all physical contact with the male of the species.

'What did they get away with?' she barked.

'Four boiler suits,' answered Sutton tearfully, hoping Rita might offer him a shoulder to weep on.

'Get yourself cleaned up,' she said abruptly, dashing his hopes, before striding back to her office to telephone her good friend DCI Harrison.

* * *

Shortly before six p.m., DCI Harrison beckoned DCs Benson and Clarke into the two chairs opposite his paper-littered desk.

'Just had a call from the lovely Rita at Chapman's,' he began casually. 'The Mafia are definitely on the move. Two of the team just robbed Chapman's of four boiler suits, so they're ready to go. You heard from your snout today?'

Clarke smiled at Benson and then replied: 'Spoke to him about an hour ago and had a meet with him after. They're hitting the gun shop at Tamworth about ten thirty Monday morning. The shotguns they blagged from Gunnels Wood House have been cut down for the job, but Jones has got a real problem with the motor.'

'What problem?'

'He's got to lay hands on a decent one, something that's not going to screw up like the pile of shit they took to Gunnels Wood House. Problem is, he hasn't got a clue where to get one. If he doesn't come up with one, the job's off.'

'Job's off be fucked,' snorted Harrison. 'We'll get a motor for him.'

'Get a motor for him, guv? How?'

'We'll hire one.'

'Hire one?' repeated Clarke, glancing at Benson, who was sitting back in his chair, grinning broadly.

'Fucking right,' continued Harrison, beginning to fish around in his bottom drawer before placing his bottle of

Bushmills on the desk. As he poured the three of them a drink, he continued: 'No way this job is being called off because he can't lay hands on a motor. I've got Ozdemir's balls in a fucking vice and I'm not going to let go. I want you two in early on Monday to go and see a mate of mine with a car rental business out at Darrick Wood. I'll sort it with him over the weekend. You get the motor to Jones first thing Monday, he takes the other Mafia out to Tamworth, where our guys will be waiting. We've got a fucking great opportunity and we're not going to lose it for the lack of a motor. Cheers, boys,' he toasted them, throwing his drink back in one and banging the glass on to the table in front of him.

'Guv,' replied the two detectives, raising their glasses in salute to their ballsy boss and also draining their glasses in one.

'Tell Jones you'll have what he needs first thing on Monday. Tell him to keep cool and he'll be fine. He'll be allowed to get away after the job but I'll want to speak to him later, understood?'

'OK, boss,' said Clarke. He and Benson got to their feet and left the room. Closing Harrison's door behind them, they walked back to the CID office talking quietly to each other.

'Fucking hell, Bob,' began Benson, laughing as he spoke. 'The crazy old bastard's going to hire the Mafia a motor to blag the gun shop. Fuck me, he's unbelievable.'

Clarke nodded his assent. 'He's got it in aces, John. Anything goes wrong on Monday, his arse is in a sling, you know that?'

'Yeah, I know, but I'm pretty sure he'll have it all boxed away for kick-off. Fuck me, ever heard anything like it before?'

'Nope,' said Clarke simply, shaking his head, 'but Harrison is a fucking original.' As they entered the general CID office, which was full of other detectives smoking and enjoying their traditional Friday afternoon glass or two of Scotch, he winked at Benson, who understood that the subject was now off limits to anyone else. The fewer people who knew what was being planned, the better.

Benson was absolutely right that Harrison intended to have all the angles covered for Monday morning. Once the two DCs had left his office, he telephoned Chief Inspector Pete Stevenson at the far end of the corridor. Stevenson was just slipping a civvy coat over his uniform shirt as the phone rang, but he glanced at his watch and decided to take the call.

'I need a word, Pete,' said Harrison simply.

Half an hour later, as Stevenson sweltered in the traffic on his way home, he could scarcely contain his excitement. On Monday he would be commanding his first live firearms operation. Over the weekend he would contact the patrol group inspector and brief the on-call unit who would undertake the job with him. As luck would have it, it would be Unit Three, two of whose officers had been at the ill-fated raid at the Grant Flowers flats where Bovril had been murdered. The Mafia were walking into the biggest shit storm they could ever have imagined. What a fucking great job this was, mused Stevenson.

As the traffic started to move, he resolved that he would after all put in an appearance at the fancy dress party planned for the station bar that evening to raise funds for the Royal Ulster Constabulary Widows and Orphans Fund. It would be a great opportunity to introduce himself to members of his new nick in a less formal setting, and also to let his hair down and celebrate his escape from Mengele.

Chapter Seventeen

H had been on the road for about five minutes from his home in a similarly depressing new town a couple of miles north of Handstead. His drive to work usually only took him ten minutes, and he had left bang on nine thirty to give himself time to change into his uniform before the ten p.m. muster. He glanced casually at the cloned factory and light engineering complexes that hugged the never-ending dual carriageways, bathed in sodium light, crisscrossing his dreary home town, and wondered what the coming week of night duty would turn up.

He felt the familiar stab of fear of the unknown mixed with the exhilaration that he always felt when he began his journey to work. His routine at home had followed a familiar pattern. He had eaten a light supper before reading a story to his infant daughter, something he had become quite strict about since Bovril's murder. Although none of the group would ever admit it to each other, not even a pair as close as the Brothers, they were all now acutely aware that a split second was the difference between life and death, the lights being switched off for ever. In common with the others, H was determined that if his lights were ever turned off, there would be nothing left unsaid or undone. With his daughter, anyway. Relations with his wife continued in the same businesslike but remote manner, and he had shut the front door behind him without either of them saying a word. It was not that they had argued – simply that neither had anything to say to the other any more.

As he turned his 1971 Ford Escort on to the motorway that linked his home town with Horse's Arse, H tried to relax and calm his racing mind. Whilst he always got tense before duty, night duty in the summer was a time when he had to work particularly hard to hold himself together. The current heatwave had really stoked up tension on the Park Royal estate, and he was all too aware of the mayhem that the group they were following had endured during their seven-night tour of duty. It had included the indecent assault on the female officer in the Park Royal pub, and most groups at Horse's Arse now operated an unofficial policy of keeping the WPCs inside until things calmed down. Somehow, mused H, he just couldn't see that the Blister would ever be at risk, but all the same she too was confined to barracks for the next seven nights. With all the windows in the car wound fully down, the slightly cooler night air rushed around him as he drove quickly towards another shift in the maelstrom that was Horse's Arse.

About two miles from Handstead the motorway crested a long slope, and as H looked ahead he could see the glittering expanse of the town spread in a huge panorama before him. From this distance and height, the place looked quiet and pleasant, its sinister glowing heart hidden from view. He imagined it was how it might look from the cockpit of a plane, and the butterflies in his stomach began to leap about again. He continued on in the light evening traffic to the Handstead exit, and ten minutes later pulled up at the huge razor-wire-topped rear gates to the nick and pushed the intercom button. All officers at Horse's Arse drove their own private vehicles to work, and would move heaven and earth to park inside the secure rear compound. Any vehicles left in the unprotected rear car park or on the street would inevitably be targeted by local thugs, who would conduct regular surveillance on vehicles coming and going from the nick to identify police officers' motors. On a number of occasions, officers leaving work had been followed home and both their vehicle and their home vandalised. They all now routinely employed anti-surveillance techniques when driving home – altering routes, going round roundabouts twice or more, pulling over, jumping red lights, anything to ensure they didn't have an unwelcome tail.

H was eventually answered by the late-turn switchboard

operator, who warmly welcomed him back to hell and opened the rear gates remotely from his desk. Pleased to find a space inside the garage block, which would afford his prized Escort even more protection from the locals, H parked up, pulled the armoured concertina doors shut and walked to the back doors of the nick past the lines of liveried police vehicles, where he was buzzed in by the switchboard operator. Walking briskly along the brightly lit ground-floor corridor, he was greeted by Jim, who had arrived slightly earlier and had been catching up with the switchboard operator.

'OK, big man?' asked H with a smile, always pleased to see his partner in crime, his virtual right arm.

'Fucking right, H,' replied Jim, patting him on the back of his sweaty shoulders as they walked together towards the locker rooms at the far end of the corridor. 'Late turn's been murder apparently, one punch-up after another. Late-turn Yankee One's tucked up at the hospital with a nasty stabbing. We might not have the motor until later.'

'Bollocks,' said H, pushing the locker-room door open and allowing Jim to pass. 'Long as they're not all fucking night. Need be, mate, we'll run a spare panda up to them and get Yankee One off them. I'm fucked if we're taking anything else out.'

'Good idea, H,' agreed Jim as he opened his locker door and began to sort through the numerous wire hangers for a shirt for the night. Opposite him, H did likewise and the

Brothers quietly chatted about what the night might hold. The others were also filtering in, and soon the locker room was filled with the sound of D Group's male officers swapping stories and anecdotes, insulting each other and trying to hide the apprehension they all felt.

Sergeant Andy Collins surveyed the group sitting in front of him and smiled benevolently. They all looked tired, their faces pale and lined and baggy eyed – evidence of another sleepless day before an eight-hour tour of duty in Horse's Arse. Hardly ideal preparation. He smiled again at the faces he knew and looked slightly worried as he glanced at one he knew only by reputation. Dave Baines's replacement, Andy Malcolm the Mong Fucker had arrived. He sat aggressively at the front, arms folded, mouth turned down in a deathly pale face topped by a mop of strawberry blond hair. He was sitting next to Ally, his kindred spirit and the only person he knew at Horse's Arse. They were both hoping to be paired up for the night, hopefully for the entire week, to give Malcy time to settle and get to know the ground. Whilst Malcy knew of the reputation of Horse's Arse, in common with anyone who had not worked there, he had absolutely no idea how quickly he would have to settle in. Fit in or drown was the maxim.

'Listen up, guys,' called Collins, glancing over his shoulder to where Inspector Greaves sat in a chair facing the noticeboard talking to a Police Mutual Assurance Society poster. Shaking his head and sighing quietly, Collins turned back to the group. Only Malcy appeared to think Greaves was a bit odd – the others no longer even noticed what he was up to.

'OK, guys, here we go,' he began. 'We've got a new addition to the group with us tonight. Welcome to Horse's Arse, Andy Malcolm. You'll be working with Ally Stewart tonight. Just go with the flow, he'll see you all right, OK?'

'OK, Sarge,' growled Malcy, glancing over his shoulder to see how the others were reacting. The Brothers were not looking at him, but Psycho was beaming merrily. Pizza looked less pleased to see him and Piggy was gazing into space, the evidence of his last hurried meal at home smeared around his mouth. Ally was delighted to be free at last of the flatulent millstone that was Piggy, and it had occurred to Pizza that he might now get lumbered with him. To his undisguised relief Collins continued, 'Ally, you and Andy take Two One, show him the Park Royal, OK? Psycho, you and Pizza take Two Two. Brothers, you've got Yankee One if it gets back, otherwise you'll have to take a panda. Piggy, take the dirty van. We're going to be busy fellas, late turn was a zoo. Mr Greaves and I will be out and about in Bravo Two,' he finished, glancing over at Inspector Greaves, who was still chatting to the poster. Collins looked down at Greaves's feet and noticed that he had come to work in a pair of brand-new Green Flash tennis shoes.

'Fucking hell,' he murmured to himself – he was in for a difficult night with that lunatic. The group had begun to chat amongst themselves again and Collins called them back to order.

'Heads up, guys, listen in,' he called, opening up the General Occurrence Book and determined to send them out on the ground in the best mood possible. 'The cells have been busy, but they're turning the bodies round quickly so there will be room for your prisoners. Couple of quality jobs to tell you about, but this is a fucking peach,' he said. 'Late-turn Two One dealt with an interesting sudden death this afternoon. "Sudden death – Grant",' he read from the entry in front of him. '"Officers called to 26 Farmers Grove, Handstead, on report of an explosion. On arrival officers found the body of Alan John Grant, twenty-two years, resident at that address, wedged into the washing machine in the kitchen. There was evidence of an explosion in the kitchen but no other persons had apparently been injured. Grant was declared dead at the scene by the FME. A dog in the house had sustained minor burns. Enquiries by late-turn CID officers have established that Grant had apparently tried to cram way too much laundry into the ancient machine by getting on top of it and pushing it down with both feet".' The group were now laughing loudly as they waited for the expected punchline. Even Greaves had stopped his conversation with the poster to listen.

'Fucking hell, this bloke's a genius,' continued Collins.

'Anyway, it appears that as he stamped the laundry into the machine, he got stuck and accidentally hit the on switch. The agitator went into gear and began to thrash him about.' The group were now braying like donkeys and Collins continued: 'As he's thrown around, his arm knocks a box of baking soda on to the floor which spills everywhere. His pet dog, alerted by the noise, walks into the kitchen and, terrified by what it sees, pisses on the baking soda. The piss and the baking soda react together and explode, slightly burning the dog, and as the washing machine goes into its spin cycle and hits top speed, Grant still inside, he cracks his head against a wall and is killed outright. Fucking quality,' he roared, sitting back in his chair, tears running down his face.

The group laughed until it hurt, exchanging high fives and more quips. After a minute or two of continued hilarity, Collins calmed them a bit and continued to pass on the events of the early- and late-turn tours of duty. He was interrupted by the Blister, who appeared at the muster-room door looking flushed and sweaty. She had obviously trotted down the corridor from the front office as fast as her chubby legs would allow.

'Disturbance at the youth club across the road,' she panted. 'Late turn are still tucked up, someone's got to go.'

'We'll take it,' said Jim as he and H got to their feet. There had been no conversation between them but each had instinctively known that the other would want to take the job. 'Yankee One's still out and about, so we'll deal with this until they get back.'

'OK, boys, good luck,' said Collins, waving them away. He confidently expected at least one badly battered prisoner to be locked up fairly soon.

'What's the story?' asked Jim as he and H walked up the corridor with the Blister and slipped on their gloves and caps.

'One of them punks been sniffing glue apparently,' she replied. 'Started laying people out,' and she handed the Brothers their personal radios.

'Shouldn't be long,' observed H as they stepped out into the front office and then on to the front steps of the nick. As always, there was the distinctive sweet smell of disinfectant around the steps, which were regularly used as a toilet by a couple of the local homeless persons, no doubt indicating their feelings for the occupants of the nick.

'Got everything?' queried Jim.

'Yep, ready to go,' answered H, flexing the pair of Northern Ireland military-issue gloves that Jim had given him, and which Jim also wore. The knuckle area of the gloves, which had high elasticised wrists, appeared to be padded. In fact they were packed with lead flats and could be used either as a lethal boxing glove or a cosh. Both men patted their slim mahogany lead-pipe-filled issue truncheons, which were slipped into the truncheon pocket of their trousers, the leather straps pulled clear and wrapped around their belts, before striding purposefully across the road to the Bolton Road East Youth Club directly opposite.

As they arrived at the front door, they were greeted by a sight they had grown used to over recent years. The resident bouncer on the door, Gary 'Boneface' Hilton, was busily punching lumps out of a large youth he had pinned to the ground by the throat. He glanced up as the Brothers walked towards him.

'Everything OK, Boneface?' asked H pleasantly. 'This the one who's been playing up?'

'Nah, this is his mate,' replied the perspiring Boneface. 'The other one's inside, big fucker off his face on glue. I'll give you a hand with him in a moment,' he added, landing another clumping right-hander to the struggling youth's head. Boneface had earned his nickname because of his craggy features, which appeared to have been carved from bone. None of the local cops knew his real name – he was always referred to simply as Boneface at the youth club.

'You deal with him, Boneface,' laughed Jim as he and H stepped into the foyer of the youth club and opened the double doors. The noise was intense, the packed bodies in the darkened interior appearing to boil and move around like a heavy swell at sea. Lit only by flashing disco lights and accompanied by the deafening blast of 'Baba O'Riley', the scene was positively devilish. None of the occupants of the hall, all scruffy teenagers up to the age of seventeen, noticed the Brothers arrive. They were too busy enjoying the spectacle of the obviously deranged and very large punk with an enormous stiff green Mohican haircut staggering around the centre of the dance floor, offering to take on all comers.

Graham Aitchison, yet another stalwart from the Park Royal, and descended from an unadulterated line of scum, had recently put two tubes of Airfix glue up his nose through a bread bag, and he was flying. His mate, who Boneface was cheerfully beating to a pulp outside, had also indulged in the glue frenzy, and the pair had gatecrashed the disco intent on trouble. It hadn't been long in coming, and so far Aitchison and his mate had had the upper hand. They'd taken a few lumps but none had registered in their befuddled brains – the knocks had only reinforced their feelings of invincibility. Now, as Aitchison squinted into the heaving crowd in front of him, he saw it part like the Red Sea and two hated uniforms moving towards him. His eyes lit up. What an opportunity to take out two of the enemy, the bastards who seemed to live to make trouble for his extended family. With a whoop of joy, he rushed at the pair, expecting them to be shocked by the attack and fail to react.

When the Brothers caught sight of Aitchison, their first reaction had been to draw their sticks. Like clockwork, they gave each other room, as they had done numerous times before, and as he closed on them, hit him simultaneously in the face with their sticks. Aitchison appeared to leap into the air, his legs flying above shoulder height, before he crashed back on to the floor, his nose broken by Jim's stick, his left eyebrow split to the bone by H's. Blood streamed from his wounds and he lay quietly on his back, eyes closed, breathing heavily. The Brothers stood over him replacing their sticks as they eyed their audience, gauging how they would react to what had happened. The omens were not good. A couple of full cans of lemonade were thrown out of the dark, followed by a broken bottle, which smashed against the wall behind them as they ducked. Their sticks were again quickly drawn as they bent down to drag their prisoner out of the hall. Then the chant began, quietly at first but quickly rising in volume, drowning out even The Who – 'Kill the Bill, Kill the Bill!'

'We might have a problem here, H,' said Jim, picking his first target.

'Hmm,' agreed H, also earmarking his first hit. One of the crowd now ranged in front of them, detached itself from the group and moved closer to H, who felled it instantly with a strike across the top of its head. The sound was audible above the din. As the troublemaker slumped next to Aitchison, another went for Jim, who smashed his truncheon into the assailant's raised arm. The youth's scream as his elbow disintegrated stunned the simmering mob who, apparently now leaderless, seemed unsure how to take out two seemingly vulnerable and outnumbered coppers. The evidence displayed in front of them in the form of two prostrate bodies was that they were in fact anything but vulnerable.

Despite their early successes, the Brothers quickly assessed that they were still in a lot of trouble. The group was not dispersing and there was only one way out of the club – the way they had come in.

'We're going to need some help in here, Jim,' remarked H casually.

'Yeah, I know,' he replied in a resigned tone. Pulling his personal radio out of his pocket, he spoke quickly. 'Hotel Alpha, night-duty Yankee One, Ten One, Ten One, Bolton Road East Youth Club.'

The code was the designated call for a police officer requiring urgent assistance. Only used in dire circumstances, a Ten One call superseded everything: one of your own was in the shit. Radio traffic was cleared down, channels opened up, and if need be, divisions surrounding the call put on standby to come in. Horse's Arse accounted for 90 per cent of Ten One calls in the county, with the surrounding divisions regularly brought into the town to help out. But it was the first time anyone could remember the Brothers calling one. Back at the muster room and in the front office, the rest of the group stared open mouthed at their personal radios as the sound of Jim's voice faded.

'Fucking hell!' shouted Psycho eventually. 'The Brothers just put up a Ten One? Come on, you lot, across the road. This is going to be a good one,' he added cheerfully.

Leading the charge into the front office and out across the street, causing passing traffic to screech to a halt as a stream of coppers raced across the road, seemingly oblivious to the risk, Psycho, at the head of the pack, paused outside the club, where Boneface had finished pummelling his yob and was getting to his feet.

'You OK, Boneface? Where are the Brothers?' he shouted.

'Gone inside. I'll give you a hand,' he began, but was pushed to one side as the rest of the group piled into the still darkened youth club. No questions were asked as Psycho led the group in search of the beleaguered Brothers. Using their sticks like the Light Brigade amongst the Russian gunners at the end of the Valley of Death, they ploughed into the mob, laying them out like ninepins and smashing their way to the back of the hall, where they found the Brothers standing like a pair of stags at bay.

'OK, boys?' called Psycho manically, turning quickly to lay out another would-be assailant.

'Good to see you, Psycho. We just need a hand to get this shitbag out of here. Grab yourself a body if you want one.'

None of the others needed a second bidding, and soon they were all cutting a path back through the crowd, which was now less keen to get within striking distance. Aitchison was grabbed unceremoniously by the Brothers and Malcy and hauled quickly through a gap cleared by the others and out into the foyer. There Malcy smashed a chair to pieces on the floor and, pulling the double doors shut, wedged a chair leg through the handles, trapping the infuriated mob inside.

'That'll give us time to get away,' he said to the others, a few of whom had their own bruised and bleeding prisoners in tow.

'Nice one, Malcy,' said Psycho, patting him on the back. 'Welcome to Horse's Arse.'

The raiding party departed back across Bolton Road East accompanied by Boneface, who'd brought his unconscious body along for the ride, through screeching traffic with incredulous drivers looking on at the spectacle. A few minutes later they were in the sanctuary of the custody suite, panting from the exertion and exhilaration of the fight, waiting to book their prisoners in with Sergeant Mick Jones. He had looked up from the drink-driver he was dealing with as the door opened with a crash, the Brothers using Aitchison's head as a battering ram. As they threw him to the floor beside the terrified drink-driver, Jones groaned. He had noticed the queue behind the Brothers, all with prisoners. He was in for a bastard of a night.

'I need a piss,' he announced, getting to his feet and walking out to the front corridor.

The drink-driver was quickly marched off to the cells to wait for a police doctor to come and take a blood sample. As they waited for Jones to return to start the booking-in process, H glanced down at Aitchison and noticed something was amiss.

'Where's his fucking hair, Jim?' he hissed.

'Hair?'

'His fucking hair's missing, look.'

Jim glanced down. Aitchison's huge, stiff green Mohican had indeed vanished, leaving only a strip of livid red flesh where it had once been.

'Fucking hell, where's his hair?' repeated H, looking behind him at the rest of the group, who were crowding in through the door.

'You mean this?' said Malcy, stepping forward to show them a strip of skin and hair that had once, quite clearly, been Aitchisor's Mohican.

'Oh, quality,' enthused Psycho delightedly from the side. 'Malcy's only gone and scalped the bastard.'

'For fuck's sake, Malcy, how did that happen?' asked Jim quietly.

'Came off in my hand as we lifted him from the floor. Couldn't have been attached very well.'

'Put the fucking thing away, Malcy, before Jones sees it.'

Malcy rolled the piece of bleeding skin and green hair into a ball and shoved it back into his pocket with a wide grin, then pushed his way back through the group to the corridor. Jones returned shortly afterwards, pulled another A3 custody sheet out of the drawer in his desk and glanced up at the Brothers.

'What you got?' he asked.

'One for threatening behaviour and assault on police at the youth club, Sarge,' replied H.

'Name?' Jones asked the prostrate Aitchison.

'He's not going to be answering questions for a while, Sarge – off his face on glue.'

'Stick him in the drunk cell with the others,' said Jones resignedly, starting to fill out the detention sheet with the usual details – 'not fit to provide personal details'. He was thinking of getting a rubber stamp made up with that legend, so often was it used for prisoners under the influence of drink or drugs. 'Get his property off him and fill out the details when you've got it,' added Jones. He had not even noticed that Aitchison was missing his hair.

Not wanting to encourage the sergeant to start asking questions, the Brothers quickly dragged their prisoner away to the cell corridor and followed the gaoler into the drunk cell. There they quickly emptied Aitchison's pockets of a few coins and rolled him on to his front alongside two snoring drunks, with his face in one of the gulleys in case he was sick. After filling out his property sheet, they retired to the report-writing room to write up their pocket books. They found the late-turn Yankee One crew doing likewise.

'Early start for you then, boys?' laughed the late-turn crew, who had seen the prisoners being dragged across the road from the youth club.

'You've been busy then?' said Jim by way of reply.

'Fucking murder. Nasty stabbing at the Hedgehog earlier. We've been up at the hospital.'

'Got anyone for it?'

'Not yet. Got a name, though.'

'Good luck. Reckon we're in for a fucking shedload tonight,' said H.

Now that it had kicked off, all H's nerves and trepidation had gone. He was doing what he understood best, and sitting opposite his mate as they discussed what they could recall of events in the youth club, he knew he was doing the finest job in the world.

Piggy, not surprisingly, had not taken a prisoner at the youth club, arriving some time after the others. Not for nothing was he known, amongst many other nicknames, as the Fat Gurkha. Now, as the sole Hotel Alpha night-duty officer not closeted at Handstead custody with a prisoner, he was on his own. The main Force control room was on the ball, though, and had begun to call in double-crewed cars from surrounding divisions and had them running in clockwise and counter-clockwise holding patterns on the periphery of the town to respond when appropriate. Piggy, however, got the next Hotel Alpha call: to the rear of an Indian restaurant on the Harvest Mead shopping parade, an anonymous 999 call reporting a man screaming. All officers hated calls as vague as that because it could mean absolutely anything.

With a bit of luck, thought Piggy, by the time he had spent an age getting there and searching around aimlessly, he could close the call as 'area searched, no trace', having killed another hour of his shift.

His luck was out. As he drove the van into the service road at the rear of the parade of shops, the vehicle's headlights immediately picked out a man writhing around on the ground alongside a pair of large metal wheelie bins. Probably gang related, thought Piggy. Even better, the male was on his own, so Piggy wouldn't have to worry about any suspects in the area and could kill the better part of his shift fannying about at the hospital. He booked his arrival on scene and requested an ambulance before leaving the van and walking over to the man, who was screaming in agony and clutching at his left leg, which was obviously broken, the jagged edge of the tibia clearly visible through the leg of his jeans.

'What happened to you?' Piggy asked nervously, looking round to ensure he wasn't about to be ambushed. The man didn't reply, continuing to scream at the top of his voice. Piggy kept his distance and wished he had some back-up, even though he was in no apparent danger. He was startled when a door to the right of the bins was suddenly flung open and a shaft of light from inside the building flooded out into the yard. Two men carrying meat cleavers appeared from within the building. They stopped when they saw the trembling Piggy, conversed with each other in a foreign tongue, and returned from where they had come. A few seconds later they were back without the meat cleavers. With difficulty they introduced themselves as waiters from the Indian restaurant, and shook hands with a massively relieved Piggy, who had initially feared he was about to be slaughtered like his namesake but now saw a very good chance of a free meal.

'D'you know what happened to him?' asked Piggy. The two waiters began to jabber away, pointing animatedly at the screaming man but making absolutely no sense to Piggy. He held his hands up for silence and asked, 'Anyone inside who speaks English?' The waiters looked quizzically at one another, then one of them disappeared back into the restaurant whilst his colleague began to shout and point at the injured man. As Piggy tried to calm him, the other waiter returned with a third Indian, this one dressed differently and clearly the manager. His two waiters gabbled away to him loudly before he turned to Piggy with a wide smile.

'Good evening, officer, how can I help you?' he asked in perfect English with barely a trace of an accent.

'I was hoping someone could tell me what happened to this bloke.'

'Certainly, officer. He was a customer here.'

'Oh,' replied Piggy, worried now that he might have suspects in front of him and that he'd have to do some work. The manager had read his mind.

'Don't worry, officer, this is nothing to do with my staff.' He smiled. 'This is all self-inflicted damage.'

'Self-inflicted?' snorted Piggy indignantly. 'Broke his own fucking leg, did he?'

'Most certainly, officer,' said the manager, spreading his arms innocently. 'If you'd care to look upwards, the window two storeys directly above this unfortunate gentleman is the window in the gentlemen's toilet in my restaurant. My waiters tell me that when he was given his bill for a quite substantial meal, he told them he just needed to use the toilet first. The idiot apparently tried to leave via the window to avoid paying, forgetting he was two floors up. Rough justice, wouldn't you say, officer?'

Piggy put his head back and roared, and he and the manager and his two waiters stood around the wounded man laughing until tears ran down their faces. Usually the scales of justice were loaded the wrong way, but every now and then natural justice reared its head and gave the right person a good kick in the nuts. Tonight was such a night, and it got better twenty minutes later as the screaming man was loaded into an ambulance and Piggy sat down to a plate of freshly fried onion bhajees.

Shortly after eleven p.m., as the noise and chaos in the custody area reached an almost overwhelming level, yet another group approached Sergeant Mick Jones's desk. He spread out another detention sheet and without glancing up said, 'What you got for me?'

'One for the indecent assault on our WPC two nights ago, Sarge,' replied DC John Benson.

Jones looked up, immediately interested; the attack on the WPC had angered everyone at the nick. He glared at Paul Collier, another Park Royal Mafia member, who stared back at him with an arrogant and defiant sneer on his face. Collier had been identified as one of the attackers from his fingerprints, lifted from the glossy finish to the WPC's issue leather handbag, which he'd tried to wrench from her grasp after he'd stopped trying to rip her skirt and tights off.

'Fucking prove it,' he mumbled through one side of his swollen mouth, a legacy of the fierce right-hander Benson had given him as he answered the ring at his front door. 'And I want to complain about that bastard; he decked me.'

Behind him, Benson and Clarke smiled knowingly at each other, contemplating another interview with a Park Royal Mafia member at the end of a piece of packing case elastic.

'Bang it up your arse,' replied Jones. 'Name?'

Reluctantly, and as awkwardly as he could, the spotty, lank-haired Collier gave his personal details whilst Benson roughly patted him down, giving him a sneaky punch in the nuts to be going on with. Sergeant Jones glanced up briefly as Collier collapsed to the floor, but said nothing and resumed his frantic scribbling. Eventually, looking up at the almost filled cell allocations chalkboard, he called to his nearby gaoler, 'Double him up in number five,' and waited as Benson and Clarke hauled Collier to his feet and whisked him away to the wall of noise that led to the cells.

'Who's next?' called Jones to the group of officers waiting at the custody block door.

Once they had thrown Collier into an already occupied cell to stew, the two detectives decided to nip upstairs to the bar, where the fancy dress party was still in full swing. A quick snifter would set them up for what promised to be a busy night. The thumping music was clearly audible from outside the nick, with all the windows open to try to bring some respite from the horrendous heat inside. As Benson and Clarke pushed through the double doors, they were briefly stunned by the sheer number of people packed inside, the eye-wateringly loud music and the incredible wet heat that swept over them.

'Fucking hell!' exclaimed Benson as he began to squeeze past various Napoleons and Hitlers, a couple of hippies, a Roy Wood, a matching pair of Gary Glitters and an enormous yellow chicken.

Chief Inspector Pete Stevenson was having a great evening but was bitterly regretting his choice of costume, in which he was dripping sweat. His usually red face was now the colour of a ripe tomato, and encased in the chicken's head with the beak flapping over his forehead, he looked absolutely ridiculous. But he had broken a lot of ice with some of the members of his new nick and he had drunk like a fish with them. He was three parts pissed, and as so often when he had had a drink, he was beginning to feel a little belligerent.

Benson eased past the massive chicken and leant on the bar to try to attract one of the girls behind it. The chicken glared angrily at being brushed against and hissed, 'Was I in the fucking way there?'

Benson turned and raised his eyebrows. 'What's up?'

Stevenson quickly assessed the big man facing him as quite a handful. The last thing he needed on his first day at Handstead was a pitched battle with someone who looked as though he'd give as good as he got.

'You're OK, big man,' he growled, smiling and offering his hand. 'I'm Pete Stevenson, new uniform chief inspector here.'

'Hello, guv,' responded Benson, shaking his hand. 'DC John Benson, day-shift CID. This is Bob Clarke, he's on the day shift as well.'

Stevenson leant forward to shake Clarke's hand. 'Get you two a drink?' he asked.

'Couple of Scotches would do us a treat, boss,' shouted Clarke above the din.

As Stevenson's huge frame dominated the bar area, he was soon served, and he and the two detectives were shortly after toasting each other at the top of their voices.

'First day, boss?' asked Benson.

'Yeah. Place is something else, isn't it?'

'You're not kidding, but you'll get used to it.'

'I've worked in some shitholes before, but from what I know about this place, I've really landed in it.'

'Could be worse, guv. You've moved over from Mengele's lab, haven't you? Wouldn't fancy working for that twat myself. At least here they like you to get on with locking up the bad guys.'

'Yeah, wasn't a lot of fun over there,' agreed Stevenson. 'What you dealing with so late?'

'What *aren't* we dealing with?' laughed Benson. 'Just got one in for the assault on the WPC last week.'

Stevenson had been briefed about the assault and the threats made to abduct and rape a female officer, and was keen to know more. This would be a significant development and a great start to his new career at Horse's Arse.

'How'd you get him?'

'Came up on prints, got him bang to rights as being present, but I'm not sure whether the plonk will be willing to pick him out on a parade, if you know what I mean. We can put him at the scene but we're struggling to show he actually assaulted her.'

'Bollocks,' snorted Stevenson, who hated to see a scumbag walk away from anything on a technicality. 'It's just not right, is it? We all know he was there and involved, but some righteous cocksucker of a solicitor or stocking-wearing old transsexual of a judge would be happier he was walking the streets because we can't prove beyond a reasonable doubt that he did it. It's just not fair,' he mumbled to the bottom of his empty glass as his inherited Highland melancholy enveloped him.

'We'll work on him, boss, don't you worry,' said Clarke encouragingly, noticing that Stevenson seemd to be taking the news quite badly.

'Aye, I hope so, boys, I hope so. Same again?'

'Not for us, boss, we've got loads to do yet. Thanks for these, though. Welcome to Horse's Arse; I'm sure we're going to be seeing lots of each other.' Benson and Clarke shook Stevenson's hand again and left him propping up the bar, staring mournfully at his empty glass and muttering to himself. The two detectives pushed their way out of the heaving bar and back into the slightly cooler stairwell, where they loosened their ties a bit more and pulled at their sodden shirts.

'Jesus, how fucking hot was it in there?' asked Clarke as they jogged downstairs to their office to start writing up their reports. Their handover sheet for the early-turn CID officers due in at eight the following morning would include a separate, disposable and deniable note to brief the attacked WPC on what would be required at a subsequent identification parade.

'Stevenson seems OK,' offered Benson as they sat behind their desks, piles of paper and files balanced precariously around them.

'Seemed a bit upset that Collier wasn't a dead cart.'

'Yeah, he'll get used to it, I guess.'

As they began to update the initial crime report and prepared a contemporaneous interview for Collier to sign his life away later, Stevenson suddenly stood upright and shouted, 'It's just not right!' startling the two women behind the bar and causing the man next to him to bite through his pint glass. Then he turned and ploughed unsteadily through the crowd towards the double doors like a tornado through a wheat field.

A minute later, Sergeant Mick Jones heard the custody doors bang open. As usual he didn't look up from his detention record but merely called, 'Next,' and reached into the drawer for a fresh A3 sheet. There was no reply. When he looked up, he saw a large chicken examining the custody board, swaying slightly from side to side.

'Who are you?' he said, getting to his feet.

'Chief Inspector Stevenson,' replied the chicken, turning to show Jones his puce perspiring face. 'Which one's in for assaulting one of my WPCs?'

'Why?'

'Never fucking mind why, Sergeant,' snarled Stevenson,

striding over to Jones and glaring down at him from what seemed an enormous height. 'Which one assaulted one of my WPCs?' he repeated.

Jones sensibly decided not to make a fuss and meekly replied, 'Number five, Collier.'

'Keys!' shouted Stevenson, holding his ham-like hand out to the open-mouthed gaoler. He too capitulated and stood alongside Jones as the enormous chicken swayed off towards the cacophony of noise in the cell passage, swinging the keys.

Paul Collier got to his feet and folded his arms arrogantly as he heard the key in the lock of his cell door. He was expecting his arresting officers back for what he intended to be a no-comment interview. He glanced down at the unconscious drunk at the far side of the cell and waited for Benson and Clarke to walk in. His mouth dropped open as a huge, perspiring chicken ducked under the door frame and into the cell.

'What the fuck?' he managed to gasp before the chicken floored him with a swinging roundhouse punch to the chin that nearly took his head off his shoulders and sent him flying to the other side of the cell, where he crashed unconscious against the wall. He slipped down alongside the drunk, who momentarily came round and opened a watery eye. As he noticed a giant red-faced chicken screaming abuse at the man lying next to him, he resolved to give up drinking for good.

Slamming the cell door shut, Stevenson lurched back to Jones and the gaoler, tossing the keys to them with a broad grin before disappearing out of the cell area and into the rear yard where his car was parked. Shortly afterwards, bemused late-night passers-by saw a Ford Capri careering away along the main road without its lights on, being driven by an enormous yellow chicken singing merrily at the top of its voice. This being Horse's Arse, they merely shrugged their shoulders and went on their way.

A little after midnight, all the night-duty Hotel Alpha units were back out on the ground, the crews having completed their initial, rudimentary, notebook entries. Should it get quieter later, they would endeavour to complete all that was required before six a.m., but the reality was that they would all be late home in the morning. They resumed the patrols of their assigned ground, dealing with the numerous petty squabbles and fights as the hot evening continued into the slightly cooler early morning. It was good fighting weather, and the surrounding divisions' vehicles, which had been returned to their own ground, had all been told to expect to go back into Horse's Arse. An unmistakable air of tension and menace gripped the town as it waited to boil over like an unguarded pan of milk.

As the cars cruised the town, the Force main Channel One operator had been keeping them up to date on a chase involving a stolen Saab in an area to the south of Manchester. On two occasions the chase had come around Manchester on the motorway in the direction of the Handstead Force area only to veer away again. But it had kept going, and once again the operator opened his channel to alert local traffic units that the Saab was once more northbound on the motorway and well into their area. It was being chased by ten three-litre Rovers, and was being driven by a category A prisoner who had escaped from a prison van in Birmingham two days earlier. As the pursuing Rover crews switched to the local Force area radio frequency to give commentary, they could barely be heard above the screams of the numerous sirens. The chase was continuing unabated at ninety miles an hour plus, often hitting three figures and with little prospect of a happy ending. The villain driving the Saab had no intention of going back inside and was determined that his capture would be an onerous affair for the police. He was, unfortunately for him, heading for a group of officers all too willing to help him achieve his desired notoriety.

'Fuck me, H,' said Jim, adjusting the volume on Yankee One's radio set. 'This keeps coming north, we'll get a piece of it. Why don't we get up to the Crofton Road bridge?'

'Great minds think alike, Jim,' smiled H, who was already racing Yankee One towards the bridge, which sat over both carriageways of the motorway and carried a usually deserted B road across its back. It was a favourite spot for Hotel Alpha units to observe motorway traffic and also notorious around the Force as the spot used to bring to an end any number of chases in either direction.

'Still coming our way,' said Jim happily as H turned on to the bridge. 'Oh fuck me, look at this lot, will you?' The headlights of Yankee One had picked out all the other Hotel Alpha units parked up on the bridge, as well as the Alpha Tango area car. The crews were leaning over the railings in the dark, peering south down the motorway waiting for the chase to arrive. They had all collected what they would need to help stop the pursuit.

'Quickly, H, we're going to miss out,' said Jim urgently as H brought Yankee One to a halt behind Piggy's van.

'Hello, Delta Hotel,' said Jim into his handset as there was a brief lull in the radio traffic. 'Show Yankee One and other Hotel Alpha units on the Crofton Road bridge for this chase,' he continued as H dived out of the car. There was a pause before the operator, who knew exactly what was coming, replied.

'Thank you, Yankee One, all Tango units northbound, be advised Hotel Alpha units are on the Crofton Road bridge to assist with this pursuit. Tango Two,' a local traffic unit that had joined the chase, 'give me your location now, please.'

The Tango Two crew also knew what was coming. 'Delta Hotel, we're now two miles south of the bridge. Speed is ninety-six miles an hour, all over the road and still failing to stop. We are the lead vehicle.'

'Understood, Tango Two, two miles and closing. Give them room; back off, back off,' instructed the operator.

'Yes, yes,' said the Tango Two operator tersely. His driver began to come off the gas, and both officers wound down their windows and began to flag down the other pursuing traffic vehicles.

In his stolen Saab, the prisoner saw the headlights and blue lights in his rearview mirror begin to drop back, and whooped with delight. Fucking police have lost their bottle, he thought happily, been called off because it's getting a bit hairy. He floored the accelerator again, pushing the big Saab past the hundred-mile-an-hour mark, and raced north-bound, singing 'Brown Sugar' at the top of his voice and popping another tab of acid.

Ahead, in the dark of the unlit motorway, he could see a motorway bridge and what were obviously police vehicles parked on it. Deciding to give them a greeting as he passed, he slowed the vehicle, wound down his window and delivered a two-fingered salute. As he did so, he began to see dark objects coming at him from the bridge, hitting the carriageway in front of him and slamming into the front grille. Fifty yards from the bridge, they began to hit the vehicle full on. A fusillade of large stones slammed into the car, and about thirty yards from the bridge half a house brick hit the windscreen.

Stunned and blinded, the prisoner began to brake heavily, just as half a breezeblock came through the windscreen and smashed into his left hip. Still travelling at around seventy miles an hour, he let go of the steering wheel to grab at his cracked hip. The vehicle veered to the near-side, struck the bridge hard and then overturned, rolling four times, all the glass in the vehicle shattering, pieces of bodywork detaching themselves, before coming to a screeching, smoking standstill just the other side of the bridge. Up above the Horse's Arse crews were celebrating as though an important goal had been scored, jumping up and down, hugging each other, yelling with delight and delivering vigorous high fives.

'Delta Hotel, bandit vehicle has been stopped at the Crofton Road bridge,' transmitted the Tango Two operator. 'Serious RTA, we'll need an ambulance down here and a full northbound closure until further notice. No details of injuries, but I'll get back to you.'

'Thank you, Tango Two,' acknowledged the Force control room operator, as the staff there also celebrated the successful conclusion to the pursuit with loud cheers and a round of applause. No injuries other than to the bad guys was the best possible result – job done. The previously pursuing traffic cars made their way gingerly through the debris thrown at the stolen Saab before pulling up around it. Remarkably, the escaped prisoner was soon being hauled out through the windscreen alive and uninjured other than the breezeblock-inflicted hip injury. The coppers on the bridge began to make themselves scarce, all except Psycho, who saw an opportunity to stick one to the hated traffic police, or Black Rats as they were generally called.

'Come on, Psycho,' hissed Pizza urgently. 'We don't want to hang about here.'

'Won't be a moment,' called Psycho, hauling a heavy sand-filled motorway cone across the roadway to the other side of the bridge. Peering over, he saw that a traffic car from the other Force had very conveniently parked directly below. He hauled the twenty-pound cone on to the parapet, carefully lined up the shot and then dispatched it neatly through the rear window of the traffic car, causing the crew standing near by to leap in fright as their vehicle crashed down on to its springs and the alarm went off.

'Hallefuckinglujah!' shouted Psycho, diving back into the car alongside Pizza. 'Let's get down to the railway sidings, my tanks need emptying again after that.'

'Oh no, not again,' protested Pizza, who had become tired of having to sit quietly in the front seat of the car whilst the monster had his hairy plums sucked dry by an on-duty tom.

'Just a quick one, Pizza, just a quick one,' promised

Psycho as he drove off the bridge with the car's lights off.

By the time two of the traffic cops had clambered up the embankment on to the bridge, it was deserted except for a white liveried dog van, which appeared to be unoccupied. The two furious traffic officers peered into the warm darkness and at the far end of the bridge could just make out a shape.

'Hey, you!' shouted the larger of the pair. The figure stopped and began to wander back to them, soon revealing itself to be Ooh Yah Young. He had arrived too late for the vehicle stoning but had decided to give Alfie the opportunity to stretch his legs.

'You talking to me?' Young asked the sweaty red-faced traffic cop.

'Fucking right I am,' he replied aggressively, sizing up the scrawny dog cop in the ridiculous aviator tinted specs. He pushed his white-topped flat cap on to the back of his head and put his hands on his hips, planting his feet wide like a western gunfighter. Ooh Young looked at him and smiled. Divisional cops had a theory that traffic cops, as well as being eunuchs and kiddie fiddlers, had grooved pointy heads that they screwed their caps on to, because they never, ever took the fucking things off. Even in this unpleasant heat they all had their caps firmly screwed on, though the one addressing Ooh Yah had pushed his back a little further to reveal his grooved pointy head.

'What do you know about the fucking cone through my

back window?' whined the traffic cop in a flat Black Country accent.

'Fuck all, mate. Don't know what you're going on about.'

'Is that right? By my reckoning, pal, it's down to you. No one else up here, is there?'

'Just my mate,' replied Ooh Yah Young. 'Why don't you ask him?' he finished, before whistling loudly and bellowing, 'Arthur Scargill!' at the top of his voice. The traffic cops then saw what appeared to be a small horse with a crocodile's head streaking out of the dark towards them.

Young stood to one side as Alfie launched himself at the gobby traffic cop, whilst his mate disappeared down the embankment in a cloud of dust. As Alfie tried to swallow the man's head, Young wandered to one side of the struggling duo and picked up his hat, which had become unscrewed as Alfie ate him. He walked over to the van, opened the rear double doors and whistled loudly.

'Here, fella,' he called, and began to wave the white-topped cap around his head. Alfie glanced up from his screeching meal and his mean coppery eyes lit up. With a roar, he leapt away from the cop and raced back to the van, leaping into the cage as Young tossed the cap inside. Slamming the doors shut, Young got back into the front, started up Delta One and did a U-turn on the bridge. As he drove slowly past the bedraggled traffic cop, who was just getting gingerly to his feet, nursing several large puncture wounds in his scalp, the sound of the raging monster in the back tearing his prized cap to pieces filled the warm night air.

'Was it my mate?' asked Young pleasantly. The traffic cop scowled at him but wisely declined to reply.

'Thought not. Why don't you bang that cone up your arse, you gelding,' said Young cheerfully before heading back towards Horse's Arse, where he hoped the monster would get a bit more business before the end of their shift.

The early-morning hours of the shift continued much as the evening before. None of the cars closed for refreshments, either eating their sandwiches as they lounged on the bonnets of their vehicles listening to the radio traffic, or blagging a disease-ridden spongy burger from the twenty-four-hour greasy spoon a couple of miles off the motorway. There was no way any of them wanted to miss out on a decent job by being off the road. Even Piggy stayed on the ground in case natural justice chose to show him another example of what was occasionally possible.

The Brothers were driving around the ring road in light early-morning traffic, comprising mainly clubbers making their way to late-night venues, scrutinising the occupants of passing vehicles for a likely stop, when Jim suddenly called out, 'Fucking hell, H, stop, stop!' and looked urgently back over his shoulder. They had just passed the large new sports centre on the outskirts of town and he was pointing back towards it.

'What you seen?' asked H, indicating over to the nearside lane and an adjacent exit slip road.

'In the fucking car park, H, there's a blue Mini Cooper tucked away down the side. Quickly!'

'You're fucking joking. Please let it be JP,' answered H, powering Yankee One down the slip road back towards the sports centre. Killing the lights, he parked in the service road and they quickly ran up the approach drive and into the deserted car park.

'Where?' asked H.

'Down here,' hissed Jim, leading the way past serried ranks of wheelie bins and roaring extractor fans. Halfway down, and otherwise well concealed, was a battered old blue Mini Cooper. The Brothers quickly identified it as the vehicle H had found the log book for at John Patrick O'Neil's house.

'You fucking beauty,' whispered H. 'Let's have a quick look inside.'

Stealthily the Brothers crept up to the vehicle, which had both its front windows open, and peered in. Curled up on the back seat under a thin blanket was the object of all their recent attention and humiliation – John Patrick O'Neil. He was fast asleep and blissfully unaware that his undeserved liberty was about to come to an abrupt end.

'Yes,' they mouthed triumphantly at each other in

unison, before withdrawing silently behind a wheelie bin to plan their next move.

'The little bastard's got a shedload due,' observed H. 'He's really fucked us about and made us look a right pair of mugs. We've got to make the most of this, Jim.'

'Wait here,' whispered Jim. He crept back to the Mini Cooper and silently tried the boot. It was unlocked, and by the light of his Maglite torch, Jim carefully rummaged about in the clutter inside before his eyes lit upon a small red metal petrol can. Easing it carefully out, he shook it gently from side to side and was pleased to find it still had a small amount of fuel left inside. Certainly enough for what he had in mind. He returned quietly to H and outlined his plan.

'Let's torch him,' he said simply.

'What?' exclaimed H. Even though he operated on the same wavelength, he could scarcely believe his ears. 'Set fire to the car with him inside?'

'Yeah, scare the shit out of him. We'll get him out in time, use the extinguisher from Yankee One, and we can say we rescued the little turd.'

'You mad bastard,' laughed H quietly. 'Love it, though. Hang on, I'll get the extinguisher.' He hurried back to Yankee One, returning shortly with the small red extinguisher from the boot of the area car. Jim was ready with his Zippo when he got back.

'Ready?' he asked. H nodded his assent and they crept back to the Mini Cooper.

JP was still snoring contentedly. He had spent the last week sleeping in the car at various locations around the town as he had become aware of the Brothers' increasingly aggressive campaign to get hold of him. He had gone home soon after they had last visited his wife, and realised that living at home was no longer an option. He was unsure how long he would have to stay away, but whilst the heatwave lasted it was no real hardship. The prospect of another period inside really didn't appeal to him, especially as his time in prison usually coincided with his wife becoming pregnant. He'd had a good drink earlier in the evening and had fallen into a deep sleep, dreaming happily of a new life back in the old country with the family. Bizarrely, his dream seemed to involve flames leaping around him, smoke billowing, and he started to feel uncomfortably warm. He began to stir, and then rolled on to his back and opened his eyes, smacking his dry lips. At first he thought he was still asleep and dreaming. Flames lapped around the rear window and he could hear cracking and popping sounds. He rubbed his eyes, sat up and took in fully what was happening. The Mini Cooper was engulfed in flames, and outside he could just make out two expressionless coppers, standing with their arms folded, their pale faces devoid of any emotion.

'Fucking hell!' he screamed, throwing off the threadbare blanket and rolling over on to the front seats. The bonnet was also ablaze and he began to tug desperately at the driver's-side door handle. As he did so, he heard a loud whooshing noise and the car was engulfed in a huge white cloud, which flooded into the interior of the Mini Cooper, choking him. The door was wrenched open and a hand grabbed him by his long, lank hair and pulled him out of the car on to the tarmac. He scrambled away from the smoking wreck and looked up at his grinning saviour.

'You were lucky there, JP,' said Jim cheerfully. 'Lucky we were passing and saw your motor on fire. Otherwise you'd have been toast, son.' Open mouthed, JP looked round to see H dousing the flames on and around the Mini Cooper.

'No need for any thanks, JP,' continued Jim pleasantly. 'By the way, you're fucking nicked under the terms of a no-bail warrant. It's back into the bin for you, mate.' He hauled JP to his feet, spun him round and quickly cuffed his hands behind his back.

'JP!' exclaimed H, approaching with the empty fire extinguisher over his shoulder. 'Fancy finding you in that motor. Lucky we came along, old son. Come on, in the back of our motor with you and we'll get you off to prison as soon as we can.'

Speechless and stunned, JP was taken back to Yankee One and pushed on to the back seat. He really wasn't sure what had just taken place and simply couldn't countenance one of the possibilities – that these two crazy bastards had set fire to his car with him inside.

'Whose motor was that, JP?' continued H as Jim

informed the main Force control room that they had just come across a car on fire and extracted its sole occupant unharmed, fire extinguished, no need for the Brigade. A quick check of the Mini Cooper's registration number confirmed that the previous keeper, a female from south Manchester, had informed Swansea she was no longer the owner.

'No current keeper, JP,' commented Jim blandly. 'You've not been nipping about in an unregistered motor, have you, especially with you being disqualified?'

'Some unscrupulous cops might be minded to say they saw you drive on to the car park, JP, but not us,' said H. 'No need to fit you up, son, not with that fuck-off warrant with your name on it,' he laughed.

As H took Yankee One back to Handstead nick with their morose prisoner, Jim updated Control that they had just nicked the person they had rescued from the blazing motor on a no-bail warrant. The control room operator closed the call ticket on her desk with the final result and turned to her colleague alongside her who was also monitoring the Handstead channel.

'Only in Horse's Arse,' she said with a grin.

Ten minutes later, as the Brothers marched JP across the back yard to the rear doors, Sergeant Collins appeared alongside them in Bravo Two. He had dropped Inspector Greaves off for a nap a little earlier and continued patrolling alone.

'Got him then? About fucking time,' said Collins aggressively. He looked angry.

'Been sleeping rough, Sarge,' answered Jim, glancing at H. 'That's why it took us a while, but we told you we'd get the little bastard.'

'That's right, you did,' agreed Collins. 'Get him booked in and get yourselves into my office. I want a word with you two.'

The Brothers again glanced at each other but said nothing. They'd never seen Collins like this before.

'Yeah, no problems,' they chorused as Collins took Bravo Two up to a parking bay near the back doors and stormed into the nick.

Sergeant Jones hardly looked up as the Brothers bowled into the custody area. He was working like an automaton, processing his prisoners now in under five minutes each. It was a skill custody sergeants at Horse's Arse learned to embrace very quickly if they were not to be totally overwhelmed. There was no time for any niceties or legal entitlements. Name, address, date and place of birth, place and time of arrest, reason for arrest and arresting officer, off to the slammer – next. Name, address, date and place of birth, place and time of arrest, reason for arrest and arresting officer, off to the slammer – next. No room? Double them up. Next.

'What you got?'

'Wanted on warrant, no bail.'

'Name?'

'He's a bit shook up, Sarge, we pulled him out of a burning motor,' said Jim.

'Not his night, is it? What's his name?'

'John Patrick O'Neil.'

'Date and place of birth?'

'Twenty-fourth of August 1946, Howth, Dublin.'

'You know a lot about him,' said Jones, looking up for the first time.

'Been after him for a while.'

Jones nodded. 'Address?'

'Twenty-six Pinehurst Gardens, Park Royal estate.'

'Warrant details?'

'Handstead Magistrates, eighteenth of March this year, non-payment of fines. No bail.'

'Got it. Time and place of arrest?'

'Handstead Sports Centre car park, one twenty-five a.m.'

'You the arresting officer?'

'Yes.'

'Got it. Any property?'

'Nothing.'

'Bin him, number six,' Jones said to the harassed gaoler behind him. 'Next.'

'What about a brief?' said JP, his first words since he had encountered the Brothers.

'Bang it up your arse,' said Jones, spreading the next detention record out in front of him. Whilst he sometimes yearned for his former life at a quiet rural nick, he now took a perverse pride in the fact that he was part of a small group of officers trying to make a difference in the devil's kitchen.

The Brothers knocked quietly on the closed door to the sergeants' office. They received a cursory shouted 'Come in!' and stepped inside, where a red-faced Andy Collins was pacing the floor.

'You wanted to talk to us, Sarge?' asked Jim.

'You pair of stupid arseholes!' shouted Collins, taking a step towards them.

The Brothers fancied themselves in most situations, but the enormous Andy Collins in this sort of mood was a dangerous proposition. They kept quiet.

'What the fucking hell do you think you're doing?' continued Collins, tears welling in his eyes. 'You're supposed to be the difference.'

'What you on about?' queried Jim, already fearing the reply.

'I was fucking watching you, you pair of idiots,' raged Collins. 'I saw you at the sports centre. I was in the petrol station on the other side of the dual carriageway and I saw you. Jesus Christ, I saw you.'

'Oh,' said the Brothers simply, hearts thumping in their throats.

'I fucking saw you, you idiots; what the fuck did you

think you were doing?' Tears were streaming down Collins's face, a combination of anger and disappointment.

'He's scum, Sarge,' said Jim quietly.

'They're all fucking scum!' bellowed Collins. 'That's supposed to be the difference between them and us. That's how *they* behave. We're the good guys; we're supposed to do things differently. How are you two any different to any of the shit on the Park Royal?'

'Sorry, Sarge, we just wanted to give him a hard time. We never meant to hurt him or anything,' offered H.

'Are you both fucking mad?' stormed Collins. 'I watched you commit a criminal offence. I should have nicked the pair of you. What if it had all gone wrong? What if you couldn't get him out? You set fire to his car with him inside. Fucking murder – Jesus Christ, you'd get lifted for murdering a piece of shit like JP O'Neil. Where's the sense in that?'

'We hadn't thought of it like that,' said Jim. The Brothers were in trouble; they knew that, but any blame would be accepted jointly. They took the rough with the smooth, the praise with the criticism, the accolades with the bollockings, as a pair. They were a joint enterprise.

'You're out of control,' continued Collins, slightly more quietly. 'All of you are out of control. The difference between you and the scumbags is hardly clear any more. You could be nicked for what you did.'

'Is that what you're going to do?' asked Jim nervously.

Collins didn't answer immediately, but slumped into a

chair and dropped his head into his hands. The Brothers looked anxiously at each other. He was right: they had been veering closer and closer to the invisible line that separated the good from the bad, frequently crossing it, and now it had all gone wrong.

'I need you all back on the straight and narrow, you two especially,' said Collins finally, looking up at them with red, watery eyes. 'You make a difference here and it matters, but you can't carry on like this. Guys, you're this close to getting locked up for some serious stuff.' He indicated with his thumb and forefinger close together.

'What happens now, Sarge?' asked H.

'It finishes as of now,' said Collins, getting to his feet. 'All of you, it finishes now. There's got to be a difference between them and us, and if it means that sometimes we don't win, then we don't win. We can't be like them. You carry on like this, we're all finished. Christ, I know the strokes you pull out there; done a few of them myself in the past, but this is different. Too much. It's got to stop. Go on, fuck off, the pair of you.'

'OK, Sarge, it stops,' chorused the Brothers.

They left Collins's office and walked quickly to the locker rooms to catch their breath. Relief swept through them both. They knew they had escaped justice by the skin of their teeth. They'd been given a break they would never have offered a resident of Handstead. They would change – a little.

* * *

It was just after two a.m. and getting cooler, but the calls kept coming. Piggy was busier than most, with the van being used for as many prisoner runs as possible. The group had been working flat out since ten p.m. and they needed a lull to draw breath and regroup. Sergeant Collins called all vehicles to a rendezvous at a town centre multi-storey car park just after three to give them a pat on the back whilst Inspector Greaves, who had had his nap, remained in the rear of Bravo Two like royalty, singing quietly to himself. The group no longer paid him any attention and he was little more than the nominal leader. Collins wielded all the real power and influence and commanded the respect of the troops, but he remained professionally loyal to Greaves.

'Doing a fucking great job, boys,' he began. 'Mr Greaves and I really appreciate what you're doing. Keep it going, because it doesn't look like it's going to get any quieter. Keep an eye on each other, back up where and when you can and be careful,' he emphasised. 'Go on, guys, get out there and get your revenge in first.' He glanced meaningfully at the Brothers as he finished and was relieved to see them nod at him. He was sure the message had got through. He saw the Brothers as absolutely vital in the effective policing of Horse's Arse. They were rough, tough, took risks, bent the rules and got the job done, but he wanted them the right side of the line.

The group dispersed back to their vehicles, reinvigorated. Collins hadn't said much, but it was all they needed to let them know that someone in a position of authority valued what they were doing and cared that nothing untoward happened to them. Bovril's murder had affected Collins more than he wanted to admit; it was like losing a member of the family, and he was determined not to lose another.

The remaining hours of the shift were relatively quiet. At five a.m., Collins called the group into the nick for a cup of tea, which the Blister had been tasked to get ready. As they sat around the front office, chatting quietly about what had happened overnight, anticipating the paperwork that awaited them before they went home, the sun rose over the horizon, throwing long fingers of light across the simmering town. The temperature began to rise again as a malevolent sun god cast a livid, bloodshot eye over Horse's Arse. With the exception of Piggy, who true to form had remained prisonerless and was out of the door like a greyhound at six, and of course the Blister, who had been in the front office all night, the rest of the group had a few hours of writing ahead of them. Collins and Greaves remained at the nick with them even though their early-turn reliefs were in, in a show of solidarity that did not go unnoticed. For Andy Malcolm it had been something of a baptism of fire. He wasn't afraid of a bit of hard work, but his first night at Horse's Arse had been a real eye-opener. It wasn't going to get any better, but he had come through it with flying colours, and scalping Aitchison had endeared him to all of them. It would not take long for him to become fully incorporated into the Horse's Arse way of things.

Shortly after eight a.m., the Brothers made their way wearily out to their cars, parked in the rear compound garages. They were hollow-eyed and quiet. It was hot and humid and the early-morning sun already had an edge to it. It was going to be another scorcher, which could mean no sleep for any of them.

'We had a close one tonight, H,' said Jim quietly. 'Reckon that's the end of it with Andy?'

'Yeah, reckon so. Let's face it, if he was going to nick us, he would have done it there and then. He's on offer now if he decides to do it subsequently. No, I reckon that's it over with. We had a right result, Jim.'

'You're not fucking joking. We're going to have to tone things down a bit, mate.'

'I know, but he's right. Shit like JP aren't worth going away for. End of the day, who gives a fuck if his warrant never gets executed. It's not that important. We need to wind our necks in a bit, that's all.'

'See you tonight then, H,' Jim said by way of reply, unlocking his Vauxhall. 'Have a good one.'

H laughed at the sarcasm in his partner's voice. 'Some

hope! Sleep well, mate.' He followed Jim out of the yard and down the side road to the main Bolton Road East, where they went their separate ways.

It was Saturday morning and quiet, with little traffic about. Winding down his window and luxuriating in the cool breeze that enveloped him, Jim headed for home in the village of Bathurst about eight miles away. His routine on a Saturday when he was working nights was always the same, despite the risk from unwelcome observers. Stopping at a small newsagent's on the edge of town, he picked up a copy of the *Telegraph* and then went next door to the baker's, where he bought a freshly baked loaf and had a quick chat with the old dear behind the counter, whom he had known for years. It was all a part of his process of shedding the armoured skin he wore at work, throwing it off by doing and saying normal things – things that everyone else did.

The shedding continued as he stepped quietly into his silent house and stood in the hallway listening to his grandfather's old clock on the wall and straining to hear if his children were awake yet. The house remained as quiet as a church, only the clock ticking rhythmically telling him he was safe, as it helped him morph back into Jim the husband and father. Quietly shutting the kitchen door behind him, he made a large pot of fresh coffee and began to cut the fresh loaf. The aroma of the coffee and bread began to permeate the whole house, and as usual he was soon joined by his two tousle-haired, warm, sleepy daughters, who rushed him as he and H would rush a suspect, falling to the ground on top of him as he tickled them, ruffled their hair and smothered them with kisses. In later adulthood, his daughters would always associate the smell of coffee and fresh bread with their father's return from work Leaving them munching warm doorsteps dripping with butter as they watched the TV in the kitchen, Jim set a tray with the pot of coffee, a mug, a small china jug of cream and a plate with two hunks of bread for his wife. Hurrying upstairs, he pushed the bedroom door open with his knee and peered into the dark, sweet-smelling room. His wife was awake, lying on her side under the sheet, smiling at him.

'You're late, darling,' she said sleepily. 'Been busy?'

'Same old shit, had a few in,' he replied, putting the tray on the floor and leaning to kiss her on the forehead. Then he buried his head in her warm neck and inhaled deeply, smelling her trust and love for him.

'You OK?' she asked, turning slightly and hooking an arm round his neck. She didn't know the details of what he did at work, but she had read enough about Handstead, and heard plenty from the wives of other cops there, to know that her husband would not have had an easy shift. Sometimes his eyes betrayed the fact that he had been through the wringer, but he had told her the day they met that what happened at work stayed there. He never, ever talked about his job and apart from some bad dreams, never brought it home with him.

'Yeah, I'm OK now,' he murmured into her neck.

'Good. Go and have a shower, honey, you'll sleep better, and besides, you smell like a bear,' laughed his wife.

Getting to his feet with a wry smile, Jim stripped off his sweat-drenched clothes, tossed them into the wicker laundry basket in the bathroom and treated himself to a powerful lukewarm shower. The strong jet washed away the filth of Horse's Arse, embedded deep in his pores and stained into the roots of his hair, running away in the spinning whirlpool at his feet. He was cleansing himself of all guilt and questions – he was nearly back in the land of the living. Five minutes later he crawled under the sheet next to his wife and lay on his back with his eyes closed, sighing deeply twice. She rolled over, hooked a leg over him, and he felt her slim, warm body begin to cover him. She snuggled her head into his chest and threw her arm across him. The transformation was complete; he was back. His brain shut down, and as he fell asleep he murmured, 'I'm in the safe place,' and she smiled in the darkness and hugged him closer.

Chapter Eighteen

Clarke and Benson had not worked on Sunday night, swapping their shift to a quick-changeover late turn so they could be in early on Monday morning to pick up the motor from the car-hire garage at Darrick Wood.

'Off down to London to take some statements and pick up a prisoner, I hear,' said the owner conversationally as he walked the detectives over to the freshly valeted vehicle.

'Huh?'

'Off to London?' repeated the owner, and Clarke realised that Harrison had spun him a line about why he needed the car. Telling him it was going to be used for an armed robbery would probably not have been the smartest move.

'Yeah, yeah, that's right. We'll drop it back later today if that's OK,' replied Clarke.

'Whenever, that's fine,' said the owner. 'Always happy to help Mr Harrison out,' he added, and he walked back to his office leaving the detectives alone. Tired but excited by the prospect of what was coming, they were surprised to be handed the keys of a superb Rover 2.2.

'Fucking hell, he's done all right, hasn't he?' remarked Benson as he and Clarke paced around the gleaming car.

'Hope that cunt Jones doesn't wreck it or we'll have a few questions to answer.'

'Best we let him know, then. What time are we meeting him at the sidings?'

'Eight thirty, I said.'

'Come on, let's get going then. You can drive, you look like you're wetting your pants to have a go.'

Shouting their goodbyes to Harrison's mate in his Portakabin office, Benson jumped back into the CID motor and led Clarke back to the Handstead railway sidings, where they parked up behind the metal skips and waited in the early-morning sun for Brian Jones to arrive. He was late. The detectives were starting to get worried and were on the verge of going to look for him when he walked into the sidings yard glancing furtively over his shoulder. He was ashen faced and looked terrible.

'Where the fuck have you been, you useless tosser?' asked Benson unsympathetically.

'John, John,' chided Clarke, patting Jones on the shoulder. 'He doesn't look well at all. You OK, Brian?'

'Didn't sleep a fucking wink last night,' replied Jones, glancing over at the Rover and adding, 'You got one then?' in a very disappointed voice. All night he had prayed the detectives would fail to supply him with a motor. He knew he'd have to face the wrath of Briggs and Travers, but that was infinitely preferable to doing this half-baked robbery.

'She's a fucking beauty, isn't she?' said Clarke proprietorially. 'Only fair to point out now, though, Brian, you put a mark on it and we're going to take a baseball bat to you, understood?'

'Fucking hell, you pair of bastards. I'm taking it out on a fucking armed robbery and you're giving me grief about a mark? There's a fucking good chance it's going to look like a colander by the end.'

'You look after it!' shouted Benson, jabbing a big finger into Jones's chest. 'Any damage and I'm going to shove the exhaust pipe up *your* exhaust – are we clear?'

'Fuck's sake, yes, clear,' replied Jones despondently. If he got through today, emigration was starting to look like an extremely appealing proposition.

'Right, listen very carefully, Brian,' continued Clarke. 'This is what you're going to do. You pick the others up as arranged and take them to Tamworth, where they go in to blag the shop. Our guys will be waiting for them.'

'Your guys are waiting? What, to shoot them?' asked Jones, for the first time considering the full implications of what was about to occur.

'No, no, not to shoot them, just arrest them. Anyway, you stay outside in the motor, you hear them get nicked, so you fuck off a bit sharpish and meet us back here. We'll get the undamaged motor away, job done, OK?'

'Fine,' said Jones flatly. He sounded unconvinced, as he had every reason to be.

'Go on then, fuck off,' said Clarke, tossing him the keys to his pride and joy. 'And fucking take care of it.'

Jones got in and fired up the Rover, revving the engine loudly.

'Treat it carefully, you twat,' shouted Clarke. 'Where are you going to tell Briggs and Travers you got it from?'

'Found it on the drive of a house with the keys in the ignition, I suppose.'

'Tell them you found it with the keys in, on the forecourt of Baxter's Garage at Darrick Wood,' said Clarke. 'That'll make more sense, seeing as it's got loads of markings for the garage on it.'

'OK, see you later,' shouted Jones. He left the sidings at speed, causing Clarke to hold his head in his hands.

'He's going to fucking wreck it, I know he is,' he wailed mournfully.

Shortly after nine a.m., Brian Jones parked the hired Rover outside the block of flats occupied by Briggs and Travers. In his hand-painted ex-Post Office van, PC Phil Eldrett watched him go into the foyer and picked up his personal radio. He was operating on a back-to-back channel with

DCI Harrison, who was waiting half a mile away in an unmarked CID vehicle driven by DS Dave Mathews, with Dl Barry Evans in the front passenger seat.

The radio Harrison was holding burst into life.

'Brian Jones just turned up at the flats in the Rover. He's inside.' There was a click as Eldrett switched off his radio to avoid any risk of sudden radio traffic or static giving him away. Harrison nodded grimly and stared out of his window.

'Dave, head out towards Tamworth but keep off the main roads,' he finally instructed.

'OK, boss,' replied Mathews, swinging the two-litre Cortina into a U-turn.

'What you got then?' asked Travers as he opened the flat door to Jones.

'Only a fucking Rover,' replied Jones triumphantly.

'Fuck me, right result,' said Travers. 'Where'd you find that?'

'Car-hire forecourt at Darrick Wood. Some dozy wanker left the keys in the ignition.'

'Brian got you a proper set of wheels this time,' announced Travers as he led Jones into the kitchen, where the rest of the team were drinking coffee. None of them seemed even slightly pleased with his recent acquisition.

'Good news, isn't it, Pat?' said Jones mockingly to the

scowling Patrick Allen. Ian Chance and Dave Martin just looked sick. Handing Jones a mug of coffee, Briggs tossed a plastic bag to him.

'You need to put this on for the job,' he said quietly, 'and a pair of these,' indicating a box of surgical latex gloves.

'What's in the bag?'

'Boiler suit. Those useless bastards didn't get any balaclavas, so make sure you keep the hood up,' he replied, glaring at Chance and Martin, who were already close to folding up like cheap deckchairs.

'I'm driving, not going out into the shop. Why do I need to wear a boiler suit?' whined Jones.

'Just put the fucking thing on!' shouted Allen, who was furious that Jones had come up with a motor and would once again be sitting out the real graft.

Briggs appeared from the living area of the flat carrying the two sawn-off Purdeys and a box of rifled slug cartridges.

'Pat, you can take one,' he said, tossing one of the guns to Allen, who caught it by the shortened barrel. 'Which of you two wants the other?' he asked the trembling Chance and Martin. They looked fearfully at the menacing shotgun and then at Briggs, but neither replied. Their nerves had been stretched to breaking point, and they now posed a real threat to the plan. They were both shaking with fear.

'Pair of fucking pussies,' snorted Briggs contemptuously. 'Ian, you take it,' and he threw the weapon at Chance. It landed in his lap, knocking his arm and spilling hot coffee on to his legs. Yelping like a pup, he leapt to his feet, the shotgun clattering to the floor, and rushed towards the toilet to douse himself. Jones and Allen glared at each other. The omens were not good, but Briggs and Travers appeared unconcerned by the two obvious weak links.

Once Chance had returned, his trousers damp, Travers instructed the team to get themselves dressed, whilst Briggs loaded the Purdeys with a single cartridge each. Five minutes later, the four robbers stood in the flat in their blue boiler suits.

'You useless pair of idiots!' shouted Briggs at the trembling Chance and Martin. 'Didn't you look at the fucking sizes? The fucking things are massive, you'll have to roll the arms and legs up.'

'At least the hoods are big enough to hide their faces,' observed Travers, shaking his head. 'Just make sure you can see where you're going.'

Handing the loaded shotguns to Allen and Chance, Briggs glanced out of the living-room window at the deserted street outside. Nothing seemed out of place. All the usual motors, except the gleaming new Rover that Jones had brought along. With the shotguns tucked into the voluminous sleeves of their outsize boiler suits, Allen and Chance left the flat and walked quickly to the locked Rover, followed by Jones and Martin.

'Come on, for fuck's sake,' hissed Allen as he waited for

the doors to be opened, painfully aware that he was dressed like a circus clown and carrying a sawn-off shotgun.

The team were soon all seated in the sweltering car, Allen in the front passenger seat, Chance and Martin shaking uncontrollably in the back. With their hoods still pulled up over their heads, they resembled a quartet of monks on a road trip.

'I can't drive like this,' gasped Jones, pulling his hood down, his face red and dripping with sweat. The others followed suit, and once Jones had got the car moving, the breeze helped to cool them, though they continued to cook inside the thick cotton boiler suits.

'All four are in the car, all wearing boiler suits with the hoods up, can't see the shooters,' transmitted Eldrett from his van, followed shortly afterwards by, 'Unbelievable, the hoods are down. Allen's in the front seat, Chance and Martin are in the back,' before he switched off and waited for his driver, who had been briefed to return to the van once the Rover moved away. He was on board a minute later, calling over his shoulder to Eldrett in the sweaty rear, 'You OK, Phil?'

'Pretty good, thanks. Got them in sight yet?'

They picked up the Rover quickly, travelling out of town on the main Tamworth road, and Eldrett switched his radio back on and left it open for his commentary. Peering through his letterbox spy hole to the front, he began to update the rest of the police team.

'Behind the Rover now, on the Tamworth road, still four up,' he reported.

'Keep well back, Phil,' urged DCI Harrison from a mile away. 'Don't worry too much about losing them; we know where they're going. Don't show out whatever you do.'

'Understood,' replied Eldrett. 'Mike, drop right back, give them loads of distance. It doesn't matter if we lose them.' His driver obliged, and soon the Rover was lost from view as both vehicles began to wind their way through the lanes towards Tamworth.

'You'll have to pull over,' snapped Allen to Jones. 'I've got to have a dump.'

'What?' exploded Jones. 'You're fucking joking, right? Why the fuck didn't you go before we left? We can't stop now.'

'Couldn't go at the flat,' replied Allen a little shamefaced. 'Fucking stop or I'm going to shit myself.'

'Bollocks, you'll have to wait,' shouted Jones.

'Fucking stop or I'll blow your fucking head off,' said Allen simply, slipping his sawn-off shotgun down his sleeve and holding it to the side of Jones's neck. 'Pull over here,' he continued, indicating a small lay-by.

Resignedly, Jones pulled the Rover into the lay-by. He

glanced in his rearview mirror at the wide-eyed duo in the back and took a deep breath. We are fucked, he told himself.

'Wait here and I'll be right back,' hissed Allen, slipping the sawn-off back up his sleeve. 'You two keep an eye on this windy bastard. Ian, he tries to drive away before I get back, shoot him in the fucking back, understand?'

Open mouthed, Chance nodded like an idiot from the back. As Allen left the Rover, Eldrett's van swept past the lay-by.

'They've pulled over, Allen is out of the vehicle,' he transmitted urgently. 'What should I do?'

'Keep going, don't stop,' shouted Harrison quickly. 'Don't worry about them, Phil, we know where they're headed. Fuck knows what they're up to, but just don't show out. Get yourself over towards Tamworth but well out of the way, OK?'

'Understood,' replied Eldrett. 'Keep going, Mike. Park us up somewhere they won't notice us.'

Jones watched as Allen picked his way through long grass and thick bushes before disappearing from view behind a large hawthorn hedge adjacent to a small copse of trees. He looked into his rearview mirror again at Chance and Martin, who were staring wide eyed at the hedge.

'This is all going to rat shit, boys,' he said quietly. 'If we fuck off now, we might be OK.'

Ian Chance snapped out of his trance and glared back at him. 'Shut your fucking mouth, you bastard,' he snarled, slipping his shotgun out of his sleeve and pointing it at Jones's head. 'We're fucking waiting for Pat.'

Jones held his hands up in surrender. 'Whatever you say, Ian, it's your fucking funeral,' he shrugged. He tried to relax as he waited for Allen to return. The beautiful, silent countryside shimmered gently in the early-morning sunshine, the air was full of dandelion spores floating this way and that in the breeze, birds flitted in and out of the hawthorn hedge, the sky was a perfect, unblemished blue, and the light breeze rustled the leaves on the copse of lime trees like waves breaking on a stony beach. The tranquillity belied the murderous mission they were embarked on, and even a philistine like Jones appreciated the contrast.

Behind the hawthorn hedge, Patrick Allen unbuttoned his boiler suit, awkwardly pulled it down to his calves, then dropped his pants and squatted painfully in a large clump of grass. It was a close call but he had got there in time and quickly dropped the kids off at the pool. Giving his arse a cursory wipe with a large rough leaf growing near by, he re-dressed and hurried back to the Rover and his reluctant partners in crime. Without a word, Jones started up the engine and pulled back out on to the quiet country road. Within a minute the complaints started.

'Fucking hell, what's that smell?' asked Jones, glaring accusingly at Allen.

'Fuck knows, not me.'

'It stinks,' shouted Martin from the back, where he and Chance were gagging.

'It smells like human shit,' gasped Jones, his eyes watering.

'Fuck all to do with me,' said Allen defensively.

'Did you shit yourself or step in something?'

'Did I fuck.'

The smell was overpowering, the breeze coming in through the open car windows doing nothing to alleviate it. Chance and Martin were hanging out of the rear windows, gagging and honking like migrating geese.

'Fucking hell, Pat, it's you, you dirty bastard, you fucking stink.'

'It's not fucking me, I told you!' shouted Allen, but even he was beginning to find the smell overwhelming.

'Then you've trodden in something, you tosser.'

'I fucking haven't,' protested Allen, quickly checking the soles of his trainers. 'Fuck knows what it is.'

'Fuck this,' shouted Jones, pulling the Rover on to the grass verge and baling out into the road. The others followed, and the team of armed robbers staggered about on the verge in their ill-fitting boiler suits, coughing and spluttering, eyes watering. Then Jones spotted it.

'It's in your fucking hood, you twat!' he shouted at

Allen, walking quickly away. Allen looked quizzically at him.

'What is?'

'In your fucking hood,' gagged Jones. 'Get rid of it.'

'What?' bellowed Allen.

'You've shat in your hood, you wanker.'

Across the adjacent field, Eldrett and his driver observed the extraordinary events.

'What the fuck is going on now?' asked the driver.

'Fuck knows,' replied Eldrett, picking up his radio. 'They've pulled over again,' he transmitted. 'Allen's taken his boiler suit off and is prancing about like the sugar plum fairy on the verge in his pants. Fuck only knows what's going on.'

DCI Harrison exchanged a look of bemusement with DI Barry Evans.

'Fucking Fred Karno's,' he observed. 'Relax, they'll be there.'

In the gun shop at Tamworth, Chief Inspector Pete Stevenson and two PCs from Unit Three of the patrol group were monitoring the same channel. PCs Peter Tomlinson and Barry Knight had received a detailed briefing from Stevenson first thing, and now the three of them, all in civilian clothes, were the only people in the shop. The staff had been quickly spirited away as they arrived for work, and so far, as luck would have it, no customers had presented themselves. Stevenson had left Knight and Tomlinson in no doubt about what was coming their way.

'They've got a pair of sawn-off shotguns and plenty of ammo, and they won't be playing nicely or asking too many questions when they get here. Give them a quick warning if you can and then waste them,' he said simply.

Knight and Tomlinson looked at each other and swallowed hard. It was what they had been trained for, but now, on the threshold of actually shooting someone, it took on a different complexion. Stevenson felt the same apprehension gnawing away at his insides. What none of them had considered for a moment was the risk they all faced at the hands of the armed Mafia. It simply did not occur to them; the only thing any of them wondered about was what it would feel like to shoot someone.

'Won't be long now,' remarked Stevenson in a calm voice that belied the tension he felt as he heard Eldrett report that the Rover was on the move again, travelling time to Tamworth now about three minutes. He walked quickly to the front of the shop and peered out into the deserted high street. The small post office directly opposite seemed to be the only source of life in the village, with a couple of customers browsing through the limited supply of groceries on the shelves.

Inside the post office, Sercan Ozdemir's minder, Ahmet, was casually inspecting the freezer cabinet, glancing up occasionally to look across at the gun shop. Ozdemir wanted to know about the raid as soon as it happened.

'One minute, one minute,' called Eldrett. Stevenson, Knight and Tomlinson ducked down behind the counter, glanced grimly at each other and for the thousandth time checked their issue Smith and Wesson .38 specials.

In the Rover, the tension was palpable. Chance and Martin were panting with fright and both shotguns were now on display.

'Hoods up,' commanded Allen, who then cursed as he pulled his own shitty hood over his head. The smell was appalling but he didn't intend to suffer it for long.

The Rover pulled up directly outside the gun shop and stopped. There was a brief pause. The high street simmered in the heat and the only sound was the purring engine of the Rover. Dark Turkish eyes glanced up from the freezer cabinet. Inside the gun shop, Stevenson hissed, 'Here we go, boys,' through gritted teeth, and Knight and Tomlinson took deep breaths and set their trembling jaws firm.

'Now!' shouted Allen, pushing open his door. He waited briefly as Chance and Martin joined him on the pavement, then pulled Chance close to him and with Martin a step behind barged through the front door of the gun shop.

A bell tinkled on the ceiling above them. There was no sign of any staff behind the counter, but Allen screamed loudly anyway, 'Hit the deck, this is a fucking robbery!' and pulled the trigger of his Purdey. The blast noise was intense as the single round tore into the plaster ceiling above him, the slug hitting a rigid support joist, cracking it along its length. Plaster, dust and debris began to shower down.

The unexpected noise was too much for Chance's fragile nerves, causing him to jump with fright and inadvertently pull at his own sawn-off's hair trigger. The gun leapt from his grasp as the shot exploded from the single barrel. The one-ounce solid lead shot left the sawn-off barrel at fifteen hundred feet a second and entered Allen's head where his skull met his neck. It travelled upwards, severing his brain stem and pulverising his brain before his entire head exploded as the enormous pressures generated pushed outwards. The ceiling and far wall were sprayed with a mixture of blood, brain tissue and skull fragments as though from a hosepipe, and Allen's corpse pitched forward, still clutching his shotgun in a death spasm, blood hosing against the counter in front.

Chance's shotgun clattered to the floor and he and Martin stood frozen to the spot, staring aghast at the corpse in front of them, the remains of its head plastered around the walls and ceiling.

'Fuck!' shouted Stevenson from the floor. He pointed his handgun over the counter without getting off his haunches and began to pull the trigger wildly, hoping his weapon was aiming generally in the right direction. Knight and Tomlinson did likewise, and all three emptied their handguns into the front of the shop. The noise in such a confined space was deafening and numbed their senses.

On the other side of the counter, the air was alive with hot lead. One round hit Martin in the top left of his chest, tearing through the skin and passing clean through his chest cavity and out under his armpit. It didn't really register with him, such was the shock he was in, but the next round that got him put an end to all his worries. The 158-grain jacketed soft-point round punched a hole through the side of his skull and began to plough a furrow through the brain mass. The round began to distort and bounce around the skull cavity, pulverising more brain matter. He was unconscious before he hit the ground, blood pouring from his nose and ears. The vagus nerve had been severed and as his breathing and circulation ceased he died quickly.

One of the other eighteen police rounds loosed off into the shop smashed into Chance's chest, tearing through his heart and causing a huge hole. Immediately unconscious through the shock of the hit, Chance collapsed on to his back, haemorrhaging massively into his chest. The round severed the coronary artery, travelled into and through his left lung and into his rib cage, where it eventually lodged under the skin of his left armpit. He suffered a massive heart attack seconds later and like Martin died quickly.

Outside in the Rover, Jones had heard the first two shotgun blasts and then the fusillade of small-arms fire. He ducked as all the glass in the door and windows of the shop seemed to explode in slow motion, only peering up once he was sure it was over. Not bothering to wait for anyone to come out of the shop, he rammed the Rover into first gear and blasted it away down the high street, leaving a trail of rubber on the hot road surface. Ahmet also quickly left the post office and walked to his car, parked further up the street. He departed in a more sedate fashion so as to not draw attention to himself.

In the still-ringing and smoke-shrouded shop, Stevenson, Knight and Tomlinson got nervously to their feet and peered over the counter. A scene of unimaginable carnage greeted them.

'Jesus fucking Christ,' whispered Stevenson, glancing from the corpses on the floor to the gruesome material running down the walls and dripping from the ceiling.

'Fucking hell,' said Knight quietly as he stepped from behind the counter and up to Allen's headless body. He had bled out quickly and the thick blood was literally everywhere.

'That's a fucking own goal,' said Knight, who was well aware that their handguns could never have inflicted such damage.

'There were two shotgun blasts,' agreed Tomlinson. 'First one went into the ceiling; the second one must have got him in the head. Definitely an own goal.'

'We must have done the other two,' said Stevenson, looking down at the lifeless, pale faces of Chance and Martin, both with shocked expressions, eyes wide open, the blood on their faces still fresh and wet.

'All three in the shop are dead,' transmitted Stevenson into his personal radio. 'No injuries to any of us.'

DCI Harrison nodded grimly as DS Mathews drove him quickly to the scene. As he surveyed the carnage in the shop, he resolved that his next visit would be to Ozdemir. He needed to know quickly that he was on offer.

'You all OK?' he asked Stevenson and the patrol group officers. They looked shaken but otherwise all right.

'Yeah, fine,' replied Stevenson wearily.

'Great job, guys. Get your van to pick you all up, get back to Handstead and start writing your statements,' he instructed. 'Pete, you know what's required. Make sure the i's are dotted and the t's crossed, OK? Dave, Barry, get this scene under control and keep me in the loop. I've got a visit to make.'

The reverberations around the Park Royal estate in the next few hours would be immense – as significant as those after the murder of PC Dave Baines six months earlier. Then, graffiti had appeared on walls around the estate mocking the police with the legend: Mafia 1–Pigs 0. The graffiti had been altered after the demise of Driscoll to 1–1, and would be updated again soon to reflect the death of Baker in Strangeways and the shooting of the three Mafia members at Tamworth. The police were getting back on top of things again, and with Harrison and Stevenson firmly in charge of the CID and uniforms, and with similar outlooks on policing, there was no sign that the initiative would be lost.

Ozdemir took the news from his minder in silence, but he was deeply shocked.

'The police were waiting?' he asked.

'They walked into an ambush. No one got out.'

'What about the driver?'

'No, he got away, as far as I could see.'

Ozdemir laughed grimly. 'A bit obvious, isn't it? We don't have to look far for the leak.'

Ahmet nodded. 'You want me to find him?'

Ozdemir shook his head, got up from his chair and began to pace his office as he quickly assessed the situation and his options.

'No,' he said finally. 'He's not the problem right now. Get hold of Briggs and Travers and bring them here.'

Ahmet and the other minder turned and left quickly. They knew the severity of the situation Ozdemir now faced, and also that if the family decided to punish him, their vengeance would in all likelihood include his close associates.

They found Travers and Briggs waiting for news at their usual table at the Park Royal pub like a pair of triumphant generals. They were unceremoniously bundled into the waiting Mercedes and ten minutes later stood nervously in front of Ozdemir, who regarded them as a patient headmaster might a pair of naughty schoolboys.

'The police were waiting for your boys,' he began, smiling at them.

The colour drained from their faces. 'Oh fuck.'

'Indeed, oh fuck,' repeated Ozdemir. 'Who went into the shop with the guns?'

'Pat Allen, Ian Chance and Dave Martin. Have they been nicked?'

'They're all dead,' said Ozdemir quietly. 'Who was driving?'

'Brian Jones,' said Briggs slowly. 'He dead as well?'

'No, he drove away unhindered. What do you know about him?'

'Know about him?'

'Yes, you fucking idiot, know about him!' shouted Ozdemir, raising his voice for the first time. 'Do you trust him? Could he have been working for the police?'

'Brian a grass? No way,' said Briggs, glancing desperately at Travers, who looked worried and was chewing his bottom lip.

'Has he been arrested lately?'

'Yes, but—' began Briggs.

'Oh fuck,' interrupted Travers, who was busy fitting pieces together. 'He got nicked for a burglary at the Marshes Social Club. Pat Allen was on the job with him but got away. Far as I know he's not been charged: still on bail for further inquiries.'

'Further fucking inquiries,' snorted Ozdemir. 'You pair of cretins!' he shouted. 'Didn't it strike you as a bit odd that he hadn't been charged? He's probably been working for the police ever since.'

Travers and Briggs remained silent as Ozdemir sat back in his chair and thought desperately.

'The police will be coming for you two soon,' he said finally. 'We need to get you somewhere safe. My boys will find you a safe house away from Handstead.'

'Where?'

'My aunt has a farm just off the M6,' said Ozdemir, glancing up at Ahmet, who nodded his understanding. 'Go with Ahmet now and he'll sort things out. Don't worry, we'll take care of you.'

'Thanks, Mr Ozdemir,' said Briggs, offering him a handshake that was pointedly ignored.

'Go now,' said Ozdemir, getting to his feet and waving them away to squealing oblivion. Travers and Briggs followed the two minders out of the office like cattle towards the abattoir.

* * *

Ten minutes later, Ozdemir opened his office door to DCI Harrison, who strode in and slumped down on the expensive sofa opposite the desk. The office was nice and cool.

'The wheels all came off for you this morning, Sercan,' he smiled.

'What can you mean, Mr Harrison?' said Ozdemir, breathing a massive sigh of relief that he'd got Briggs and Travers away quickly.

'I know what you've been up to, and I intend to use what I know against you.'

'Mr Harrison, I run a legitimate haulage business. What are you talking about?'

'I know you do, Sercan, amongst other things, but it's the other things that I'm going to nail you to the wall for. I know you had Alan Baker topped in prison and I know you sent that Mafia team to Tamworth this morning. They're all dead, you know.'

Ozdemir's blood ran cold as the scale of his betrayal became apparent. He licked his lips as he looked at the bulky detective smiling at him, and desperately tried to slow his racing heart and respond calmly.

'If you could prove any of this, we wouldn't be having this wild conversation, would we, Mr Harrison?' he replied quietly. 'As I said, I run a legitimate haulage business.'

'Of course you do, Sercan, of course you do,' said Harrison, getting to his feet and walking to the office door.

He looked over at Ozdemir and saw the fear in his eyes. 'I'll be in touch,' he said, leaving as quickly as he had arrived. Ozdemir was on the end of his leash, and he intended to give it a fucking good tug soon.

Sercan Ozdemir slumped into the chair behind the desk and pondered his predicament. He needed to start clearing away some potential problems, and quickly.

'Listen up, guys,' called Collins as the night-duty group chatted loudly amongst themselves. 'You've probably heard the rumours, so here's the story. The Mafia walked into an ambush at the Tamworth gun shop this morning. Three of them were shot dead by our guys in the shop. They've been named as Pat Allen, Ian Chance and Dave Martin, all from the Park Royal. There will be repercussions on the estate, you know that, so be careful, OK?'

'Praise the Lord!' shouted Psycho, getting to his feet, arms outstretched like a gospel preacher, as the group celebrated the demise of three of the enemy.

'He won't help you,' said Collins loudly above the cheers. 'Just watch your fucking backs out there tonight. Those arseholes will be looking for revenge.'

As the group continued to celebrate and chat, Collins began to fiddle with the new overhead projector on the desk alongside his lectern. It had arrived that morning from Divisional Headquarters, with instructions that it was to be used to display the collator's bulletins so that the troops could see them for themselves, rather than have a sergeant read them out to them. It was another example of the job embracing utterly pointless technology, but what no one had bothered to check was whether the projector was 'policeman proof'. Collins flicked irritably at the on and off switch, but the delicate projector refused to start. It was already broken, after less than twenty-four hours' service.

'Fucking thing's dead already,' said Collins, giving it a slap and picking up the collator's bulletin to read it aloud.

'Hey, Sarge, it's started to rain,' called Pizza, pointing to the darkened rear yard.

The group ran to the windows, where they could see that the weather had finally broken and the first few welcome drops of rain were falling. The humidity had lifted and a cool breeze flapped the muster-room curtains.

'Fucking typical,' called Collins to their backs. 'Telex from Headquarters came through this afternoon. The Chief's relented: you can all take your ties off.'

'He moves in mysterious ways,' shouted Psycho. 'What a cunt.'

Author's Note

Whilst I have dedicated this book to my wonderful and forgiving children, I would like to take the opportunity to thank three men who shaped the young Charlie Owen into the person who joined the Police Service in 1976. I was sent to boarding school from the age of nine and missed the presence of my father during the most influential years of my life. I didn't get to know him until I too was a father. Far too late and a waste.

But three men unwittingly became surrogate fathers to me whilst I was at Milton Abbey School between 1970 and 1974. Simon Smail encouraged me to play sport, which subsequently dominated my life; Pete Traskey imbued in me a love of writing and the poetry of Robert Frost; and David Baggaley was simply the coolest man I have ever met, a dude way, way before being a dude was cool.

Gentlemen, I thank you.

During the writing of this book I had the guidance of a

number of individuals whom I must thank: Dr Freddy Patel from the London Hospital Forensic Medical Centre, Mark Walton, Roger Holt, and his brother Matt, and Paul Major, all offered invaluable support and assistance. I am also indebted to numerous serving and retired police officers for a continuous supply of stories every time we meet up: Ken Stewart, Dave Cronin, Mike Reed, Graham Poulter, Mark Newton, Billy Bryden, Martin Kosmalski, Andy Williams and many others. Thanks to them all.

Close

Martina Cole

Keep your friends close and your enemies closer. And your family should be closest of all.

Patrick Brodie is on the way up. He knows exactly how far he's prepared to go to get what he wants. And he wants it all. Now. Before long, Patrick has become a legend in his own lifetime. Violently.

The kind of women Patrick Brodie is normally attracted to have no illusions, no foolish dreams of marriage, children or, God help him, love. But Lily Diamond is different. Together they are determined that their children will have everything they didn't, no matter what.

But the unthinkable happens, and Lily is left on her own to look after their family in a dangerous world. A world where you can trust no one. The Brodies must stay close to survive. But as everyone knows, your sins will find you out . . .

Praise for Martina Cole's phenomenal No. 1 bestsellers:

'The stuff of legend . . . utterly compelling' *Mirror*

'A blinding good read' Ray Winstone

'Her gripping plots pack a mean emotional punch' *Mail on Sunday*

'Intensely readable' *Guardian*

978 0 7553 2861 1

headline

Now you can buy any of these other bestselling
Headline books from your bookshop
or *direct from the publisher*.

FREE P&P AND UK DELIVERY
(Overseas and Ireland £3.50 per book)

Horse's Arse	Charlie Owen	£6.99
I Predict A Riot	Bateman	£7.99
Nothing to Fear	Karen Rose	£6.99
Stalked	Brian Freeman	£6.99
Death's Door	Quintin Jardine	£6.99
Blood Test	Jonathan Kellerman	£7.99
Power Play	Joseph Finder	£6.99
The 6th Target	James Patterson and Maxine Paetro	£7.99
A Passion for Killing	Barbara Nadel	£7.99

TO ORDER SIMPLY CALL THIS NUMBER

01235 400 414

or visit our website: www.headline.co.uk

Prices and availability subject to change without notice.